NUCLEAR DENIAL

NUCLEAR DENIAL

A CHANCE LYON NOVEL

By Van C. Torrey

NUCLEAR DENIAL
A CHANCE LYON NOVEL

This is a work of fiction. Names of the characters and the incidents portrayed herein are the product of the author's imagination or are used fictitiously. Any resemblance to actual characters, living or dead, is coincidental.

For information concerning this novel please contact the author at: torreyvan@gmail.com

Copyright © October, 2013 by Van C. Torrey

All rights reserved. Except as permitted under the U.S. Copyright Act of 1976, no part of this publication may be reproduced, distributed, or transmitted in any form or by any means, or stored in a database or retrieval system, without the prior written permission of the publisher.

Printed in the United States of America.

ISBN-10: 1492292281
EAN-13: 9781492292289

Library of Congress Control Number: 2013916027
CreateSpace Independent Publishing Platform
North Charleston, South Carolina

© 2013 Signal Hill Press

IRAN AND NUCLEAR WEAPONS

"I believe that if Iran were to acquire nuclear weapons, there would be three very negative consequences. One is you would have a nuclear-armed Iran with missiles that could reach Israel today and would be able to reach Europe in the not-to-distant future. Second a nuclear-armed Iran would ignite a nuclear arms race in the most volatile part of the world. And third, a nuclear-armed Iran would be significantly more aggressive in places like Iraq and Afghanistan, throughout the region, in terms of trying to throw their weight around. The only acceptable alternative is that the economic sanctions bring enough unpopular unhappiness that the region decides it's in its best interest (to cooperate)...if there is one thing the Iranians and the North Koreans have in common, it's they don't care how many of their people get killed."

Robert M. Gates
Former U.S. Secretary of Defense, 2006-2011
(Credit: Interview with Bloomberg Business Week, December, 2012)

U.S. NAVY SEALS

"The only easy day was yesterday."
"Earn your Trident every day."

U.S. Navy SEAL training mantras

U.S. ARMY RANGERS

"Sua Sponte"
(Of Their Own Accord)

U.S. Army Ranger motto

"I'd rather be going down the river with seven studs, than a hundred shitheads!"

Colonel Charlie Beckwith, Founder of Delta Force

ACKNOWLEDGMENTS

Writing a story, especially a work of fiction, is an intellectually demanding exercise, frequently requiring the writer to spend hours of solitary time thinking, creating, and reworking what was previously set down. In addition, creative writing takes intellectual courage and patience, two characteristics which in my case have required a great effort to improve from my original base skill set. Perhaps this is penance for matters of my past. If so, such effort has been gently encouraged by my skillful and patient editor, Francine Hardaway, Ph.D. I am equally grateful to Ms. Terry Parker, Esq. for her invaluable professional assistance in making this manuscript suitable for publishing.

Those same friends and associates who encouraged me to go forward with the original Chance Lyon story (<u>Point of the Trident</u>) deserve my continued thanks here. I gratefully acknowledge the ongoing encouragement and suggestions from Louis 'Buzz' Sands, Robert Palmer, Bevan Olyphant, John Guerrero, and JALM, as well as two other professionals who prefer not to be mentioned by name, as they continue to work in the noble and frequently underappreciated profession of bearing arms for the benefit of the United States of America and her fortunate citizens.

Finally, I would be remiss if I did not acknowledge those teachers from my past, Thelda and Chris, who taught me to understand and appreciate the power of the written word to inform and entertain.

For Emma, Andrew, and Will
May you know a life without the threat of nuclear conflict.

Van Torrey
Phoenix, Arizona
September, 2013

Cover by Mike Vera

TABLE OF CONTENTS

Nuclear Denial	iv
Iran and Nuclear Weapons	v
Acknowledgments	vii
Table of Contents	ix
Forward - 2019, A.D.	xi
Cast of Characters	xv

BOOK I - A SEAL WARRIOR'S FLASHBACK — 1
Lieutenant Chance Macklin Lyon, U.S.N. — 3

BOOK II - FATEFUL PLOT — 25
Chapter 1	Trouble on the High Seas	27
Chapter 2	Aftermath – Chaos and Intrigue	39
Chapter 3	Plots and Counter Plots	47
Chapter 4	How Do We Play This?	55

BOOK III - DENIAL BY STEALTH — 63
Chapter 5	Intelligence from the Mossad	65
Chapter 6	A Daring Plan – With Risk!	83
Chapter 7	Sandia – Doorway to Doomsday	93
Chapter 8	Dry Run	113
Chapter 9	Mid-Ocean Drama	119
Chapter 10	Wounded Warrior	151

BOOK IV - REACTION — 159
Chapter 11	Frustration and Resolve	161

BOOK V - THE CONSPIRACY — 169
Chapter 12   Shopping For Nukes — 171
Chapter 13   The Pakistani Connection — 175
Chapter 14   Striking a Deal — 181
Chapter 15   Success and Wealth, or Failure and Death — 191

BOOK VI - THE GAMBLE — 205
Chapter 16   Bankers and Spooks — 207
Chapter 17   Abrupt Change of Plans — 213
Chapter 18   North Korean Connection — 233

BOOK VII - DENIAL BY FORCE — 245
Chapter 19   Fateful Test — 247
Chapter 20   Nuclear Forensics — 261
Chapter 21   Out – Recruit – Double — 283
Chapter 22   End Game — 295
Epilogue — 355

FORWARD
2019, A.D.

Beginning in the late half of the 20th Century and continuing into the early 21st Century the Middle East has evolved from an 'Area of concern' to a status of 'Flashpoint of grave strategic importance' to the governments of the United States and her allies in Europe and the Far East.

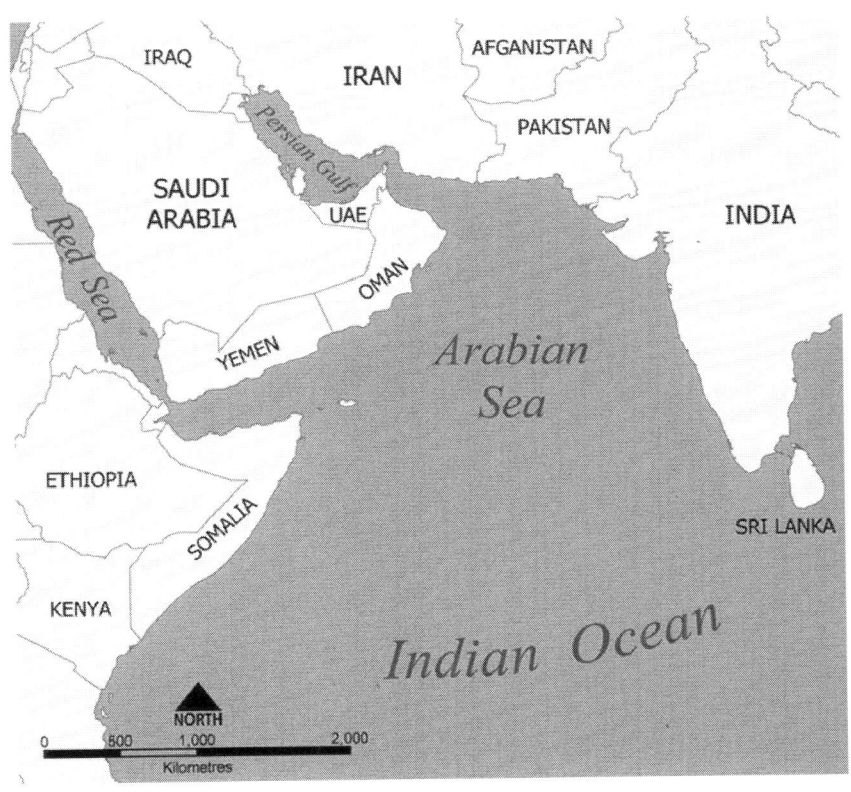

Despite the substantial efforts of political and industrial leaders in America and the industrialized free world to deemphasize the use of fossil fuels for energy use in favor of alternative energy sources, the worldwide consumption of crude oil has continued unabated as the economies of emerging nations drive up both demand and price of this readily available and convenient commodity. Although the price of crude oil, still precariously based on the U.S. dollar, is in the neighborhood of $150 per barrel, thus encouraging new sources of crude, the undeniable fact is that nearly 30 percent of the world's supply of crude is produced by the oil-rich countries of the Persian Gulf, and is shipped through the Strait of Hormuz in Very Large Crude Carriers into the Arabian Sea for distribution throughout the thirsty industrialized world. This simple fact alone makes the stabilization and protection of this vital waterway and the surrounding sea lanes the top international priority of interest for the United States of America.

The Islamic Republic of Iran holds vast quantities of crude oil reserves. However, Iran's insistence on developing a home-grown nuclear infrastructure that could potentially fuel a nuclear weapons capability, combined with a vociferous belligerence on the part of her religious and secular leadership toward Israel, has resulted in economically restrictive trade sanctions being imposed by the United Nations. Such sanctions have made it difficult for Iran to freely market this valuable export commodity and produce revenues that would keep her on a par with her OPEC partners. Nevertheless Iran will not abandon her nuclear ambitions that, if realized, would make her the only OPEC country with substantial reserves of crude oil and an arsenal of nuclear weapons. This combination could make Iran the most powerful Islamic country in the world.

The country in the region most potentially threatened by Iran reaching her goal of becoming a nuclear state is Israel. In addition to a delivery mechanism such as a guided missile, Iran could also transport a crude nuclear device relatively unimpeded across Iraq and Syria, bringing it to the doorstep of Israel unchallenged. For years the United States – primarily covertly – has been working in concert with Israel, its only solid ally in the Middle East, to deny Iran's acquisition of this lethal capability. Now Mossad, Israel's Intelligence Agency, has made a startling discovery about Iran's top secret plans to get even closer to developing a home-grown nuclear weapon in the near term. Mossad has suggested a bold and ingenious plan to thwart this effort using the unique covert military assets of the United States.

The two powerful forces – Iran's unquenchable desire to acquire a nuclear weapons capability, and the United States-Israel cabal's determination to prevent this - foretell a new dynamic about to unfold that will unite the two enemies in a drama involving courageous, cunning, and desperate men and women from Asia, the Middle East, Europe and America - all with competing agendas, but with a common goal of seeing their hopes and dreams realized or fears abated. Iran seeks to become the de-facto leader in the Islamic world and establish a new caliphate based on Sharia law, displacing the Sunni House of Saud with such new leadership. Those in positions of power and influence in the United States and the Middle East are motivated to remain so, bolstered by their political and religious beliefs that are so firmly held. How these conflicting forces play out against each other is the subject of this story.

Our odyssey takes the reader from secretive military bases on both coasts of the United States, to the halls of power in Washington, D.C., cities and combat outposts in the Persian Gulf, the strategic waterways of the Indian Ocean and the Arabian Sea, the vast uninhabited deserts of Iran, and the mysterious private banks in Zurich, Switzerland, and beyond. The characters encompass a range of fascinating people, from powerful political and religious leaders, highly motivated and courageous military men utilizing complex surveillance systems and deadly weapons employing unimaginable new technology, intellectually gifted and cunning spymasters, unethical scoundrels motivated by potential riches, and sinister nuclear technicians. In the end there will be winners and losers and the stakes could not be higher in this game of nuclear intrigue.

Amidst an underlying theme of the protection of the national security of the United States and her closest allies, we witness the courage and resolve of an American Navy SEAL warrior, Lieutenant Chance Lyon, as he struggles with the memory of the loss of a close friend and fellow warrior, and the demons surrounding the murder of his former lover. His sense of duty and dedication to the culture of his profession become a jarring counter reality that influences a chain of events stunningly plausible in outcome and consequence.

Admiral (Ret.) James Morgan, USN
Former Director of National Intelligence
Annapolis, Maryland
September, 2019

NUCLEAR DENIAL
CAST OF CHARACTERS

President Jonathan Braxton: Current President of the United States, re-elected in 2016, he is serving his second term.

Rachel Hunter, Ph.D.: Director of National Intelligence (DNI). She is a former Wall Street Lawyer at Goldman Sachs, holds a Ph.D. from the London School of Economics and a law degree from Harvard, as a former classmate of Jonathan Braxton. She has many connections in the international banking community.

Jack Duggan: National Security Adviser to President Jonathan Braxton.

Raymond (Ray) Rollins: Director of Central Intelligence.

Jonas Southworth: CIA Station Chief in Tel Aviv, Israel.

Justin Roberts: U.S. Secretary of Defense.

Alexander Randolph: U.S. Secretary of State.

Philip Johnson: Chief of Staff to President Jonathan Braxton.

Sarah Whittington: White House Communications Director.

Lieutenant Chance M. Lyon, U.S.N.: Decorated veteran Navy SEAL operator having served multiple deployments in Afghanistan, where he worked out of Bagram Airfield with SEAL Team Two. From there his team carried out intelligence gathering and combat operations against Taliban and al-Qaeda insurgents. He previously participated in the mission carried out by a joint force of Navy SEALs and Army Rangers that freed captive U.S. prisoners from a prison camp in Northern Pakistan, one of whom was his Navy SEAL father, Commander Bernie Lyon.

Admiral Steve Wheeler, U.S.N.: Chief of Naval Operations.

Commander Ryan 'Buck' Buckholder, U.S.N.: Commander, U.S. Navy SEAL Team Two.

Max Jenkins: Shadowy 'trouble shooter' and 'problem solver' for the executive staff of the CIA. He reports directly to the Deputy Director – Operations (DDO), Central Intelligence Agency.

Captain Mir Assad: Captain of Iranian 'Kilo' class submarine, hull # 454, sunk by U.S. Naval forces in the Strait of Hormuz.

Vice-Admiral Sidney Kineer, U.S.N.: Commander of U.S. Fifth Fleet; Doha, Qatar, (United Arab Emirates).

Rear-Admiral Nicolas Reardon, U.S.N.: Deputy Commander, U.S. Fifth Fleet.

Lieutenant Riley Pornier, U.S.N.: Pilot of F-35C fighter jet from the aircraft carrier U.S.S. Abraham Lincoln (CVN-72) tracking the Iranian Kilo submarine. His radio call sign is 'Porn Star.'

Mahmoud Abdul Rashad: Secular President of Iran. A Shiite Muslim.

Sharif Rashad: High ranking Iranian Trade Minister and secret plotter with his brother, Mahmoud Rashad, President of Iran.

General Pervez Ali al-Zarcash: Commander of the elite Pakistani Army Corps and Chief of Pakistani Army Security Forces. Second in Command only to General Jamil Muhammed, Commander of the Pakistani Military. He has a serious integrity problem.

Colonel Young Ho Kim: North Korean Commander of Korean nuclear technicians working on and maintaining nuclear warheads in Pakistan. An eventual co-conspirator with Sharif Rashad.

Hugo Delagarde: Executive Director Emeritus of Banque Switzerland et Cie, a venerable international banking concern with offices throughout Europe. A Grand Master at contract bridge with an impressive contact list that includes Heads of State and many international business executives.

Rene Delagarde: Managing Director of Banque Switzerland et Cie and son of Hugo Delagarde. Educated at the London School of Economics and Harvard Business School. Once employed at the U.S. Federal Reserve as Special Assistant to Allen Greenspan.

All characters are creations of the author, Van C. Torrey, and are purely fictitious. Any similarity with actual people, living or dead, is purely coincidental. Copyright, September, 2013. All rights reserved.

BOOK I

*

A SEAL WARRIOR'S FLASHBACK

LIEUTENANT CHANCE MACKLIN LYON, U.S.N.

"What's past is prologue."
Shakespeare (The Tempest)

Chance Lyon was groggily coming-to on a Stryker hospital bed in the recovery area of the sick bay of the aircraft carrier U.S.S. Abraham Lincoln as it steamed in the northern region of the Arabian Sea. Gradually he became aware of several other unoccupied beds and the fact that he was the only occupant of the cramped area, probably meaning that the huge vessel was operating at an unbelievable safety status at the moment. With a crew of over 6,000 sailors and airmen operating an array of complex mechanical equipment, it was rare that the place wasn't full of bodies in some state of recovery after surgical repair of an injury.

The SEAL team commander was beginning to shake off the effects of the general anesthetic from the surgery, and he was lucid enough to request his surgeon, Doctor (Commander) Jennifer King, to cut back on the pain meds that he was getting IV at the moment. Chance, like many other Navy SEALs, subscribed to the philosophy that relying on pain meds for moderate pain only increased one's vulnerability to pain when the luxury of pain medication was not available, as during a combat operation where clear thinking was required to accomplish a mission and support the actions of the team. An individual SEAL's personal comfort came in a distant third in that dynamic.

His attention immediately turned to his left thigh and the heavy bandaging around it. Through the fog Chance began to remember the sequence of events that brought him to this sterile medical cocoon where he was flat on his back and uncharacteristically helpless. His last conscious recollection was shooting it out with an unknown person in the cargo hold of an ocean freighter that he and his SEAL element had taken down many hours ago. Chance had killed the man but not before the man had wounded him with a piddling small caliber handgun. Even so, the projectile had penetrated his muscular thigh and managed to rupture his femoral artery, causing a sustained loss of blood that gradually eroded his cognitive processes. Chance vaguely remembered detonating the explosives his SEAL team had set in the cargo hold, but the rest of the night - getting back to the submarine in the Zodiacs, his transfer to the med-evac helicopter, and his arrival on the flight deck of the Abraham Lincoln was a hodge-podge of momentary images that had no continuity. *'For better or worse, here I am.'* Chance thought as he drifted back and forth from awareness to blissful nothingness.

"Good morning, Lieutenant Lyon," came the calm, professional voice of a woman in green scrubs with a print hair cover looking down at him with a warm smile. "I'm Doctor King, your surgeon. You're going to be just fine now that we have that ruptured artery put back together."

"Thank you, doctor. I can't believe that guy could cause all this trouble with that little cap pistol."

"Well Lieutenant, if it will help your ego, I'll tell your friends that he shot you with a forty-four magnum. That should enhance your war story bona fides in their eyes."

"No worries, ma'am, they'll know I'm just lying anyway," Chance replied playfully.

"Care to tell me what this was all about, Lieutenant?" asked Commander King. "There's no one here but us officers."

"Love to, doc, but it's classified. I could tell you,…but you know the rest."

"Do you know how many times I've heard that from you SEALs? What is it with you guys anyway? You sure seem to be injury prone," the doctor replied.

"Basically we're just a bunch of adrenaline junkies who overdose on our own testosterone sometimes. Guess I'm looking at the antidote right here."

"Well, I wouldn't push it Mr. Lyon," she replied good naturedly. "Speaking of antidotes, without surgery here on the Lincoln this could have gone very badly for you."

Chance and the doctor spent the next few minutes in a more business-like and professional conversation about his aftercare, during which he discussed his wishes about pain meds and revealed that his grandfather was a physician. Commander King told Chance that she would e-mail Doctor Mack Lyon about his grandson's condition and they agreed to have coffee in a couple of days after Chance was permitted to be up and around.

The next day the recovery nurse told Chance he was about to receive an important visitor. "We'll be clearing the room of all other personnel so you and Captain Turner can talk privately," she said with a wink.

When the Captain of the Abraham Lincoln, Captain Walter J. Turner, entered the recovery room he was greeted by Doctor King and her medical staff. "Good morning, sir," she said professionally. "Let me introduce you to our star patient, Lieutenant Lyon. We received him by special delivery from an undisclosed vessel two nights ago, after being assisted by some undisclosed colleagues, who were returning from an undisclosed mission at an undisclosed location. That's all he's willing to tell us."

"Damn, Commander King, do we even know if he's in our Navy?" replied Captain Turner. "He could be one of those Somali pirates."

The good natured banter continued for a brief period after which the skipper of the Lincoln requested to be left alone with Lieutenant Lyon.

After professional introductions Captain Turner confided to Chance that he had been in touch with Admiral Kineer, Commander of the Fifth Fleet, after Chance had been transferred to the Lincoln for treatment. "The Admiral wanted me to pass along his regards, Lieutenant Lyon. Apparently what you and your people were doing a couple of nights ago is classified way out of my pay grade, but he said that the mission was a complete success. Your team is probably in Diego Garcia by now and the freighter you were visiting is limping along to Iran, bruised, but still miraculously afloat."

"Thank you, sir. I'd like to give you a blow-by-blow, but I don't think I'm authorized...no disrespect, sir."

"None taken, son. I have enough to concern myself with, but I'm glad you're doing okay. None better than Doctor King and her staff. I'm Proud to have them aboard. They're going to transfer you to the hospital in Doha in a couple of days, then on to Ramstein. I understand you're a frequent flyer at that facility."

"Unfortunately, yes," replied Chance ruefully, referring to his neurosurgical procedure of two-and-a-half years ago there after being the victim of a Taliban sniper during a SEAL ambush of insurgent fighters in Afghanistan.

"Lieutenant, I've been a blue-water sailor since I got out of the Academy twenty-two years ago. I've never understood you commando types, but I'm damned glad you're on our side. I look at you here all bandaged up and I shudder to think what the other guy looks like," he said with a wink. "You're welcome in my sick-bay anytime!"

As a precaution, Chance was confined to his hospital bed for the next two days as he awaited transfer to a shore hospital in Doha, Qatar, United Arab Emirates, which was headquarters of the U.S. Fifth Fleet.

Chance did some reading and sent a few carefully crafted - ever mindful of the security aspects surrounding his recent mission - emails to his family and, especially, to his close friend, Judy Zavier.

Dad & Anne -
Just a quick note to tell you I'm making a 'detour visit' to a carrier while they do a little tune-up on my left leg. I had a little dust-up that required some surgery. No structural damage and I'm in pretty good shape despite the drama of getting here. Great medical staff fixed me up just fine. Going to Doha in a couple of days and then on to my old stomping grounds, Ramstein. Doc Mack should be getting an e-mail from my surgeon. Probably see you soon before I go back to work.
Chance

Chance then began to think about how he would break the news to his girlfriend Judy Zavier. In spite of Judy being a Naval Academy contemporary and the fact that she knew the risks of Chance's life as a Navy SEAL, she had always expressed concern about his welfare during long deployments. Chance hoped that a guarded message would not upset her unnecessarily.

Hi Judy -
Hope you are well and happy at work. I've had a little reversal and am being treated medically on a carrier. I'm getting excellent care from the staff and am going to be transferred to Doha in a couple of days. Some vascular damage to my left thigh, but I'll be okay in a few weeks they say. I'll call you from Doha. Please don't worry, this is not life or career threatening - just part of the job. Everybody else is okay. I've got a lot of time on my hands and have been thinking about our Jamaica adventure. What a way to end our vacation! Maybe we can go back and have a more relaxing finish. I love you!
Chance

Chance Lyon used the remote control to adjust the hospital bed back into a horizontal position and let his thoughts wander back to the happy days with Judy Zavier when they vacationed in Ocho Rios on the Jamaican coast many weeks ago. The two Naval Academy alumni had made a serendipitous reconnection at the Sandia nuclear training site where Chance and his fellow SEALs were training for an upcoming mission, and where Judy was assigned as a technical instructor.

Chance Lyon bolted upright from his sweat-soaked sheets, breathing in short gasps as he slowly began to comprehend that what he had just experienced was a nightmare and not reality. The ceiling fan circulating above his bed provided little relief in the humid sleeping porch of his tropical hotel suite.

Now fully awake, Chance looked anxiously around the area for Judy Zavier, his good friend and companion with whom he was sharing a brief vacation at the Sandals Grande Riviera Resort Ocho Rios, on the North shore of Jamaica in one of his rare breaks from duty.

Chance unwound from his sitting position and stayed seated for a moment at the edge of his bed, clearing his head of the vivid dream images of close and violent combat before venturing into the air conditioned comfort of the hotel suite.

"Judy, are you in here?" Chance ventured tentatively. He found her dozing in one of the large overstuffed lounge chairs in the living area adjacent to their sleeping porch.

"What are you doing out here, Judy? It's still dark."

"You were having one of your nightmares, Chance. I needed to escape the bed and your flailing around. Are you alright?"

"Yeah, I guess so...the same old shit," he answered absently.
Chance Lyon flashed back to tonight's dream and the one the night before. In it he and a number of his fellow SEALs were navigating a tropical river in one of the famous Zodiac boats when they were ambushed from the shore by a numerically superior force throwing spears and shooting arrows that were puncturing their rubber boat, causing it to lose steerage and founder. The dream ended with Chance and his

fellow SEALs clumsily attempting to reach shore encumbered by all their equipment and supplies as they dodged projectiles being hurled by their attackers.

"Chance, two weeks ago it was Stephanie, and then it was Walt Richard's death that had you going," Judy said as she uncurled herself from the chair and went over to give him a hug. "Maybe this break will help clear your mind of some of the built-up stress of that trauma," she continued. "Let's sleep for a couple more hours, have an early breakfast and then go snorkeling. The water looks really inviting. I haven't done much diving, but I bet you're a good teacher...Mr. Big Time Frogman," she said teasingly.

Judy's comments made Chance briefly think back to past events that made deep impacts on his psyche. Lieutenant Walt Richards had been a close friend and fellow SEAL warrior in Afghanistan before being ambushed and killed during a midnight raid on a meeting of Taliban cadre in a remote village just 25 miles from their Bagram base. Chance had escorted his friend's remains back to the United States, which had turned out to be the catalyst for a domino-like series of events that had culminated in the rescue of his Navy SEAL father and two other Americans who were being held as prisoners in Pakistan. The death of his friend had hit Chance hard, but, ever the warrior, Chance had put it behind him to continue his professional duties with distinction. Still, there was the occasional negative memory that sneaked into his thoughts to remind him of his past.

Stephanie Morris' death was another matter. Their romance, born out of a set of common experiences anchored in their education at the Naval Academy, was the first genuine romance for both, and held great promise for the future. Chance would always hold fast to the thought that the facts uncovered by the FBI investigator regarding her death pointed to Stephanie being identified as a close friend of a Navy SEAL and, therefore, a soft target for revenge planned by a domestic terrorist cell sympathetic to al-Qaeda in Afghanistan. Guilt trips were not Chance Lyon's specialty, but as with the Walt Richards tragedy, those thoughts invaded his otherwise healthy mind from time to time causing him significant angst and an occasional nightmare.

Chance and Judy Zavier rented some snorkeling gear from the Sandals' cache of recreational equipment and took bikes along a trail bordering the oceanfront. In thirty minutes they found a quiet cove with a secluded beach where warm, azure waters invited them to explore the beautiful scenery and sea life below. After a few minutes of expert instruction from Chance, Judy found herself at home, swimming effortlessly through calm water buoyed by the subtle foam life belt around her slim waist. Chance, a very strong open water swimmer, eschewed any such encumbrances and made adventurous free dives to the relatively shallow depths to retrieve small objects that caught his eye. He never strayed too far from Judy, who watched him enviously as he propelled himself through the water with the ease of a powerful sea creature. In the eyes of Judy Zavier, Chance Lyon - at one inch over six feet and weighing 190 pounds - had the physique of a well-toned athlete and was ruggedly handsome. *'He's definitely a keeper,'* she thought. *'I wonder if he thinks I am.'*

After their leisurely swim the couple returned to the hotel, had a light lunch and returned to find that the housekeepers had tidied up their suite, ensuring restful privacy for the balance of the day.

Judy showered to remove the salt from her short blond hair and washed her body with a lotion that had a scent of fresh tropical fruit. She dried herself, wrapped the towel Turkish style around her wet hair, and walked completely naked into the darkened living room of the suite. Chance had drawn the blinds to enhance the sense of a cool, dark refuge from the tropical heat, and was dozing lightly when Judy entered the room silently. As she bent down to kiss Chance on the forehead one of her bare breasts brushed against his shoulder causing him to startle to wakefulness.

After a brief moment of reorientation, Chance broke into a wide smile and pulled Judy to him and kissed her gently and fully on her lips.

"At first I thought I was dreaming, but waking up to this is way better that what I have been used to lately," he said softly to Judy. Chance explored Judy's athletically slim body with the lightest of touching that elicited whispers of pleasure from her. She reciprocated by breathing endearments and acknowledgments of his efforts into his ear while caressing him erotically in return.

"Chance, it's such a perfect day. Please make love to me. When we were swimming earlier I watched you being at one with the ocean and dreamed that you could be that way with me. I wanted you right there...right on the beach, in front of everyone," she giggled softly. "I feel so tuned into you right here...take me now."

Soon all pretense of propriety was abandoned by both of them, and they began consummating their mutual lust as young lovers do with complete abandonment to the moment. In contrast with his fierceness as a warrior, Chance was a sensitive lover, intent on giving pleasure to Judy. She responded with gratitude as their individual oral ministrations drove them to the heights of mutual pleasure, craving for release. After Chance sensed that Judy had achieved full arousal and experienced numerous states of physical gratification, he, too, gave in to the moment and then collapsed into her willing arms, spent of body and the spirit of the moment, to dream thoughts of intimate pleasure as a welcome change from his recent past.

They woke at sunset, sexually satisfied and rested, but hungry and re-energized by their recent intimacy. Chance and Judy had drinks and dinner on an open-air dining area of the resort that was bathed in the gentle tropical ocean breezes and the music of a steel band, as they spoke of things past and yet to be.

"Judy, to quote from an old Eric Clapton song: 'Yes, you look wonderful tonight.'"

Judy adroitly followed with..."Yes, I *feel* wonderful tonight;" and they both laughed at the thought of how two minds that were normally consumed in such seriousness of purpose in their daily work could also be in synch over such a triviality as old popular music lyrics.

As Chance and Judy walked the moonlit beach after dinner, their conversation turned to how they had reconnected after their days together at the

Naval Academy. Since Chance and Judy had not been in the same class there had not been any significant social contact between the two, but in such a closed society with so much culturally in common, acquaintances frequently evolved into future close friendships as cadets became commissioned officers and launched their careers in the fleet or the Naval specialty services. In the case of Chance and Judy, he had become a Navy SEAL operator and she had been attached by Navy BUPERS to Sandia National Laboratories by virtue of her degree in Nuclear Engineering, engaging in highly classified nuclear weapons research.

The two had reconnected professionally when Chance was ordered to bring his SEAL team to Sandia a few months ago for a Top Secret briefing and training session by Sandia staff concerning a portable weapons system developed there. The SEALs were planning to use the device in connection with the stealthy interdiction and disabling of critical uranium enrichment components headed for Iran. Much to the surprise of Chance, Judy had been one of the briefers for the SEALs when they arrived at Sandia.

The Sandia trainers and the SEALs had been cautioned by their respective leadership to maintain an arms-length relationship during their week-long stay. The fact that Chance and Judy were alumni of the Naval Academy, and knew of each other from that environment served to make their professional conversations more strained and artificial under the security circumstances.

Sometime after the training was finished, Chance had contacted her cautiously through an e-mail address he obtained from the Academy alumni directory and they began a tentative correspondence, always overly respectful of the security imperatives incidental to their respective highly classified professional duties.

As they walked the beach, Judy, in her usual cautiously forward manner, remarked to Chance "In spite of what your commander may have told you guys before you showed up in Albuquerque, we knew you were SEALs and the weapon we were training you on was going to be used by you to gamma radiate some unidentified cargo in the future. Sandia can be a little creepy at times as they go overboard on the security stuff. I'm glad you were straight with your C.O. that you recognized me, because I was also with mine, and the fact that we did so on a mutually exclusive basis eliminated any perception of an integrity problem for us then and in the future. That's one of the things the Academy experience does for us."

"And, by the way, I was pretty happy to hear from you after your training," she continued, as she took his arm with hers.

"I think the weekend a bunch of us were all together after Sandia for the Army-Navy game iced it for me, Judy. It was time for me to move on after Stephanie and I was ready for some down time after the last op, so you came along just at the right time."

"Is that over? Stephanie, I mean," she asked quietly.

"Yes, but I'll always be sad that she had to become a victim for what I had done in Afghanistan. At least that's what the FBI investigator concluded. I have to be honest, I'll probably always carry a little bit of that around with me."

"Chance, I have to be straight with you," said Judy, as they came to a halt during their walk, holding hands and absently scrunching the brilliant white sand with their bare feet. "I hope I'm not being presumptuous, but I'm becoming attached with my feelings for you and I know how your work can negatively impact a relationship. If we become closer, I'm prepared to work real hard on this if you are."

Chance thought for a moment before responding. "I'd be disingenuous if I dismissed that, Judy. My father was a SEAL operator and his marriage to Anne would not have lasted without her being a strong and committed woman. I understand what you're saying and know it's the truth based on my experience with my dad and my guys. I love and respect you and I promise to consider this as we move forward."

In an attempt to lighten the moment Chance continued. "Since you know something about what we have up our sleeves in the next few weeks, would you care to tell me what else you Sandia spooks have been up to these days?"

"You know the old joke, Chance. I could, but then I'd have to kill you."

"You are such a bitch," said Chance playfully. "But I have a soft spot in my heart for high quality bitches, and you're a Mercedes!"

"Seriously," continued Judy, as they resumed their walk, "I know we have to be careful with what we talk about, but we're on vacation, so let's forget about work for a while. How about a moonlight swim?"

"Are you suggesting that a classy, conservative, U.S. Naval Officer and gentleman like me risk it all by going skinny-dipping with a fellow officer? I mean, what would they say at the club? Ooops, I guess they don't have clubs anymore!"

"What I am suggesting, Lieutenant," answered Judy in her best conspiratorial tone, as she doffed her clothes and took Chance's hand, "is that this gentleman establish his territory like any good Navy SEAL would by doing so on sea, land, and air. We already took care of that on land this afternoon, the sea is beckoning, and, depending on the size of the head on the plane home, we can take care of the air aspect later. So, are you ready Lieutenant Lyon?"

It was well after midnight when Chance and Judy returned to their room at the hotel. In spite of the idyllic nature of the past few days of vacationing pleasure, neither Chance nor Judy was under any illusion about the time ahead. Both had chosen difficult professional disciplines that promised to tax them intellectually and, in Chance's case, perhaps physically. Any sustained romance would have to be on-the-fly and perhaps not entirely on their own terms. But, as with all military professionals speaking philosophically about their work with each other, the conversation frequently ends with, "...it's the life we chose."

∗

Jamaica is a tourist-driven, eclectically populated, laid-back, tropical paradise on the outside, shrouded in mystery and indigenous superstition in the inside. Along the waterfront and Victoria Avenue one can see the World on parade. In the deeper parts of Kingston, one can also see the dark side of that same world. That was the world of a man known as The Falcon.

Ty'anie Francis Marcone, known to his friends as 'The Falcon' due to his close-set eyes and widow's peak, was a recent and hard core convert to the Islamic faith. As an immigrant, and an illiterate and poverty stricken teen in the South Bronx of New York City, his frequent brushes with the law had finally scored him a one-way ticket to Riker's Island, the central jail facility just a couple of miles from the teeming streets of the city, but a world apart from gracious humanity itself. There, living in a survivalist culture, his life was saved but his soul was hijacked by Islamic fundamentalists who drowned him in the literal tenets of the Holy Quran and then brought him back to life as a jihadist for Islam.

After Marcone was released, he drifted in the streets during a drab winter in New York. Motivated by his dislike for the cold and wind, and fueled by proceeds from a number of petty thefts, he managed to accumulate enough money for a one-way plane ticket back to his native Kingston, where he fell in with some small-time criminals in a loosely organized street gang. It was there that he was noticed by some Jamaican Islamic fundamentalists and identified as the ideal conduit for an act of terror they hoped to launch against America.

The American Airlines flight from Kingston to Miami was only half-booked, which suited Chance just fine. After his experience with Stephanie, Chance took pains to enter and leave public places such as airports without Judy Zavier, primarily for her protection. Although it was a matter of personal preference, many Navy SEALs went to great lengths to protect their identity - mostly for the sake of their families, and rarely did they identify themselves as members of the SEAL community to those they did not know or trust.

By virtue of his training Chance was also ultra-sensitive to the concept of in-flight security. He always had a plan stashed in the back of his mind about reacting rapidly in case a flight on which he was a passenger was threatened with a criminally disruptive act.

His basic strategy was to sit as close to the front of the aircraft as possible so he could react quickly in the event of a threat, which statistics showed nearly always originated from that part of the aircraft. If such a threat did materialize it was also wise strategy to confront the threat immediately before a potential terrorist - and his co-conspirators, if any, - could get organized and establish control over the aircraft.

Chance, again by virtue of his SEAL training, knew that decisive and aggressive action gave him the best potential for a successful intervention. Time and again, the SEAL instructors had emphasized to SEALs in training the maxim of *'never letting an adversary gain a tactical advantage.'* Such an admonition was never far from Chance Lyon's thoughts.

As they left the cab from the hotel, Chance turned to Judy and said, "I'll see you inside. Your seat is in the back of the aircraft. Just remember, if there's a serious threat, get up and make a scene. Men never know what to do with crying women. See you in Miami."

Security in Kingston, Jamaica, will never rival that of the TSA at a busy American urban airport. Third World tourist hotspots are all about making sure the clients have a positive experience. The need for regularly returning travelers and their easy money make it an imperative for governments to do the absolute minimum from a security standpoint while still barely meeting international standards. Even then a lapse or two brings only a mild rebuke from a low level bureaucrat who has little or no enforcement power. Such was the situation in Kingston at the moment. Frequent changes in the government, combined with an unexplained drop in seasonal tourism, resulted in airport funding being reduced with many employees doing double or triple duty to cut down waiting times for those exhausted tourists waiting impatiently to board the flight home.

Ty'anie Marcone caught Chance's attention while they were in line for the carry-on scanner. Unless he had checked a large bag at check-in — unlikely in Chance's view as he assessed the tall, but scrawny looking person wearing ill-fitting new clothes — it didn't compute that he was holding only a small gym bag and was carrying a large set of boots to be scanned. Boots were hardly the footwear of choice among the Jamaican hipsters, who favored loose fitting minimalistic sandals. No baggage for a trip to the mainland and big, bulky boots?...red flag! Although it was just a hunch, this guy seemed out of place to Chance and way too uptight for a laid-back Jamaican dude jamming away at the airport.

As the line progressed Chance covertly watched the Jamaican passenger through his darkened Ray-Bans and thought he detected a glance of recognition between the security person operating the scanner and the Jamaican hipster. The boots and the small bag had barely exited the scanner before the Jamaican quickly retrieved them and went all the way to the furthest chair away from security before he tugged his boots on, grabbed the bag and walked rapidly to the waiting area where he checked in. To Chance, this act of checking in at the boarding area was proof enough that the person had not previously checked a bag. In the U.S.A., it was unlikely that the 'Masta Rasta,' as Chance had come to think of him, would have made it this far. Based on everything Chance had seen so far with this passenger, his antennae were on high alert. Lacking the level of training that Chance Lyon had, and his instinctive sense for imminent danger, it was unlikely that anyone other than Chance would have suspected a possible future problem.

Since the flight was not full, Chance hung back during the boarding process, making sure he boarded after the Jamaican, and took an empty seat a couple of rows behind him on the aisle. Chance also noted that Judy had taken an aisle seat in the rear of the aircraft that would make it convenient for Chance to pass her a note on the way to the aft head if he suspected something suspicious and had to communicate with her. Having a disciplined and intelligent ally — however physically unimposing she might appear — was better than having to rely on unknown strangers in a pinch.

After takeoff Chance pretended to read a magazine and refused any refreshment service so he could be unencumbered by a tray. When the person in the seat next to him, an older woman obviously returning from holiday, attempted to engage him in conversation, Chance replied in passable French, which ended that potential conversation abruptly. All his thoughts were focusing on the Jamaican three rows ahead.

The flight time between Jamaica and Miami is a little over one-hour and half way through the flight nothing had occurred. *'Maybe I'm a little oversensitized,'* thought Chance. *'Some of my fellow SEALs might say I need a week at the beach…but I just had a week at the beach,'* he reasoned darkly. Chance started to feel what is known as stress fatigue, which is what happens when stress is suddenly relieved and the body returns to an unthreatened and semi-relaxed state. He knew to defend himself against such vulnerability and forcefully refocused on the man three rows ahead. *'I still think something is amiss here,'* he thought.

Chance's highly refined sense of imminent danger, forged by the hours, days, and weeks of constant combat, and honed by the heavy burden of responsibility for the lives of his fellow SEAL warriors, was suddenly vindicated as a flight attendant walked up the aisle past his seat toward the galley at the front of the aircraft. As she passed the Jamaican he rose rapidly from his seat wielding a large knife that he had apparently extracted from his boot and held it to the neck of the visibly terrified attendant. He managed to turn her around so her body was between him and the majority of the passengers, who could see the point of the knife pointed to her carotid artery.

"You!…you," he shouted to another flight attendant several steps behind the captured woman, "call the Captain and tell him we are going to Havana. I will kill this infidel dog unless we change our destination immediately. Tell the Captain to make his turn immediately," he shouted, jabbing the point of the knife menacingly for emphasis.

From the back of the plane came the terrified wails of a woman, who Chance hoped was Judy, doing exactly as he had coached her in case of such an event. Ty'anie was momentarily distracted by the scene in the rear of the aircraft and craned his neck to see what the disturbance was.

Without Chance's ingrained notions of security, his suspicions regarding the Jamaican, and his pre-planning for such an eventuality, it was unlikely that even a warrior would be prepared for such a moment. However, Chance, ever assuming the consciousness of a highly trained Navy SEAL, was totally ready and made his move. The fatal flaw for the terrorist was that neither he nor his handlers anticipated that a credible response would come from an aircraft full of tired tourists nursing hangovers and sunburns. To their great future regret they didn't count on the actions of Lieutenant Chance Lyon.

True to his belief that a response should be swift and deadly, Chance sprang from his seat and lunged toward the victim as she was being held by her attacker. As Chance had been taught by Delta Force anti-hijacking experts, two predictable human reactions on the part of the attacker were in play here and they both came true. First was the element of surprise. The attacker was counting on everyone on the flight freezing in fear as he made his move. In his distraction about what might be happening in the rear of the aircraft, the attacker was not prepared for an immediate counter-assault from another passenger. Chance's violent lunge toward the victim and the Jamaican, so quickly after Marcone made his original assault, was completely unexpected.

Second, it is against the nature of a person holding a hostage to stand his ground if attacked. The natural reaction is to retreat a few steps to avoid the lunging counter attacker and prepare a defense. Such a movement was made by Ty'anie and Chance used that as momentum, sending the three of them crashing down violently onto the aisle of the aircraft.

In this evolving defensive dynamic the Jamaican lost the tactical initiative so important to the success of his mission, and the knife went sliding across the deck harmlessly. Chance pulled the screaming flight attendant off the prostrate body of the startled Jamaican, hurled her roughly into the seats adjacent to the aisle and straddled the Jamaican, placing his hands firmly around his neck. He put his face down close to the sputtering Jamaican and said in a surprisingly quiet tone, "This is over, you crazy motherfucker. Do not attempt to move or I will kill you with my bare hands right here. I will rip your fucking throat out. I love killing assholes like you! Do you completely understand? DO YOU?!"

Ty'anie Marcone was now shaking violently; he knew his reckless plan had come to grief and he was being straddled by a very strong and very angry man who was threatening to snuff out his life. To Marcone, right now the old mean streets of New York looked pretty good by comparison. What he didn't know was that his next stop in the long-term would probably be to a place known as SDX-Supermax in Florence, Colorado, where his body might be safe from harm, but he would probably, day after long day in solitary confinement, slowly and completely lose his mind.

As the flight crew attempted to reassure the passengers, the Co-pilot and Chance secured Ty'anie Marcone with hand-cuffs and tie wraps while isolating him from any passenger contact. The Captain was in touch with American Airlines security, and after brief introductions with Chance telling the Captain he was an active duty Navy SEAL, the Captain put him on the radio with the FBI team who would be meeting the flight in Miami.

"Just a precaution, Lieutenant Lyon, please give me your service number so we can verify with the Pentagon who you are. We're all very grateful for your quick thinking up there…you probably saved many lives today."

The American flight was cleared for priority landing in Miami, but would not be going directly to the gate. After landing, the Boeing 777 was directed to a secluded area of the airport and several busses were sent to take the passengers to a secure site where they would be interviewed individually by FBI and American Airlines personnel. Before the passengers were allowed to leave the aircraft, Ty'anie Marcone, Chance, and all the flight crew were taken off the aircraft and moved by FBI vans to a secure hangar area where they could be interviewed by federal law enforcement authorities.

Marcone had been subdued on the aircraft with a powerful sedative and was unconscious when he was removed on a gurney. To any casual observer, he would appear to be dead. This fact might work to the long-term advantage of the FBI.

After Chance gave a statement to the lead FBI investigator, the two had an opportunity for an off the record conversation. "Look, Lieutenant Lyon, if it weren't for you, this could have been a very bad outcome. We stopped using air marshals on most flights a long time ago, and something like this was bound to happen again. Unfortunately, we can't keep the press out of this. They're pounding on the door wanting to know details of the thwarting of this hijacking."

"You'll have to make up a story, Agent Hancock," said Chance firmly. "We don't do publicity unless the Navy dictates and that isn't frequently. There's also the security issue for me and my family. I've already had one bad situation occur that is classified. If you want to know about it you'll have to go through channels, but I'm not going to tell you about it here. That's between the Navy and the FBI. Anyhow, I don't want a repeat."

"I understand Lieutenant. We'll think of something. There's going to be some paperwork, but I'll run it through the Navy BUPERS and it will probably trickle down through your command. Believe me, Lieutenant, we'll do everything we can to protect your identity."

"Agent Hancock, there's one other thing. I'm traveling with another Naval officer; a Lieutenant Judy Zavier...she wasn't sitting with me...it's our protocol. Take it easy on her in the interview room. She knows nothing and she also has a highly classified job in the Navy. It wouldn't be good for her name to get out either. We both need to be John and Jane Doe as far as this goes."

"What about her, Lieutenant? Can you tell me something to help me with this?"

"Well, yeah; she works with nukes at Sandia. She probably has a higher clearance than the president."

Special Agent Hancock looked at Chance in dismay and shuffled his paperwork as he thought. "Lieutenant Lyon, may I ask you to sit tight for a few minutes? This whole thing is getting a little out of my pay grade."

Special Agent Anthony Hancock came back in ten minutes and sat down across from Chance Lyon. "Lieutenant Lyon, I just got off the phone with the Deputy Director. Lieutenant Zavier is being bussed over here as we speak and the two of you will be flying to Andrews tonight in a FBI private jet. You'll be meeting with the Director and some Navy and Delta Force types tomorrow morning. This may have been the cleanest outcome of a hijack attempt ever. I don't know who you are Lieutenant, but when your name came up, alarm bells all over Washington went off."

"Well, I didn't think it was that big a deal," remarked Chance with a deadpan expression. "It's not like there were a half dozen of them."

"Yeah, well, the Secret Service detail that you're getting in D.C. is not for you...it's for her!" answered Special Agent Hancock, raising an eyebrow and pointing his thumb toward the door to the hanger, through which Judy Zavier was expected to appear at any moment.

ONE MONTH LATER

Chance Lyon had been reassigned back to one of the East Coast SEAL teams as an Operations Officer when he was called into his C.O.'s office.

"Lieutenant, I've just been on the phone with the Deputy Director of the FBI. We both thought you might be interested in the longer-term results of the FBI follow-up of the attempted hijacking you foiled. It turns out that Ty'anie Marcone had no family, so the FBI put out a story that he had been killed in the hijacking attempt. This was meant to lull the terrorist cell in Jamaica who planned this into a false sense of security that Marcone would not be able to give us any information. Instead, the FBI has him on ice somewhere and he's singing like a choirboy, hoping that he won't be sent back to Riker's Island. Likely he doesn't know about Gitmo or Supermax. If he did he might be getting sentimental about old home week at Riker's.

Anyway the information he was able to give was enough to finger the jihadists in Jamaica. After diplomatic consultations with the Jamaican authorities these guys were arrested by Jamaican police and American FBI and the Jamaican government was only too happy to give them the boot. Right now they're all cooling their jets in Gitmo...as the travel agents say, 'the only resort in the Caribbean catering exclusively to terrorists.'"

"Also, about the identity thing. The FBI came up with a good one for that. They told the media that the person who foiled the hijacker was a Sky Marshal. Most people have heard of that program, so the feed was plausible. I don't think you have anything to worry about."

"Thank you, Commander," replied Chance. "I suppose you know that another naval officer was traveling with me. She's a ring-knocker and is working black, too. Just so you're in the loop."

"I'm vaguely aware, Lieutenant. That's all I want to know. Just keep that wrapped tight and you'll both be cool with everybody; ...and Lieutenant, sometimes it's dangerous to know too much."

"Yes, sir," replied Chance knowingly.

"You're dismissed. We've got a lot of work to do."

As the memories of Jamaica and Judy Zavier gradually faded from Chance Lyon's awareness, and the cutting edge interdiction mission behind him, he wondered what his professional future might bring next.

BOOK II

*

FATEFUL PLOT

CHAPTER 1

TROUBLE ON THE HIGH SEAS

"Without a decisive naval force we can do nothing definitive; and with it everything honorable and glorious."
George Washington

On a moonless overcast night in February, an Iranian SSK Kilo Class submarine lay in wait at the north side of the Strait of Hormuz bordering the Gulf of Oman. Having left the Iranian naval port of Bandar-e-Abbas at 23:00 hours the *Spirit of Revolution* proceeded on the surface for two hours before diving to a depth of 150 feet and crawling along at 6 knots in a southeasterly direction. The Kilo Class boat, built in the Russian Federation at the Admiralty Shipyards in Saint Petersburg and sold to several navies throughout the world, had a reputation for being one of the quietest diesel submarines ever produced. In the narrows of this busy waterway with the huge volume of surface traffic making passage at all hours, there was a very low noise signature from this deadly warship, or so it was thought by the Iranian Navy.

KILO CLASS SUBMARINE

NUCLEAR DENIAL

TYPICAL VERY LARGE CRUDE CARRIER

Earlier the previous day the Very Large Crude Carrier (VLCC) *International Galaxy* had left the crude oil deep water offloading port at Manamar, Bahrain with a fresh load of 300,000 dead weight tons of Saudi Arabian crude oil, heading for the Japanese port and oil refinery facilities of Ichihara in Tokyo Bay. The International Galaxy was a perfect target for the sinister plans of the Islamic Republic of Iran's President Mahmoud Rashad.

At 04:00 hours the skipper of the Kilo submarine, Captain Mir Assad, brought his submarine to periscope depth and lay in wait for the perfect moment when he could fire three of his Iranian made Val-Fajr high explosive torpedoes toward this pre-determined target. Iranian intelligence assets had notified their contacts at the Iranian Naval headquarters of Bandar-e-Abbas of the exact time of sailing of the *International Galaxy* and the navy had tracked her progress toward the Arabian Sea via the Strait of Hormuz by aircraft radar, plotting her exact course and speed. This information was, in-turn, simultaneously passed on to the *Spirit of Revolution* as she transited from the Iranian naval base. By simple navigational projection the submarine captain was able to position his boat at the precise point where he could make his intercept, fire his spread of torpedoes, and make a clean get-away.

Although the moonless sky provided little celestial lighting, the fact that the captain knew exactly where to look made detection of the lumbering VLCC relatively easy. Equipped with a massive array of running lights as a precaution against collision with another vessel in this narrow waterway, with twin thirty foot diameter bronze propellers churning away as she made way at 10 knots in this busy shipping lane, the huge oil tanker was easy to identify and target.

When *The Spirit of Revolution* was three thousand yards away, hovering at periscope-depth and abeam of the fully loaded tanker, Captain Assad made an initial calculation of his firing solution and prepared to fire a spread of three torpedoes. Assad was so sure of his firing solution and the fact that the tanker was taking no evasive action that he didn't even bother to submerge deeper and wait for the range to close further. Instead he activated the recording mechanism in the periscope to document the attack that was likely to have reverberations throughout the world.

PREDATOR DRONE AIRCRAFT

But Captain Assad was unaware that for the past 60 minutes his submarine had been tracked by a U.S Air Force unmanned Stealth Hawk drone aircraft being controlled out of Fort Rucker, Alabama, nearly 6,000 miles away. This super-secret, seventh-generation stealth drone was equipped with two advanced technology sensors that gave away the Kilo's position just as if it were traveling on the surface with a full complement of running lights blaring jihadist slogans from powerful speakers.

First, the drone had a sensitive infrared sensor that was able to sense temperature variations in sea-water down to 200 feet with a sensitivity window of 5 degrees, C. The submerged Kilo's external temperature near the rotating screw was easily greater than ten degrees compared to the surrounding seawater. Once a deviation above that window was detected, a tiny wireless acoustic sensor was launched by the drone that landed on the sea surface within a 500 yard radius of the submerged submarine's temperature signal. Although the noise of the many vessels transiting the strategic strait was a confused cacophony of sonar signatures, this advanced acoustic sensor split frequencies so thinly that it immediately picked up the Kilo's unique signature, identified by the U.S. Navy's exhaustive database of acoustic identities of most of the World's fleet of seagoing vessels, friend and foe alike.

Once detected by the drone, the tracking telemetry of the Kilo from the drone was carefully monitored by computer at both Fort Rucker and U.S. Fifth Fleet Headquarters in Doha, Qatar, in the Persian Gulf. This identification of a potential enemy submarine in an area fraught with tension set off a series of events that had been carefully and exhaustively war-gamed many times over by planners at the highest level in the Pentagon.

Once the Kilo was identified by the drone, a U.S. Navy F-35C fighter carrying a newly developed version of a Mark 50 torpedo was launched from the nuclear aircraft carrier U.S.S. Abraham Lincoln, flagship of the U.S. Navy Carrier Strike Group Midway that was patrolling in the northern reaches of the Arabian Sea.

The Mark 50 was a scaled down but technically superior version of the formidable Mark 45 torpedo that had served the navy so well in the early

U.S.S. ABRAHAM LINCOLN (CVN-72)

part of the 21st Century. Lighter, faster, yet with a powerful warhead, the Mark 50 was capable of being launched by naval aircraft or by the new San Antonio class amphibious transport dock ships (LPD's), such as the U.S.S. New York, built to patrol and protect vital American interests in the littoral waters of world trouble spots.

UNITED STATES F-35C JOINT STRIKE FIGHTER

Vice-Admiral Sidney Kineer, Commander of the U.S. Fifth Fleet, was immediately notified of the identified Kilo by his Fleet Deputy Commander, Rear-Admiral Nicolas Reardon in the Fleet Combat Decision Center (CDC). Kineer and Reardon had been classmates at the Naval Academy as well as roommates playing quarterback and tight end, respectively, for the Midshipmen. This current teamwork, the groundwork of which had been laid on the football field of Annapolis, had prepared the two men exceptionally well for the command responsibility they shared in one of the world's greatest potential flash points.

"Admiral, we have a Kilo moving in the Strait of Hormuz," Reardon reported by secure telephone to Kineer. "Her acoustic signature was identified by a drone. Computer tracks are identical between Fort Rucker and Doha Fleet Tracking Command. I think there is a 95 percent chance this is Iranian, sir. They are the only ones in the Gulf using Kilos these days. One hundred percent it is not Russian."

"Can we be any more definite about the boat, Nick? See if you can get a better workup," replied Kineer. "I'll be in the CDC in five minutes to join you." Admiral Kineer was an old school sub-driver, and his juices started to flow as he knew a deadly game of undersea cat-and-mouse was about to begin right in his back yard.

When Admiral Kineer arrived in the Fleet CDC he was greeted by his Deputy Commander, Nick Reardon. "As I told you, sir, I think we have a developing situation in the Strait." The Fleet Combat Decision Center was a large underground room at the sprawling U.S. Naval Base at Doha. The CDC was darkened and quiet; the glow of large computer consoles reflecting off the faces of the analysts and communication specialists gave each technician a ghost-like appearance.

A huge video screen dominated the CDC on the north wall of the building, showing in real time the positions of every U.S. Naval and air asset active in the Middle East Theater of Operations. The technicians controlling the display could also superimpose a view of any foreign air or sea asset being tracked by U.S. radar.

The only asset not shown on the Flag Plot, as it was known to those working in the CDC, was the position of several stealth drones operated by the U.S. Air Force out of Al Udeid Air Base in Qatar. These airborne intelligence assets were considered so highly classified that only flight control technicians at Fort Rucker, the Command level of the Fifth Fleet, and the technical personnel at Al Udeid could be aware of their presence and approximate position.

The number of drones and their disposition was considered so highly classified that if either Admiral Kineer or Reardon wanted to see the location of any drones he could do so only by placing a password known to him in a special computer terminal in a separate Marine-guarded room at Flag Plot. "Admiral, it looks like we have a bogie that might have bad intentions. We've been tracking for about an hour and she has slowed to nearly a complete stop. There are oil tankers transiting the area and we're keeping a sharp eye on this guy," remarked Deputy Commander Reardon steadily.

"Any further I.D., Nick?" asked Kineer.

"Yes sir, Admiral." *Even though Sid Kineer and Nick Reardon were the closest of personal friends from many years back, when in the Fleet CDC with so many others present they maintained a very formal communications protocol. The two Admirals believed that this professional behavior set the example for all junior officer and enlisted technical staff that, in time of crisis, would have to work in professional unison to accomplish the assigned mission.*

Reardon continued, "We ran the signature through the computer and we think it's Kilo 454 or 456. Both were sold by the Russians to Iran ten years ago. We have good acoustic data on both boats, and they have nearly identical signatures because their hull numbers are close and they were built concurrently in the Admiralty Shipyard in St. Petersburg to identical specifications."

"What is the status of our blocking assets, Nick?" asked Admiral Kineer. (In this case a four star admiral was free to use any form of address to an officer his junior).

"We've launched an F-35C from the Abraham Lincoln with a Mark 50 as ordnance, sir. He's closing on the area and will be able to fire in less than two minutes if we need him," replied Reardon.

"We also have a SSN, U.S.S. Phoenix, en route. I didn't want to break her off from the Midway strike group, but we doubled the air cover and launched another drone out of Muscat to provide additional cover for the strike group. We still have a second SSN on Midway's station. Standard protocol dictates placing the Lincoln on DEFCON two for the time being. In addition to F-35s flying high cover, that means we have armed F-35s positioned on both catapults of the Lincoln with engines hot, and four more fighters staged. AWACS cover shows no aerial or surface threats and the CSG's destroyers are darting around like snarling dogs looking for submerged threats. We could have ten fighters in the air in eight minutes. Captain Turner and his Air Boss, Glenn Forsey, on the Lincoln have their people pumped, sir."

"Can we get a live TV feed from the drone, Nick? Probably can't see much if Kilo is submerged, but let's take a look anyway."

Admiral Kineer was correct that the drone was showing nothing except surface ships, especially a large VLCC entering the narrows of the Strait of Hormuz. Suddenly, a speaker crackled from the encrypted communications link to Fleet Command - Doha from Alabama. "Doha Command, this is drone control Sierra," came a transmission from Rucker control in Alabama. "Our drone Alpha Tango 13 is currently under joint command link Doha. We are designating the Kilo as target Victor 23. To take command of this asset, please authenticate *Charlie Victor Two-Niner-Six*."

This was a coded Signal Operating Instruction (SOI) coming from drone command that required the local commander, in this case Admiral Kineer, to read back a coded alpha-numeric sequence corresponding to the coded sequence just read by Fort Rucker Drone Command. This code changed every three minutes by a random number generator in the Pentagon. Admiral Kineer, or his designee, had less than three minutes to validate the authentication request or Fort Rucker would abort the drone's mission and return it to base.

Admiral Kineer plucked a small book attached by a chain from around his neck and motioned for his deputy to do the same. They found the alphabetized code in the small signal books and saw a series of letters that appeared next to the code they had received. The two admirals went to different computer terminals and typed in the code they received from Fort Rucker and the corresponding code from their books. In an instant a series of numbers and letters flashed up on the two computer screens. Both officers copied the letters before the code disappeared from the screens. They immediately compared the code each had copied and verified that they were identical.

Admiral Kineer nodded to Reardon, who picked up a secure telephone set and said, "Rucker, I authenticate *Whiskey X-Ray Seven Five Eight*."

Rucker drone control responded, "Authentication valid. Doha, you now have command of the Alpha Tango 13. It is your mission. Thank you, sir. Rucker out."

If the authentication from Doha had not been valid the communications link between Alabama and Doha would have been immediately terminated and all hell would have broken out in the Chief of Naval Operations (CNO) office in the Pentagon, CENTCOM, and the CIA. Admiral Kineer and his staff at Fifth Fleet Flag Plot would have a lot of explaining to do.

"Okay, Nick," commanded Sidney Kineer to his deputy, "It's your show."

Minutes went by until the data stream that was steadily coming from the drone signaled CHANGE OF TARGET STATUS in large red letters. Additional data updates flashed on the screen in red letters. TARGET COMING TO PERISCOPE DEPTH...HOVERING AT PERISCOPE DEPTH...
RADAR DETECTING PERISCOPE...DEPTH STEADY...TARGET NOT MAKING WAY...SPEED ZERO...DEPTH STEADY...

"Nick, I'm an old sub driver and I say this skipper is lining up a shot. I say have the pilot arm the Mark 50. If the Kilo opens his torpedo tube doors, order the pilot to fire," ordered Kineer.

"Aye, sir," replied Reardon. The pilot in the F-35C had been designated call sign Barn Burner Three.

"Barn Burner Three, this is Alpha Tango 13 actual. You are authorized to arm your ordnance. Stand by for command to fire. Fire **ONLY** on my command."

"Roger 13," replied the F-35C pilot laconically. Lieutenant Riley Pornier, U.S.N., otherwise known by his radio call sign 'Porn Star,' knew that if commanded he would drop his torpedo but have no control over its trajectory after it left his aircraft. Control of the deadly weapon would be totally under the control of the telemetry from the drone he could not see. If it hit the target, the drone, not 'Porn Star' would be the hero here. *'I'm supposed to be a fighter jock but, today, I'm just a delivery boy,'* he thought.

Captain Assad, satisfied that his firing solution was correct to destroy the Very Large Crude Carrier in a hellish inferno of flames that would send the tanker to the bottom of the shallow strait, gave the order to open the forward torpedo tube doors. He planned to shoot a spread of three torpedoes ten seconds apart to hit the tanker in three different spots, assuring her complete destruction with a maximum amount of flames. In this pre-dawn environment the flames would be seen for many miles in the still waters of this strategic waterway. *'The Strait will be closed for weeks because of my actions here tonight,'* Assad thought smugly. *'I will surely be awarded a medal by President Rashad and be looked upon with great favor by Allah.'*

"Opening torpedo tub doors, Captain," said the Kilo's fire control officer.

One final thought occurred to Captain Assad; he asked his sonar officer if he saw any threats on his waterfall display. "No submerged contacts, Captain."

Captain Assad, cautious man that he was, hesitated. He had set up his shot carefully and his sonar man detected no threats on his waterfall, so Assad had no sense of urgency about taking his shot.

*

The telemetry from the drone virtually shouted out to the Admirals in the Fleet CDC in a re-lettered crawl across the screen, CHANGE OF STATUS...TORPEDO TUBE DOORS OPENED...

Rear-Admiral Nick Reardon, a man of steady nerves and firm resolve, and knowing that the possibility of him getting his third star hung in the balance of this moment, spoke into his microphone, "Barn Burner Three, this is Alpha Tango 13 actual; FIRE. I say again, FIRE."

Within a split second, 'Porn Star' triggered his already hot weapon and got an immediate confirmation of a green light from his heads-up-display (HUD) that the deadly torpedo was away. "Roger, 13; ordnance away," as casually as if he had executed a simple task.

"Roger, Barn Burner; stay on station to confirm results. How's your fuel?"

Pornier fudged a little and replied, "My HUD says I'm good for eight minutes, sir; then I'm bingo." Porn Star was already making provision for an afterburner get-away that would probably be his only excitement for the day.

"No sweat, Barn Burner; this will be all over in three minutes," replied Reardon.

Captain Assad looked nervously over at his sonar officer, a mere youth of 20 years, as he intently watched the waterfall display cascading in front of him. *'So young...so little experience'* thought the Captain. *'Does he really know there are no contacts to thwart our mission?'* For a moment, Captain Assad was lost in thought and hesitated for a fatal moment.

"CAPTAIN, CAPTAIN," shouted the freshly panicked sonar officer; "TORPEDO IN THE WATER...TORPEDO HAS ACQUIRED US... RANGE ONE THOUSAND METERS...NINE HUNDRED METERS."

Captain Assad turned from his periscope and looked at the young sonar officer in stunned disbelief. *'This cannot be...I've been so careful setting this up... Allah has betrayed me.'*

"EIGHT HUNDRED METERS, CAPTAIN!"

The last words commanded by Captain Assad to his unknowing crew were, "DIVE...CRASH DIVE! ALL AHEAD FULL!

The Mark 50 torpedo homed in on the fleeing Kilo, made a short course correction and slammed into the doomed submarine at a full 50 knots, simultaneously setting off its one hundred pound warhead. The combination of the torpedo's impact on the hull of the Kilo and the powerful explosion caused the submarine to implode violently, splitting it nearly in half. All hands were killed in moments and the intensity of the impact could be heard on the surface for ten miles and on the sonars of ships up to thirty miles away.

"Alpha Tango 13, this is Barn Burner. I have a surface visual of impact. Looks like you got your man. Request permission to vector off station and head for the barn," Pornier asked.

"Roger, Barn Burner. Permission granted; fine flying, son," responded Admiral Reardon.

Porn Star put the victorious F-35C into a snap roll to a 180 degree turn, locked on to the Abraham Lincoln's omnidirectional navigation signal and pushed the sleek fighter to a bone jolting after-burner thrust just as the sun broke over the eastern horizon. *'Man...that's better than sex...,'* thought Pornier. *'Looks like I'll be back for breakfast.'*

CHAPTER 2

AFTERMATH – CHAOS AND INTRIGUE

News of the sinking of the Iranian Kilo was known within a few moments at CENTCOM, in the office of the CNO, and simultaneously at the Middle Eastern desk at CIA headquarters in Langley, Virginia. Within moments Jack Duggan, the President's National Security Adviser, Rachel Hunter, Director of National Intelligence (DNI), and Ray Rollins, Director of the CIA (DCI) were connected by secure land-line to compare what each of them had been told by their respective briefers. In this case, the information was essentially identical and it became Jack Duggan's job to notify the President of this event. Early morning in the Gulf region was just past nine at night in Washington, and Duggan guessed correctly that the President, a notorious early-to-bed guy, was either reading or had dozed off. He decided to go through the White House switchboard as this President preferred to use the White House internal communications system with his staff for security reasons.

Duggan dialed a private number that was immediately routed to an automated switchboard in the basement of the White House and after hearing a series of beeps, punched in a numeric code unique to him that routed the call directly to the President's private residence. A tone from his bedside phone jerked Jonathan Braxton's attention from his e-reader and as he glanced at the caller I.D. he winced slightly as he saw the name of Jack Duggan, his National Security Adviser. *'This can't be a bedtime story,'* thought Braxton, as he picked up the receiver.

"Evening, Jack, I trust this can't wait 'til morning; I've had a long day already."

Duggan decided to forego the preliminaries and spoke directly.
"Mr. President, a U.S. Navy fighter, under the command of the Fifth Fleet Commander in Qatar, just sunk what we believe to be an Iranian Kilo-class submarine in the Strait of Hormuz. We have strong intel that she was targeting a loaded crude oil tanker transiting the Strait and was about to fire a torpedo."

"Jesus, Jack, sorry; I guess that rates a wake-up. What more do we know?"

Duggan did a quick brief for the President and told him that the Navy was rushing assets to the scene to gather more intelligence particularly relating to the sunken submarine. "I'm sure we'll have more info in a few hours, Mr. President."

"Okay Jack, better gather the members of the National Security Council in the Oval Office at 07:00 tomorrow. That'll give CIA a chance to develop more intel. Hang on, will you? I want to check something." Jonathan Braxton reached for the TV remote control on his bedside table and clicked on to CNN. It looked like normal news programming, but in a moment a crawl across the bottom of the screen screamed in large red letters, 'BREAKING NEWS'...*al Jazeera TV is reporting that a large explosion has been heard in the Persian Gulf in the vicinity of the Strait of Hormuz. There has been no visual sign of any explosions in the area but al Jazeera reports intense air activity about 20 miles south of the busy naval port of Bandar-e-Abbas.*

"Jack, CNN has a crawl reporting an explosion in the Persian Gulf... nothing visual. I'm sure this will break more later tonight. Do we have lockdown on this?"

"So far it's black for us, Mr. President; nothing to tie us to any action so far. It's possible Iranian radar knew that we had air assets in the area and when they discover they've lost a Kilo they may blame us. I recommend we keep a lid on it and play dumb at the press briefing tomorrow. The press corps are going to see a connection between the news that develops out of there and the National Security Council meeting, but we can just say that was a precautionary meeting."

After a moment the President replied, "Jack, let's just keep this meeting between you, Rachel Hunter, CIA, and the SECDEF for right now. We can always expand it if we have to. This will cause less of a commotion. I see you guys every day anyway, so if we keep it low key it'll look routine. I'll call the Secretary of State and brief him in after I ring off with you. Please call SECDEF and have him show up at 07:00. We can talk before that and have current information lined up for him. And Jack, brief my Chief of Staff in on this ASAP."

Duggan rang off, knowing that there would be little sleep for him this night. Braxton turned off the sound on his TV and stared across the bedroom at nothing in particular, reflecting, as he sank back into his bed, on the sequence of events that had led up to this initial crisis, which might be the first real test of his administration's second-term foreign policy expertise.

Shortly after he had been inaugurated, his wife, Jane, had been diagnosed with a particularly virulent form of pancreatic cancer and had died six months later. In spite of his presidential duties, Braxton had been able to apply the appropriate amount of time and energy to this deeply personal ordeal.

In the roughly six months since her death, he had concentrated on doing what government was capable of doing to reinvigorate the economy by improving opportunities for job growth and reducing regulatory interference for the private sector. He had been fortunate to be able to forge a strong coalition of enlightened congressional leaders and private sector leaders, and the U.S. economy was beginning to improve steadily. Now, he was on the verge of his first real foreign policy crisis, the management of which might be the basis on which his second term might be judged.

In the past, Jonathan Braxton had relied on the sound and steadying advice of his academically gifted and politically savvy wife to help him find his way through the murky corridors of personal and professional crises. Now he no longer had Jane's support to lean on. Instead, he would have to rely on the intellectual skills, judgments, and gut instincts of the national security team he had assembled when he was elected. Braxton wondered if they were up to the challenges of this latest crisis, and whether he and his team would be able to control it to the safety and benefit of the United States of America.

President Braxton flashed back to the incident in a previous administration involving a U.S. aircraft carrier in the northern reaches of the Arabian Sea. After a series of provocative moves – initiated by the Iranians and responded to clumsily by U.S. Theater Commanders who were out of sync with the National Command Authority – the Iranians shot at a U.S. aircraft carrier with an Exocet missile that managed to infiltrate the protective counter-measures surrounding the carrier. The carrier was heavily damaged and over four-hundred U.S. Navy personnel were killed or wounded.

As bad as that was, a U.S. Navy nuclear submarine responded by launching two sea-launched cruise missiles with non-nuclear warheads that substantially damaged two of Iran's suspected nuclear processing facilities. Fortunately these were far away from any significant population centers and damage was limited to the facilities and personnel working there. Only the immediate intervention of Russia and China at the United Nations Security Council prevented the situation from spiraling out of control, possibly involving Israel and Saudi Arabia.

In the end the big losers were Iran – losing two advanced processing and R & D facilities while further exposing their strategic military impotence, by having no capacity to respond to a retaliatory attack – and the U.S. President himself. His bungling of the initial provocation was soundly condemned by the media, which had supported him blindly up to this point, as well as by congressmen from his own party. In the end he was exposed as an emperor with no clothes and he lost the election to Braxton by a landslide.

But Braxton's honeymoon was now over and he knew that a new bungled crisis on his part would be damaging to his reputation as a leader in the arena of global geopolitics. This new crisis required skillful management with little margin for error.

IRAN

The news about the mysterious explosion heard in the Persian Gulf Tuesday morning started taking bizarre twists almost immediately. As dawn broke over the Strait of Hormuz immediately after the explosion was detected, Iranian patrol boats zeroed in on the area that their acoustic triangulation determined to be the likely site and soon found flotsam that could be identified as belonging to the Kilo. In a matter of hours a press release from the Iranian military made a cautionary statement that one of their submarines had been lost in the Strait due to 'unknown' causes.

The secular President of Iran, Mahmoud Abdul Rashad, was confronted with the news of the loss of the Iranian Kilo submarine immediately after morning prayers.

In contrast to the disingenuous humility he had just displayed in his exhortations to Allah as he bowed toward Mecca on his elegant prayer rug, the short but muscular Rashad ran his hands in frustration over his closely cropped hair and flew into a violent rage at the news.

Only Rashad and a few of his closest military staff were aware of the plan to confront the West in the Strait, and now the tables had been turned on them by an unknown military assassin. Iranian diplomats were already flooding the foreign ministry asking for instructions on how to respond to the speculation leaking out on news feeds that debris from a ship thought to be sunk in the Strait in today's early hours might have been Iranian and a military vessel as well.

But by whom and under what circumstances? That question, and the fact that he had been foiled in his grand plan, confounded him immensely. What would he tell the Shiite clerics – the omnipotent ayatollahs – who were the true source of his power?

THE WHITE HOUSE

The CIA reviewed the sound data gathered by the US Air Force Drone and its acoustical buoy and confirmed with one-hundred percent certainty that the sub was Iranian Kilo, hull number 564. This information was immediately given to Jack Duggan as he was about to make his way into the Oval Office for the meeting scheduled the night before with President Braxton. So far, the only people who knew all the pieces of the puzzle unfolding in the Gulf were at the highest levels of intelligence of the United States. The purpose of this meeting with Braxton, Jack Duggan, DNI Rachel Hunter, Director of Central Intelligence Raymond Rollins, Secretary of Defense Justin Roberts, and Braxton's Chief of Staff Philip Johnson, was to share ideas about how to achieve containment of what they knew and how to manipulate the situation to the best advantage of the United States.

The meeting convened in the Oval Office informally, as the Director of National Intelligence, Rachel Hunter, reviewed the events of the past twelve hours. "Mr. President, we had sound intel that an Iranian submarine was about to fire on a crude oil tanker coming out of the Strait of Hormuz. This was an overtly hostile act with no provocation. The Fifth Fleet Commander, in whom we all have complete confidence, took appropriate action based on our national policy, *that had previously been made clear to all stake-holders in the region"* she said for emphasis, "and eliminated this threat by forceful, aggressive action, thereby keeping this vital international commercial waterway safely open to all traffic."

"Very well, Rachel," replied President Braxton, "What's next?"

Jack Duggan stepped up next. "Mr. President, we believe this was done with a maximum of stealth on our part using the most sophisticated weapons in our arsenal. Both the U.S. drone aircraft operating out of Al

Udeid airbase in Doha, Qatar, and the F-35C Joint Strike Fighter from the Abraham Lincoln were unlikely to have been detected by the Iranians. In addition, the Mark 50 torpedo that took out the Kilo probably exploded into so many pieces that it would be impossible to trace this back to us. Therefore, we think it is reasonable that this action can be contained to this room at the moment. Sure, there are some military personnel involved, but these people know this was a classified mission and we shouldn't expect any leaks there."

"Okay," continued Braxton, "I guess this makes us the Lone Ranger in this little skirmish. Any recommendations for the path forward?"

Jack Duggan continued, "Sir, I think I speak for all of us when I recommend we keep a low profile on this. Many in the press and in diplomatic circles are going to speculate that this action was taken by U.S. forces. Let them do just that...speculate. I recommend that our position be one of *"we don't know what actually happened, and therefore we have no comment."* If asked directly if U.S. forces were involved we answer 'No,' as simply as that."

"Okay, unless there are objections or alternative suggestions from anyone, this will be our public position. Phil, give Sarah Whittington some guidance on this so we're all on the same page. Oh, and by the way people, my guess is that this is going to be a bumpy ride before it's over. You know, those *unintended consequences* that keep us all awake at night." President Braxton paused for a moment, then said, "I expect this to develop significantly during the next 24 hours; we meet again at 07:00 tomorrow. If you have sources, work them discreetly like you don't know anything. I'll need your input and recommendations. Thank you!"

PAKISTAN

Ali El Hakim, President of Pakistan, upon being made aware of the cautious early news out of Iran by his Security Minister, placed a telephone call to the head of the Pakistani Defense Ministry, General Jamil Mohammed, and asked him if he could give an assurance that no Pakistani Naval assets were active in the area of the Strait of Hormuz. Mohammed, a clandestine political foe of the Pakistani President, replied cautiously that there was no such activity. Once the conversation was terminated, the Pakistani military chieftain arranged an urgent meeting with his naval commander to discuss this potentially troubling news out of the Gulf.

Pakistan was now geographically caught between two neighbors, India, which possessed a nuclear weapons capability, and with whom Pakistan had fought a short but brutal war in 1971; and Iran, with which political and religious relations were not friendly, and which seemed intent on acquiring a nuclear weapons capability of its own. Any flare-ups in this regional tinder box had to be carefully watched by Pakistan, whose primary military strength was in its possession of a sizable number of potent nuclear weapons.

The actual location, as well as command and control of these weapons, within Pakistan, was another question altogether, which made the political and military dynamic of Pakistan the lynchpin of the entire Middle East and Asian subcontinent region.

CHAPTER 3

PLOTS AND COUNTER PLOTS

"Oh what a tangled web we weave when first we practice to deceive."
Sir Walter Scott

President Mahmoud Abdul Rashad was being bombarded on all sides by those requesting information and those offering advice in light of the increasing amount of speculation and questions about the sinking of Kilo 564. Most of the advice he brushed aside as coming from Iranian officials he deemed intellectually inferior or for whom he felt a measure of distrust. The people he was accountable to unquestionably were the ayatollahs of the ruling Council of Clerics who, at this point, only had questions about the sinking.

He had to fabricate a story that would be plausible to their inquiring natures. Rashad might be the president, but his power was ultimately in the hands of the Muslim clerics who were the religious leaders of Iran.

Late in the day the Iranian president was summoned to a meeting of the Supreme Clerical Council, the group of Shiite Muslim mullahs who were the real power behind Rashad's presidency. Rashad spent the final two hours prior to the meeting feverishly trying to determine the facts behind the Kilo loss; more specifically trying to understand with clarity exactly what foreign force had thwarted his plans.

He had summoned his intelligence chief and the admiral who commanded the Iranian naval forces to his office. After the briefest of formalities, Rashad, shaken with frustration and concerned with what he would tell the ayatollahs in the impending meeting, tried to remain calm as he questioned his colleagues. "What have you learned about the Kilo lost this morning? Do we know who did this thing to us?" he asked in a low voice.

Admiral al-Hamish, the Naval Commander, replied tentatively; "Mr. President, we have patrol boats on the scene who are recovering items on the surface that we are sure came from the Kilo. Unfortunately, we don't know how the boat was lost. However the depth near the site is only about 70 meters, so we are in the process of getting divers on the wreck as we speak. We should know something very soon."

Rashad nodded his head anxiously, but remained calm while thinking. *'Best not to let my colleagues know that this is a stressful moment for me. They, themselves, knew nothing of this plan, nor did the clerics with whom I must meet shortly. Hopefully I can keep this contained so they will see no evidence of scheming on my part. I want them all to see this as an overt act of aggression on the part of whoever did this.'*

Aloud he said, "Brothers, we must determine who committed this act of blatant aggression. Allah will judge us harshly if we do not find out who attacked us and punish them."

Mahmoud Rashad's strategy for the sinking of the large oil tanker had been clear in his mind right from the beginning. The fact was that Iran's desire to become a 'real' nation, in the geopolitical sense, by developing a homegrown nuclear weapons capability, had been consistently and frustratingly stymied by those powerful forces in the Western democracies who saw Iran mainly as a 'service nation,'- a lowly, non-threatening dispenser of crude oil to the developed world in her current non-nuclear status. Further, her bellicose posturing toward the end of 'driving Israel into the sea' had gained her pariah status throughout most of the free world. Gaining a nuclear capability, however, would instantly elevate Iran to peer-group status in the eyes of her adversaries and make Iran into a global power and force to be reckoned with among world councils.

Nuclear weapons, however controversial, were nonetheless a currency to be respected behind closed doors in the capitals of the world. The combination of the Israeli commando raid on the highly classified fuel enrichment facility in 2014 and the American retaliatory cruise missile attacks one year later had caused severe damage to Iran's nuclear development program by destroying these facilities and killing many skilled technicians and some of Iran's top nuclear scientists. These were assets that were not easily replaced in terms of time, money, and human treasure. The Iranian nuclear weapons program had been set back by several years by these blows. Rashad was now seriously considering a 'Plan B,' the essence of which was, if he couldn't develop a nuclear weapon on his own soil in a reasonable period of time, perhaps he could procure one or more from another source.

A means to that end would be to create chaos in world oil markets, perhaps creating an opening to acquire weapons technology by illicit means from an oil dependent nuclear nation such as Pakistan or North Korea.

By sinking the tanker, with the subsequent undetected escape of the Iranian Kilo, Rashad had calculated to close the Strait for an indefinite period and, in the process create chaos in world oil markets, thus driving up prices for the foreseeable future, even well after the Strait had been re-opened.

If the Kilo had managed to escape undetected, there would have been little but suspicion to indict Iran in the court of world opinion. Many countries had submarines – if, in fact, the sinking could be traced to a submarine using a torpedo – and there were several states that could have a legitimate interest in closing these strategic straits, resulting in a significant uptick in oil prices. Iran would be a prime suspect, of course, but lacking a 'smoking gun,' there was suspicion only, thus making military retaliation by the West highly unlikely and potentially risky.

Now Rashad's planned attack had been thwarted by some unknown force and his mind was racing trying to understand both the long-term and near-term implications of this event. President Rashad had not risen to his current position by a lack of cunning or being unable to balance his political ambitions against the absolute and rigid theocratic thinking of the powerful ayatollahs, whose frequent passive acquiescence assured his continued secular presidential power.

He would have to fabricate a story that would not only satisfy the Council of Clerics, but convince them to grant him even more power to seize this moment and seek alternatives to becoming a nuclear power, as the Iranian mullahs were anxious to increase their reputation and standing in the eyes of the Muslim World. The acquisition of nuclear weapons, along with their vast reserves of crude oil would give the mullahs status among their Muslim brothers that would rival or even supplant that of Saudi Arabia. The fact that the Saudis relied on the tacit protection of their major oil client, the United States, was often a source of ridicule among many Shiite Muslims, who decried the perceived 'Westernization' of Sunni dominated Saudi Arabia, abetted by the passive acquiescence of the pampered princes of the mighty House of Saud.

In their view, the minority Shiite Muslims had suffered under the rule of the Sunni majority for too long! Possessing the ultimate in weapons would force the rest of the world to finally grant Iran the respect she had for so long desired, and expand her influence in a fractious Muslim World.

It began to dawn on President Rashad that the thwarting of his original plan by the loss of the Kilo might just work to his advantage – perhaps even more so than if the tanker had been sunk. Now the Iranians could publically proclaim that the mysterious explosion in the Gulf had, in fact, been the result of an attack on one of their submarines. All hands had been lost and no one had come forward to take responsibility for this blatant act of piracy. The underwater photos taken by the Iranian navy divers confirmed that the Kilo had been sunk by a torpedo. Lacking any firm forensic evidence of the identity of the attacker, President Rashad decided to send up a trial balloon during his meeting with the clerics later in the day to see how this might be received by a prejudiced set of ears.

The meeting took place in the Imam Khomeini Grand Mosque, the center of religious activity in the Iranian capital of Tehran, immediately after prayers the day of the sinking of the Kilo. The Supreme Ayatollah took the lead in questioning President Rashad. "Tell us of the events of this long day, al-Rashad," as he was known to the mullahs. "There seems to be disturbing news out of the Gulf that apparently involves one of our warships."

"Yes, Mullah Superior; we have determined that one of our warships, a submarine, patrolling the borders of Iranian waters and the Strait of Hormuz early this morning, was attacked without warning by an unknown warship and lost with all hands. We suspect that it was an Israeli submarine that was deliberately stalking our vessel. We do not have proof yet, but if we can recover parts of the torpedo we can determine its origin by a process of elimination."

The president paused for effect here and then continued, "This was not only an attack against the country of Iran, but against Allah, himself! It must be avenged or we will appear weak and impotent in his eyes."

Rashad knew that in bringing suspicion on the Israelis that he could possibly turn the mullah's thinking away from more rational thoughts and play to their emotions as haters of the Zionists who, in their eyes, were occupying lands legitimately owned by the Palestinians for centuries and given to the Jews by the victorious allies illegally after World War II.

Rashad could see the combination of hate and resolve well up in the mullah's eyes as he further embellished his fanciful story by telling them that the Kilo was named 'The Spirit of The Revolution' and was captained by a devoutly religious Shiite Muslim who came from a well-respected family.

The interrogation of Rashad by the mullahs continued with questions that the clever Rashad easily answered to their satisfaction with conjecture and half-truths that could easily be rationalized later if necessary. As Rashad spoke – in an ever increasing respectful manner – he noticed that the mullahs were nodding in agreement. Rashad knew he had his audience convinced that Israel had indeed engineered and conducted this despicable act against Iran and Allah himself.

If *means, motive and opportunity* were uttered in the same sentence as 'Israel,' the Shiite mullahs would convict Israel every time with little other corroborative evidence.

After an hour of interrogation by the mullahs, the Supreme Mullah asked Rashad to leave them for a while so they could discuss what they had heard among themselves. Rashad excused himself and had tea in an anteroom adjacent to the Ayatollah's meeting chambers.

Rashad never ceased to be impressed and emotional as he observed the beautiful inlaid tile and grand frescos of the great mosque. It was as if being in this beautiful place was to be in the threshold of Heaven itself. For a brief moment he felt humble indeed, a feeling greatly out of character for this rogue of a sinister plotter. In his heart he knew that under his able administrative and political leadership, his secular actions could mesh with the religious ideals of the Shiite clerics who ruled Iran as dictators of the Sharia law, under which all faithful Shiite Muslims found themselves, to the greater glory of Allah.

After nearly 30 minutes Rashad was summoned back in to the grand chamber by a servant of the mullahs, a tall glowering man who showed no particular respect or lack thereof to the president. In the house of the mullahs, the only ones to whom respect was consistently and carefully given were the mullahs themselves. Rashad felt that by the look in this man's eyes, he might as well have been an infidel.

The Grand Mullah cleared his throat and addressed Rashad clearly, as a teacher to a student. "Based on your report to us today, the ayatollahs and I have reached our conclusion relative to this grave matter. You are quite correct; this attack is an attack upon Islam itself by an infidel with whom we are constantly at war, and we are powerless to strike back at them strategically. Israel cannot be permitted to continue these attacks on our sovereignty and against Islam. We must get in a position – if it pleases

Allah – to defend Iran and the Islamic faith against the infidels. To gain the respect of the West we must find a way to get the necessary weapons to put ourselves on a level field with them. Since our internal development of our nuclear program has been set back by these ruinous attacks, we must find a way to get such weapons elsewhere. The Supreme Clerical Council hereby authorizes you, as president, to take whatever means you deem expedient and appropriate to obtain these weapons. We shall expect a report from you in a month's time as to your plan for making this possible."

Rashad left the meeting with a feeling of exuberant pride and a strong sense of freedom. At last he felt free from the conservative and restraining hands of the ruling clerics who were continually interjecting the fundamental precepts of Sharia law into matters of international politics. He felt the West would never understand Islam and there were times when dealing with the West required that religious fundamentals – as important as they were to Muslims – be temporarily abandoned for the practical convenience of reaching a political accommodation that would have long-term benefits for Iran.

Rashad went to his office to consider the alternatives that lay before him in his new strategy to acquire a nuclear bomb. *'What are my realistic options?'* he thought.

There were two countries with which Rashad had passable relations that had a nuclear capability, the Democratic People's Republic of North Korea (DPRK) and Pakistan. All other countries that were members of the 'nuclear club' were either Western nations, who were in lockstep in their firm opposition to Iran becoming a nuclear power, or fair weather friends such as the Russian Federation and the People's Republic of China who were reasonably apathetic to Iran having a nuke. Both of these governments knew it would be contrary to their fundamental best interest in their relations with the West to help Iran get a weapon.

As Rashad considered further, he knew that North Korea, due to the fact that they too had suffered at the retaliation of the U.S. in the aircraft carrier incident years ago would be only too glad to be a willing accomplice, but the logistics of transporting a nuclear weapon from North Korea to Iran would be formidable. Therefore, the obvious choice would be to take advantage of the inherent political instability of Pakistan and try to enlist rogue Shiite colleagues in that country in a plot to acquire not only one, but several nuclear weapons. The potential for cooperation was surely there due to the natural enmity between Shiite and Sunni factions in that country, and the logistics would be far simpler. Now, with the encouragement of the mullahs, Pakistan was emerging as a distinct possibility.

Meanwhile, in the White House, very early the next day, Jonathan Braxton and his close advisers, Director of National Intelligence Rachel Hunter, National Security Adviser Jack Duggan, and Secretary of Defense Justin Roberts, were huddling to assess the fall-out from the Kilo sinking while trying to develop a follow-on strategy that would allow the most international wiggle room for the U.S. in this delicate situation; one that presented so many challenges and also so many potential opportunities.

CHAPTER 4

HOW DO WE PLAY THIS?

"Appearances are often deceiving."
Aesop – Ancient Greek Story Teller

TWO DAYS AFTER THE IRANIAN KILO SINKING.
THE WHITE HOUSE OVAL OFFICE.

Jonathan Braxton was a poker player. While he was in college he used his natural intelligence and affinity for mathematical logic to win many a pot - unfortunately mostly student small change - as he gained the respect of his fraternity brothers, who also fancied themselves astute poker tacticians. Today, he and his close intelligence chiefs and strategic staff would be playing a hand for far greater stakes and he had to make the final call.

The meeting convened in the oval office at 07:00 with Braxton, his SECDEF Justin Roberts, DNI Rachel Hunter, Director of Central Intelligence (DCI) Ray Rollins, National Security Adviser Jack Duggan, and his Chief of Staff, Philip Johnson, all present.

Braxton started by saying, "I called this meeting to follow-up on the initial decisions we made yesterday. I think it's important that we re-think this based on any new intel we've received since then and after we've had a chance to sleep on it – that is if any of you got any sleep; I know I got very little. So, let's get a summary of what we know and, if possible, what the

Iranians know. I guess the goal for today is to decide how we continue to play this, internally as well as to the outside."

Rachel Hunter as DNI was in the dock first. "Mr. President, we have excellent intelligence that the Iranian Navy has been diving the wreck scene and has taken off a large amount of flotsam that presumably came from the Kilo. I think it is safe to say that they will soon have solid evidence that the submarine was, in fact, torpedoed."

"Depending on how much of the torpedo is left, if any, they may even conclude that this was a U.S. device. However, that does not automatically give them a smoking gun that it was us as we have 'sterilized' these weapons and even altered the explosive signatures to make them indistinguishable from other makes of explosives. Our explosive material is almost identical to the Czech Republic's C-4 that they sell to everyone."

"I think it might even be difficult for the FBI to trace this back to a U.S. Navy torpedo. Besides, we have sold similar devices to the Israelis and the Pakistanis – without the firmware and software, of course."

Jack Duggan was next to speak up. "Mr. President, I think we have an opportunity here to play this one close to the vest. It appears that only we know exactly what happened here. Since there has been very little information out of Iran, we can assume that they don't know themselves, so we have an opportunity to use plausible deniability here even if this becomes conjecture. They have no hard evidence."

At that exact moment Rachel Hunter received a coded text on her cell phone. She looked twice at it and turned to President Braxton. "Sir I need to use the encrypted phone to my office. We have some new intel coming in...I think it may pertain to this."

The DNI, a one-time Harvard Law School classmate of Braxton's and a former Wall Street lawyer, was every man's dream and nightmare all rolled into one. She was a tall brunette with a striking figure and a mind like a trap. Her ability to instantly absorb all the details of a complex situation and issue an analysis that was spot-on correct had earned her the grudging respect of the top executives at Goldman Sachs, a notoriously difficult place for female talent to rise to the top.

A few years ago she had abruptly resigned, telling the CEO at Goldman that Wall Street was no longer for her.

When asked where she was going, she simply said, "I'm taking a position in Washington."

With that she virtually disappeared from the private sector for the next several years. Only a select few knew that she had been recruited by the legendary (within the upper echelons of the CIA, at least) spymaster Nehemiah Jamison - now in retirement in Switzerland - to help engineer a scheme that had resulted in the CIA's capability of virtually reading the former Russian Federation President Vladimir Putin's mail and listening to his telephone conversations for the last four years of his term. At Goldman, Rachel Hunter had developed many valuable contacts within the international banking community. Putin was a voracious consumer of sensitive financial information, some of which was closely held by certain institutions. His access to this information was not always legitimate, but it had helped make him one of the wealthiest men in Russia. By utilizing some of her contacts and reversing some of Putin's unauthorized ports of access, it had become possible to use his secret communications system against him. Greed always creates a vulnerability that can be exploited by a patient and skillful opponent, and the CIA was nothing if not patient and skillful. This was classic CIA vs. KGB tradecraft stuff that was viewed within the intelligence community as payback for the infamous Robert Hanssen spying affair - perhaps the greatest intelligence compromise in U.S. history. (The relative competitive value of the Putin communications intercepts operation vis-à-vis the Hanssen affair may never be quantified in our lifetime, but the fact that the CIA made the choice to shut it down rather than risk compromise of the technology had to mean that the data collected was extremely valuable and CIA wanted to keep open the option of using these tools again). If there was any intangible satisfaction to be enjoyed by Rachel and her colleagues who worked on the 'Payback Intercepts,' as the program was code-named within CIA, it was that Vladimir Putin and Robert Hanssen had, ironically, been working for their respective spy agencies during the same general time frame, neither knowing that their professional paths would be like ships passing in the night to the benefit of their adversarial intelligence agencies.

After this success Rachel Hunter's stock began to rise within CIA and she was soon was promoted to Deputy Director (Intelligence) of the agency. Her keen intellect, attention to detail, and organizational skills soon made her the logical choice for Jonathan Braxton's choice for his first Director of Central Intelligence.

Rachel Hunter punched some numbers into the secure phone on the President's desk, heard a tone and responded with another set of numbers.

Instantly she was connected on the other end and simply asked, "Hello Ken, what do you have for me?"

She listened intently without saying a word for approximately 30 seconds, and then signed off with, "please work this up and fill in the content. I'll see you in an hour," and rang off.

"Gentlemen," she said, "the Iranians are making this easy for us; Rashad is telling the Iranian press that he has evidence that the Kilo was sunk by an Israeli submarine."

Jack Duggan got off the couch and began to pace. "This is really going to get interesting," he said to no one in particular.

"What do you think, Justin?" asked Braxton of his SECDEF. "This surely has implications for us," he continued, "do you think the Iranians will try something against Israel in retaliation?"

"Actually, Mr. President, lacking a nuclear weapon, there's not too much that Iran could do to them that would make as much of a statement as the sinking of the Kilo. Maybe Rashad has been convinced that the Israelis actually did this..."

"...And maybe his tirade against the Israelis is just a ruse," interjected Rachel Hunter. "Rashad is a crafty SOB and he may have something up his sleeve here. This much we know for sure: These guys are lusting big time for a nuke and they have been foiled significantly in the past couple of years not only by us, but by the people they have vowed to eliminate. I believe this dust-up has the potential to tip the strategy of the Iranians away from making a home-grown weapon and to procure one on the black market."

Duggan had gathered his thoughts and jumped into the discussion: "When this crosses the wires the Israelis will deny it; first because it's not true and, second, because there would be no sense provoking the Iranians by admitting it even if true. The Israelis are between a rock and a hard place - damned if they do and damned if they don't. I wouldn't want to be in their shoes right now," he said ruefully.

"The other thing is that the Israelis will be pointing the finger at us, at least internally. You know, sometimes it's a good thing to have the Israelis as an ally...takes the pressure off in situations like this."

Duggan was interrupted by the buzzing of the telephone on the President's desk. This could only be one of his department secretaries. Few had direct access except SECDEF and SECSTATE. Since Justin Roberts was sitting in the room Braxton knew with ninety-nine percent certainty that this was Alexander Randolph, his unflappable and highly reliable Secretary of State. Braxton picked up the phone on the second ring and punched in the speaker for all in the room to hear.

"Morning Alex...you in the air? Guess you've heard the news. Jack told me he talked to you last night, so you know the deal. We've tentatively decided to play dumb about this – no jokes please," he smiled grimly. "Yes, well I've got some people in the office and we're discussing it now. Can you call me when you land and I'll have some more on it. We're still getting intel...it's developing."

Randolph replied, "You're going to love this Mr. President. I just received a call from the Israeli Ambassador, and since he can't see me today, he wants to see *you*...ASAP! I asked him what the subject matter was and he said he would prefer not to say. Maybe he doesn't trust the Iridium phone, even if it is encrypted."

Braxton filled the SECSTATE in on the information Rachel had just learned from CIA, which immediately connected the dots on the unusual request from the Israeli Ambassador. "Any suggestions, Alex?"

"Well, Mr. President, protocol would dictate that he sees me first, but since I'm seven miles above the Pacific right now, I guess he has a right to at least ask to see you. I think it would be showing our hand if you stalled him. My recommendation is to see him sometime today – perhaps not right away – and then to be coy with him. Moshe is pretty cagey and he's going to try to get you to spill the beans. Casually deny we had any part in this and show concern that we are trying all the back channels to find out ourselves. But, don't speculate, as he might leak this and place us in an embarrassing situation. Freshman law school strategies, sir - deny and delay!"

"I always appreciate your sound advice, Alex. Call me later after you've landed; I should have more by then."

Braxton turned to his Chief of Staff and asked him to call in the White House Communications Director, Sarah Whittington.

"Phil, you take the lead on this. If it comes from me she'll think it's a big deal. I think it would be consistent with our strategy of downplaying this incident if it looks routine. Maybe we should have Rachel and Ray leave through the other exit so Sarah doesn't see them here. I don't want her to think this is at too high a level right now."

Braxton nodded at Rachel Hunter, and said, "Thanks Rachel, call me later if you get updated intel."

HOW DO WE PLAY THIS?

Sarah Whittington was one of the first people Jonathan Braxton had placed on his staff when he was elected. She was a handsome African-American of medium build and exceptional intellect. She had gone to work for the Washington Post as a cub reporter immediately after graduating from Columbia School of Journalism and steadily worked her way up. Her work on the National Political Desk had honed her political skills and earned her the respect of those from the left and the right, who appreciated her accuracy and her maintenance of confidences with her sources.

The Post had a decided liberal bent and her editors occasionally raised an eyebrow when they felt she wandered a little too far to the right on an issue, but she had demonstrated courage by not revealing sources on an important political story that was not flattering to the left and offered to resign if pushed on the matter. She was fond of telling those close to her, paraphrasing former Secretary of State Dean Rusk after the Cuban Missile Crisis, "I was eyeball to eyeball with him (her editor) and he blinked."

"Sarah," Chief of Staff Phillip Johnson, said, "We have information the national press will soon get, that Iran is accusing Israel of deliberately sinking one of their submarines in the Strait of Hormuz two days ago. Our position has not changed since yesterday's briefing; we simply don't know the details of what happened. We have very little hard intel about this ourselves and are completely in the dark about who perpetrated this act and what their motives may have been. The reason for this meeting here is that our national interests are at stake in this area and we are concerned. In fact, the President has asked the Israeli Ambassador to come in today, to learn what he knows about this matter. We'll release more information as it becomes available."

Sarah Whittington drummed her fingers on the leather case of her iPad and replied, "Phil, do you really think Moshe Mendue is going to tell you anything other than the sky is blue and the birdies sing?"

With that she smiled broadly at everyone there and exited to her press office. *'Something big is up,'* she thought.

BOOK III

*

DENIAL BY STEALTH

CHAPTER 5

INTELLIGENCE FROM THE MOSSAD

"By way of deception, thou shall do war."
Motto of the Israeli Mossad

President Jonathan Braxton hung up the phone after spending fifteen minutes talking on the encrypted line with the Israeli Prime Minister, Moshe Barkev. *'Another uninspiring conversation,'* thought Braxton. *'Every time I talk to him I get the feeling that he's tattling like a schoolboy,' he mused.*

Despite the Currier and Ives view of the snow-covered White House lawn from the Oval Office and the crackling fire of the rustic fireplace, Jonathan Braxton was far from content as he paced the historic room, occasionally stopping in front of some memorabilia - a portrait or a bronze bust - from another presidential era as if hoping to get inspiration from the ghosts of men who had toiled in this office before him. But today, no such telepathic exchanges were forthcoming and Braxton, for the hundredth time in his presidency, realized how fundamentally lonely this job was for whomever sat behind the presidential desk.

Like those who had gone before, Jonathan Braxton had sincerely believed when he took office that a fresh approach, with a positive attitude and new faces, could confront pre-existing problems and find novel solutions to the complex challenges facing the world. The Braxton Administration had not been without its successes, both domestically and in foreign policy, but many of the same old issues remained resistant to the mightiest efforts for even slight improvement. Braxton, educated in the disciplines and exactitude of engineering, as well as the practicalities of compromise when it came to matters of law and discord between individuals or entities, knew that human nature was often immune to movement by the laws of nature or by man.

The case in immediate point was the Islamic Republic of Iran and her relations with her neighbors in the Middle East. Ever since the Shah of Iran was deposed in 1979 and replaced by a Theocratic Democracy led by Ayatollah Khomeini, Iran's belligerency toward her neighbors, most notably Israel, became the source of a potential flashpoint in that region. Now, many years later, that hostility had been exacerbated by Iran's relentless quest to acquire nuclear weapons. In spite of the overwhelming opposition by the world community, Iran continued on a path to nuclear independence by rationalizing that other countries in the region, including Israel, Pakistan, and India already had such a capability and Iran needed to be able to defend herself against these potential enemies.

Up until now, through the covert actions of Israel's Mossad and, to a lesser degree, the United States, as well as a semi-permeable barrier of economic sanctions put in place by the United Nations, Iran had been foiled in her attempts to build a workable warhead. But Jonathan Braxton knew that time was on the side of the Iranians and the United States must take the lead to deny Iran obtaining this class of weaponry if peace were ever to prevail in the Middle East, and beyond this volatile region.

Braxton looked at his watch as his telephone rang. His secretary, Margaret Finch, announced that his Chief of Staff Philip Johnson, National Security Adviser Jack Duggan, and Director of National Intelligence Rachel Hunter were assembled for the scheduled meeting.

"Please send them in, Margaret; I'm ready."

"Welcome everyone," greeted Braxton. "I just got off the phone with Moshe Barkev and he had some interesting news for us. I wanted to get all of you in the loop as quickly as possible. But first, is there anything on your hot-list, Rachel, which we ought to know?"

Rachel Hunter, former Director of the CIA and now, with the retirement of Admiral James Morgan, Braxton's Director of National Intelligence, waited a thoughtful moment and replied, "Mr. President, as our old litigation professor used to say, 'regardless of how bad you're losing, it's important that you rationalize to yourself that you're really winning.' I'd prefer to say that we're winning."

"How so, Rachel? After talking to Moshe I could use a fresh point of view."

"Well the good news is we're getting a little more info out of North Korea about their economic situation and their nuclear program; the bad news is the new guy who managed to topple Kim Jong Un last year has complete control of the military and appears to be even more determined than the young kid to intimidate South Korea and Japan with nuclear-tipped missiles. The really bad news, gentlemen, is if North Korea decided to make a preemptive strike on either its brothers to the south or even Japan, we couldn't stop their missiles even with our interceptor technology. There just wouldn't be enough time to react. If we retaliated with a Sea-Launched Cruise Missile from one of our boomers parked in the East China Sea it would take a miracle to keep China out of the fray."

Jonathan Braxton rose from behind his desk, went over to the Jack Kennedy rocking chair salvaged from the White House furniture archives and settled in. "Well, it seems like today is 'Axis-of-Evil' day, as Mr. Bush 43 quipped. I'd like to brief you all in on my conversation with Moshe this morning, as it has to do with another member of the Bad Boy Club, in this case Iran."

"It seems that Mossad has been able to recruit a mole in Iran's VEVAK - their State Intelligence and Security Service - who claims to know a high level nuclear scientist ideologically opposed to Iran's nuclear weapons program and willing to help the West sabotage it - gently and subtly. Well, there are two problems that I see here. One, we have no way of verifying this as it is internal information known only to Mossad. Two, the scientist says he can only help us passively as he fears for his family's safety. Any thoughts from anyone?" Braxton concluded.

Jack Duggan was quick to step in. "Why is Moshe telling us this? If they have the mole why don't they take some action of their own? They have more to fear - at least initially - if and when Iran gets a bomb they can deliver."

President Braxton rocked back and forth as he pursed his lips and prepared to answer. "Jack, I think we all know what Moshe is thinking. If he supplies the raw intel, maybe we'll do the dirty work - if indeed that is what is called for - taking the heat off them for a change. Rachel, this was a courtesy call from Moshe to me offering few details. May I suggest that you get our CIA Station Chief in Tel Aviv fully briefed in by Israeli intelligence on what they know and then get him back here to brief us? We have so little good information coming out of Iran, and I don't want to lose this opportunity – if, in fact, it is one."

One week later the Tel Aviv CIA Station Chief, Jonas Southworth, his boss - DCI Raymond Rollins, Rachel Hunter, and other members of Braxton's inner circle were assembled in the White House Situation Room listening to a fascinating story directly from notes taken by Southworth during his meeting with Mossad three days ago.

President Braxton called the meeting to order and asked Rachel Hunter to begin. "Mr. President, Director Rollins and I have spoken extensively to Mr. Southworth since he returned from Tel Aviv this week, and I must say he feels the Israelis have some interesting information they are willing to share with us. With Ray's permission, perhaps we should have Mr. Southworth go ahead with his narrative."

With a Presidential nod, Southworth began.

"Mr. President, Director Hunter, gentlemen, as you all know, Israel's highest intelligence priority, as well as one of the Top Five for us, is trying to understand where Iran stands with their nuclear weapons program. It wouldn't be an exaggeration to say that Mossad is *obsessed* about this, enough so that Prime Minister Barkev called President Braxton about this late last week."

"Shortly thereafter I was asked to meet with my Mossad counterpart and he - quite uncharacteristically - was most open to giving me total access to this information they claim to have on exceptional authority. To be brief, they claim to have a mole in VEVAK who knows an Iranian nuclear scientist opposed to their weapons program and wants to help the West delay it. As to Mossad's motives in making us aware of this, my guess is they want us, meaning the United States, to do the *delaying* component. Kind of like '*we fixed dinner, you do the dishes.*'"

"My suspicions exactly, Mr. Southworth, but please continue," remarked Braxton with a hint of distaste.

"The most surprising aspect of this - at least for me - is that we have been concentrating on the Fordow nuclear facility near Tehran as Iran's primary uranium enrichment site. But, according to Mossad's mole in VEVAK, that is no longer their primary site. Most of their centrifuges were damaged in an act of sabotage - the source of which is still unknown to us, but suspected to be Israel - in 2013 and they have not been replaced."

"So how are they proceeding," asked Braxton.

"Sir, twenty miles southeast of Fordow, connected by a series of caves, is a new site. It's ten times the size of Fordow, containing all the centrifuges undamaged by the sabotage on the Fordow site and expanding with new centrifuges arriving every day. This is their primary uranium enhancement facility."

"The Iranians continue to show the world that Fordow is their main site and pretend that any damage there is being remedied, but that is just a ruse. Fordow is a Potemkin Village and has been for some time. The real entrance to the facility is many miles away and hidden by a tunnel that appears as a roadway pass under a mountain. Within the confines of this tunnel is a turn-off so trucks carrying supplies to the facility may exit and deliver their loads. They leave under the cover of night, showing an image exactly as it appeared as when it entered. This may be confusing to satellite imaging, but confusion is exactly that...confusion. This information could be plausible."

Rachel spoke next. "So, what you are saying, Mr. Southworth, is that we - Israeli intelligence and the CIA - may have been laboring under the misconception that Fordow was where we ought to be centering our surveillance when, in fact, the real site was over 20 miles southwest of there and being fed while we were asleep at the wheel."

"I'm afraid that the information uncovered by Mossad points to that conclusion, ma'am," answered Southworth cautiously.

Braxton broke the silence produced by Rachel Hunter's conclusion by asking, "Is there any good news out of the meeting you had with Mossad, Mr. Southworth?"

'Well, yes sir there is - in a manner of speaking," ventured Southworth, gaining more confidence in briefing at this level.

"The Mossad have proposed the genesis of a plan to seriously delay Iran's enrichment plans. I think it may have some merit."

"I can hardly wait to hear how much this is going to cost in money and lives - ours, not theirs," remarked Jack Duggan with a snarly smirk from across the room.

Braxton broke in saying, "Jack, I know where you are coming from. I tend to agree, but let's hear what else Mr. Southworth has to say."

Southworth took that as a sign to continue. "Mossad's source seems sure that Iran's strategy for a do-it-yourself device is to use highly enriched uranium rather than Plutonium. Plutonium requires a reactor that gives off a serious infrared signature and is difficult to hide. HEU, on the other hand, can be made from uranium-235 in a gas diffusion process that can be accomplished using centrifuges. Iran already has the technology for that and can make them right at home. That avoids any inconveniences caused by import sanctions."

"But significant amounts of weapons grade U-235 requires many centrifuges working in what is known as a 'cascade.' Even a relatively low yield weapon of 20 kilotons - like we dropped on Hiroshima - requires a couple hundred kilograms of ninety percent U-235. This takes a few thousand centrifuges working twenty-four-seven to just make the fissile material for the warhead."

Southworth concluded with, "Therefore, in summary, Mossad - and I'm sure our people have concluded this as well - thinks that Iran has the technical knowledge to make a crude uranium bomb of relatively low yield. What they don't have is enough fissile material to make several and then sustain production enough to modernize the weapons as their development continues. Starve the beast and he can't grow enough to be a threat."

"So, let me guess here," replied Jack Duggan. "We cut off their capacity to produce HEU, and their project dies from lack of nourishment. I must say, Mr. Southworth that is hardly a new strategy. We've speculated on this for years."

"And the Israelis have actually done some of this back a few years ago when they allegedly raided one of Iran's processing sites and killed off a few Iranian and North Korean scientists in the process," interjected Rachel Hunter.

"Correct, Director Hunter," responded Southworth. "Except for the fact just revealed to me in my recent meeting with my Mossad counterpart. This is a shocker, because it's an embarrassment to Israeli intelligence. Although they raided a uranium enrichment facility, it was a small one - not the major facility they thought.

"Yes, there was damage and some technicians were put out of action, but the overall damage to their development program was actually very slight. In fact Iran played along with this by complaining loudly to the world that this raid had 'set their peaceful nuclear development program back for years.' In fact it did not. It did expose Israel to the scathing denunciations of many third world countries who branded them as an aggressor. Make no mistake, from a practical value and PR standpoint, this raid was a loser for Israel and the Mossad."

"Okay, Mr. Southworth, there must be something more other than Mossad doing a mea culpa on a previous dust up with the Iranians," offered Jack Duggan with a trace of irritability. "Why are we all here today? We're a long way from swapping war stories at cocktail hour."

Southworth knew he was in rarified air sitting in the White House Oval Office with some of the most politically powerful people in the free world and it was his time to deliver or fade to irrelevance within the CIA power structure.

"Yes, Mr. Duggan. Everything I've said so far was on background, and now I'll get promptly to the point. Mossad's contact in VEVAK knows where the real uranium enrichment site is located and has given me the approximate grid coordinates." Southworth reached inside his jacket pocket and extracted a simple three-by-five index card which he slid across the table to his boss, Ray Rollins. "This explains why it is so difficult to see from any aerial surveillance."

Rollins examined the card for a moment and handed it to Rachel Hunter for her perusal as well. She handed the card back to the CIA Director, who punched the grid coordinates into a laptop next to a large video screen at the end of the room. Within moments the screen divided into two side-by-side views showing a relief map and political map of Iran respectively. A blinking red dot identified the grid coordinates typed in by Director Rollins. The assembled National Security Team stared in silence for a brief moment in complete surprise.

✱

INTELLIGENCE FROM THE MOSSAD

Lieutenant Chance Lyon dozed in First Class of a 747 as it began its descent into Reagan International in Washington, D.C. His stint as an instructor at the U.S. Navy Special Warfare Training Center in Coronado, California had been a welcome change from the previous intense months of constant deployment in Afghanistan, but training a new class of potential SEAL warriors had soon become boring and repetitive. The original class size of over one-hundred-fifty young men had steadily declined to a more manageable 70 or so in six months and Chance's request for transfer back into SEAL Team Two at the Naval Amphibious Base - Little Creek, VA, had been approved.

Chance had told his commanding officer in Coronado that he simply didn't have the temperament for training new SEALs. When asked to be more specific, Chance could only reply "Sir, out in the teams, most everything is black and white to me. We either do this or we do that to accomplish the mission. End of story. With these new trainees, I find myself vacillating between giving a guy who is busting ass but failing an evolution another chance or kicking him out during evals. I don't mind being judge and jury to a bad guy on a mission, but I see myself in some of these guys and know that failing them may simply be a gut reaction on my part. I'd prefer to leave that to someone else. I don't mind being out in the shit, sir, but Coronado is not for me."

As the wheels of the giant jetliner touched down, Chance was looking forward to two weeks leave and getting back into whatever SEAL Two was getting spun up for.

Chance Lyon called his father, Captain (Ret.) 'Bernie' Lyon and caught him as the Captain and his wife, Anne, were leaving their home for dinner. "Hey dad, I'm at Reagan and wondered if I could crash at your place for a couple of nights until I can get a place at the Fort Story BOQ."

"We'll do you one better, son. Cool your jets and we'll bulldoze our way through the traffic to the United terminal and pick you up at the curb. If you're hungry, perhaps you can join us for dinner. I'm sure Anne is anxious to see you! We'll call your cell when we're about five minutes away."

Two hours later, over drinks, conversation and a dinner far superior to what Chance had been accustomed to at Coronado, they were on their way to the same condo where Chance and his step-mother, Anne had shared their common revelations many months ago about the unexplained sensations of Bernie Lyon's mysterious presence to them against the backdrop of his presumed death.

As the three enjoyed dessert in the spacious living room, Chance explained to Bernie and Anne that he had requested a transfer out of his training duties at Coronado back to duty with SEAL Team Two in Little Creek.

"I was surprised that they granted it, but I'm taking what I can get. At this point I can't imagine doing anything else in the Navy. I'm committed to at least three more years. I've got two more weeks to get back into shape, so it's off to the gym early tomorrow."

The next day Chance reluctantly returned to the same gym where he had met Stephanie Morris many months ago. Standing at the doors of the facility a flood of memories dominated his senses as he remembered the all too brief times of love and companionship the two had shared before and at scattered times between his deployments to Afghanistan.

'If she wouldn't have been involved with me, she would still be alive today,' was the mantra of guilt that stopped him from entering the gym. *'But she would not have tolerated me retreating into that and using those events to prevent me from moving forward. We were strong together. I'm going to stay strong in honor of her memory,'* thought Chance Lyon, as he pushed open the glass door to the gym and steeled himself for whatever lay ahead.

President Braxton's National Security Team in the White House Situation Room continued gazing intently at the large video screen projecting the location of the uranium enrichment facility based on the grid coordinates provided Southworth by his Mossad counterpart days earlier. This new location bore no resemblance to any Iranian nuclear facility previously known to the CIA.

Ray Rollins continued to add and subtract layers of information to the map images based on stored information the CIA had in its database, but the new location still stood alone. The only conclusions Rachel Hunter could draw from this was that either Mossad had solid information about a new facility that may have been in operation for a long time, or their mole in VEVAK had supplied them with bad information. Both scenarios were troubling to the Director of National Intelligence and she knew they had to be vetted before she could be confident in her analysis.

Jack Duggan took the floor once more after the National Security Team had digested the images shown on the video screen. "Okay, Mr. Southworth, that's one piece of the puzzle. Now we know there might - emphasize *might* - be a new and improved uranium processing facility in Iran. What does Mossad, and I presume this means the Prime Minister as well, suggest as a course of action?"

"Well, sir, *nothing*...I mean nothing *directly*."

The three members of Braxton's National Security Team looked cautiously at each other and then to President Braxton, who by now had his hands linked together behind his head and was looking at the ceiling as if deep in thought.

"NOTHING?" asked Jack Duggan, incredulously.

"Well, yes and no, sir," answered Southworth cautiously.

"God damn it, Southworth, this is not some stupid game. Spit it out man. We're not playing games with Mossad. Either they have some suggestion, or they do not. So far, everything we've learned here could have been taken care of by a routine cable between Tel Aviv and Langley."

Southworth detected a new sense of urgency in the room that was confirmed by making eye contact with Director Rollins, his ultimate supervisor. *'Well, for better or for worse, I've got to tell them the Mossad plan,'* he thought.

Southworth continued, "When I said 'nothing directly,' I was referring to Mossad's reasoning that attacking the Iranian uranium enrichment facility either by air or ground directly carries too many risks to predict a positive outcome. First there is the potential for aggressive retaliation on the part of the Iranians against whoever initiates such an action. In addition, there is sure to be ancillary condemnation by Iran's allies in the Islamic world to such an action, regardless of our motives. Finally, if the actions against the facility were carried out by the Israelis, this would only serve to be a propaganda victory to Iran that could justify future military action in retaliation. In summary, Mossad is suggesting something more subtle and possibly even more effective."

"The Israelis subtle? We're all ears," interjected a mildly amused Rachel Hunter.

"There are several pieces to the puzzle," continued Southworth.

"First, the real enrichment site is buried in a natural cave complex within a mountain that has required minimal excavation to be made useful for this purpose. That's one of the reasons it hasn't been detected by overhead surveillance by our satellites. Second, the entrance to the complex is from a roadway that passes as a tunnel through the mountain. Therefore access to the complex is indirect, making security exceptional. A direct attack on the complex by air or ground would require a substantial military operation with marginal probability for success. Third, and finally, we don't want the Iranians to know that we've discovered the site and therefore potentially expose our intelligence source. In summary, it's not important that we *know* of the site, but what we *do* at the site that has an impact on their enrichment program."

Southworth was encouraged that Jack Duggan had calmed down and was listening more intently now, so he continued confidently. "Mossad is suggesting that we infect the site with virus that spreads from within rather than beating down the doors with a proverbial sledgehammer."

This time Director Rollins broke in.

"Mr. Southworth, you may recall that we and the Israelis gummed up the works a few years ago with a so-called Stuxnet computer virus that attacked their site network. The Iranians overcame that easy enough and were back in business in a couple of months. I'm sure their firewalls are much improved at this point."

"Yes sir," answered Southworth. "It's not that kind of virus they are suggesting. They want to nuke the facility metaphorically."

A cloak of silence dominated the Situation Room as the impact of such a notion reverberated throughout. President Braxton immediately seized the irony of the moment and spoke softly.

"So in order to keep Iran from developing a nuclear weapon we're going to use one of our own on them. I don't know about the rest of you, but I might find this somewhat difficult to justify at the U.N. I'm afraid this would be another Colin Powell moment there."

He was referring to Secretary of State Powell's presentation to the U.N. Security Council in February, 2003 that Iraq could be preparing to use "weapons of mass destruction."

Jack Duggan waited a respectful moment before he spoke again. "Let me guess here, Mr. Southworth. Mossad is suggesting that we march right in there, nuke their main uranium processing facility from inside, and then catch the next flight out of Tehran?"

"Oh, no, sir. The Chinese with the help of the South Africans and the Japanese are going to do it for us."

In a rare moment of dramatic levity, Rachel Hunter placed the back of her hand against her forehead and declared, "My God, I think I'm going to faint."

Southworth continued briefing the President and his National Security Team in the White House Situation room after assuring the semi-astonished group that what he was about to propose might actually contain a germ of reason and effective strategy. "Actually, what Mossad is proposing is not as much of an Armageddon moment as it may sound."

Braxton broke in with, "Well, Mr. Southworth, when you use 'nuclear weapons' and 'someplace in the Middle East' in the same sentence, that's exactly the image that comes to mind. But we've come this far, please continue."

"Sir, Mossad's mole in VEVAK reports that Iran is planning a major expansion of the enrichment facility. The primary component of such a facility is what is technically referred to as gas diffusion centrifuges. They will need thousands more of these to stock this facility. Iran can and does make these with its own resources, so this is not an import sanction issue - at least not in a macro sense.

"However, there is a point of vulnerability that we could possibly exploit that would significantly render this facility unfinished and unusable for the foreseeable future, and not leave a detectible fingerprint. In other words, Iran would be scratching its head after the fact, seeking solid evidence of who the culprit was. Lacking a smoking gun, they would be left shaking their fist at the world in general and receiving little more than lip service support from their few friends."

"And what would that be?" asked Jack Duggan.

"One of the most critical components in a gas centrifuge is a couple of very special magnets made up of an exotic metal alloy," explained Southworth. "The Iranians have to buy these on the market and one of the few suppliers of this item is the Chinese. That dynamic makes the transaction natural because the Chinese are huge importers of crude oil - of which Iran has plenty - so there is synergy here. Cap that off with the fact that the Chinese have largely thumbed their noses over the years at cooperating with sanctions that have negative commercial implications for them and you have a good deal for both parties."

"So, Iran needs these magnets and the Chinese have them. What can we do about that?" asked Ray Rollins, the DCI.

"Actually, not much according to Mossad," replied Southworth. "The Iranians, through a front company, cut a purchase order to the Chinese company that makes the magnets and the Chinese have ignored a request from the International Monetary Fund to not fill it. It's a done deal. The magnets will ship within a month directly to the company in Iran that makes the centrifuges. After assembly, the centrifuges will be shipped to the uranium enrichment facility where they will be assembled into cascades, and then the fun begins."

"Fun?" asked Jack Duggan lightly.

"Well sir, with enough centrifuge cascades working in tandem, they can carry on a parallel program of processing uranium to the 20 percent level, stockpiling that, and then taking the 20 percent product and further enriching it to the 90 percent level required to make weapons-grade uranium. With enough uranium 235 ore and enough cascades it is just a matter of time before you are in the uranium bomb business."

At this point Rachel Hunter broke in and said, "So, the key ingredient here seems to be the precision alloy magnets being shipped from China. Keep these from being installed in the centrifuges and that reduces Iran's ability to enrich uranium. So Mr. Southworth, how does the Mossad suggest we accomplish this?"

"Starve the beast!" answered Southworth cryptically.

"How so?" continued the DNI.

"We don't attack the enrichment site directly," responded Southworth. "We attack Iran's ability to produce the key ingredient to carry out their enrichment process - the centrifuges. We render the centrifuge manufacturing facility dead in the water by irradiating the magnets for the centrifuges to a dangerously high level of radioactivity while they are en route between China and Iran by ocean freighter. This would render them useless and set their program back for a long time."

"And how would you propose to irradiate these magnets while in transit?" asked Jack Duggan, skeptically. "I don't speak for the President, but I doubt that he wants to start a nuclear war over this latest provocation - and that's what it is at this time, only that."

"Sir, I think I can speak for everyone - including Mossad - that no one wants to start a war over this provocation. There are advantages to everyone in taking a far more subtle approach. We don't have to invade sovereign geography, blow anything up, inflict any human casualties, or even make our identities known to damage their enrichment program. Mossad has proposed a diabolically clever plan."

Chance Lyon reported to his old familiar SEAL Team Two at the U.S. Naval Amphibious base - Little Creek, Virginia on the Monday morning after his leave expired. About half the personnel he had served with previously were still with the unit. Some had retired voluntarily, and a few had been released for medical disability reasons. The rest had migrated to other SEAL Teams or other Special Operations specialties out of necessity or personal reasons, replaced with new graduates from the SEAL Qualification Training program. The former commander, 'Rusty' Fortenzo had been promoted and was now in a slot at SPECWAR/CENTCOM at MacDill Air Force Base in Tampa. The new C.O. of SEAL Two was Commander Ryan 'Buck' Buckholder, a veteran SEAL from one of the West Coast SEAL Teams.

After some time becoming reacquainted with fellow SEALs he had known prior to his assignment to Coronado, Chance met privately with Commander Buckholder.

"So, you couldn't cut the nine-to-five life out in Coronado, huh Chance?" remarked Buckholder good-naturedly. "Try to give a guy a break from working the twenty-four-seven and he just wants to come back for more punishment. Can't say that I blame you, however. Training's not my thing either unless it's with my own guys. I never liked to see a guy with good potential ring out."

"Well, sir, I'd be lying if I said I didn't miss the unit. This is where I want to be right now. I'm not married or attached and can afford to give it my complete focus," answered Chance.

"Okay, Chance. You have a damned good record here and I'm going to give you the second platoon now that Lieutenant Johnson has been moved to another specops slot in Europe. Very hush-hush. Even I don't know what he's doing. I don't know very much about what's up for us, but we've been back here for over a month and I got to believe we're headed back to the shit pretty soon."

"Thank you, sir. I'm looking forward to it."

"And Chance, please don't get shot in the head again…You know the drill, two neurosurgeries and you're out of here. The only place for officers who are drooling is out in the fleet."

Jonas Southworth spent the next twenty minutes explaining the outline of Mossad's plan to irradiate the centrifuge magnets to President Braxton and his National Security Team. After many questions and substantial discussion, President Braxton summed things up.

"Actually, not too bad a plan - at least conceptually. This has the potential to be a very clean operation while achieving the end results we want. If the Iranians squawk - and they will to Holy Hell - about their magnets being unusable, everyone involved will have plausible deniability. I would like to reconvene tomorrow morning including my Secretary of Defense, the Chairman of the Joint Chiefs, the CNO, as well as Admiral Williams, the SPECWAR Commander from CENTCOM. I have a feeling that this is going to be another Navy SEAL operation.

CHAPTER 6

A DARING PLAN - WITH RISK!

"First ponder, then dare."
Helmuth von Moltke

President Jonathan Braxton's National Security Team reconvened in the White House Situation Room at noon the next day, and the session was opened by Braxton himself.

"Thank you all for being here. Recently we have been made aware of significant developments in Iran's continuing quest to develop a home-grown nuclear weapon. This administration, as well as others before us, has made it a very high priority to resist Iran's acquisition of such weaponry for many reasons. One of Secretary Roberts' predecessors, Robert Gates, said it well when he expressed the view that such a development would be very disturbing to the balance of power in that region, as well as threatening to America's interests in the surrounding area. I have said before and I will repeat to all of you; 'It will be a matter of the highest priority for my administration to actively resist the acquisition of any nuclear weapon by the Islamic Republic of Iran.'"

"With that said as background, I would like to turn the intelligence aspect of this meeting over to Director Hunter, who will then allow Jack Duggan to ask for your comments on a potential military response to this situation. After Jack's comments we will adjourn for a light lunch and continue with your recommendations on how we may proceed."

Without disclosing to the military professionals present the fact that Mossad's source was a mole deep within VEVAK - such information required guarding strictly on a need-to-know basis at the very highest levels of the Braxton Administration - Rachel Hunter briefed the team on what Jonas Southworth had told the group yesterday and gave a brief outline of the Mossad plan concerning the irradiating of the centrifuge magnets as a means of thwarting Iran's planned expansion of their uranium enrichment facility.

"Gentlemen, our own Central Intelligence Agency discovered around six months ago the existence of a purchase order cut from a front company, possibly working under the aegis of the Islamic Republic of Iran, to a Chinese company for a very large number of specialty alloy magnets. These are very expensive and require a long lead-time to produce. We decided not to confront the Chinese directly about this issue, but rather to have a representative of the International Monetary Fund inquire about this through their - shall we say - more genteel international financial channels. Our source was so sensitive on this that we didn't want to risk exposing it by letting the Chinese know the U.S. knew."

"In the end the Chinese banker said he would pass the concern - along with a suggestion that they not fill the order - up the food chain and that's the last we heard of it. This is not overly surprising as the Chinese basically do their own thing as far as international cooperation goes. They have never been enthusiastic supporters of any sanctions on Iran because they need her oil."

"The other part is to annoy the United States. If we could ever break away from borrowing so much money from China, maybe we could make some progress here...with respect, Mr. President," concluded Rachel Hunter carefully.

Jack Duggan, President Braxton's National Security Advisor was next in the dock. "Thank you, Director Hunter," Duggan began. "Before we break for lunch I would like to suggest the broad outlines of a potential plan to thwart Iran on taking delivery of these magnets that are a key component to the gas diffusion centrifuges they are planning for the expanded enrichment facility."

A DARING PLAN - WITH RISK!

"One of the primary goals of any military operation to thwart the usefulness of these magnets must be to give plausible deniability to any entity along the chain of delivery of the magnets that they had any involvement in the contamination of the product. This, of course, will minimize the potential for retaliation by the Iranians when they find that these things have essentially become useless to them for many years while they wait for radioactive decay."

"In spite of the secret nature of this transaction between the Chinese company and the front company who cut the mysterious P.O., a little back channel investigating after the initial intel was received led us to learn where the Chinese manufacturing plant was located, how these items were packaged for shipment, and from what port they would be shipped. Iran is not the Chinese's only client for this type of item and they are eager to expand their high-tech trade. We intend to focus on learning more about their operations very soon to assist us in figuring out how we might corrupt their transaction with Iran."

Jack Duggan concluded his remarks with, "So, in summary prior to our lunch break, we are thinking that allowing the shipment of the magnets to take place from China and allowing the Chinese company to get paid in the process will give plausible deniability to the Chinese Company and keep them happy. The tricky part will be intercepting the shipment on the high seas, planting some type of device within the shipping containers that will irradiate the magnets, and escaping undetected."

"In whatever period of time it takes from that part of the operation, the shipment will arrive in Iran and be found to be radioactively contaminated. At the end of the day, the Iranians are out many millions of dollars paid the Chinese company - creating a tremendous amount of ill-will in the process - and they are stuck with a shipment of radioactively contaminated magnets that they can't use for many years, perhaps never at all. I realize the devil is in the details, gentlemen, but it's an intriguing idea. If we can pull this off it would be a real winner for the West. Admittedly, this is high risk - high reward," summarized Duggan.

During lunch Vice-Admiral Clayton Williams, the SPECWAR Commander at CENTCOM sought out Admiral Steve Wheeler, the newly appointed Chief of Naval Operations (CNO) for a one-on-one consultation.

"Sir," began Williams, "I think this has all the makings of a SEAL mission. If we're going to place people on an ocean freighter at sea, my people are the ones trained to do this. The only other option would be SOF-Delta, but if this is going to involve submarines, water, and Zodiacs, it's probably going to be SEALs."

"I think you're right Clay. I'll speak to this after the SECDEF has his say and asks for input," replied Wheeler.

"I better let the Chairman know my thinking here just as a courtesy. I have a feeling he's going to defer to me anyway since this is something that's probably going to happen at sea."

After the luncheon meal and a short break where the various military commanders had a chance to consult among themselves, the National Security Team reconvened with Justin Roberts, Braxton's SECDEF taking the podium.

"Mr. President, I've spoken to the Chairman and the CNO. The consensus is that the plan outlined up to now is conceptually doable. The Navy has the resources to pull this off, but there are many, many details that would have to be carefully worked out and rehearsed. In addition, there is much intelligence that would have to be gathered to make the risks acceptable. May I suggest that the Chairman, the CNO, his SPECWAR Commander, and the appropriate intelligence assets start work on an operations plan and bring the first draft back to this group within a time frame specified by you? We would need to get a written authorization in the form of an Executive Order from you to me to start the ball rolling with some general guidelines."

Braxton looked around the large conference table making eye contact with each member of his National Security Team and replied, "You've got it,

A DARING PLAN - WITH RISK!

Justin. Stay back and we'll get something drawn up immediately. I guess this operation needs to have a name. Any suggestions?"

Admiral Steve Wheeler, looked over at his SPECWAR Commander and said, "Clay, since this is probably going to be your show, you want to give it a name?"

Williams thought for a moment and responded, "Thank you sir. How about Operation Trinity?"

After the briefest of moments, President Braxton gave it his blessing by announcing, "Operation Trinity it is. May we have an initial brief on a draft op-plan a week from today right here? If there are no objections, we are adjourned."

Justin Roberts asked his commanders to remain after the President left the room and asked Rachel Hunter to do the same. "Rachel, I'd like to spend some time with my commanders and draw up a punch list of things we need to do, and then spend some time later this afternoon going over some intel requests from you. Perhaps all of us could meet with you and your team at the Pentagon tomorrow morning."

"Can do, Justin. I've got a feeling this is going to be a very busy week for all of us."

Armed with an Executive Order signed by President Braxton, the next morning Admiral Wheeler, Vice-Admiral Williams, Rachel Hunter and DCI Rollins met in a secure conference room at the Pentagon to begin discussions on Operation Trinity. Rachel Hunter began with an intelligence estimate.

"Here's what we know, gentlemen. We know the physical location of the manufacturing facility in China where these magnets are manufactured. The South Africans have purchased similar items from China recently and we have been able to get some information from them about how these items are packaged for shipment. For example, our intelligence sources there have been able to provide us with imagery of this packaging. We intend to verify this with a dummy purchase of similar items through a front trading company we sometimes use and have them shipped to a location in Japan by surface, which means they will have to be shipped by sea from the FOB point we believe to be Shanghai. We'll track the shipment to verify the logistics. We should be able to have this information within two weeks."

Vice-Admiral Williams followed up.

"If we are sure that these items will ship by ocean freighter, that's a start. Now we have to decide at what precise point we intercept the shipment to plant the nuclear contaminating device. That's the key element to be decided, because it will dictate how we get the SEALs onto the ship and then extract them after they complete their job."

"Well Admiral, I think we may be of additional help here," interjected Ray Rollins, the DCI.

"NSA is intercepting the electronic mail traffic between this Iranian front company that ordered the magnets and the Chinese company. The terms of the purchase order and the supplier's acknowledgment are very specific about shipping date and carrier of the items. Once we verify that the shipment has left Shanghai we can easily track the ship along its path. Nearly all ocean freighters delivering goods to Iran stop in Karachi, Pakistan, before heading for the Iranian ports through the Strait of Hormuz and into the Persian Gulf. Likewise, there is never another stopping point after Karachi. If our intelligence is correct, it looks like placing your SEALs on board somewhere between Karachi and the entry to the Straits would be opportunistic."

Admiral Williams and Admiral Wheeler looked at each other for a brief moment and nodded in agreement before Williams asked that a map of the region be displayed on the monitor in the conference room. "It looks like it's about 720 sea miles between Karachi and the entry to the Straits," remarked Williams. "At 12 to 15 knots, that's roughly a two and a half day transit. That would give us plenty of time to execute," he concluded. "Thinking out loud, I would say that we would try to do this at night by boarding the ship, getting my SEALs into the cargo hold, placing the device, and leaving before it gets light; conceptually that's doable."

"Sounds very dangerous - and very tricky," interjected Rachel Hunter."

"Everything SEALs do is dangerous, Director. Otherwise it's not challenging," replied Williams as he smiled grimly.

"How are you going to place your people on a moving ocean freighter in the middle of the night without being detected?" she continued.

"Only two ways," replied Williams. "Either by helicopter or Zodiac - depends on how stealthy you want to be. Here are two potential scenarios," he continued.

"The freighters working the Arabian Sea are used to seeing our two carrier strike groups working that area. They would think nothing of being shadowed by American Naval vessels as they headed toward the Straits. We could board my SEALs from a carrier-based helicopter but that would most likely be detected. That's still a possibility if we could come up with a plausible reason to do so. You can bet that everyone in the region would know about this and there could be a lot of explaining to do on our part."

"The other way would be for SEALs to sneak up on the freighter in a Zodiac, board the ship stealthily, do their thing, and extract. This would require more effort, but the stealth factor would work to the advantage of the strategic objective of deniability. I think there are some political considerations that may drive how we do this. Those are out of my pay grade." summarized Williams.

"Meanwhile," spoke Admiral Wheeler, "Rachel, can you start getting us aerial images of the freighter - or at least the class of freighter - that will be carrying these items so my people can begin to start assessing how they can board this vessel."

"We're already on to that Admiral. We're getting satellite images of her sitting by her berth at the Shanghai docks and hope to get some real-time footage of how they load her with a stealthy drone launched from a 'phantom freighter' belonging to us cruising in the East China Sea. By the way, I think we can help you slow this ship down so she will be easier to board," answered Rachel Hunter with a coy smile.

"With respect, Director," asked Vice-Admiral Williams carefully, "how do you propose to pull that off?"

"Admiral, this freighter is going to be cruising along in the dead of night minding her own business, and we're going to send a stealthy drone overhead and zap it with an electromagnetic pulse that's going to fry its electronics. Navigation, propulsion, communications, lighting - everything - is going to come to a grinding halt. Even their emergency generator and auxiliary power units are going to be zapped," explained Rachel Hunter.

"This freighter is going to be bobbing like a cork in the middle of the Arabian Sea until her engineers can come up with some workarounds that can get her going again. Depending on how talented the ship's engineer is and how many spare parts he has on board, I would say they're going to sitting there for two or three hours before they can even think about starting to move again. By that time your SEALs should be able to do their thing and be gone."

"I assume this technology has been tested, Director," remarked Admiral Wheeler.

"If so, are there countermeasures that are known to protect against this - not just for our enemies, but could this technology be used against our naval assets? This sounds like very advanced physics. How far ahead is the United States on this technology?" concluded the clearly concerned CNO.

A DARING PLAN - WITH RISK!

"Admiral, I am not qualified to give a detailed brief on this. You and the other members of the Joint Chiefs will be getting a classified briefing on this as early as next week from the scientists at Sandia who have been working on this for a long time. All I can say is there has been a recent technical breakthrough and Operation Trinity may be the ideal platform to test this in a real operation. With regard to our technical lead, all I can say is that the fundamental technology has been known theoretically for years, but, as usual, closing the gap between theory and reality is the trick. My understanding is that no one else has done this yet. You'll have to discuss this in greater detail with the geeks."

Vice-Admiral Williams was the next to speak.

"So, perhaps a summary is in order here for us to begin detailed planning. If I may, here's what I think we are zeroing in on from an operational standpoint. An ocean-going freighter takes on a load of highly sensitive machine parts at a Chinese port and makes way for an eventual delivery to an Iranian port in the Persian Gulf. Somewhere during the transit between Karachi, Pakistan, and this port, this freighter is disabled by an electromagnetic pulse from a U.S. military air asset. Immediately thereafter, a group of U.S. Navy SEALs stealthily boards this freighter, makes their way to the cargo hold, identifies the cargo bound for Iran, plants devices on this cargo that will irradiate it and exfiltrates to safety.

"Presumably, these devices subsequently detonate, contaminating the cargo and rendering it useless for the next dozen or so years. At the end of the day, the Iranians are out-of-pocket many millions of scarce hard currency lost to the Chinese, a ton of strategically essential - but now useless - machine parts, and no hard evidence of who the perpetrators were. As the kid from the Peanuts cartoon would say, 'Rats!'"

"That pretty well sums it up, Admiral," replied Rachel Hunter, "except that I think 'Rats!' might be putting it mildly."

CHAPTER 7

SANDIA - DOORWAY TO DOOMSDAY

"Our mission is national security. We apply science to help detect, repel, defeat, or mitigate threats."
Mission statement: Sandia National Laboratories

At zero-eight-hundred hours, two days after the initial planning meeting in the Pentagon, SEAL Team Two in Little Creek, Virginia, received a warning order from the office of the Chief of Naval Operations, filtered through CENTCOM and the Office of the SPECWAR Commander at MacDill Air Force Base that they were on notice of imminent deployment.

Commander 'Buck' Buckholder, Commander of SEAL Team Two gathered the team in the team room of the SEAL complex at Little Creek.

"I can't tell you exactly where we're going, but it's somewhere in the Middle East and this one is going to be a water-oriented operation. So, your packing and pre-positioning at Oceana will be the Zodiacs, extra engines, dive gear, and boarding equipment. In addition, pack all the combat gear you would expect to use for a land combat operation. Where we're going has minimal support for what we do, so if there is any doubt - and if will fit in a C-17 - pack it.

"One more thing. Lieutenant Lyon and his platoon will be leaving at noon tomorrow for an undisclosed location to train on the special aspects of this mission. You'll be traveling on a C-37A and wearing civilian clothes - business casual. When you arrive at the destination you will be met by a civilian security team and taken by bus to the training site. Once there you are to speak to nobody other than the staff, who will all be wearing green jumpsuits at all times while they have contact with you and, of course, others on the team. If anyone other than staff dressed in a green jumpsuit tries to establish contact with you, you are to inform your security handlers immediately.

You will be at the site for five days and four nights. Better bring a good book, because there will be no off-site activities authorized. The weather is of no consequence as you'll be indoors all the time. You will have access to a gym and an indoor swimming pool. No one else will have access to those facilities when you are using them. Leave your cell phones here at the detachment. This is a 'black' trip. Are there any questions?"

One of the Senior CPOs spoke up and asked light-heartedly, "Yes sir, as usual I have a lot of questions, but I don't suppose it would do any good to ask."

"That's right Chief. Anything else?" replied Buckholder with a smile.

Chance Lyon had settled-in to his position as a SEAL Platoon Commander with the enthusiasm of a highly trained leader finely honed over many years, beginning with his adolescent and teen years at Mount Union Military Academy, his education at the United States Naval Academy, his rigorous SEAL qualification training, and finally, his several deployments to the harsh operational conditions of Afghanistan.

Within the closed culture of U.S. Navy SEAL Teams, Chance Lyon was making a name and a reputation for himself as being a mission-focused leader, while staying true to the team culture that bound the SEALs together as a tightly knit and effective fighting force. Chance had the respect of his fellow SEALs and returned that in kind by keeping his men in the information loop whenever possible and working harder at readiness and personal fitness than anyone else. None of the other SEALs ever heard Chance Lyon utter an excuse about anything that was his responsibility.

Chance's platoon spent the balance of the day making sure both the team gear and their personal gear were accounted for, checked for operational fitness, and pre-positioned for loading on the C-17 transport that would depart at a future unknown time from Oceana Naval Air Station and fly them to the undisclosed takeoff point for their final objective. The only clue for Chance as to the nature of the mission was Buckholder's cryptic remark that this was to be a 'water-oriented' mission. His admonition that they were to take their combat gear as well only served to add mystery to the final destination.

It was well past eight o'clock in the evening when Chance and the other members of the team gathered one final time and compared their respective pre-deployment checklists to ensure that nothing had been forgotten.

"Okay guys," Chance said. "I think we're done for the night. I know that some of you have to go home and break the news that you'll be gone for a few days - and after that you'll be gone again to 'wherever' until 'whenever.' I can't say I envy you doing that. See you back here for P.T. tomorrow and then we're flying out at noon to Bumfuck-ville. Have a couple of beers and get some sleep."

Chance waited until everyone cleared out and then drove his HUMVEE back over to the pre-positioning area, where the Team's gear was steadily piling up waiting for the loading of the C-17. As he walked among the complex assortment of specialized equipment his heart swelled with pride that he had become a part of such an elite and deadly efficient combat organization that stood at the point of the trident defending America. Then he allowed himself to think wistfully of the departed Stephanie, but he shut down those thoughts as quickly as they had begun lest the demons of the past return to cloud his judgment.

Chance Lyon's SEAL Platoon was wheels up from Oceana Naval Air Station at precisely twelve-hundred hours the next day. Once airborne the co-pilot summoned Chance to the flight deck and handed him a sealed envelope that was addressed: **Lieutenant Chance Lyon, USN. EYES ONLY!**

Chance thanked the pilot and went back to the cabin where he sat and read the contents. After absorbing the message, Chance stood up and took the microphone in the forward part of the cabin and announced to the passengers: "Okay, listen up. I have a memo from Commander Buckholder regarding our destination that I will read to you at this time."

> MEMO TO: Second Platoon, SEAL Team Two
> FROM: Commander Ryan Buckholder, USN
> SUBJECT: Destination.
> **CLASSIFICATION: Top Secret - Nuclear.**
>
> This memo will be read to you by your Commander, Lieutenant Chance Lyon, once airborne and en route to your destination.
>
> Your official destination today will be Kirtland Air Force Base, New Mexico, and then on to Sandia National Laboratories located there. You will be housed and sequestered in a secure section of the facility that is off limits to all personnel that do not have a need to know. From Kirtland airfield you will be taken to this site in a bus with no windows.
>
> Your quarters will be Spartan, but comfortable, and your meals will be brought in by security personnel indigenous to the site. The only conversational contact you will be permitted is within the team and with your instructors who will be wearing identical forest green jumpsuits. Do not speak with anyone else unless it is to one of the security people in a red jumpsuit, and then only if you suspect a security breach. Sandia personnel will wear badges with a first name and a number. While on duty there U.S. Navy SEAL personnel will wear black jumpsuits with a badge showing your first name and a number. These badges must be worn at all times.

<u>**DO NOT**</u> reveal to any Sandia personnel the fact that you are members of the U.S. military or the fact you are Navy SEALs.

The purpose of your visit to this facility will be to receive training on a device indigenous to an upcoming mission for which you have been previously alerted. This training is extremely important and will require intense concentration as there will be no written takeaways after the training. Subsequent use of this device will be by memory only.

On the last day of the training, there will be a practical exercise based on the training you have received immediately prior. Failure to complete this exercise with a grade of one-hundred percent as judged by the exercise proctor will have a negative impact on each participating operator's efficiency report and may be cause for dismissal from the teams and being sent back to the fleet or discharged from the Navy altogether.

The next briefing will be from one of the Sandia senior instructors at your final destination.

(Signed) R. Buckholder: CDR, U.S.N.
COMMANDING

"Well guys, if that little love letter from Commander Buckholder doesn't get your attention, nothing will. If there was any doubt that this isn't a business trip, I guess that clinches it."

After reading the letter Chance noticed that the atmosphere within the team during the balance of the flight was considerably more serious and subdued than usual. Whatever this group of SEALs would be doing at Sandia for the next few days was going to be very serious business indeed.

The C-37A militarized executive jet rolled to a stop within a private hanger at Kirtland Air Force Base and the co-pilot released the door, allowing the SEALs to descend the staircase to the gleaming grey epoxy-coated floor. After a pit stop in a guarded restroom within the hanger itself, the team was escorted by several security people to a black, state-of-the-art Prevost luxury coach that was idling near the hanger doors.

For the SEALs, the mystery of their journey was made even deeper now as they noticed their actions were carefully scrutinized by the half-dozen serious-looking security types who were protecting the area from unauthorized personnel. Once Chance Lyon verified to the lead security person that all his personnel were aboard, the bus buttoned up and they were on their way to the top-secret site.

In twenty minutes, the SEALs reached their destination and were escorted into a large concrete block building. All but two of the security men left the group and they were greeted by a middle-aged man wearing a forest green jump suit adorned with a plastic badge with the name 'Art' and the number '4' in large block letters.

"Welcome to Sandia, gentlemen. In a few moments I will escort you to your quarters, where there will be a buffet set up in two hours. Meanwhile, if you would like to relax or take advantage of the recreational facilities, please do so. My team and I will look forward to seeing you after breakfast tomorrow at zero-eight-hundred. I'm sure your Commander has told you that this training will be very important and perhaps intellectually challenging."

The energetic SEALs were eager to work out the kinks imposed by their long plane ride and took to the gym and the large indoor pool after settling into their dormitory settings. After some spirited competition among the SEALs swimming several laps both underwater and free-style, one of the Chief Petty Officers approached Chance Lyon as they rested at the end of the pool.

"Sir, what do you make of this? They're taking the security here damned seriously. One of the guys has been to Sandia for some Nuclear 101 training, but it was never buttoned up like this."

Chance thought for a moment and answered, "Schultz, this being Sandia and the memo from Buckholder being classified Top Secret - Nuclear, you can bet your retirement this has got to be some kind of advanced nuke training. If I knew more I'd tell you, but I'm in the dark too. That paragraph about passing the practical exercise means this is very serious shit, however."

Schultz continued, "Sir I wasn't a science major in college and Physics 101 is as far as I got. I hope there's not too much theory in this training. I mean, half the people working here are probably Ph.Ds.'."

"Chief, don't worry about that. Just everybody put their ears on and listen up sharp. In the evening we'll get the team together and go over everything as a group to make sure we're all on the same page and totally understand the material. We're a team and our culture is we do everything together, and together we're going to ace this, Schultz. Spread the word."

Chance had 30 minutes before the evening meal and he decided to pass the time by doing lazy laps and clearing his mind for what might lie ahead. As he back-stroked easily his thoughts turned to what had happened in his life in the past year and a half since becoming a SEAL Operator. Chance knew that everything he had accomplished professionally since graduating from the Academy had surpassed his every personal expectation, but that was only the good side. The multiple jolts of losing his best friend, Lieutenant Walt Richards, to a Taliban sniper in a night raid in Afghanistan and then the brutal assassination of his girlfriend, Stephanie Morris, by al-Qaeda sympathizers in Washington had hardened his psyche against thoughts of random acts of kindness or even momentary weakness of purpose.

Although participating in the dramatic rescue of his father and his colleagues from captivity in Pakistan had been emotionally and professionally satisfying, that had been more of a rescue mission involving incidental contact with a passive enemy, and it provided Chance with little satisfaction that he was settling scores with the ones who took the lives of those he loved.

His subsequent assignment as a training officer in Coronado - free of the daily stress of combat as it had been - was unrewarding and soon became an irritant. Chance had been out in the mud with his fellow SEALs in Afghanistan for so long and endured so many demanding missions that he felt he could look into the eyes of the BUD/s trainees and tell in a heartbeat who would survive and even prosper under the harsh training environment and who would not. He felt fortunate to get back with the teams and the reality of laying it all on the line every day for Stephanie, Walt, and the teams. Chance knew he was in the ideal position to avenge the wrongs that had been perpetrated against his family and friends and he vowed to make those who had tormented them pay dearly.

The next morning started early for Chance Lyon's platoon. They gathered at 06:00 for group PT and swimming for one hour before eating a hearty breakfast. All the SEALs had the gut feeling they were about to be deployed on another tough mission and each man felt a sense of personal responsibility to his fellow SEALs, and to himself, to maintain a fitness edge that would serve him well for whatever lay ahead.

At 08:30 the SEALs assembled in a modern and brightly lit classroom with tables arranged in an elevated semi-circle above and around a large stainless steel table. It was obvious that there were several objects of different shapes and sizes arranged on the table, but they were covered by a dark green cloth. A half-dozen men and women clad in green jumpsuits were in the room along with the man they recognized as 'Art' (# 4), who had greeted them the previous day. Art began by addressing the SEALs.

"Good morning, gentlemen. I trust you have settled in comfortably. Before we begin the instruction, I would like to go over a few administrative matters. I am 'Art' - we don't use last names in this particular training facility - so there will be no socializing while we are here together, no exchanges of e-mail addresses or social media information, promises of staying in touch later, or things of that nature. My staff sees only your first name as well. Just so you know, we do not know who you are or what organization - if any - you belong to. You may safely assume that we are professional associates of Sandia Corporation, period."

Art continued, "The purpose of your visit to this facility is to learn the operational theory and the practical application of a very low yield nuclear device in a conflict environment. It is my understanding, and you may safely assume as well, that in the near future you may be called upon to deploy this device in such a manner that will further the strategic goals of the United States of America."

"That is consistent with the mission of this facility. You may have noticed that I have not categorized this device as a weapon. Because of its unique design and yield, detonating this device may produce a passive deterrent that is more powerful and effective than the initial detonation itself. Although my staff and I are not aware of how this particular device will be deployed by you - if at all - I can tell you that several uses for this device were taken into consideration during its design phase. I urge you to be open-minded during this training concerning the potential this device has for causing damage to enemy combatants and/or infrastructure."

Art continued, "If you have not been formally trained on the deployment and use of nuclear weapons you may be under the assumption that they are inherently dangerous. This could not be further from the truth. Despite the enormous potential for destruction these devices have, an accidental detonation of one of these weapons is highly unlikely. To demonstrate this point I direct your attention to the large video monitor in the front of the room. The object held above this concrete surface is a live nuclear bomb of several kilotons yield. It will be dropped from a height of fifty feet onto the concrete surface below to simulate accidental mishandling. Prior to the release of the device a technician will sweep the concrete surface with a Geiger counter. This will show no significant signs of radioactivity."

Art directed that the video proceed. Just as he predicted, the bomb was released and fell to the concrete surface. There was significant external damage to the bomb housing caused by the impact, but no explosion. The same technician returned to the device lying on the concrete and swept the device itself and the area around it with the Geiger Counter. A close up of the meter showed the same amount of negligible radiation as before.

"You see gentlemen, these are robust devices that do not detonate unless they are fused and armed, allowing them to do so," he summarized.

'Impressive,' thought Chance, *'they must have had my guys - and the way they throw stuff around - in mind when they designed these things.'*

Now that the demonstration was over, Art continued with the briefing.

"Gentlemen, now that you know that you don't have to walk around on eggshells here, we can get started with the substance for which we are gathered today."

"You will be with us here for the next few days, and the program will be broken down as follows. Today will be mostly theory of nuclear physics and how nuclear weapons and similar devices work. Although it is important that you understand the theory, don't worry, there won't be a test on theory - it's just background. Tomorrow, we will be carefully walking you through the design and component parts of the actual device you will be working with. A practical aspect of this will be the assembly and disassembly of this device until you know that cold and can do it in very low visibility situations.

"The following day you will be rehearsing the actual conditions - as closely as we can approximate them - of the actual deployment of this device in a simulated mission. You will be doing this dressed in garments shipped here for the exercise by your employer. The final day you will be going through a practical exercise that you rehearsed the day prior. This will be a proctored exercise overseen by me and my staff that will be graded. There will be only one run-through of this practicum, so you must make it count.

Once this exercise is complete you will receive a meal and transportation back to the air base to board your aircraft. The results of the exercise will be made known to you by your employer," Art concluded.

The first day passed with the SEALs absorbing an amalgam of theory concerning nuclear fission and fusion, plutonium and uranium based weaponry, arming and fusing devices, safety-and-security systems, and fail-safe mechanisms. In the afternoon they were taken to another area - once again in the bus with the blacked-out windows - on the sprawling facility, where they were shown many varieties of actual nuclear weapons in various stages of assembly. This tour was conducted by an attractive blond female member of Art's staff who carefully explained what the curious SEALs were observing.

"Gentlemen, what you are seeing here covers a substantial overview of the United States' nuclear weapons inventory. You are being shown this because of your ultra-high security clearance and - by what we have been told - the possibility that you may come in contact with weapons such as these during your line of work."

As she continued with her tour, Chance noted that her nametag said simply, 'Judy' with the number '8.' It did not escape Chance that 'Judy, # 8' cut an attractive figure even wearing the standard green jumpsuit worn by all Art's staff. This combined with her articulate explanations and obvious intelligence got Chance thinking. *'I've seen this woman before'* he mused. *'I just can't place her...but she's definitely familiar.'*

As the tour continued with the staff explaining the components of the various nuclear weapons, Chance noticed that 'Judy' kept giving him glances, and shortly there was a spark of mutual recognition between the two. During a break when the SEALs continued to walk around the various devices asking questions of the staff or simply gawking at the awesome display of deadly weaponry, Judy came up to Chance and remarked, "Either you are a guy named Chance from a famous military academy on the East coast, or you are his twin," she smiled.

"Bet you don't remember me!"

Chance looked around nervously, not knowing quite how - or if - to respond. Now it was making sense to him. 'Judy' was ahead of him at the Naval Academy and was one of the Middie's star female athletes as well as number four or five academically in her class. But what was she doing here at Sandia? Wasn't she still in the Navy? Hell, with all the spookiness going on around here, maybe she was detailed here by BUPERS. Who knew?

"Yes, now I remember," answered Chance.

"Is it okay...I mean is it okay to talk? You know, the security briefing."

"Yeah, sure," Judy said easily.

"This isn't Russia with the KGB lurking about. To be perfectly ethical, I'll have to report this encounter to security, but this is a chance encounter - no pun intended" - she chuckled.

"It's happened before with special visitors...the fact that we were at the Academy at the same time can't be helped. The cat's out of the bag now - between us anyway. Better we not get too personal here, though. The quick read is that I'm detailed here by BUPERS for a year, and I don't even have to guess what you and your buddies do for a living. After working with these things like I do, I can smell danger from a long way away and you guys are it with a capital D!" she concluded with a wink and a smile.

"We'll be talking - discreetly," Judy said, as she turned and walked away.

The next day Chance and the other SEALs assembled in the classroom for their hands-on portion of the training. The previous day's experience around the deadly array of nuclear weapons had been sobering for everyone and had given the men a fresh perspective on how a careless miscalculation by a political or military leader who possessed such weaponry could cause the deaths of hundreds of thousands and incalculable physical destruction.

Chance saw that all Art's crew was present, with the exception of Judy # 8. He hoped their brief and casual conversation had not been the source of her absence. Perhaps he would never know.

As usual, Art began the briefing and training session.

"Gentlemen, in spite of what you witnessed yesterday both in the session on nuclear theory and 'The Grand and Morbid Tour' - as I prefer to call it, - showing you examples of this country's nuclear arsenal, what we will be working on for the balance of this training will be very far removed from the atomic and thermonuclear weapons you saw yesterday. Those weapons were designed to cause massive destruction of an enemy's infrastructure and, unfortunately kill many humans in the process. The most dramatic examples of this were the bombs exploded at Hiroshima and Nagasaki that ended World War Two."

"The device we will be training you on for the balance of your training is not so much a bomb as it is a radiological dispersal device, or by its acronym, a RDD. Yes, this device does indeed explode, but the explosion is made by a conventional explosive - in this case TNT - and the purpose of the explosion is to disperse radioactive material into a confined area for the purpose of contaminating everything in that area with gamma radiation. Very few of the items exposed to this effect will be physically damaged, but they will become radioactive to the point that humans cannot come in contact with them for years without the risk of radiation sickness. For example, if you had a tool that you used in your daily work that became exposed to the radioactive material dispersed by the explosion, you could never safely use that tool again in your lifetime."

One of Chance's men asked Art, "Isn't what you are describing the general theory behind detonating a so-called Dirty-Bomb?"

"Precisely," answered Art, who strained to look at Chief McClusky's nametag.

"Unfortunately, given a source of radioactive material such as cesium-137 or strontium-90, it may be relatively easy for a motivated amateur to build a dirty-bomb and detonate it in an urban area in an act of terrorism. The results in terms of property damage in the form of denial of use could be quite disruptive in the short and, possibly, the long term, but substantial loss of life would be unlikely if remediation steps are started promptly."

"Your purpose here, gentlemen," continued Art, "is to learn how to use such a RDD - as we would prefer to call it - and deploy it in a very specific situation that has been described to us in general. We will begin this today."

For the first time the green cloth covers were removed from the hardware that had been placed on the large stainless steel table below the SEALs seating arrangement. Chance noticed that Judy # 8 had entered the room and he was further pleased that she was the person actually doing the training that was about to start.

For the balance of the morning, the SEALs were briefed in great detail on the component parts of this so-called RDD and watched as Judy, aided by another technician, repeatedly assembled and disassembled the device, showing the SEALs the component parts and how they related to each other.

After a break for lunch, the SEALs were securely bussed to yet another area where there were what appeared to be four sea-going containers placed together to create one large steel container. Upon closer examination the containers had their interior walls removed to form a very large open space with only exterior walls. In the center of the room was a wooden shipping crate.

Once again Judy # 8 and some technicians appeared with a device that appeared identical to what they had been briefed on that morning and they placed it on top of the shipping container.

Once again, Judy addressed the assembled SEALs.

"Gentlemen, what we have here is an exact duplicate of the device you will be using in your professional activities. However, in this case the materials to be dispersed are extremely fine metal particles, ground finer than talcum powder, that have been coated with a white material. These particles represent the radioactive material that will be present in a live RDD. Planted throughout the steel container are many magnets of various sizes, some placed in nearly inaccessible places in the container. We are going to shut the container doors and detonate the RDD, which you will be able to observe on the video screen. After the detonation we will open the doors to the container and observe the effects of the RDD. I am confident you will be impressed."

Chance Lyon had sat through more than his share of Dog-and-Pony shows in his career as a student at the Academy and during the more technical aspects of his SEAL training, but this had all the makings of strange. His attention was more on the physical attributes of Judy # 8 than the sealing of the doors of the large container. But Chance snapped back to reality and dutifully watched as a technician counted down from five and fired the explosive package remotely. There was a muffled report from inside the container and the video screen immediately turned a stark white and stayed that way for several minutes until some gray, then darkness, gradually began to saturate the screen.

In a few moments a technician opened the steel doors of the container and invited the SEALs to take a close look inside.

"Please observe, gentlemen, that the wooden crate is largely destroyed but the metal parts inside are still intact. But even more important, I would like you to look at the spots throughout the container on the walls, floors, ceilings, and even in the most remote corners and crevices where there is a high concentration of white particles. Please keep one very important fact in mind as you assess what you are seeing here. Those spots where there is the highest concentration of white powder are *magnetic*."

For fifteen minutes Chance and his SEALs inspected the inside of the container and came away impressed about how ubiquitous the white powder had penetrated the internal surfaces of the steel container. If the white particles had been radioactive, everything inside the container would be 'hot.' Since it had been emphasized to the SEALs, it was not lost on them that the magnetic surfaces were caked heavily. But what was the point, they all wondered?

On the morning of the third day - rehearsal day - the SEALs were surprised to be greeted in the classroom only by Art, the leader of the Sandia staff who had been with them from the beginning.

"Gentlemen, for security reasons I will be leaving you for the balance of the training. Judy # 8 will be the only one of my staff who will remain with you. Your rehearsals will begin in a few minutes, after a briefing from another person. Thank you for your attention the past two days and I wish you the best of luck in your future endeavors." With that short greeting Art left the room.

After Art exited, a door from the other side opened and in strode Rachel Hunter, Director of National Intelligence and Admiral Clayton Williams, the SPECWAR Commander from CENTCOM. The SEALs immediately rose to their feet and came to attention for the Admiral, for whom they all had the greatest respect and who was, essentially, their boss.

Admiral Williams told the SEALs to take their seats and began.

"Gentlemen, for those of you who may know her by reputation only, I would like to introduce you to Doctor Rachel Hunter, the Director of National Intelligence. Today, Director Hunter and I will give you background on an upcoming mission and a briefing on the specifics of how we expect you to execute it. After that we will go into a realistic rehearsal phase for the balance of the day and into the evening, if necessary. This rehearsal will be a prelude to the practical exercise you will conduct tomorrow. After the completion of the exercise you will return to

Little Creek for further preparation and eventual deployment. I wanted to be here personally to ensure you understand the importance of this mission as an instrument of United States' national policy. I expect you to do your best!"

Director Hunter took the podium and from that moment had the SEAL's complete attention. It is a universal truth that people of accomplishment are drawn together by an invisible force that speaks to them beyond the mundane, cutting through the trivial, and pushing their collective thinking toward the fundamental truths of their discipline. Except for her obvious femininity - accented by tasteful and understatedly expensive clothing - Rachel Hunter was a commanding woman with the heart and mentality of a Navy SEAL.

The Director spent the next twenty minutes briefing the SEALs on the background of the mission just as it had been described to the National Security Team - leaving out, of course, the details of the mole that Mossad had developed in VEVAK - and the various options that had been considered for countering Iran's increased enrichment plans.

"What we have decided, gentlemen, is that we will adopt a policy of starving the beast, as it were, and deny the Iranians the use of a vital commodity incidental to their enrichment activities by stealth, rather than fly directly into the teeth of the storm. In doing so we accomplish the same ends without giving them the opportunity for a propaganda diatribe that could surely come after an overt strike in their territory. In the end President Rashad may rail against the wind, but his protestations will fall on deaf ears."

Admiral Williams took the podium next to give a mission overview brief. Everyone knew that more thorough briefings would soon follow, but in order to rehearse realistically, the SEALs had to know the strategy of the mission. The actual tactics would be worked out in the first rehearsal phase and refined from there.

"Gentlemen, the basic outline of the operation - known from today forward as Operation Trinity - will be for a SEAL Team, composed of two

SEAL elements, to board a freighter adrift in the Arabian Sea and place a number of radiological dispersal devices especially designed and built by the people here at Sandia in the cargo hold. Once these devices have been set, the SEAL Team will extricate to their Zodiacs and detonate the RDDs remotely. The detonation will compromise a shipment of precision machine parts – more specifically, magnets, by irradiating them. At a predetermined time and place the Zodiacs will rendezvous with the U.S. Navy submarine that delivered them and return to port. The operation will begin and end at the U.S. Naval base at Diego Garcia in the Indian Ocean."

Admiral Williams continued, "Gentlemen, more to the specifics, you will depart from Diego Garcia in a U.S. Naval submarine at a time coincidental to the progress of the freighter, intercept the freighter that has been previously disabled and is no longer under way, move from the semi-submerged submarine via your Zodiacs, proceed to the freighter and board her in two groups."

"The security group will move all of the personnel in the freighter to a secure location on the vessel so they may not interfere with the SEAL assault group that will board shortly thereafter and make their way into the cargo hold, find the shipment of magnets, place the charges and exfiltrate to their boats. The security group will follow and be the last to return to the Zodiacs, and all will proceed together to the rendezvous point for extraction."

"I might add here that this operation will take place entirely at night. We can't control the phase of the moon, but we can control the timing, which should work to our advantage. This is SEAL Operations 101, gentlemen, simple, straightforward, and efficient. I would estimate time on the boat to be one hour, max. I know you will have questions. I can take some of the more basic ones now," Williams concluded.

Chance Lyon, being the officer of this group of SEALs, took the lead.

"Sir, you say the freighter will be disabled and adrift. How will that be accomplished?"

Admiral Williams explained about the use of the electromagnetic pulsing technology that would disable all the electronics on the ship, rendering it powerless and giving the SEALs a two- or three- hour window to have their way on the ship before the ship's engineer could find workarounds to restore power.

"About the only thing that might work for the skipper might be an Iridium telephone, but who is he going to call for help halfway between Karachi and the Persian Gulf? Anyway, by the time they get the essential electronics back on line, you guys will be long gone. The bottom line is that the crew may suspect you people are Americans, but there will be no evidence left behind except radioactive cargo, so there's no smoking gun."

"If you don't have any further questions at the moment, let's board the bus and proceed to the area where we will be rehearsing for the rest of the day," concluded Williams.

CHAPTER 8

DRY RUN

"Practice is the best of all instructors."
Publilius Syrus (Roman philosopher)

Chance Lyon's SEALs were bussed to a remote area of the Sandia reservation where they would practice for their upcoming mission.

The SEALs had by now named the luxurious Prevost coach with the blacked-out windows 'The Magic Bus' because, as if by magic, entering it whisked them away to a new environment without being able to see what lay between.

The practice environment was inside a large austere cement block building. The ceilings were perhaps 30 feet above the polished epoxy-coated floor and housed many fluorescent lights that gave the building its only sign of life. At the center of the cavernous building was a set of intricately placed scaffolding that soared to within a few feet of the ceiling. The seasoned SEALs immediately realized that the scaffolding was there to simulate the freighter skeleton they would have to negotiate in fulfillment of their mission. Laid out along one edge of the building were boxes and bags of the gear the SEALs would have to wear and carry.

Once again Rachel Hunter greeted the SEALs as they gathered in front of a large video monitor.

"In the past few weeks we have been able to get significant footage and stills of the freighter tied up at the quay in Shanghai designated to transport the magnets to Iran. In addition we have video footage of some freight loading that has been carried out up to now. This gives us valuable information about access to the cargo hold and the pattern used to load the freight. Hopefully, this will reduce the amount of time the assault team will have to spend in the hold searching for the containers holding the magnets."

The SEALs spent an hour viewing images obtained from aerial reconnaissance satellites and stealthy drones that had been launched from U.S. intelligence gathering vessels disguised as commercial ships in the international waters off the coast of China.

In addition to the aerial images the SEALs were provided still images of the freighter. Many vessels of this iteration of ocean freighter were produced in the Polish shipyards of Gdansk, so this data was available from many public marine data bases. The images showed the outside and inside layout of the freighter in great detail. The SEALs would commit these to memory as they ran through their simulations prior to the mission.

One of the many strengths of the SEAL warrior culture was their collective ability to look at the basics of an operation and then, based on the intelligence available, plan the execution of the operation down to the last detail. The SEAL team's combination of training and experience gave it the tools they needed to decide how they would execute as a team to accomplish the task. For an hour the SEALs poured over the images of the freighter discussing and deciding the most advantageous places to board her and what boarding tools and combat gear they would need.

"As Admiral Williams has previously said, the only thing we won't be able to control," remarked Rachel Hunter, "is the phase of the moon you will be working under. Ideally, I know you would prefer no moon - just the light from the stars to augment your night vision devices. This would also give you more stealth in approaching the freighter in your Zodiacs. Regardless, I think there will be enough confusion on the part of the crew dealing with a no power situation that they will not be suspecting a boarding party."

Admiral Williams then spoke for the first time since the SEALs had entered the building.

"Once the security team has boarded the freighter, four men will immediately go to the bridge and secure that area and collect the Captain. The rest will provide security against any potential resistance by the crew. You will order him to gather all hands on the bridge immediately. If you receive any resistance from him you will threaten to dump one of his men overboard. I'm confident he will comply."

"Once you have the crew secure, signal the assault team to board and do its job. While you are waiting you will take headshot photos of each crew member and have the Captain produce the manifest of all the items of cargo. Have the ship's second officer produce all weapons that may be on board, catalog them as best you can and throw them overboard. The Captain will probably have an Iridium telephone - or two. Secure that and bring it with you. Once both teams have made it back to the Zodiacs, get a head count and blow the RDDs. The extract point will be approximately five miles from the freighter and that is where you and the submarine will rendezvous. Once you meet, stash the boats and motors, re-board the sub, and you will be on your way back to Diego Garcia for some beach time. Are there any questions?"

Judy # 8 then produced several 'dummy' RDD devices the SEALs had worked with previously and they spent 30 minutes deciding how those would be secured and transported during the mission.

Over the course of the next few hours the SEALs worked in the totally darkened room aided only by their NODs, with only enough auxiliary lighting to simulate a worst case scenario of a moonless night with an overcast sky. They simulated the entire exercise several times until Chance Lyon announced to Admiral Williams and Rachel Hunter that his men were ready for the practical exercise.

Chance and the other SEALs knew that this simulation - in a dry, inside, cloistered environment - was hardly realistic for what they would encounter at night on the high seas, but it was important that they establish a rhythm of action and a protocol for transporting and deploying the RDDs that were so central to the success of the mission. This would have to do until they could train more realistically in the waters around Norfolk. "I think we're ready, sir...Director Hunter. We're good to go. Just add cold, choppy water, announced Chance, with a dose of dark humor."

The next morning 'The Magic Bus' conveyed the SEALs to the simulation building where they were surprised to be greeted by none other than their Commander, 'Buck' Buckholder. There was no sign of Rachel Hunter, the Admiral, or Judy # 8.

"Gentlemen, I've been staying in touch with the Sandia personnel and am satisfied that this week has been productive in terms of prepping for the mission. I am told that the simulation yesterday - as wholly unrealistic as it may have been - went well and you are ready for the practical exercise. We'll be getting to that after we have an informal meeting where all of you will be asked to give input in the form of ideas to improve the execution of the mission. Do not be reluctant to come forward with your ideas."

After Commander Buckholder concluded his remarks Chance asked to speak privately to his commander.

"Sir, I need to make you aware of a certain situation that came up this week...something unexpected that probably could not have been avoided," Chance explained.

"One of the instructors here was a contemporary of mine at the Academy and we recognized each other. Her name is Judy and she was wearing badge number eight."

"And?" asked Buckholder.

"Well, sir, given our admonition in the initial briefing that there was to be no follow-on contact and socializing, between the two groups - Sandia staff and SEALs - we both felt it was only ethical that we let our respective superiors know about this. She said she would take it up with her security people. In my case, I'm taking it up with you."

"You know, Lyon," replied Buckholder, "that's why I value my SEAL billet so much. Nowhere else in the Navy would I have the opportunity of dealing with people on an everyday basis who value personal integrity so much as to be up front about something like this. Just so you know, your Academy colleague, Judy, did make her security people aware of this and they, in turn, notified me. I had a feeling you would come forward, and I'm very pleased you did."

"Thank you, sir." replied a suddenly relieved Chance Lyon.

Commander Buckholder thought for a moment and then continued.

"It's not an issue, Lyon. I know she put two-and-two together and figured she was working with SEALs. She's a very intelligent person and is apparently on a fast track in the Navy. We'll have a talk with her and encourage her to keep a lid on it. She's got a very high clearance anyway and probably knows about a lot of stuff that's way out of our pay grades. Let's get to work, so we can blow out of here - no pun intended...this place gives me the creeps."

Before the actual exercise began the SEALs briefed Commander Buckholder on how they had decided to execute the mission, paying particular attention to the final assembly of the Radiological Dispersal Devices to be deployed on the shipping containers and the arming and fusing mechanisms that would be the final items installed on the RDDs before leaving the freighter. With those in place the remote detonator would do its job up to one-quarter mile away.

The SEALs geared up and the exercise began. The room darkened to what would be the equivalent of starlight with overcast-level lighting and everyone was working with the benefit of their NODs -- as they would surely be doing on the actual mission. Commander Buckholder positioned himself inside the skeleton of the scaffolding so he could observe his SEALs clamoring up the sides of the structure and then in the direction of their assigned objectives after successfully boarding the freighter. He was also in the communications loop that helped him understand how the security and assault teams would be working together.

Near the end of the simulation, as the two teams were preparing to exfiltrate the practice structure, the Commander threw a curve at the security team, telling them that one of their group had been shot and wounded by one of the ship's crew. This required the assault platoon leader to adjust his exfil plans in mid-stream and divide his platoon in order to neutralize the shooter and also get the wounded SEAL off the vessel. Dealing with the unexpected was a situation the SEALs had practiced many times before and they adjusted seamlessly, going through the motions of handling it like the professionals they were. But in the operational world of the SEALs, simulations were one thing and reality was frequently another.

As cobbled together as that the simulation was, Buckholder and his SEALs were confident that the week at Sandia had given them valuable insight into theory and deployment of the unique device they would be pioneering and the overall operation plan that had been devised. Given the successful implementation of the plan to disable the freighter and reasonable weather, Chance Lyon and his brother SEALs were confident of its outcome.

After the SEALs secured from the exercise and the lights came up, they spent another thirty minutes critiquing with Commander Buckholder. It was clear that he had approved their efforts and after packing their gear and having their mid-day meals, the SEALs were transported one final time in 'The Magic Bus' to their chartered V-37A and departed for Oceana Naval Air Station in Norfolk.

Now the more strenuous training was about to begin.

During the long flight back and for the first time since the death of Stephanie Morris nearly six months ago, Chance Lyon had a fanciful curiosity about another woman. He vowed to look Judy # 8 up through the Naval Academy alumni database and begin a tentative correspondence.

CHAPTER 9

MID-OCEAN DRAMA

"To hell with luck, I'll bring the luck with me."
Santiago (The Old Man) - <u>The Old Man and the Sea</u>. Ernest Hemingway.

Once back at the Navy SEAL base at Little Creek, the SEALs refined their plans for Operation Trinity as they continued to study the images and internal plans that had been obtained for the freighter vessel Pacific Dawn that was moored to at a quay in the bustling Shanghai harbor.

The NSA was continuing to intercept the electronic mail between the manufacturer of the magnets and the bogus trading company fronted by the Iranian government. In doing so they learned both the exact loading day of the parts ordered and the departure date of the Pacific Dawn. Although a precise delivery date to Iran was not given, a window based on the ports to be visited by the freighter gave the SEAL operations planners a close approximation of when to attack the shipment. The attack would be carried out in the middle of the night after she departed Karachi en route to Iran.

Based on the approximate date of the month, the predicted moon phase the SEALs would have to deal with was either the third quarter-to-the waning crescent phase. Although the ideal phase would be no moon, either of these phases would be better than the hated full moon, which would illuminate their Zodiacs on the open sea from perhaps a mile away from the ship. Now they could only keep their fingers crossed for fair seas on which to navigate in their small rubber boats.

OPERATION TRINITY - OPERATIONAL PLAN

Since it would be a relatively simple matter to track the Pacific Dawn along its route, it would be easy to calculate when the U.S. Navy submarine should leave Diego Garcia with the SEALs and their equipment on board to intercept the freighter. Likewise, positioning the aircraft carrier from which the drone carrying the Non-Nuclear Electromagnetic Pulse Generator (NNEMP) would launch would be a simple navigational calculation.

The plan was for the carrier to lay off the freighter between fifty and one hundred miles, allow the drone to deliver its low yield package to the target, and then confirm that the freighter had been disabled with its hi-res camera package by sending live infra-red images back to the Combat Direction Center at the carrier. The drone's electronic and propulsion systems were protected by special shielding, making it immune from its own NNEMP strikes. Once confirmed, a signal would go to the submarine for the SEALs to deploy.

Barring any passive sonar or periscope detected surface threats, the submarine carrying the SEALs - lying off the disabled freighter approximately one mile - would surface just enough to expose the sail and the deck hatch to the lock-out chamber located behind the sail. The SEALs would emerge from the lock-out chamber in groups of nine, and unlock the hatches in the Submarine's sail, holding their Combat Rubber Raiding Craft (CRRC, also known as 'Zodiacs'), boarding gear, and weapons - most critical of which would be the Radiological Dispersal Devices to be planted on the magnet shipping containers.

Once the SEALs loaded into their boats, the vulnerable submarine would submerge to safety and retreat to the pre-arranged extract point a few miles away to await their return from the raid.

The SEAL security group, consisting of 14 SEALs, would lead the way to the freighter, board her from both sides aft with boarding ladders, and secure the crew forward on the bridge. Once the freighter crew was secured, the leader of the security team would signal the SEAL assault team with an IR strobe that the freighter was secure. The assault team would board the boat and proceed to the hold of the ship, where they would locate the precision magnet shipping containers and set their RDD charges.

The assault team would leave the freighter first, followed by the security team. Once both teams were back in their Zodiacs, they would detonate the RDD charges with the remote detonator and exfiltrate to the rendezvous point, guided by their GPS navigation device. The SEALs would wait for the submarine to partially surface so they could re-board, stow their gear and extract. The exact GPS locations for the SEALs and the submarine would be separated by a few hundred yards to avoid the submarine inadvertently capsizing a Zodiac in the surfacing operation.

The SEALs were most vulnerable at the beginning of the exfiltration phase when the security team left the boat and moved away from the ship. Commander Buckholder emphasized the importance of the security team confiscating any weapons on board the freighter and tying up the crew on the bridge immediately prior to leaving. They would undoubtedly soon free themselves, but not before the SEALs had escaped in their Zodiacs. Having no propulsion or electronics, the freighter was in no position to pursue the departing SEALs or call for help until well after the fact.

Prior to briefing his SEAL Team, Commander Buckholder shared the plan with his SPECWAR Commander, and it was quickly approved. "With a little bit of luck, this should come together just fine," remarked Admiral Williams.

"Just right, sir," replied Buckholder, "but I'm expecting my SEALs to bring their own luck."

OPERATION TRINITY - THE EXECUTION

For two of the following nights, Chance Lyon's SEALs were able to practice boarding a freighter anchored around Norfolk that had a similar design to the Pacific Dawn. There was a Virginia class nuclear submarine in the area that was detailed to support the SEALs that was equipped with a lock-out chamber and a sail configured with storage where they could stow their Zodiacs in a knocked-down mode. It was important to the success of the mission that every possible detail be practiced as close as possible to the actual situation, and the area and naval assets around Norfolk provided all of this - except for the sea conditions the SEALs might face in the Indian Ocean.

Meanwhile satellite images from Shanghai harbor showed the Pacific Dawn making preparations to get underway. Chance Lyon and his SEALs were put on 24-hour notice to pre-position their gear at Oceana. In two days Chance and 20 SEALs were on a C-17A headed for the American base on the Indian Ocean island of Diego Garcia (7.3133 S, 72.441 E).

Diego Garcia is some 9,600 direct air miles from Norfolk. In a C-17A transport that would involve nearly 21 hours of flying time and at least three mid-air refuelings. Therefore the trip for Chance Lyon and his SEALs was broken up into three legs, Norfolk-to-Ramstein Air Base in Germany, Ramstein-to-Kandahar, Afghanistan, and finally, Kandahar-to-Diego Garcia. On the third day after leaving Norfolk, Chance's SEAL team landed at Diego Garcia and was taken to a small isolated compound on the Indian Ocean atoll where they could work out the kinks from their long flight and check their gear. Once unloaded from the cavernous C-17, Chance and his senior enlisted Chief Petty Officer were met by a Navy liaison officer and whisked to the high security anchorage where the U.S.S. North Dakota (SSN 784), a Virginia class nuclear attack submarine, had been docked for the past two days.

After passing through security Chance and his Senior Chief made their way down the gangway connecting the quay to the North Dakota, saluted the colors, and were guided on board by a U.S. Marine security guard. Once inside they were met by the ship's Executive Officer and the Chief-of-the-Boat (COB), who escorted the SEALs to the Captain's cabin. While the three officers met with the Skipper in his quarters, the SEAL Senior Chief and the Chief of the Boat met in the boat's mess area to work on the administrative and logistics of the SEALs joining the crew while they were transported to and from their mission.

MID-OCEAN DRAMA

Chance was introduced to Commander Werner Hoffman - a Naval Academy Graduate a year before Chance's father, Captain (ret.) Bernie Lyon, and whose great uncle had been a U-Boat Captain in the latter stages of World War II.

"Welcome aboard, Lieutenant Lyon," greeted the Skipper. "You and your men may find the quarters somewhat cramped, but such is life aboard even the newer attack submarines."

"Thank you, sir. My men and I will try to stay out of the way."

The skipper continued, "I have sealed orders that I have been instructed not to open until you and your men arrived in Diego Garcia. Now, with the XO and you present we'll open these up and see what all the fuss is about. This is not our first experience in delivering SEALs, but this one seems a lot more elaborate, if nothing but the location itself. We usually don't hang around Diego Garcia too much. Good place to get island fever, I'd say."

Commander Hoffman went to his safe and extracted the large envelope with the red 'Top-Secret' security banding on it, broke the security seal and extracted the contents. There were three identical copies of standard U.S. Navy orders, one for each officer. The contents were surprisingly concise, but specific:

	CLASSIFICATION: TOP SECRET
To:	Commander; U.S.S. North Dakota
From:	Chief of Naval Operations
Subject:	Orders - Operation Trinity
	<u>EYES ONLY: CDR HOFFMAN, LCDR ROBERTS, LT LYON</u>

1. Upon arrival at Diego Garcia, take on a complement of U.S. Navy SEALs and their equipment under the command of Lieutenant Chance M. Lyon, U.S.N.

2   When alerted, proceed directly to 'Point Alpha' as indicated on the attached map of the Northern Arabian Sea. There you will remain submerged while you identify and track the ocean freighter Pacific Dawn when she departs Karachi, Pakistan, harbor on a date that will be communicated to you.

3   In the late evening hours of the first night out of Karachi the Pacific Dawn will be disabled and will lose all power, causing her to lose way. When the Pacific Dawn stops you will pull to within one mile of her and surface enough to discharge the U.S. Navy SEALs. After they have collected their equipment and departed your vessel, you will submerge to periscope depth and proceed to 'Point Bravo' to await the return of the SEAL Team from its mission.

4   When the SEAL Team has returned you will take the SEALs back on board and proceed directly to Diego Garcia where the SEALs will disembark. New orders will await you there describing the continuation of your patrol.

5   Your crew will have minimal contact with the SEALs who are aboard the North Dakota. This will be strictly enforced by the Chief of the Boat and the SEAL Senior Chief Petty Officer. Any communication with the SEALs by your command structure will be between the Captain or XO of the North Dakota and Lieutenant Chance Lyon, SEAL Commander.

S. Wheeler: ADM, U.S.N.
Chief of Naval Operations

END OF MESSAGE

"I have to say, Lieutenant," commented Commander Hoffman, "it is highly unusual for an individual boat captain to receive written orders from the CNO that don't come through Fleet Command. Perhaps he copied the Commander of Fifth Fleet Submarine Forces, but it does not say that."

Chance Lyon replied, "Sir, when we do get the word to board from you, we will have our gear staged for pickup and I would prefer to board my men and our equipment after dark. We'll be working with our NODs so any lighting on the quay or on the boat can be killed. We've practiced this many times on one of your sister boats in Norfolk, so we've got the routine down. It won't take us more than an hour to stow our gear and board."

"Okay, Lieutenant Lyon, once your Chief and my COB get their coordination down, we can break."

"Sir, one more thing," added Chance somewhat awkwardly. "Could we speak privately for a moment?"

Chance shot a glance at the XO and said, "No offense, sir. I've been instructed to speak about this privately to the Captain."

Not accustomed to deferring to a mere Lieutenant, the XO gave an annoyed glance to the skipper, who asked him with his eyes to excuse himself.

When the two officers were alone, Captain Hoffman began. "Okay Lyon, this is getting creepier by the minute. First I get a direct order from the CNO, and then I'm being asked to cut my XO out of something that I assume is extremely important to the mission. The XO and the COB are seldom out of the loop when it comes to operational matters of this boat. This better be good!"

Chance paused for a moment for dramatic effect: "Sir, I've been ordered by the CNO to tell you that we will be bringing what is essentially a form of nuclear weapon onto the boat with us that we will be using on our mission. I brought a letter from him about this which I have here."

For a long moment the skipper looked at Chance Lyon in silence and amazement, eventually responding softly with, "Goddam, Lieutenant...I think I'm having a fucking heart attack!"

"What's wrong, sir?" responded Chance, genuinely concerned.

"Wrong?! Wrong? Well, I'll tell you what's *wrong*, Lieutenant. My father was an Admiral and when I got command of this one-point-six billion dollar boat he told me, 'this is your big chance, son. Don't let anything go wrong that can kill your shot for a flag.' So, here I sit with a flash order directly from the CNO, getting ready to take on twenty or so spooky Navy SEALs who are carrying some sort of nuclear weapon, and who want me to tool them stealthily around the Arabian Sea looking for a ship to hijack... WHAT COULD POSSIBLY GO WRONG?" he smiled grimly.

"It's a damn good thing there's no alcohol aboard this boat son. I'd be into it."

"We'll try to be careful, sir." responded Chance lamely.

Chance spent the next few days intensively training his SEAL Team for the mission. The mornings were taken up with long runs around the periphery of the atoll, open water swimming, and night boat drills in their Zodiacs. Afternoons the SEALs gathered in their isolated quarters going over diagrams of the Pacific Dawn and rehearsing every possible scenario that could threaten the accomplishment of their carefully planned mission. After their evening meal was brought to them by Navy stewards from the combined mess, the men could relax by reading or playing video games. The waiting was tedious.

The National Reconnaissance Office (NRO) had been tracking the Pacific Dawn with its orbiting satellites, and as she rounded the southern tip of India the freighter headed for Mumbai where, based on past history, she would be for one day or two at the most. Captain Hoffman received a warning order for imminent deployment that he immediately forwarded to Chance at the SEAL base by messenger. The plan was for the North Dakota and the SEALs to depart Diego Garcia as soon as the Pacific Dawn left Mumbai for Karachi, her last stop before steaming for the Strait of Hormuz and Iran.

*

Even after many months of intensive focus on his work in SEAL Team Two in Afghanistan, then as an instructor in Coronado (hardly the kind of SEAL work that Chance enjoyed), and now back with SEAL Two as they embarked on a top-secret and cutting edge mission with unique weapons, Chance occasionally found himself waking in the middle of the night from disturbing dreams involving Stephanie Morris. He seldom remembered the details but there was always a backdrop of conflict and violence, ending with Chance frantically searching in vain for his murdered lover. A trained dream interpreter or psychologist might help Chance understand these repeating and troubling visions, but Chance elected to ignore them, hoping they would cease in time.

After their experience at Sandia, Chance considered whether he should reach out to contact Judy # 8 (her real name from the Naval Academy Alumni Directory turned out to be Judy Zavier) given the admonition of no post-training socializing they received when they arrived at Sandia. But since they already had a history - thin as it was - Chance took a calculated step of contacting her through her private email address. Thinking that even her private email was possibly under NSA scrutiny due to the highly classified nature of her work, Chance kept it light in his initial contact.

> Hi Judy -
> After no contact since the Academy, it was a pleasure to see you. At least neither one of us is riding a tin can out in the choppy waters of the fleet. I know we're both busy but maybe we can write or text. Who knows, maybe even an Army-Navy Game? I don't do social media, so that's out. Wish you the best in your career...this is what we signed up for!
> Chance.

Trial balloons are frequently that - a flyer. They usually fizzle with little fanfare. In this case Chance was pleasantly surprised the next morning to find a reply from Judy # 8 in his personal mail account.

Hi Chance -
Thanks for writing!
I thought you would be an old 'sea dog' by now, regaling the ladies with tales of derring-do, fighting pirates or something ;-). Yes, it was good to see you again. I heard through the grapevine - you know how that is - about Stephanie (we women stuck together regardless of class) and I'm sad about that. Let's try to find a time when we can be social.
It's really okay...just have to be cool about it. Let
me know when you have some leave coming up. I am somewhat flexible regarding timing if I have a little notice.
Judy

Even the most paranoid security type at Sandia or NSA would not find anything sinister in that exchange (if intercepted at all), and there was certainly no hint of what either of them were doing in their specialties. But Chance was encouraged - and relieved that he wouldn't have to explain about Stephanie to another woman. It was a start, and he suddenly felt better that perhaps there were brighter days ahead that didn't involve work.

Commander Hoffman's messenger caught up with Chance just as the SEALs were finishing their noon meal. He handed Chance a sealed envelope and waited for him to read the contents. Chance then handed it back to the messenger. "Thank you, yeoman. Please send the vehicles at nineteen-hundred."

Chance then gathered his men and said simply, "Let's get our gear together. We're boarding the North Dakota tonight. As they say in the old movies, 'We sail with the tide.'"

THE ARABIAN SEA

Commander Hoffman's navigator calculated it would take a little over three days moving at 25 knots for the North Dakota to reach the approximate intercept point where the SEALs would take down the disabled Pacific

MID-OCEAN DRAMA

Dawn. These were rough calculations to be sure, as there was no guarantee of the date and time the freighter would leave Karachi. But aside from being in relatively cramped quarters, the SEALs would be comfortable aboard the newer Virginia class submarine. This iteration of nuclear attack submarine had been designed with the delivery of Special Operations forces such as Navy SEALs in mind and provisions for their presence for short periods were in place. Most of their bulky gear had been stowed in the sail area of the boat and the 20 SEALs would simply have to make do for a few days in their spaces, isolated from the rest of the crew. Such isolation was necessary for the security of the mission.

After the Pacific Dawn departed Mumbai, the North Dakota began its run to the rendezvous point on an imaginary line from Karachi to the entrance of the Straits of Hormuz. This was calculated on an average steaming speed of the freighter of 15 knots between the two ports and a stay of 24 hours in Karachi, with some built-in flex time for the American submarine having to maneuver to make the intercept. The top speed of the North Dakota was nearly twice that of the freighter, so if any time had to be made up the North Dakota had a distinct advantage.

At the same time, movement data on the Pacific Dawn was being periodically updated to the U.S.S. Abraham Lincoln (CVN-72), the flagship of Carrier Strike Group Midway cruising in the northern portion of the Arabian Sea. A drone from the Lincoln would deliver the knockout punch to the Pacific Dawn, which would signal the North Dakota to surface and discharge Chance Lyon's SEAL Team on its mission.

Life for the SEALs in the cramped quarters of the U.S.S. North Dakota was tolerable at most. In spite of the amenities designed into the Virginia class boats by the builders charged with designing for SEAL warrior delivery as a secondary mission of this class of boat, their isolated quarters were cramped. But the SEALs had been trained to ignore discomfort and focus on the mission and took advantage of every opportunity to exercise and plan for the mission. They were determined to take down the Pacific Dawn and leaving her crew shaking their heads in confused disbelief.

After the Dakota had been underway for two days, Chance Lyon gathered the other 19 SEALs together and gave them a final brief.

"Okay guys, let's try to look at this from the Pacific Dawn's perspective for a moment, just so we can get into the heads of the people we are going to meet face-to-face very soon."

The skipper of this freighter is a German who has been a merchant mariner for 20 plus years. He's a professional working for China Sea Lines, the boat's owner, and one of its senior captains. On the other hand, his crew, except for the Second Officer and the ship's Engineer, is mostly a hodge-podge of multi-ethnic merchant seamen, just working for wages. Collect the three professionals and the rest should be easy, typically these guys have no loyalty to anybody."

"Senior Chief Schultz is going to be leading the security team. Because he is fluent in German he will confront the Captain in that language and deliver the orders to gather the crew on the bridge. All orders for the crew will be delivered to the skipper in German by Chief Schultz and delivered, in turn, to the crew by their skipper."

"The key to obtaining and keeping the Pacific Dawn's skipper's cooperation will be Chief Schultz getting the skipper aside under the pretense of searching his cabin for the ship's manifests. While they are alone Chief Schultz will give the skipper an envelope with twenty-five thousand Euros in cash along with a note explaining that he may present a letter that will also be in the envelope at a specific bank in Hamburg by a date certain for an additional twenty-five thousand if he cooperates. He's a smart guy, he'll probably get it; if not, the worst case scenario is we'll be out some drug money the DEA has confiscated and he'll be kicking himself in the ass later for making a bad decision."

"Once Chief Schultz has the crew under control, I will lead the assault team aboard and we will proceed to the hold where we will search for the cargo containing the magnets. Based on what we have learned from the purchases of the South Africans and the Japanese, who have made similar purchases, we should be able to isolate the magnets fairly quickly. When we do, we'll set the RDDs and leave the hold of the ship. The last thing we do is to post radioactive warning stickers on the entrance of the hold so no one enters this area unwarned...it's going to be hot...for a long time!"

At five AM the next morning Chance was summoned to Commander Hoffman's quarters on the North Dakota. Once there the Captain handed him a print-out of flash message traffic from the Fifth Fleet Commander in Doha, Qatar, addressed to both the Captains of the North Dakota and the U.S.S. Abraham Lincoln.

T-O-P S-E-C-R-E-T
EYES ONLY!
FROM: CDR, U.S. FIFTH FLEET - DOHA
TO: CDR, USS NORTH DAKOTA
CGR, USS ABRAHAM LINCOLN
CDR, NAVY SEAL TEAM / USS NORTH DAKOTA
RE: OPERATION TRINITY

PACIFIC DAWN LEAVING KARACHI 0500 LOCAL TODAY. AUTHORIZE CDRs TO EXECUTE OPERATION TRINITY AT 2300 HRS TODAY. REPORT TO CDR, US FIFTH FLEET UPON EXECUTION AND COMPLETION. GOOD HUNTING.
S.KINEER: VADM, USN
COMMANDING
END OF MESSAGE
T-O-P S-E-C-R-E-T

Chance Lyon handed the message back to Commander Hoffman, who then continued, "Lieutenant Lyon, we'll be getting satellite intercepts of Pacific Dawn and when my sonar guys get an ID on the freighter we'll stay about ten thousand yards off her port beam on a parallel course.

When the drone launches from the Lincoln we'll change our track to bring us within two miles of her. As soon as they put her out of action, I'll bring the Dakota to within a mile. We'll surface just enough for your people to exit the lock-out and secure your gear from the sail. When my video shows you away, we'll submerge and proceed to the extract rendezvous at Point Bravo. After we submerge, you'll be on your own," the Captain concluded with a note of finality that was not lost on Chance.

He and his fellow SEALs would be in their three Zodiacs in the middle of the Arabian Sea in three-to-four foot seas and fifty-five degree water temperatures headed for their own version of 'Mission Impossible.' This is what BUD/s and the arduous training beyond had prepared the SEALs for.

"Okay, people," remarked Chance, when he returned to the SEAL enclave on the submarine. "It's game on. Let's synch our watches to ship's time and go through the plan one more time. We'll have our last meal at seventeen-hundred and be ready to go at twenty-two-thirty hours. Things will begin to start happening fast at twenty-three-hundred. With optimum performance, we should be back on board no later than zero-five-hundred tomorrow and on our way back to Diego Garcia. This is what we trained for. We're going to earn our Tridents today - again!"

Chance had gotten into the habit of writing a note to his family and placing it with his personal belongings prior to jumping off on an operation. Although the contents were never specific about any particular operation, Chance always expressed the general thought that he was embarking on an 'op' that might be dangerous and last for an unknown period of time. The rest was a recitation of sincere thoughts of appreciation for the love and support he had received from his family and the assurance that if he came to grief, he was at least doing something that he loved. Fortunately none of these last messages ever got back to his family, but Chance knew that this op was challenging even by SEAL standards and one never knew what might lie in store. He signed it with a simple 'CL' and stashed it in his personal things hoping that it, too, would never find his family.

By twenty-two-thirty Chance Lyon's SEALs were prepared to enter the lock-out chamber on the North Dakota. Commander Hoffman came to the assembly area where the SEALs were gathered in their wetsuits.

"Good sailing out there gentlemen," he declared. "Your job in this man's Navy is second only to commanding this boat, but tonight I wish I was one of you. I'm proud of being part of your transportation on this mission. I'm looking forward to eating a hearty breakfast with you a few hours from now."

Hoffman picked up the intercom in the SEAL area and asked, "This is the Captain. Do you have a confirm from Lincoln?" A few moments passed and Hoffman said, "Roger that; XO come to lock-out depth. I'll be in the conn in 30 seconds."

Hoffman looked at Chance Lyon and said, "Lieutenant, the Pacific Dawn is dead in the water one mile to starboard. In less than 30 seconds we'll be at lock-out. Good luck."

Two minutes prior to Commander Hoffman's pronouncement, a United States Navy drone - a Boeing Counter Electronics High Power Microwave Advanced Missile Project (CHAMP) remotely piloted aircraft - that had taken off fifteen minutes previously from the aircraft carrier Abraham Lincoln fifty miles away, flew over the Pacific Dawn at two thousand feet and emitted a burst of high powered microwave energy directed specifically at the freighter. Once such weaponry had existed solely in the realm of science fiction, but now, after being in development for the past several years, this technology was being battle-tested for the first time in Operation Trinity.

Consistent with the results produced during many testing scenarios, the millisecond-long burst of microwave energy produced by the stealthy drone fried the electronic control and communications systems of the Pacific Dawn, plunging her into total darkness and changing the familiar pulsing mechanical systems of life on the large freighter into an eerie silence. Seconds later the twin propellers of the ship stopped their rotation and the Pacific Dawn's momentum through the Arabian Sea slowed to a crawl before stopping altogether. Within five minutes she was bobbing like a cork and a victim of the currents as well as the rapidly approaching SEALs in their Zodiacs.

After failing to reach the captain by ship's telephone, the watch officer on the bridge of the freighter immediately dispatched a messenger to Captain Friedrich's cabin. When he reached his quarters be pounded on the door and shouted, EMERGENCY...EMERGENCY, Herr Kaleunt! We have lost all power. Even back-up power has been lost! You must come to the bridge immediately."

Two minutes later Friedrich staggered onto the darkened bridge cursing the darkness and the confusion of the three men on watch. "What the hell has happened?" he thundered.

"We have no power - none at all Herr Kaleunt!" replied the Second Officer. "We are in total back-out and have lost propulsion. All ship's systems are down. We have no communications, no emergency power, and no back-ups. We are dead in the water."

"Send a messenger to get the ship's Engineer," shouted the veteran captain. "This is catastrophic. We must resume some power, even if it is lighting only. We could be rammed by another ship in this darkness."

As the North Dakota surfaced just enough to expose the sail and the hatch cover of the lock-out chamber, the first group of SEALs scrambled on deck of the swaying nuclear submarine and went directly to the sail. They accessed the interior storage spaces through the watertight doors and recovered their knocked down Zodiac combat watercraft, inflating them through the boat's internal compressed air system. The SEALs then attached the outboard motors to the Zodiacs and collected their combat gear and boarding equipment.

In addition to the specialized boarding ladders attached to the Zodiacs, which were specially designed for the purpose of boarding a large sea-going vessel, each SEAL was wearing a wetsuit and was equipped with personal mission-critical items such as a Sig Sauer P-226 9mm semi-automatic pistol, Mark II combat knife, waterproof glow-in-the-dark analog watch, a comm-link radio system consisting of ear buds and a small boom microphone, waterproof Data link Information Device (DID) with video feed and GPS capability, worn on the outside sleeve of the wetsuit, and a high-tech compact personal flotation device that would inflate only on personal command of the wearer or after prolonged pressure associated with being in the water. Each SEAL also wore his night observation device (NOD) and carried his M4 personal weapon. If illumination of an object or person by a SEAL was required, an infrared LED flashlight on a band around the forehead gave the SEALs the illumination they needed without exposing the light source to a potential enemy. Finally, if a camera was needed to record and save an image or a video, a SEAL could extract a small diameter flexible cable coiled within the DID and take an eight megapixel image with a tiny camera head at the end.

After all the SEALs were on deck and the Zodiacs readied, the SEALs on the assault team who had been previously designated 'weapons carriers' retrieved the RDDs from the sail storage of the North Dakota. A total of six RDDs were assigned to the mission and each man on the assault team carried a RDD and an arming-fusing-firing device. Three men on the assault team carried remote detonators. Only one was required to detonate all the RDDs simultaneously. The other two were for back-up.

After getting a visual thumbs-up from each SEAL, Chance gave the team a simple 'go' message and the SEALs cast off the North Dakota in echelon toward their barely visible target just under a mile away. When the SEALs had made less than four hundred yards toward the freighter, the North Dakota slid silently beneath the slight chop and moved slowly to the rendezvous point to await the returning SEALs a few hours hence.

12 SEALs in two Zodiacs made up the security team assigned the task of boarding the freighter by stealth from the stern, securing the bridge and engineering spaces in two separate elements. The two elements would then assess the tactical situation and communicate the logistics of rounding up the balance of the crew and getting them to the bridge.

It would be up to Chief Schultz to communicate with Captain Friedrich in his native language to ensure that all the crew was accounted for, any and all weapons inventoried and disposed of, and cargo manifests retrieved. The mission planners knew it was a calculated risk that the cash Euros offered to Friedrich would go a long way in securing his pro-active cooperation.

Chance and the other five SEALs comprised the assault element and held back of the stern of the drifting Pacific Dawn as they watched the security element's Zodiacs draw near the freighter, hurling grappling hooks attached to the end of a rope over the edge of the stern railing. Once hooked, one of the SEALS climbed the rope from each boat to board the ship. With two SEALs aboard, one SEAL hauled up the two boarding ladders while the other provided him security from potentially curious crew members. With the boarding ladders in place the balance of the security element quickly abandoned their bobbing Zodiacs and scrambled aboard. With no gunfire and no audible commotion, Chance concluded that the boarding had been done undetected.

There were random shouts of crewmen coming from several sections of the freighter that carried across the water but they seemed to have no urgency other than cursing their totally helpless condition of the moment. Someone was now shooting a red flare into the air every two minutes as if to signal other ships in the area that they might be disabled. This activity, until it could be stopped, added an increased sense of urgency for the SEALs to complete their mission as quickly as possible before any other ship could come to the aid of the Pacific Dawn.

Chance radioed to Chief Schultz, "Eight this is one. Secure that flare gun right away...giving us away." The flare gun was indeed a vulnerability that the SEALs could not have controlled with the NNEMP from the drone. Sooner or later the crew would break out the battery-operated flashlights and battle lanterns and begin to post them around the periphery of the ship, because they feared their greatest vulnerability was being rammed by another vessel in the dark of night.

Chief Schultz split the SEAL security element into two groups that worked their way forward on the port and starboard sides of the ship, dropping four of the men off into the engineering spaces to secure crew whose duty stations might be there. Those crewmen would have found portable flashlights by now, but that would make finding them easy. Even without portable lighting, the crew would be at a decided disadvantage against the SEALs, who had NODs and infrared lighting to guide their way in the darkness.

The balance of the SEALs would work their way forward converging on the bridge from both sides, isolating the Captain and senior officers, who would logically be there trying to cope with the disabled condition of the ship.

Chief Schultz and three of the security element SEALs worked their way swiftly to the bridge aided by natural lighting from the stars and the waning crescent moon. For them, aided by their NODs, it was nearly as light as day. The SEALs came upon the bridge as at least four of the crew and the Captain were bustling about with flashlights, frantically flailing at the controls in a vain attempt to restore some power to the stricken ship. In a pre-planned move, Schultz and another SEAL tipped up their NODs to adjust to the light coming from the flashlights, while the other two SEALs provided cover for what would immediately become a darkened scene again.

"DROP TO THE FLOOR!" Schultz shouted in German, then Spanish, and finally English.

"DOUSE THE LIGHTS!" he repeated in the same language sequence.

Schultz commanded the Captain in German to immediately obey his command or be shot. The Captain looked at Schultz and the other SEALs with a horrified expression, taken completely by surprise. The apparition of four menacing men in black wetsuits, their faces covered with masks, carrying automatic weapons, appearing out of nowhere on the bridge of his disabled ship overloaded the Captain's cognitive circuits, and he simply stood slack-jawed in response.

In seconds, the seasoned skipper sensed real danger to his ship and crew, which he knew instinctively he was powerless to overcome. He gave orders to his crew on the bridge to comply.

"Do as they say. These men are pirates and will kill us if we don't comply. Do not resist," ordered Captain Friedrich. Even on merchant vessels the crew is trained that the Captain's word is law and they immediately complied. In the next instant, the crew knelt to the floor and the flashlights were extinguished.

Chief Schultz poked the Captain with the point of his M4 and asked harshly, "Herr Kaleunt, sprechen sie Deutsch?" Immediately the cowering Captain answered in perfect German that, yes, he did indeed speak German. This response made it easy for Schultz to make several rapid demands of the Captain.

"You will immediately assemble all the crew here on the bridge. Do not resist or you and those who do resist will be executed by my men. Make this clear to your crew that there must be no resistance to my orders!"

"Jawohl," responded the trembling Captain, now stressed to the breaking point.

Friedrich urgently shouted orders to no one in particular on the bridge in passable English, echoing Chief Schultz's demands. He then looked imploringly through the darkness in the direction of Schultz as if to say he was cooperating fully.

"As soon as your crew is assembled and all accounted for, you will once again command them to cooperate fully with my men. Then you will instruct your Second Officer to round up and produce all weapons that exist on this vessel and bring them to your cabin. This must be done without delay and no weapons held back. Is this perfectly clear, Herr Kaleunt?"

"Jawohl."

MID-OCEAN DRAMA

"I will give you and your Second Officer five minutes to completely comply with this order or there will be negative consequences!"

Captain Friedrich tentatively rose to his feet and shouted out the orders to his Second Officer with similar urgency as before.

"Captain Friedrich, you will take me to your quarters," growled Chief Schultz. As if speaking to his fellow commandos, but for affect only, Schultz spoke a series of threatening commands in German into his boom microphone without pushing the talk button. This was meant to keep Friedrich guessing about the nationality of the SEALs and their motives, as he would surely be thoroughly interrogated later by VEVAK Intelligence upon his eventual arrival in Iran.

Feeling confident that his security element was in control of the ship, Schultz gave the simple command of 'Clear on bridge,' to Chance Lyon and his assault element as a signal for them to board the freighter and carry out their part of the mission.

Schultz and Friedrich now made their way deliberately to Captain Friedrich's quarters aft of the bridge in silence. As Friedrich fumbled for his keys, Schultz flipped up his NODs and shined a small flashlight beam on the lock, which the Captain quickly opened. Once inside Schultz aimed the beam directly at Friedrich and spoke to him rapidly in perfect German.

"Herr Kaleunt, with your cooperation this will all be over within an hour and your men and ship will be free to go - if your engineer can get her going. If you do not cooperate, my men will make major trouble for you and your crew, perhaps placing them in mortal danger. It is your choice. Do we have agreement?"

The thoroughly flummoxed, stressed, and perspiring Captain merely nodded meekly, managing to say, "What do you want? What is wrong with my ship?"

"What I want without delay is the ship's manifest...all the papers pertaining to the cargo on board," replied Schultz. "Can you produce these papers voluntarily or do we have to resort to other means?"

Schultz's last remark was not lost on Friedrich.

"The safe. The papers you seek are in the safe," replied an agreeable Captain.

Chance and his assault element climbed the boarding ladders that were being guarded topside by two SEALs assigned to provide security for them. Once the assault team had safely boarded they were accompanied to the entrance of the ship's hold by the aft security element. Along the way Chance radioed to Chief Schultz, "Element two on deck. Proceeding to cargo hold. Report your status."

Schultz replied immediately, "Crew is cooperating. We have 10 of the 12 and are seeking the others. Seven weapons turned in so far. We are searching for the manifests. I.D.'ing and documenting the crew."

Chance was cautiously optimistic that the plan was holding - now if they could locate the shipping containers, they just might pull this off. For a brief moment, Chance saw himself and his men humorously as swashbuckling pirates or hijackers right out of the movies.

Still concerned about his element's safety given that there were two crewmen still unaccounted for, Chance and the other SEALs proceeded to the cargo hold quickly but on high alert. With a decided tactical advantage there was little danger from a rogue crewman, but the critical aspect of the mission was now before them.

Aerial reconnaissance from Shanghai had revealed a loading sequence based on sections of the cargo hold access doors being opened at specific times during the Pacific Dawn's mooring at the quay. Drone intelligence revealed that there was a three-day gap between the next-to-last item loaded on the Pacific Dawn and the items loaded immediately prior to the freighter leaving port. The loading of the last items coincided with the promised ship date of the magnets shown on the purchase order. These facts led the CIA analysts to cautiously approximate the area of the hold where the magnets might have been loaded. Although it was no guarantee that the magnets (if they were indeed those items loaded last) would be placed directly below the opening through which they were loaded, at some point an educated guess had to be made lacking further hard data.

Once in the cargo hold Chance and his SEALs removed their NODs and went to work examining the cargo with their flashlights. In spite of the access the SEALs had to the internal diagrams of this class of vessel, they were immediately bewildered by the sheer size of the cavernous cargo bay and the volume of the contents. With the ship having made so many stops along the way, they had half expected that the hold would be nearly empty as she made her way to her last stop in Iran. But even a cursory examination of the various crates in the hold showed nearly every item was slated for delivery to Iran!

Chance saw that this could mean big trouble identifying the specific shipment they were seeking.

Based on the shipments that had been made by the Chinese company supplying the magnets to the Japanese and the South Africans, the SEALs had been given photos of what Chinese characters to look for on the shipping crates as well as what the printed labels on the crates might say in English, which was still the unofficial language of international commerce. Hopefully, between the estimate of where the crates might be physically located in the vast cargo bay, and these images, the crates could be reliably located. Fundamentally, all wooden shipping containers, especially in very low light circumstances, looked alike. Right now Chance felt as if he and his SEALs were looking for a needle in a haystack.

After nearly one hour of searching through the hold of the freighter, aided only by their flashlights, the SEALs were no closer to identifying the shipping crates and Chance was becoming frustrated and concerned about their vulnerability. The SEALs were accustomed to gathering intelligence by stealthy means, or making swift and deadly efficient combat raids that minimized their vulnerability at a target. However, each hour on board the freighter increased their chances of being discovered by an enemy force stumbling upon the stranded Pacific Dawn and having to fight their way out. In such a circumstance they would be truly on their own and could expect no help from the submarine.

During the time Chief Schultz and the Captain were in his cabin, Schultz saw his opportunity to essentially bribe Captain Friedrich.

"Herr Kaleunt, in this envelope is twenty-five thousand Euros in used currency. If you cooperate with us tonight and ensure that we do not have trouble either on the ship or after leaving, you may take the enclosed document to the bank shown and exchange it for an identical sum. You will only be eligible for this transaction if the bank gets a certain password from us after this incident is over. If you go to the bank to collect the cash and they do not have the password we will be notified and you may be certain people with international tentacles will track you down and cause great grief to come to you. And yes, I nearly forgot. If you do not present at the bank and try to collect the additional funds within sixty days, these same people will track you down as well. Therefore, it is in your best interest to cooperate with us fully while we are here and when you get to port in Iran."

The portly German Captain was still in shock about the apparent hijacking of his boat and feared for his life. Friedrich took the envelope in his trembling hands and replied through the stark dimness to Schultz, "Yes, but of course I will cooperate, Herr....? I don't know your name or who you are. Are you German?"

"Schultz is all you need to know. We are an international group," he lied.

"When you are interrogated in port you may tell them that you think we are German - perhaps a reincarnation of the Red Army Faction. That will give them chills! Tell them we were looking for a shipment of gold."

Schultz was interrupted in the recitation of his charade by a radio message from Chance Lyon. "Have you got the cargo manifests? We're having trouble finding our target. Advise."

"Wait one." was Schultz's reply.

Schultz shifted from his good-cop routine to a bad-cop demeanor in a second and said to the Captain, "Do you have a shipment of precision magnets for Iranian Crescent Trading Company on board? Identify this shipment on the manifest...NOW!"

Friedrich took the cargo manifest in his shaking hands and nervously went over the contents aided by Schultz's flashlight. "I...I don't know - there is so much cargo aboard. I don't know every shipment," he responded lamely.

Schultz pulled his 9mm pistol from its holster and held it to the left temple of a visibly shaking Captain and said menacingly, "Do not fuck with me Captain. You take me to these containers right now or I will kill you right here and get your Second Officer to show me. You will never spend a dime of this money because you'll be dead!"

"Jawohl, Herr Schultz...Jawohl!" Friedrich was happy for the darkness - at least for the moment - as Schultz would not see the Captain's pants darkening as his uncontrolled bladder discharged its contents down his leg onto the floor of his cabin.

"One this is eight. Coming your way with the skipper. He's betting his life that he can lead us to the magnets." Schultz repeated his message in German for the benefit of the Captain of the Pacific Dawn.

In five minutes Schultz and Friedrich were in the cargo hold met by a concerned Chance Lyon. Leaving the Captain with one of the SEALs, Chance took Schultz aside and said. "Chief, we've already overstayed our welcome here. Get this guy to find these magnets or we're in danger of fucking this op up and having to fight our way out of here to nowhere. I'm sending one of the guys here to check on the status up front. We've got to be ready to go if we hit pay dirt."

A newly motivated Chief Schultz moved to within an inch of Captain Friedrich's face and said quietly in his best Nazi SS tone, "Captain you have less than ten minutes to find these shipping crates or you will die a long and painful death right here."

With two minutes to spare Captain Friedrich nervously identified the shipping crates supposedly containing the magnets. "But how can we be sure?" asked Chance Lyon cautiously. "I don't have time to laboriously open these crates to verify the contents."

"You don't have to," explained Captain Friedrich, for the first time in this long night feeling some sense of confidence. He pulled out a small pocket compass from his jacket pocket and placed his body between it and the shipping container. The compass pointed faithfully north to the shore that ran between Karachi and the Strait of Hormuz. Then he dramatically turned and placed the compass next to the container and the compass needle quickly snapped toward the container of magnets as simple physics would demand. He did this with five contiguous individual containers with the same result. Chance and Chief Schultz looked at each other in amazement and silently acknowledged that this must be the elusive target of their mission.

Chance hurriedly studied the images the CIA had received from the Japanese and the South Africans and tried to compare them to what he could see on the shipping containers in the light produced by his flashlight. He couldn't be sure, but there was a distinct similarity. Time was running out and Chance, as the leader of the SEAL Team, had to make a decision. Although the RDDs would make everything in the cargo hold radioactively hot to some degree, the mission was to make a direct hit on the magnets so there could be no question about rendering them useless for many years. He had to get it right.

"Place the RDD charges on these five containers," Chance ordered. "As soon as they are assembled and the arming and fusing mechanisms are installed, let me inspect each one so the ultimate responsibility is mine," he added.

MID-OCEAN DRAMA

Chance turned to Schultz and gave him a nod as if to send him off to conclude matters for which the security element was responsible. With that, Schultz told Captain Friedrich to accompany him back to the bridge. Before the two moved Chance took Schultz aside and said, "Chief, we'll be finished setting these charges in less than twenty minutes. Once we've left the cargo hold and are ready to exfil, I'll radio you and then we'll proceed to our boat. We'll move off aft about a hundred yards and try to give you all the security we can while your element exfils. Make sure that the Captain takes seriously the message on the decals we're going to place on the entry to the hold. If he and his men don't and they get fried, they will have had fair warning."

Chief Schultz and the Captain returned to the bridge to find the SEAL security element with everything in control. One of the SEALs took Schultz aside and told him,

"Chief, we've found all but one crewmember. He's a cook and is still missing - an old Filipino guy with a bad attitude. One of the crew says he may have a gun. Speaking of guns, we found eleven - can't be sure if that's all. We catalogued them and threw them over. We also photographed all of the crew and took DNA samples just to be sure. They are pretty spooked, so I don't expect any trouble with the exfil."

"Okay Mark, get these guys all seated on the floor of the bridge and secure them with the tie-wraps. They'll eventually get out, but we should be long gone by then. We've gotta get moving; it's already zero-two-thirty and this has already taken longer than we thought. We got to make the rendezvous before first light."

After Chance was satisfied that the RDDs were properly assembled and securely seated on the shipping crates containing the magnets, he counted out his SEALs exiting the cargo hold and placed the decals indicating the presence of radioactivity on both sides of the personnel access door to the cargo hold. As he was doing so, he heard a loud noise and the voice of a human uttering an oath from within the hold. *'This can't be,'* thought Chance. *'I counted my guys out individually and it can't be one of ours.'*

Chance radioed on the open net, "Give me a count. Do element leaders have everyone accounted for?" In fifteen seconds both Schultz and the Chief of the assault element radioed back, "All accounted for, sir - including you."

Chance told the assault element chief to get to the boat and shove off.

"I'll wait for the security element and exfil with them. Schultz, I think we've got a rogue crewman here in the hold and I've got to reduce him or he could spoil our plans," concluded Chance.

"Roger, one, I've got your back. We're moving aft," responded Schultz.

Chance pulled his NODs down, turned on his IR headlight and proceeded carefully back into the hold.

"Whoever is in here make yourself known. You are in great danger if you stay in the hold. You must leave now and you will not be hurt. Shine a light and I will come to you, and you won't be hurt." There was no response.

Chance waited for another minute and repeated his message. "Fuck you - you will kill me. All pirates the same. I will kill you first," replied a small voice from somewhere in the hold.

Chance spoke into his open mike, "Chief, guard the cargo entry, don't let this asshole escape. I'm going after him. Get your security element off the ship and leave a two man security element aboard. I've got to reduce this guy before I can leave."

Chance knew he didn't have any time to waste searching for the crewman. He considered all his options and took a huge, but calculated, risk.

"Okay, I'm turning on a flashlight so you can come find me," he shouted. "We'll talk. I can prove I won't hurt you. If you don't come out you will die a horrible death anyway. I can save you from that. You have to take a risk and find me."

"I kill you, pirate," came a response from the blackness of the cargo hold.

'Well, he thinks we are pirates...perhaps Somali pirates. Maybe I can use that against him,' Chance thought.

"Yes, we are in control of this ship and it is going to Somalia. If you don't show yourself now, you will be locked in the hold to die. Your life is valueless to us. However, if you show yourself and prove you are no threat, you will be released with the rest of the crew. We want the ship and the cargo, not this crew."

Having sailed the waters of the world, the cook knew about pirates and their ruthlessness, particularly in the littoral waters of the Arabian Sea. He quickly calculated that the odds of his personal survival were slightly better by revealing himself to this pirate rather than languishing for days in the sweltering hold of this freighter with no water or food. Yes, he had been courageous to defy the boarders and the cargo hold had seemed like a logical place to hide, but it was obvious that the pirates were in control. He had little choice but to surrender...but he still had a loaded gun and he might be able to overcome his adversary and escape to another part of the ship where he had better odds of survival. *Besides, even pirates need a good cook!* He rationalized.

With time continuing to slip away, Chance had to bring this to a close. "Come to the light...slowly, and make yourself known as you approach. Trust me, I will not hurt you," said Chance steadily.

The Filipino cook saw the beam of Chance's flashlight like a beacon and approached guardedly. Chance had wisely placed himself well away from the shipping crates containing the magnets so as to protect the investment the SEALs had made up to now toward advancing their mission. Nothing must trump what they had so painstakingly accomplished so far, one's personal safety included.

Steadily the cook approached. Chance could hear him now as he shuffled across the steel floor of the hold. The beam of the light was directed upward and Chance increased his visual advantage by pulling down his NODs, instantly turning twilight into brilliant green. As the cook slowly emerged from the darkness he was startled by the apparition of Chance - a very large man compared to the diminutive Filipino - made even larger and more fierce looking by being dressed in black with his face covered by a baklava and curious eyewear.

'Surely this was no mere pirate,' thought the startled cook, *'No, this was a soldier of some type.'*

Instinctively and foolishly, the Filipino cook - now threatened by the other man's stark military presence - reached for his puny .22 caliber firearm and shot at Chance without aiming. As the frightened cook turned to run, Chance, a seasoned veteran of much training and numerous kinetic encounters, pulled his Sig-9 and dropped the fleeing Filipino in his tracks. The single round from Chance's pistol severed the man's spine between the 6th and 7th cervical vertebrae and was deflected through his carotid artery, killing him before he hit the ground.

It was only after the echoes from the report of Chance's pistol had died down that Chance knew something was very wrong. It was not so much the localized pain in his left thigh, but the flood of fluid soaking through his wetsuit and boot that confirmed he had been hit by the round from the cook's pistol. *'Shit,'* thought Chance. *'Here we go again.'*

Chance spoke into his boom mike to Chief Schultz who would still be guarding the door to the cargo hold. "Chief, the target has been reduced but I'm shot. I can walk and I'm coming your way. We've got to get off this ship and get the hell out of here. We're going to have to crank it if we are to make the rendezvous before light."

As Chance labored up the steps toward the deck he was greeted by Chief Schultz who took one look at the mini-geyser of dark red blood spurting intermittently from Chance's leg and said urgently, "Sir, we've got to get that bleeding stopped right away, I think it's your femoral artery. This can't wait."

Schultz took one of the tie wraps left over from securing the crew on the bridge and pulled it as tight as he could over Chance's wetsuit immediately above where the blood was spurting and was relieved that the flow immediately slowed to a trickle. One of the SEALs radioed into the open net, "L.T.'s down. Stand by to receive him as we hand him down."

Schultz and the two SEALs remaining on the ship as security fashioned a harness out of nylon rope and attached it to Chance over his chest and under his arms. Chance was getting a little woozy from the loss of blood but managed to walk to the edge of the fantail. He stepped off toward the bobbing Zodiacs below and was carefully lowered feet first by two of the SEALs as Schultz provided security from any remaining threats.

As soon as the Chief in the number two Zodiac announced over the open net that, "L.T. is aboard. Secure the op," Schultz and the other two SEALs released the boarding ladders from their holding devices and clamored over the back of the ship, sliding down the ropes to the waiting Zodiacs.

As the Zodiacs pulled away from the freighter, Chance Lyon, still lucid enough to command the mission, retrieved the detonator from his wetsuit and entered the numerical code that reconciled with that of the arming-fusing-firing mechanisms of the RDDs.

'After all this, the damned thing better work,' he thought. As he pushed the button marked 'fire,' there was a fraction of a second delay and then the SEALs were greeted by the sounds of several muffled explosions that rolled across the water amplified by the dense night air. They were coming from the freighter.

Chance gave a thumb's up to no one in particular and the three Zodiacs carrying the SEALs turned away from the wounded freighter and, guided by their GPS units, began speeding through the cold chop and dwindling night toward the rendezvous point five miles away. The Pacific Dawn, looking like a ghost ship, faded steadily into the background and an uncertain fate.

CHAPTER 10

WOUNDED WARRIOR

"Fight on, my merry men all,
I'm a little wounded, but am not slain;
I will lay me down for to bleed a while,
Then I'll rise and fight with you again."
English Ballad - "Sir Andrew Barton"

Despite the makeshift tourniquet fashioned by now two of the plastic tie wraps, blood was still oozing consistently from the tear in Chance's wetsuit leg. It was impossible to determine the total extent of the wound as some blood was undoubtedly seeping between the wetsuit material and his leg.

Chance had been lowered into the Zodiac where Petty Officer Clete Weber was the closest thing the team had for a medic. Weber had gone to the Armed Services Combat Medic course, but had nothing except a few basic items that had been crammed into one of the pockets of his Zodiac. Weber cut off Chance's wetsuit below the wound and was startled at how much blood had accumulated, but did not let on as such to the other SEALs. *'No sense worrying about what has already happened. We gotta keep this from getting worse,'* he thought to himself.

Even though Chance was not yet complaining of pain, Weber plunged an ampule of morphine into Chance's thigh and waited for a moment to let it begin to take effect. "I've got to try to stanch this bleeding L.T.," Weber yelled to Chance over the wind and the sound of the outboard motor. "I'm going to stuff the entry with some bandage material. This may hurt, but I've got to do this. Must have been a small caliber round because there's no exit," he concluded.

Chief Schultz knew that, without surgery, Chance's wound could be life-threatening and they had to get professional help soon. But they were out in the middle of the Arabian Sea at zero-three-thirty hoping to link up to a submarine that had no doctor either. Schultz popped open the cover of the Data-link Information Device he wore on his wrist and entered a frequency from memory and typed in a short message:

> **Trinity Team moving pt. Bravo.**
> **Have wounded. Expedite link-up.**
> **Schultz, CPO**

Schultz hit button marked 'Uplink' and the encrypted radio message was immediately beamed to a U.S. military communications satellite in geo-synchronous orbit 22 thousand miles above the Earth and simultaneously downlinked to U.S. Fifth Fleet Headquarters in Doha, Qatar in the Persian Gulf. In two minutes a Navy Yeoman was in the Combat Decision Center with a flash message for Admiral Kineer.

Keener immediately dictated a message to be broadcast to the U.S.S. Abraham Lincoln and the North Dakota:

T-O-P S-E-C-R-E-T

FROM:	CDR, U.S. FIFTH FLEET
TO:	CDR, U.S.S. ABRAHAM LINCOLN
CC:	CDR, U.S.S. NORTH DAKOTA
RE:	OP TRINITY - NEW ORDERS
TIME:	0112180330 ZULU

LINCOLN PROCEED FLANK TO PT. BRAVO.

DAKOTA COORDINATE XFR OF WIA TO LINCOLN.
HIGHEST PRIORITY.

S. KEENER: VADM, USN
COMMANDING

END OF MESSAGE
T-O-P S-E-C-R-E-T

Within ten minutes of Chief Schultz up-linking his message to the satellite above, the nuclear reactors of the Abraham Lincoln were driving the propeller shafts of the thousand-foot long aircraft carrier at 30 knots through the Arabian Sea toward point Bravo.

"Sir, I have classified flash traffic from COMMFLT," the communications specialist on the North Dakota said to Commander Hoffman as he handed the decoded message to him. Hoffman initialed the copy of the traffic and dismissed the crewman.

"Navigator, confirm we are at point Bravo."

"Aye, sir; confirming Point Bravo."

"Okay, bring us to periscope depth," Hoffman ordered.

"XO, when I get an IR signal from the SEALs, we're surfacing. They have wounded. The Lincoln has been ordered to Point Bravo and we are to transfer our wounded to the carrier. Get a detail together and go topside when we surface to coordinate that. Lincoln will send a chopper and we'll transfer by their sling device. Hopefully we can do this before first light. I don't like this boat anywhere near the surface period, and especially in daylight. Get these SEALs below ASAP. If there's any problem with getting their gear stowed, jettison it. I'm not risking this boat for some Zodiacs."

"Aye, sir," replied the XO.

"Sonar, what are you seeing on your waterfall?" asked Hoffman.

"Sonar, all clear sir."

"Up periscope!"

"Maintain maximum vigilance, sonar. We're vulnerable as hell right now. Tell me when you have the Lincoln at 15 miles," ordered Hoffman as he rotated the periscope seeking signs of the returning SEALs. The North Dakota had the Abraham Lincoln's acoustic signature stored in its database and could reliably pick her up at 20 miles in good sea conditions.

North Dakota's sonar picked up the Zodiacs at four miles and alerted the skipper with a bearing. Small craft signatures were difficult to isolate, but who else would be tooling around in the middle of the ocean in the middle of the night with a bearing in line with where the Pacific Dawn had stopped except Chance Lyon's SEALs? Hoffman picked them up at one mile and shot them an IR flash through the periscope, which was immediately seen by Chief Schultz, who signaled the Zodiacs to slow as he knew the North Dakota would be surfacing within two minutes. Once he saw the sail pierce the surface he would lead the Zodiacs in to rendezvous with the submarine.

The skippers of both the Abraham Lincoln and the North Dakota, as well as Admiral Kineer and his staff in FLTCOMM in Doha knew they had a very vulnerable situation developing in the North Arabian Sea - a five billion dollar aircraft carrier crewed by some six-thousand sailors, a one-and-a-half billion dollar nuclear submarine, and twenty-one Navy SEALs congregating around a point with a radius of no more than two miles in potentially hostile waters with first light only an hour or so away.

The Abraham Lincoln's Air Boss, Commander Glenn Forsey, (call sign 'Red Dog'), had two F-35C fighters flying high cover over the strike group being spotted by a tanker and an AWACS at 30,000 feet, with two back-up F-35s with engines hot on the twin catapults ready to be shot in less than one minute.

North Dakota's sonar became very busy - albeit with friendly targets - very quickly. It wasn't just the Abraham Lincoln, but her escort vessels, two guided missile destroyers, two Aegis guided missile cruisers, two Los Angeles class attack submarines, and the various support vessels for the carrier strike group that had to be accounted for. On the North Dakota at the moment, the most stressful place was the sonar department, from the division officer, Lieutenant Commander Ian Bradshaw, down to the individual sonar man.

Chief Schultz radioed the Zodiac carrying Chance Lyon to tie up to the North Dakota first so that all efforts of the crew on deck would be directed to getting Chance on board and taking his care to the next level. At the moment there were many top priorities, but getting Lieutenant Lyon stabilized was the first among equals.

In a few moments a helicopter with flashing IR strobes appeared out of the pitch blackness and hovered over the North Dakota, adding to the multitasking that was taking place at the ground zero point that had become the surfaced North Dakota. Commander Hoffman, with his typical cool demeanor, was monitoring all the systems in his control room, with complete confidence in the officers and crew he had so thoroughly trained. In a moment of feigned levity, he shot a remark to no one in the conn in particular saying, "That chopper better be from the Abraham Lincoln or we are really in deep shit."

Hoffman's XO was in the same capability percentile as his skipper and had thought ahead on the task that Hoffman had given him. As soon as Chance - now semi out of it with the morphine - was safely aboard, he had the North Dakota's medic start two IV lines into Chance with .09 percent saline dripping into one and whole blood into the other, attached to his wetsuit with carabiner-like fasteners. After painting Chance's forehead with a large 'M' in a red marker they placed him into the lowered sling from the chopper and gave the pilot the 'go' sign. In 30 seconds Chance was aboard the med-evac chopper and headed for a waiting OR on the Abraham Lincoln.

In fifteen minutes the remaining SEALs had stowed their gear in the sail of the North Dakota and were back on board the submarine.

"Chief, make your depth 100 feet, zero bubble, remain all stop," commanded Hoffman. "Navigator, let's let the strike group move off and then plot us a course for Diego Garcia. I need to check on the SEALs. XO take the conn," remarked Hoffman.

"Aye, Captain. XO has the conn."

Hoffman made his way to the stern of the North Dakota and sought out the second in command, who happened to be Chief Schultz.
After allaying Chief Schultz's concern regarding the condition of his Team Commander, Chance Lyon, Hoffman made them aware that that they would soon be on their way back to Diego Garcia. "Chief, after your men are squared away, please make your way to the crew mess for coffee and a good meal. We'll try to keep you updated on the condition of Lieutenant Lyon."

As soon as the med-evac chopper landed on the deck of the Abraham Lincoln, Chance was immediately taken to sick bay, where three medical doctors were waiting. Chance was relieved of his wetsuit and examined by the medical team, who catalogued his triage:

> Projectile wound, left upper thigh - no exit.
> Tq. by cmbt. medic.
> BP 90/50.
> Functional airway.
> Pulse: 102.
> Respiration 50.
> Morphine for pain, cmbt. medic.
> Two IV lines started with whole blood and saline, by cmbt. medic.
> X-Ray: No structural damage.
> Diagnosis: Arterial bleeding.
> Immediate surgery indicated.

Just before Chance Lyon was rolled into one of the small surgical suites on the Lincoln, he was greeted by Commander (Doctor) Jennifer King, the Medical Officer on the Abraham Lincoln.

"Lieutenant Lyon, I'm Doctor King. I graduated from the Academy ten years ago and went to medical school at Johns Hopkins. Welcome aboard. I'm going to fix that leg of yours before you bleed out," she said professionally.

"Actually, the films show a ruptured femoral artery...could have been worse. You had excellent first response care. By the way, I downloaded your medical records from the cloud a few minutes ago...brain surgery after a head wound? You need to be more careful! Seems like all I do is patch up Navy SEALs. Care to tell me what you were just doing?"

Chance was so woozy from the morphine and the follow-up pre-anesthesia that all he could do is mumble. "No can do, doc...just patch me up. Got any coffee?"

"Lieutenant Lyon, we're going to knock you out and I'm going to put that femoral artery back together. Maybe later you'll buy me coffee and tell me why you guys are so accident prone."

Doctor King looked over at her anesthesiologist and said, "Give Mister Macho here the juice, Greg, I've got to get to work."

Three hours later Chance Lyon was looking up at a nurse and asking where he was. "You're in the recovery room in sick bay on the Abraham Lincoln, Lieutenant. You are doing very well, thanks to Doctor King and her team. You are probably going to have a sore leg for a while, but you are no worse for wear. No triathlons for you for a while," she joked.

'Shit, first brain surgery and now this,' Chance thought. *'I feel like a magnet for shrapnel. I wonder how the other guys are.'*

A week later Chance Lyon was well enough to be evacuated from the carrier and was flown to the U.S. Naval Hospital in Doha for follow-up care. From there it was on to Ramstein, Germany, and the beginning of rehabilitation and staging for a flight to Washington, D.C., with some other walking wounded from various places in the Middle East.

Once in Ramstein, Chance felt that security of the mission was no longer a factor and he decided to call his father.

"Hello, dad. Just checking to see if you're behaving...yes, I'm okay...a little worse for wear. I'm back at the hospital in Ramstein and will probably be in D.C. in a week or so...nothing very major...had a little dust up and got shot in the leg. Kind of nasty...I'll text you with the name of my doctor here and maybe Doctor Mack can call him and get the medical details. I told him to expect a call from Mack. Can't tell you any details right now...you know the security drill. I think they're probably giving me at least 30 days of convalescent leave and beyond that, I don't know. If you can connect with Buckholder, maybe he'll brief you in on the sly...gotta go. Say hi to Anne and the Doc for me."

Chance put down the phone and decided to limp around the grounds of the hospital to clear his head, and for the very first time felt like an old man who had too many miles on the odometer of his body.

BOOK IV

*

REACTION

CHAPTER 11

FRUSTRATION AND RESOLVE

The entire crew of the Pacific Dawn heard the thuds of explosions from the cargo hold after the boarders - whomever they were - had left the ship, but it was the better part of an hour before they managed to escape from the tie wraps that bound them and regain their bearings. A commercial freighter is not any part of a warship and it was some time after that that the Captain was able to re-establish discipline and bring a sense of functionality to this diverse group of merchant seamen, many of whom were still very much in fear for their lives after the trauma of the past few hours.

The Captain and the Second Officer went aft to the cargo entrance to assess whatever damage might be associated with the explosive noises they heard only just over an hour ago. What they found at the closed-off entrance to the hold were strips of yellow plastic tape stretched across the entry doors and decals posted on the doors themselves and walls on either side that showed the international sign for radioactivity. There were several other decals printed with the words, 'DANGER - DO NOT ENTER' in Spanish, German, English, and French. The two officers backed away from the door and looked at each other in astonishment.

Meanwhile, within several hours the Pacific Dawn's Chief Engineer had managed some complex workarounds with spare parts he had aboard and was able to restore basic power to the propulsion system. The ship was still without communications as the SEALs had found and confiscated the two Iridium satellite phones that were aboard. Nevertheless the freighter was now moving westward at a tentative eight knots and firing flares at ten-minute intervals, hoping to attract attention of a friendly vessel in hopes of contacting the ship's owners and informing them of her plight. Lacking instructions to the contrary, Captain Friedrich's thinking was to keep moving toward Iran.

In another ten hours, close to early evening, as the Pacific Dawn entered the eastern reaches of the Gulf of Oman, an Iranian patrol vessel saw the flares fired by the freighter and closed alongside her. The Iranian officer called out on a bullhorn to slow down and hove to.

"Are you in distress?" the Iranian asked.

"We have been boarded by pirates and have no communications. Our ship's lighting system is also faulty. We need assistance," was Captain Friedrich's response.

"May I board you to render assistance?" was the response from the Iranian Captain.

"Yes, however, we have limited steerage and cannot assist you in boarding. We need a portable telephone so I may contact the ship's owners," responded a relieved Friedrich. They were entering a busy shipping lane and running without proper lighting at night could have dangerous consequences. *'Not that we don't already have problems,'* thought Friedrich as he considered the warning signs posted on the cargo hold entry door.

Friedrich was able to contact the owners of the Pacific Dawn and relate the entire story to the freighter line's operations people in Shanghai, who told him simply to cooperate with the Iranian authorities and make them aware of further developments. They would send a representative to Dubai on the first available flight to render whatever assistance the company could give.

Once the Captain of the patrol vessel heard the story of the freighter's disabling and saw the radioactivity warnings for himself, he returned to his patrol vessel and spent an hour back and forth in communication with his naval superiors. In three hours an Iranian military helicopter landed on the deck of the Pacific Dawn, discharging several armed men who went immediately to the bridge of the vessel. Shortly thereafter the two vessels were joined by a much larger ship, an Iranian destroyer, which sent a launch with a dozen Iranian soldiers who were obviously intending to board the freighter. The Iranians were clearly very concerned with the developments of the last 24 hours on the Pacific Dawn.

Mahmoud Abdul Rashad, the President of the Islamic Republic of Iran, listened with increased impatience and rising anger as his hand-chosen director of the VEVAK Intelligence Agency poured out the evidence his investigators had found on the Pacific Dawn, now proceeding under escort by the Iranian Navy to the port of Bandar-e-Abbas in the Persian Gulf.

Yes, there was no doubt that the shipment of precision magnets, critical components of the two thousand new centrifuges that Iran had plans to build for its expanded uranium enrichment facility, were on board the ship. Yes, this evidence - mostly statements from the crew who had been initially interviewed by VEVAK and who would undergo much more rigorous interrogation once in Iranian custody - clearly indicated that the unknown boarders were interested in some specific cargo. Yes, these same boarders had set off some type of explosive device in the hold that had not significantly damaged the structure of the ship but, according to the posted warning signs, had significantly irradiated all or portions of the cargo hold.

A cursory examination of the external walls of the cargo area had shown radiation readings far in excess of those dangerous to unprotected personnel. More precise investigation of the contents of the cargo area would have to wait until the freighter docked in a quarantined area of the harbor and could be tested by nuclear scientists. But as of now, the situation looked uncertain for the crucial magnets. Worst of all for the worried Rashad, neither VEVAK nor the crew had been able to identify the nationality of the raiders whose actions had set back his nuclear development for an undetermined time period.

"All the crewmen could agree on, Mr. President was that the ship was disabled in many places simultaneously causing it to lose all power. There is no evidence of sabotage such as explosives or physical tampering. If it would have been sabotage, it would have taken the coordinated efforts of many skilled people working in concert in different parts of the ship. The only educated people on this ship are the Captain and his Chief Engineer. The rest are simple merchant seamen. There is one hole we are trying to fill, however. The Filipino cook is missing. I would be more suspicious if he were anything but a cook. He may still be hiding on the ship."

"But what about the identities of the men who did this? Do we have any clues as to who they were?" asked Rashad angrily.

"The men all say they spoke only German and English. Their leader was a large man who spoke mostly German and was extremely gruff in demeanor. The Captain told us he did mention something about the 'reincarnation of the Red Army Faction,' and 'looking for gold,' but I think that may have been a ruse. We searched the boat thoroughly and they left nothing behind. No one claims to have seen them coming or leaving."

A pensive and exasperated Mahmoud Rashad summed the matter up from the Iranian perspective thinking out loud, "Only Allah knows for sure, but I suspect only the Israelis or the Americans have the resources and the courage to pull something like this off."

"But what was the motive? They took no prisoners, interrogated no one, and did not try to seize the boat itself as if they wanted to steal cargo like pirates. What *was* their motive?"

Once the Pacific Dawn had tied up at a little used quay in the harbor of Bandar-e-Abbas and the crew taken into custody, a careful examination of the freighter could be undertaken. Although the cargo manifests had been removed by the boarders, the ships owners were able to supply electronic copies to the Iranians and an analysis could begin.

The analysis discovered immediately that the most valuable cargo on board were the thousands of specialty alloy magnets that had been ordered from the Chinese manufacturing company. Initially, the Iranians took some small comfort in the fact that the magnets were at least now on Iranian soil.

Then the nuclear technicians sent probes into the internal spaces of the cargo hold that revealed extremely high levels of strontium 90, a radioactive isotope with a very long half-life that was extremely dangerous to humans if they were exposed. This was troubling enough.

The technicians made the decision to send a remotely controlled robot into the hold with a camera and a radiation probe to map the radiation levels throughout the hold. The robot's probe revealed a pattern of radioactivity that varied widely throughout the cargo hold. After hours of laborious mapping, the probe determined that the highest - and most lethal - levels of strontium 90 were in a specific area with a radius of about fifty feet. The video feed from the camera revealed that some of the containers had been heavily damaged but markings on some of the contiguous containers that could be read by interpreters indicated that these contained the precision magnets. The investigators were coming to the conclusion that there had been a concerted effort on the part of the mysterious boarders to irradiate the specific area of the cargo hold that contained the critical magnets. If further investigation confirmed this, someone would have to present President Mahmoud Rashad with the most unwelcome news that the magnets could not be salvaged, as they were irradiated beyond human use for many, many years.

The Mossad strategy, as outlined to President Braxton and his National security team months ago had proven to be a strategic winner. It had not taken more than three weeks for it to become known to American intelligence that the daring SEAL raid produced precisely the desired effect.

There was no public outcry from the government of Iran that their sovereignty had been violated, its citizens killed or wounded, or infrastructure damaged or destroyed. There was not even a hint of that. However, NSA was still reading the electronic mail between the phony Iranian trading company and the Chinese manufacturer of the magnets, which revealed the Iranians were making vehement demands that the Chinese refund all or at least a portion of the millions of dollars the Iranians had paid for the magnets, based on a vague and unsubstantiated claim of 'unfitness for use' of the said magnets. When the Chinese asked for specifics, the Iranians countered with two proposals. One, Iran would not reveal to the IMF that the Chinese had gone through with delivery of the magnets, in spite of the request originally made by the IMF not to do so. Two, the Iranians would apply the refund toward a similar order 'in the future.'

The Chinese responded equally forcefully and angrily that they would not give in to threats or blackmail, pointing out that they had upheld their end of the bargain as the terms of the sale had been 'free-on-board' (FOB) the shipping point. When the Iranians accepted delivery of the product at the point of shipment in Shanghai, they became responsible for safe and secure transit to the point of delivery. In summary: There would be no refund!

This information was presented to President Braxton, his National Security Advisor, and the CNO by Rachel Hunter immediately after the intercepts had been made and verified for authenticity. After a subdued celebratory clapping of hands by the group, President Braxton thought for a moment and then spoke.

"It would appear that we've placed a significant crimp in their plans and didn't even get a scolding for it - at least publicly. But this doesn't mean they won't stop trying."

Rachel Hunter replied, "That's right sir. We'll just try to stay one step ahead of them."

As the group broke, Braxton held Admiral Wheeler back and said, "Steve, your SEALs did another monumental job under the most difficult circumstances. I trust the Navy will recognize them in some appropriate way, collectively and individually."

"Of course, sir. But with SEALs such recognition has to be understated and out of the public eye...we'll take care of it. By the way, the young man who commanded the raid was Lieutenant Chance Lyon."

The Admiral paused for a moment and continued, "he was fairly seriously wounded, but he's on the mend in Germany...I thought you would want to know."

"Thanks, Steve. Yes, I appreciate the information. He's a fine young man and splendid officer. Keep me informed."

As Admiral Wheeler left the Oval Office, President Jonathan Braxton thought of Anne Lyon - and warmly so - for the first time in many months. *'What a woman - what an amazing family!'* he thought wistfully.

After it was clearly determined by the Iranian nuclear technicians that the radioactive cargo did, indeed, contain the centrifuge magnets and they were so hot that they would have to be stored as nuclear waste for many years, Rashad spent many hours working the precision magnet program backward step-by-painstaking step with VEVAK in order to understand how this clever sabotage had been perpetrated. But they were stonewalled at every turn.

The most obvious leakage point was with the Chinese manufacturer. But the Chinese government was of little help partly due to its confidence that Iran would be reluctant to alienate an important customer for its crude oil, and the secretive nature of the relationship between the Chinese government and companies that produced hard currency revenues for the Chinese economy. Iran's diplomats made many discreet inquiries of their Chinese counterparts, but to no avail.

Mahmoud Rashad was now coming to the studied conclusion that the stars were lined up against Iran developing a home grown nuclear capability over the short term by conventional means. That did not mean giving up, but it clearly called for a change of strategy. This realization only reinforced his previously determined resolve to procure a nuclear weapon from a third party source – a choice he knew was potentially fraught with peril and unintended consequences.

Due to the sanctions imposed by the United Nations, it was becoming difficult to generate revenues of hard currency for their crude oil. The many millions seemingly squandered on the purchase of the centrifuge magnets would be hard to replace under normal circumstances and the sanctions were making it more difficult even at the current price of approximately $150 per barrel of oil. One obvious solution would be to produce a sudden and significant spike in the worldwide price of crude.

Rashad had been trained as an economist in school and there was one immutable law all economists knew: supply and demand. When demand remained steady or increased and supply decreased, the price for a commodity went up.

Rashad thought he knew a way of decreasing the supply of the industrialized world's most basic commodity, crude oil, of which he had an unlimited quantity.

BOOK V

*

THE CONSPIRACY

CHAPTER 12

SHOPPING FOR NUKES

"The world has achieved brilliance without conscience. Ours is a world of nuclear giants and ethical infants."
General Omar Bradley (1948)

President Rashad, now for all intents and purposes free of any significant constraints from the mullahs by tricking them into thinking the Israelis were behind the sinking of the Kilo, felt empowered by a sense of patriotism, which was brought on by a surreal rationalization composed of one part hatred of the Israelis and an equal part lust for acquiring a nuclear weapon at any cost.

By convincing the ayatollahs of his fanciful story that the Israeli navy had sunk the Kilo, he had even convinced himself that this might be true. After all, who else possessed the wherewithal and the motive for making war on Iran? The more Rashad thought about it, the more it had to be true! Now Rashad's desire to get his hands on a nuclear weapon was motivated not only by a desire for respectability among his Islamic brethren, but by a need for revenge against the Zionists who were now 'at war' with Iran. Yes, these were now desperate times and desperate times called for desperate measures.

Mahmoud Rashad was nothing if not a cunning survivor of many political intrigues through which he had negotiated all his years of rising through the ranks of Islamic religious politics. Rashad had always felt like a persecuted outsider as a minority Shiite in an Islamic world dominated by Sunni bullies who were both condescending and suspiciously fearful of ambitious Shiites like Rashad.

The Sunnis were well aware of the Shiite desire to establish a 'true Caliphate' in the Middle East and then use this as a power base to reform Islam throughout the world. Rashad had the political skills and instincts to make such a dream a reality. If Iran, with her considerable oil reserves, could acquire a nuclear weapon and be seen as a champion against the Zionists by the more moderate Muslims in the world, Rashad could possibly mount a challenge against a crumbling and incestuous House of Saud to become a hand-in-glove secular partner with the Shiite Ayatollahs, leading Iran and the new caliphate to a position of Islamic dominance. On a purely secular level, he could achieve what Adolph Hitler and his 'Thousand Year Reich' had failed to do in the mid part of the 20th Century. However grudging it might be, he would finally be shown the respect of the diplomatic councils of the World's powerful nations.

President Rashad, from day one of his rise to power in Iran, had recognized the need for the establishment of an effective domestic and international spy network to feed him the raw intelligence he would need to keep tabs on his political enemies and hold them at bay. Although lacking the analytic mechanism of America's CIA or Great Britain's MI6, or for that matter the operational mechanism of the dreaded and hated Israeli Mossad, Rashad had carefully chosen men in whom he had great trust to live in other Islamic countries and spy for him. Establishing cover for these assets had been relatively easy as Iran had an active and healthy trading relationship with most of her neighbors that was heavily influenced by the government, and his spies were given trade envoy status that allowed them to travel freely throughout the Middle East and beyond with a minimum of suspicion. Even the American CIA found it difficult to identify most of Iran's intelligence operators and this was very worrisome to the counter-espionage people at the CIA and FBI.

As Rashad sat on the veranda of his residence in Tehran the night after his meeting with the mullahs, he looked at the sky above him ablaze with the billions of stars that had acted as guideposts for the nomadic Arabs for many centuries. He thought carefully and thoroughly about his options for acquiring a suitable weapon. He preferred to get one that would not present overwhelming challenges from a transportation standpoint and, of course, he would have to find a willing partner to exchange value for value.

Finally, the weapon would have to be reliable and powerful, not an early stage development weapon that could be both bulky and unproven. The North Koreans came immediately to mind as they were starved for hard currency and for Iranian oil, but the logistics of transporting the weapon either by sea or overland would be problematic. It was unknown whether the nuclear device they had tested and presumably refined in the 2012-2014 time frame existed in quantity and quality enough to be realistically available. No, North Korea would be a long shot. China would be an ideal partner both from a logistical and quality perspective. But China was so dependent on the United States as a trading partner that they would not risk damaging that relationship even for a break on the price of crude oil by providing Iran with a nuclear weapon. Although the logistics of transporting a nuclear bomb from China to Iran could be concealed from view, the source of the uranium or plutonium from a detonated bomb was easily traceable by the Americans after the fact and China would be held accountable by many valuable trading partners if it were found complicit with the Iranians. No, regrettably China would not be helpful in this case. This left Rashad with only one other source, and one that made more and more sense as he considered it.

Pakistan, a nation in both political and religious chaos, awash in plots and counter-plots, a place of refuge for both al-Qaeda and Taliban warriors with unchallenged access to a common neighbor, Afghanistan, had possessed nuclear weapons for many years. In the 1960's America had foolishly stood by and tacitly allowed Pakistan to develop nuclear weapons thinking that such an act would bring nuclear parity to a region dominated by India's development of a nuclear capability.

In the days of a more friendly and reliable Pakistan, the United States was comfortable that they could influence the actions of the two traditional adversaries to one of détente if both parties were secure in the comfort that each had the ultimate weapon and, therefore, a strategic deterrent against aggression.

However, now, with the unreliability of the government of Pakistan and the various intrigues that threatened the fragile alliance of the Pakistanis and the Americans, the nuclear genie was out of the bottle and the American government at the highest level was exceptionally concerned about the security of Pakistan's nuclear weapons, since there was evidence that the warheads themselves and the triggers for the bombs were being stored in separate locations.

It was, as DCI Rachel Hunter remarked to President Braxton, like "herding cats" to know the exact disposition of the Pakistani nukes and what group might gain control of them. Contrary to what had been told to Congress by Braxton's predecessor, there were still nukes unaccounted for from the breakup of the former Soviet Union and that, coupled with the uncertain security of the Pakistani nukes, was the highest priority within the CIA. Yes, Pakistan would be where Rashad would concentrate his efforts to acquire the weapons he had fantasized about having for so long...and he knew just the man who could deliver.

What an ideal opportunity for President Rashad to exploit. Rashad had a genuine feeling that Allah was guiding his thinking from beyond the stars he was observing at this pivotal moment.

CHAPTER 13

THE PAKISTANI CONNECTION

"We be of one blood, ye and I."
Rudyard Kipling (The Jungle Book)

The old saying that *"blood is thicker than water"* could well have had its origins in the Arab World. Blood relations are stronger than currencies among the Arab peoples. This was nowhere truer than in the case of Mahmoud Rashad, the secular president of Iran, and his brother Sharif.

Shortly after Mahmoud rose to power in Iran, he appointed his brother to be the Iranian trade representative to Pakistan. Pakistan was an important trading partner with Iran and, although Sunni Muslims were in the majority there, Pakistan had a healthy number of Shiites, some of whom had important positions in government.

It was also true that Pakistan was a progressive nation when it came to education and many Pakistanis were well educated in technical disciplines, an asset that Rashad planned to exploit in the future to the benefit of Iran. Sharif was fluent in Persian (Farsi), the dominant language of Iran, and English, as well as Pashtu and Urdu, the two primary languages spoken in Pakistan near the border areas of Afghanistan. Yes, Sharif would someday be of great use to his brother and his long range plans for Pakistani and Iranian cooperation.

Meanwhile, Sharif was no mere tool of his brother. In his position as Principal Trade Representative, he had become very wealthy. Sharif had used his web of business and political contacts, his language skills, and access to trading opportunities to amass considerable personal wealth. He had wisely created accounts in several Arab and Western countries, of which he might have need in the future, depending on what winds of change might sweep over the Middle East and Asian sub-continent. While his younger brother reveled in being an internationally recognized political figure, Sharif preferred to remain under the radar, wielding power with a velvet glove.

Neither of the two brothers was any stranger to political intrigues and their careers had been long and successful, abetted by common survival mechanisms. None was more important than being able to communicate with each other clandestinely. Mahmoud Abdul Rashad used his control over the Iranian intelligence apparatus to acquire sophisticated communications technology for his and his family's personal use.

The most useful of these – primarily because of its commonplace underlying technology – was an encrypted Iridium telephone. Iridium technology used two-way communications via orbiting satellite for the connection. No cellular towers were required to establish the two-way connection and encryption software native to the individual phone sets made conversations between two cooperative parties a virtual private line. Although there was always the slim chance of a clandestine interception, Mahmoud Rashad trusted this means of two-way communication to be extremely useful in the execution of his grandiose plan to acquire a nuclear weapon.

In order to put his plan in place it would be necessary to have a face to face meeting with his brother in a neutral place, away from the eyes and ears of the Iranian intelligence community, the Ministry of Intelligence and National Security of the Islamic Republic of Iran, or VEVAK for short. Although this agency was headed by an appointee of Rashad's, it would be important to keep any information about the acquisition of a nuclear weapon a secret from anyone but a chosen few who could be completely trusted. Setting up such a meeting would be under the subterfuge of

Mahmoud simply phoning his brother in Pakistan and asking him to come home for a family celebration in the next two weeks.

Sharif Rashad arrived in Tehran in late July on an Iran Air flight from Islamabad, Pakistan. Even the hydraulically operated jet way from the terminal to the Boeing 747 was sweltering hot as he exited the aircraft from his seat in first class. As much as Sharif sometimes missed his native country he didn't miss the intense heat of the Iranian summers.

Mahmoud had sent a car for his brother and Sharif was relieved to enter its air-conditioned comfort from the stifling 115 F. (46 C.) degree heat outside the Tehran terminal building... The driver greeted him courteously and headed for the Presidential Headquarters in Tehran just as if he were on a business trip back to the Iranian Ministry of Trade. After taking care of some purely routine matters at his office to validate his infrequent visit there, he phoned his brother's office and was connected with his beautiful appointments secretary, who informed Sharif that his brother was in a meeting but would like Sharif to come to his office a few minutes after afternoon prayers. He was also invited to have dinner that evening at the president's home. Sharif responded with a simple, "As he wishes," and signed off. He knew any serious discussions would take place in Mahmoud's home that evening.

Sharif attended afternoon prayers in the courtyard of the large government building where the Ministry of Trade was headquartered. Unlike his brother, Sharif was a devout Shiite Muslim and took his religion seriously. In spite of the fact that much of his wealth had been the result of insider deals and a certain amount of graft resulting from political connections, he believed that Allah had truly blessed him with great wealth and he was careful to tithe a percentage back to the Mosques where he attended prayers while he was in various Arab cities. He occasionally chided his brother about his lack of 'true faith' but his admonitions about the eventual wrath of Allah on Mahmoud Rashad went unheeded.

That evening, after a plain meal of roasted lamb and rice – a favorite of Mahmoud Rashad's – the two brothers adjourned to a private room in the

Presidential residence that Mahmoud was reasonably sure was secure from any eavesdropping. Even so, the president was careful to put on some traditional Arab music on the Bose CD player so as to confuse any electronic devices that might otherwise be able to record the sensitive conversations that were to take place there.

"Sharif, my brother, how good of you to come on such a flimsy excuse of an invitation. I'm sure that coming to Tehran this time of year is not a welcome thing. Nevertheless, I have important things to discuss with you, as well as a request for your able assistance. What I am asking will be of exceptional benefit to Iran. It will also propel our country to the apex of respect within the world of Islam and cause our enemies to think twice about attacking us as they have been doing with great impunity in the past years. There will be no more Israeli commando raids against our infrastructure and no more attacks against our naval vessels. We will now have the capability of responding to such provocations with such force as they will have to negotiate with us in good faith...even the Americans!"

"So my brother," responded Sharif waiting a courteous moment after listening to Mahmoud's grand plan, "what is this plan you have for the advancement of Iran...and how can I as a humble man be a part of something so grandiose?"

This response drew a hearty laugh from Mahmoud Rashad as he quickly answered his brother. "Ha! Sharif; there is not a humble bone in your body! But you do possess the skill and cunning...and also the *courage* to help me carry out this plan. And how do I propose to foil the Zionists once and for all?"

Sharif looked at his brother with patience, nodding his head.

"Iran will be procuring not one, but *three* nuclear weapons...and not *primitive* weapons, Sharif. Not large, bulky weapons based on enriched uranium technology. We will not settle for that. We will be buying the very latest plutonium weapons. These weapons are small enough to be delivered by a missile...a missile such as that which we already have tested and we know has the range to hit the targets of our enemies...and, I might add, targets of our so-called *friends* in the Arab World. Iran will finally be getting the nuclear capability we have sought for so long. No longer will we cower like a dog at the feet of the Zionists!"

Sharif waited another moment, this time collecting his thoughts at such an outrageous thought. Iran had worked for years to develop a nuclear capability from within, only to be thwarted repeatedly by the Israelis and by stubborn sanctions initiated by the intimidation of the Americans. Now his brother speaks of buying this weaponry. The audacity!

"Mahmoud, praise Allah that you could arrange something as clever as this. But where...from whom...by what means, will you accomplish such an act of outright piracy? And that is what it will be viewed as by our friends and enemies alike...barbarous piracy!"

Mahmoud Rashad was pacing the room as he spoke, thinking as he walked. After a perfect theatrical pause he turned and looked straight at his brother and said quietly, "You, my clever brother, will buy these from the Pakistanis and transport them overland, through Afghanistan, or even Pakistan itself, right here to Tehran!"

The room grew silent save for the high-pitched sound of Arab music from the CD player. After what seemed like an eternity for Mahmoud Rashad, his brother responded exactly as he had hoped he would. "And what will I be paid to accomplish this most difficult task?"

Mahmoud, now relieved that he had received no resistance from his brother, sat back down in his chair and looked at the ceiling as if deep in thought.

"Two million dollars in gold for each weapon...above and beyond expenses, of course."

Sharif's large brown eyes bored into Mahmoud with the intensity of a high-powered laser and his expression became dour.

"Four million each…after expenses, of course."

Mahmoud Rashad allowed a slight smile to grace the craggy features of his unshaven face. "Negotiated like a true Bedouin of ancient times…done, my brother!"

The two spend the rest of the long night planning on how such an outrageous scheme could come to fruition. Sharif Rashad seemed to be thinking out loud as he and his brother considered ways of connecting with the Pakistani political and military structure about the possibility of acquiring one or more of its nuclear weapons.

"I cannot simply knock on the door of President El Hakim and ask him if I can buy some of their nuclear weapons. Corrupt as he is, he is a Sunni, and would laugh at me before having me thrown out of the country. Of course, he may say 'yes,' but for many millions and then renege after being paid. He is a dog…and one with running sores at that! It is hard enough to deal with that man for the things he wants and is willing to cooperate with us for. No, it is not possible with Hakim."

"Well, Sharif," countered Mahmoud, "I am counting on you and your connections with others inside that crumbling regime – others who might be more motivated, shall we say, to cooperate with us in this quest. You must know others at a slightly lower level that might be more flexible in their attitude and reasonable relative to their price for cooperation. Shall we meet again in a month to discuss progress? I have some time, but the mullahs have revenge on their mind and are pushing me to make progress."

"Together we will either succeed or fail, my brother," answered Sharif… "and failure is not an option I wish to contemplate."

CHAPTER 14

STRIKING A DEAL

"O conspiracy! Sham'st thou to show thy dangerous brow by night. When devils are most free?"
Shakespeare - <u>Julius Caesar</u>

Sharif Rashad could barely conceal his zeal at his good fortune. Although he had obtained great wealth by working as a trade representative for his brother, he had considerable expenses in Islamabad and two 'off budget' expenses, gambling and young women. His voracious appetites for both of these vices made him a fellow traveler among many of the wealthiest of Arab Princes. Actually, among Arab Princes, these activities were not seen as vices, but rather as interesting diversions that passed the time between regular pay-offs from oil rich families who preferred to keep their offspring at arm's length to prevent embarrassment from devout Muslims, who still valued the strict discipline of the Quran.

With another twelve million in gold upon acquisition and delivery of the weapons, Sharif could elevate his level of activity in the castles of pleasure in Dubai as well as London, while perhaps being promoted from the duties of a mere trade representative to a more lofty position of Ambassador at Large, which would, of course, be a front for becoming an enforcer of Shiite doctrine throughout Islam for his brother's new found respect as a possessor of nuclear weapons. Yes, the Sunnis would have to give a great deal more respect to Mahmoud Rashad and his brother, given the new reality of Iran's nuclear capability, if and when this good fortune came about.

Sharif set about to hatch a plan for the acquisition of these terrible weapons.

The Pakistani nuclear weapons program was begun in the mid-1970's under the aegis of Dr. Abdul Khan in response to India's testing of its first nuclear device. In comparison to America's development and testing of such a device, which took only a few short years during the early 1940's, it took Pakistan over 13 years to achieve nuclear status. These early weapons were based on highly enriched uranium technology, which made them large, bulky, and inherently more unstable like the "Little Boy" bomb produced by the United States used to bomb Hiroshima and bring about the conclusion of the war with Japan in 1945.

In the late 1990's there is evidence that Pakistan produced enough weapons grade plutonium to produce smaller nuclear devices, but there is controversy as to whether such plutonium bombs were actually produced and tested. Nevertheless, Pakistan was known to have the technology to produce weapons grade plutonium and it stood to reason that it had built additional nuclear devices based on this technology. If so, these were the bombs that Sharif would seek to divert to the hands of Iran.

Toward the end of high-level involvement of the NATO coalition's (primarily United States) military operations in Afghanistan from 2012 through 2014, Pakistan became reluctantly and increasingly involved in the conflict for two primary reasons, both related to the overall difficulty of internal governance.

First was the pure geography of Pakistan's long and rugged border with Afghanistan and the nearly impossible task of securing it from ease of transit by those Taliban and al-Qaeda forces seeking temporary refuge and reorganization in Pakistan from NATO forces fighting them in Afghanistan.

Second was the fact that the political leadership of Pakistan walked a fine line trying to remain a strategic ally of the United States, while many among its ethnically diverse population felt kinship with the forces trying to depose the corrupt Karzai government of Afghanistan, and were covertly doing this as Taliban fighters. These fighters were also using bases in Pakistan to renew and refit, and the United States felt that Pakistan was not doing enough to discourage this activity.

The final straw of the breach in U.S.-Pakistani relations came in 2011 when the CIA and the U.S. military determined after a lengthy surveillance of a suspected human courier and analysis of his movements, that it was highly likely that Osama Bin Laden, the number one most wanted international terrorist and master-mind of the September 11, 2001, attacks on the United States, was living and hiding in a large compound outside of Abbottabad, Pakistan. In a daring surgical raid by U.S. Navy SEAL Team Six in the night of May 1-2, 2011, The SEALs entered the compound, killed Osama Bin Laden and some of his family members, collected a treasure trove of useful intelligence, and left as they had come via advanced stealthy helicopter aircraft.

This raid was conducted in Pakistan and transited over Pakistani air space without the U.S. Government consulting with the government of Pakistan. Bin Laden and his family had been living in Pakistan for quite some time and not only was the presence of Bin Laden in Pakistan a very large embarrassment to the Pakistani government, but the fact that the U.S. felt compelled to conduct such a brazen raid without consulting the leaders of a sovereign government sent a message to the rest of the world about how little the United States trusted the relationship. From then on the relationship never improved and the political stability in this troubled country deteriorated further. Nevertheless, Pakistan remained a country dominated by the Muslim religion – although divided among a Sunni majority and a Shiite minority – that had one asset coveted by the many warring factions that existed in the region: An unknown number of nuclear weapons ostensibly in the control of the Pakistani military.

There were three burning questions about this fact. To what leadership, on any given day, was the military loyal? Where were these weapons being kept, and under what level of security were they stored? These were the questions Sharif Rashad had to answer before he could put a plan in place to procure these weapons.

The imports that Pakistan relied on above all else were the crude oil and gas needed to drive her economy. Iran, a large exporter of these commodities, saw Pakistan as a huge and geographically convenient trading partner. This partnership became more of an imperative as the economic sanctions imposed by the United Nations in 2011 and 2012 – led by demagogical insistence by the United States and her client, Israel - increased pressures on Iran to find new outlets for her petroleum exports.

Once again, Pakistan was caught between two competing imperatives. She desperately needed energy in the form of crude oil and natural gas being offered by Iran, but was feeling the pressure, primarily from the United States, to abide strictly by the economic sanctions being imposed by the UN. Iran was well aware of the quandary that Pakistan's leaders felt and it was within the purview of Sharif Rashad to continually remind every politician with whom he had a connection – and he had many – that Iran was standing by, willing and able to provide energy supplies to Pakistan, in spite of what the more prosperous nations of the West wanted.

At the forefront of Rashad's arguments for a "damn the West" partnership between the two Islamic nations was his reminder that this was really more about the West's subtle 'war against Islam' than it was about Iran and Pakistan being allowed to prosper and become economic competitors with the Western world.

Sharif thought that all he needed to do was to find one or two disaffected political or military leaders who were rivals of the current Pakistani leadership to cooperate with him. The price to the traitors would be their cooperation in getting him the nukes. Their reward would be Iran's commitment to them for the energy they required to move their economy forward. With such a partnership in place, they would become the new leaders in Pakistan either formally or behind the scenes. In addition, they would become rich in the process, as Sharif had included their gratuity in his definition of 'expenses' for this enterprise to his brother in the fateful meeting in Tehran. Sharif knew precisely whom to approach first. General Pervez Ali al-Zarcash, was a 30+ year veteran Pakistani Army officer and had risen to command an elite Pakistani Army Corps. He was also Head of Pakistani

Army Security forces, while surviving several changes of government since the days of Muhammad Zia ul-Haq and Benazir Bhutto in the late 1980's. After all these years, Sharif thought, wisely so, that al-Zarcash knew where all the skeletons were hidden and, presumably, the mysterious nukes as well. It helped that al-Zarcash also had the weakness of being a compulsive gambler. It helped even more that al-Zarcash owed Sharif and others over $100,000 U.S. dollars in gambling debt, and on a Pakistani Army officer's salary that amount would be nearly impossible to pay back.

Unless such a debt could be miraculously erased, his dream of retirement after many years of service and moving to a place far more pleasant than Pakistan with his wife were simply that...*empty dreams.*

Over the past two years as the gambling debt to Sharif had grown, Zarcash had made repeated attempts to get the debt reduced or even forgiven. Sometimes Sharif had relented and allowed al-Zarcash to miss a payment for several months. However, like many compulsive gamblers, the General had attempted to wager his way out of debt, which had made things even worse. The amount of the debt grew larger rather than shrank.

In America, particularly in Las Vegas or Atlantic City, Zarcash would be known as a *'degenerate gambler.'* Sharif Rashad had read the Quran many times and had been taught in the madrassas by the mullahs that Allah was merciful and that anyone expressing sincere belief in Islam must demonstrate mercy as well. Sharif was confident that he had been a merciful as well as a charitable man many times over throughout his adult life. However, in a matter this important...important to the faith of Islam itself, he knew that matters of faith must trump acts of individual mercy and he plotted to spring his trap. Besides, if his plan worked, el Zarcash would be free of this piddling debt as payment for his help. He might even be financially rewarded if things went well.

When he returned to Islamabad from Iran Sharif made contact with the General and arranged a meeting, ostensibly to talk about the gambling debt that el Zarcash owed. Sharif made the request sound positive, implying that there was a way out of this burdensome dilemma for the General. Thinking this the case, the General was only too happy to clear his schedule to meet with the Iranian Trade Representative.

Sharif had a modest apartment in Islamabad, quite humble by the standards befitting his wealth, but Sharif, being a minority Shiite and not wanting to draw unwanted attention to a lavish lifestyle decided to keep it simple. When it was his desire to indulge himself, he conveniently retreated – on a 'trade mission' - to Dubai, where gambling and women were freely available and he could retire to a five star hotel with all the expected pleasurable hedonistic amenities for the duration of his visit. He also suspected that his apartment was bugged by the Pakistani Intelligence Service, who viewed all Iranian diplomats and high level businessmen with suspicion, particularly if they were representing Mahmoud Rashad's Shiite government. No, the meeting would have to be in a trusted neutral venue so the two men could speak freely.

Sharif knew a small time gambler who also trafficked in hashish, American cigarettes, and Scotch whiskey. He did business out of a small smoke shop in one of the darker areas of Islamabad where there was a steady parade of respectable Pakistani businessmen and government types who were only too anxious to leave quietly after making their surreptitious purchases. The owner and Sharif occasionally did each other small favors. Therefore the presence of two gentlemen such as the General and Sharif would not be unusual. There would certainly be no surveillance in such a place, as the results could be embarrassing to those who came and went clandestinely to this *neutral* site. It was agreed that the two would meet in the rear upper room of the smoke shop at a late night hour.

The two men entered the shop at different times, Sharif having arrived much earlier to ensure the security of the site and to make sure that no customers were staying beyond the normal time it took to make a transaction with the owner. After the general arrived, wearing civilian clothes to reduce his recognition footprint, the owner directed him to the room where Sharif was staying and closed his shop for the evening. The General and Sharif were now alone to hatch Sharif's plot that could possibly lead to the veneration of Iran in the eyes of the Islamic world.

"Good evening, General," smiled Sharif, with the confidence of a man who held a winning hand, both literally and figuratively. Sharif had thought carefully about the potential for involving al-Zarcash in his plans and after considering all the possible outcomes, he had concluded that al-Zarcash would have no alternative but to cooperate. And if in the off-chance that he did not, Sharif had made contingency plans to make any revelations by the General lose their credibility in light of his large gambling debts to Sharif and others. Al-Zarcash would probably cooperate, if only reluctantly.

The two men exchanged pleasantries and small talk, carefully testing the waters to make sure there was nothing of ill-will on the part of either that would cause disaffection between them. After drinking tea and smoking some American cigarettes the shop owner had graciously provided, it was down to business.

Sharif continued: "General, I believe that outside our mutual love of gambling and *other activities*, we have some more practical things in common."

"And what would those be?" asked the General, his curiosity piqued.

"It is regrettable that you have had such a run of bad luck with your gambling, General. At times I feel a certain amount of guilt that you have such a debt to me. However, gamblers understand each other only too well, and as much as I would like to unburden you from much of this, I too have debts that must be paid if I am to retain my honor as a gentleman. Therefore, I must reluctantly remind you that I must be paid."

"You did not bring me here tonight to remind me that I am indebted to you, Sharif. Allah knows I remind myself of this every day. If the President knew of this my career would be in jeopardy. Even my wife knows nothing of this," he grumbled.
"As I said," noted Sharif nodding with as much sympathy as he could muster, "this is regrettable indeed."

A moment of silence filled the room before Sharif continued.

"What if I proposed to you, General, that there was a way that this burden could be removed from you and you could begin with a clean slate, perhaps even with enough of a stake to gracefully retire and even leave Pakistan for a more agreeable place? You have served your country well and deserve to live comfortably and in peace with your wife."

General al-Zarcash was astonished at the thought and his head swam in the anticipation of being relieved of this debt and the possibilities connected with it. But al-Zarcash was a cunning man and after a brief moment of exuberant optimism came back to Earth with the knowledge that there would surely be a hefty price to pay for such relief, and it would not be in financial terms.

"Of course, I would be interested," answered the General with as much nonchalance as he could project.

"Well, I have such a plan," said Sharif. "Please listen carefully and let me know if such a thing is possible."

"General, as you know, Iran has been placed in a very difficult position by the West, primarily driven by its passionate and irrational support of the Zionists. It seems as if Iran stands alone in Islam's fight against the Zionist usurpers of Palestinian lands. The price we pay for this is economic sanctions that threaten our economic health while making us a pariah country in the eyes of potential trading partners. The Americans intimidate anyone who wishes to establish mutually healthy trade with us. Even the Saudis think of us as bumbling amateurs while hypocritically making billions selling their crude oil to the infidels."

"We are in no position to be of great help, Sharif. Most of the government is Sunni and your brother Mahmoud Rashad is viewed by them as a radical. As you know, my sympathies are with you, but I must act as if I support this latest government, regardless of how I feel."

"Well, General, I can tell you that many things will soon change in the world of Islam. Iran is about to reach a far higher level of respect, not only from our Islamic brothers, but from the Zionists and their protectors. Even the mighty House of Saud will soon see Iran with a new measure of respect and hospitality."

"And how will that transpire and what does it have to do with this meeting tonight, Sharif?"

"Because Iran is going to acquire a nuclear bomb very soon – actually as many as three plutonium bombs – and we will then be respected as a member of the exclusive so-called Nuclear club!"

Al-Zarcash rose to his feet in astonishment and looked at Sharif incredulously. "How can that be? It is in the news regularly about how many more years it will take you to build these weapons given the setbacks from the Israeli commando raids."

The darkness and cool of the evening brought a sense of quietness to the small room. With little ventilation the odors of steaming tea, tobacco smoke and the body odors of the two men seemed to dominate nearly all else except their deep voices magnified by the seriousness of the moment.

Al Zarcash, blurted out, "But how...?" and before he could complete his verbal thought, Sharif interrupted him and said, "We are going to steal them from Pakistan, and you will be the thief!"

Al-Zarcash stared with a bewildered look at the grimly smiling Sharif and felt his knees begin to buckle beneath him. It was now becoming clear to the general that Sharif had hatched a devious plan from which there was no escape. To say "no" would simply drive him to a greater set of risks with little chance of acceptable outcomes. To say "yes" would expose him to extraordinary risks and possible death, assuring ignominy for his family. Allah was truly punishing him for his many sins while he was still on this earth.

'How much worse will it be when I meet him in heaven?' He thought.

"Me...a thief of nuclear bombs? With respect, even Allah himself could not do such a thing. It is too dangerous!" lamented a distraught al Zarcash.

"Yes, my friend...difficult and dangerous...but Allah does not have to do this. It is his will that together *we do it* in his name...or face his everlasting wrath in heaven! Allah Akbar!"

CHAPTER 15

SUCCESS AND WEALTH, OR FAILURE AND DEATH

"The sin ye do by two and two ye must pay for one by one."
Rudyard Kipling

General Pervez Ali al-Zarcash found himself backed into a corner with only two options. The first was to cooperate fully with the Iranian Trade Minister to steal the nuclear weapons and assist in their transport across Afghanistan or Pakistan to Iran. In this there was grave danger of being caught and tried as a traitor with the attendant consequences of execution. Conversely, if successful and against great odds, there would be wealth beyond his wildest dreams and the opportunity to live in Dubai, or even Spain, in luxury for the rest of his life. Those were the potential consequences as he considered Sharif Rashad's offer.

Failure to cooperate with the sinister plan proposed by Sharif would surely mean being exposed as a degenerate gambler and womanizer, in conflict with the strictest prohibitions of the Holy Quran. For Zarcash and his family, this would be the same as an ignoble death. As was the case for all men faced with only two options of immoral definition, he would choose the one that gave him the greatest potential reward of personal satisfaction. Consequently, he knew he would have to throw in with the devil, and the devil in this case was Sharif Rashad.

After some intellectual conflict on the part of Zarcash, he came to peace with the idea of assisting Rashad in his bold plan and began to warm to it.

After nearly 30 years of soldiering Zarcash had become inured against second guessing about consequences after a decision had been made and instead, began to plot about how this deed could be accomplished without detection. First, however, he had to establish a safety net for his wife and family.

His wife, Benazir, had been born in the Indian coastal city of Surat and had family there in abundance. She had travelled there many times for family functions and it would not seem unusual for her to get an exit visa for travel there, especially in her position as the wife of a senior military officer. Their daughter worked as a diplomat for the Pakistani government in the U.K., assuring her presence outside of the country. If the plan was exposed his family would be safe from retribution and his wife and daughter would at least have a fighting chance for asylum in those countries if necessary.

As for Zarcash, his fate would be immediate. He had no worries about torture, because he would have no qualms about revealing the plot that implicated those at the highest level of power from Iran. The fact that this was an Iranian plot would come as no surprise to the Pakistanis.

Zarcash had nothing to protect. Death would come swiftly for him after a confession. For Zarcash, there was a certain feeling of resignation on his part. The plan would either succeed, making him extremely wealthy, or fail, bringing him a swift and relatively painless death. As an inveterate gambler, Zarcash had looked at the odds and found them in his favor.

The second matter was that of compensation to Zarcash should the plan succeed. There were variables, of course. From President Rashad's perspective the ideal plan would be for a total of three complete plutonium weapons to make it safely to Iran. By 'complete,' this meant a ready-to-use weapon consisting of the complete bomb assembly; the warhead, the arming/fusing/firing mechanism, and the arming software. Also part of a complete package would be any necessary computer software associated with preparing the weapon for detonation and the detailed manuals covering all the sub-systems. The manuals would also have to be complete with all documentation relative to the manufacturing process, including quality assurance records and testing protocols that had been followed during manufacturing.

Nothing could be left to chance as the Iranians might actually have to conduct a test of one of the weapons in order to convince the UN and the other members of the so-called 'Nuclear Club' that Iran did, in fact, possess a nuclear capability.

Of course, after such a test somewhere in the vast deserts of Iran, there would be a well-orchestrated groundswell of condemnation led chiefly by the United States, and a heightening of tensions with Israel. But Israel would have to be far less bellicose in its reaction, because the remaining bombs would be well hidden and geographically separated, so a strike against Iran would be ill-advised. If such an attack did come, Iran had a contingency plan to strike back with at least one of the remaining two bombs, leaving one in reserve.

Iran now would be given far more respect and any attack would likely inflame the entire Middle East into a nuclear inferno. Oil could rocket to $500 to $1,000 per barrel and bring the economies of the West to their knees. The Christian Bible spoke of Armageddon and, indeed, such an event could come to pass under these dire circumstances.

Therefore, Rashad was prepared to pay Zarcash up to two million U.S. dollars for each ready-to-use weapon that would arrive safely in Iran. These funds would come from the "plus expenses" financial arrangements he had made with his brother during his most recent trip to Iran, where the plot had been hatched. As a seasoned negotiator, Rashad would start his offering price at a ridiculously low level to al Zarcash so he could appear generous at the end.

"So, my friend, I am inclined to throw in with you on the most ambitious project. I, too, am interested in seeing that the world of Islam gain new respect throughout the Western power structure," explained Zarcash.

"However before we go further we must discuss my compensation. There will be considerable expense incurred on my end and the payments will have to be creative. In order for me to get the cooperation I need from those providing access to the devices and actually liberating them I will need to be able to pay these men in gold. Paper money in a scheme like this is worthless."

Rashad, nodded in acquiescence as he shrewdly calculated how he could bring this much gold into Pakistan and get it prepositioned for distribution. The gold would be a complication, but he knew the general was correct. People who were engaged in criminal or treasonous acts were naturally suspicious of each other and fearful of the consequences of being caught. Given the political situation in Pakistan and her close proximity to Afghanistan, paper money in exchange for assistance in any scheme that could even hint at something illegal, or in opposition to the sitting government, would be laughed at. No, gold - the purest and most trusted form of portable intrinsic value on Earth – was the only currency that could finance this scheme at the operational level.

Fortunately for Rashad, this issue presented only a minor inconvenience, as gold was the ultimate currency – as it had been for centuries – for important transactions among the nomadic tribes of the Middle East. The British Army officer, T.E. Lawrence, known colloquially as 'Lawrence of Arabia,' had used gold, not only as a method of payment for various mercenaries he employed against the Turks, but as a lure for those with whom he famously crossed the 'impassable' Nefud desert that was the back door access to the vulnerability of the Turks at Aqaba.

Yes, gold, as it had been for centuries, was the currency that had sealed every important deal in the deserts of the Middle East and would be the key for success in this grand scheme.

Rashad thought it only appropriate that the two most common and respected commodities in world-wide commerce, gold and oil, would be thus inexorably intertwined in getting Iran the third, and newest of the valuable commodities - the monster that trumped them all, and the one most difficult to obtain – nuclear weapons. With vast supplies of the three, one could become a major player in the political and economic dynamics of the World.

Gold also had to be paid in amounts that were reasonable as exchange for goods and services. From a practical standpoint that left out using most 'bars' of gold, which could weigh anywhere from 400 ounces (12.5 kilos) on the high side (sometimes known as a London Gold Delivery Bar), down to fractions of an ounce. Although 'gold was gold' it was always preferable to deal in readily identifiable coinage, such as South African Krugerrands and the fractional denominations thereof, as most people who gave or received payment in gold recognized these coins as being authentic without going through the time-consuming and revealing activity of having to weigh an object being used as payment. In the Arab world, the one object apart from traditional coinage that was widely accepted was the one ounce of 999.9 'fine' gold, the ARY, and coined by the United Arab Emirates.

With gold hovering near the U.S. $2,000 price per ounce, fractional ounce coins would be necessary to intersperse with the 'Krugers' and ARYs as payments for the favors and services required to convert the Pakistani nuclear bombs to the property of Iran.

While one ounce gold bars and South African 'Krugers' would satisfy the currency of sovereign betrayal at the lower end of the military in Pakistan, the payments of the millions that would be necessary to get the full cooperation of Zarcash would have to be in a more sophisticated form.

Rashad flew to Dubai the very next day and checked into an inauspicious hotel there – certainly several steps below the class of lodging he was accustomed to while traveling on official business. He told the manager there that he was not to be disturbed for the duration of his stay and sealed that understanding with a generous gratuity.

That afternoon Rashad went to a medical clinic on the edge of Dubai and complained of severe headache and diarrhea, symptoms for which he was diagnosed with the flu and given a prescription for antibiotics and a medication that would ease the disagreeable gastric symptoms. In addition, he was ordered to bed for a few days. A call to his office informing them of this gave him perfect cover to be away from his cell phone for at least three days. After buying the drugs as proof of his medical cover story Rashad went to the Dubai airport and paid cash for a quick turn-around ticket on Saudi Air to Zurich.

When the banks opened the next morning, Rashad entered the Swiss bank with which the government of Iran – despite subtle attempts by the Western powers – still had extensive financial dealings.

In spite of what certain governments professed publicly, the international financial community and the diplomatic and financial managers who managed the day-to-day transfer of trillions of dollars among all countries that participated in international commerce needed a secure and, occasionally, a discreet and trusted mechanism to do so. For over a half century the 'Gnomes of Zurich,' a pejorative euphemism for the banking system of Switzerland, had been the mechanism for many such transactions. Governments of all sizes and political definitions and their leaders, who ran the gamut of despised despot to statesmen of great respect, knew they could safely turn to the Swiss banking system as a financial ally and resource. That was Sharif Rashad's mission today.

Rene Delagarde had been the personal banker to the régime of Mahmoud Abdul Rashad and, by extension, to his brother since Rashad had taken control of Iran's presidency many years ago. Rene's title of 'Executive Director' of the closely held, but financially substantial Banque Switzerland et Cie, gave him personal access to some of the bank's most confidential and important clients.

Such clients were all either high net worth individuals from across the globe, or representatives of geopolitical entities who had regular currency transactions in the hundreds of millions, or both. Such clients provided enormous profits for the bank, but also demanded substantial personal and discreet services from the Delagarde family.

Rene had been educated at the London School of Economics and received an MBA from Harvard Business School. He had spent three years working at the Federal Reserve immediately after his graduation from Harvard and because of his influential family connections in the European banking community had made extremely valuable friends within the U.S. banking structure. One of the unwritten rules of the international financial community is that the number and quality of contacts one has can be mutually beneficial to many people. Rene's father, Hugo, one of the founders of the bank and a Director Emeritus thereof, was a grand master of contract bridge and even late in his life enjoyed a spirited friendship with the American financial genius Warren Buffett and a respectful acquaintance with William Gates, a founder of Microsoft Corporation.

Such connections eventually and frequently built trust that opened doors to meeting others with whom a common interest could be established. Bankers always were looking for reliable clients, and high-ranking people in government are always looking for that most vital international commodity - *useful information.*

That is how Hugo and Rene Delagarde found their way into the virtual Rolodex of Rachel Hunter, a former executive with Goldman Sachs, and now Director of National Intelligence of the United States of America.

Contrary to the conventional notion of some demographers, the world is a very small place indeed. The number of people throughout the world whose ideas, influence and actions actually drove policy that impacts international diplomacy and relations between countries was very small. Bankers and intelligence types have one thing in common; they all wanted to know these power brokers personally and solicit the commodity they both want, whether it is financial activity or strategic information. The Delagardes and Rachel Hunter were a perfect match for each other's needs.

Rene Delagarde received Sharif Rashad in his spacious office on the 12th floor of the headquarters of his bank in central Zurich with the ease and grace of a successful European gentleman. A visit from Rashad, rather than an encrypted telephone call or e-mail, always meant that one of the Rashad brothers wanted a large favor involving discretion and a great deal of money. These were the two keys to Rene's success and he was genuinely pleased to see his old acquaintance, Sharif.

"Sharif, it is very good to see you again. You are looking healthy. How is your brother? I read about him and see him on television, but have not seen him in person in some time. At times he seems like a cornered beast fighting against many hunters."

"Thank you, Rene. Yes, Iran is under attack from many corners, but we have a right to sell our resources on the international market and will fight these hypocritical sanctions to the very end. The UN would be a paper tiger without the Americans and their IAEA inspectors are imbeciles...tools of the Zionists."

Rene Delegarde merely shrugged and raised his finely kept eyebrows in a gesture of tacit understanding.

"But then again, Rene, my brother and I know you must do business with the Israelis as well. I'll bet they warn you not to contaminate their kosher money with ours!" Both men chuckled at that remark.

"So, Sharif, what brings you to Zurich? Is this business or social? If the latter I know an excellent new restaurant; it serves lamb that literally falls off the bone. We could dine there this evening if you like."

"That is kind of you to ask, Rene. But today is important business that I must conduct in person. I must also ask for your utmost discretion as usual. Please consider this as a personal request from my brother if you will. He values your business acumen and your discretion very highly."

Rene Delegarde nodded in acquiescence and said simply, "As always, the bank and I are at your service."

There was no need for Rashad to explain why he and his brother needed some unusual personal attention. They trusted Delagarde, but not with information this sensitive. No, Rashad would simply lay out his requirement and hope the banker could suggest a solution that would be acceptable to all parties while assuring protection against non-performance and potential fraudulent receipt of the funds on the part of Zarcash.

Rashad chose his words carefully.

"Rene, General Pervez Ali al-Zarcash is an important general in the Pakistani armed forces. He is over 65 years of age and has made his career by skillfully negotiating the shifting political winds that have prevailed in Pakistan over many years. He is also a good friend of mine and has assisted me in our sometimes complicated trade negotiations with the Pakistanis."

'And he is also a degenerate gambler and womanizer,' thought the well-connected and perceptive Delagarde as he listened carefully to Rashad.

"Zarcash is in a position to do a tremendous favor for Iran that will result in our currency situation becoming much more favorable in light of these damnable economic sanctions. With his help our oil will begin to flow again and our economic situation will improve immeasurably. His assistance will be extremely valuable for us."

'I have a feeling this is all tied to this general's moral impairment and that blackmail is an operative phrase in his agreement to help Rashad and his brother,' wisely mused Delagarde as Rashad continued his explanation.

"Of course, the general will require compensation should his efforts ultimately benefit Iran, but this will take, shall we say, *considerable skill*, on his part. What I need is to tie-in his ultimate performance with his eventual payment. He is requesting payment in gold should his efforts be successful. Unfortunately our supplies of these financial commodities are quite limited and we would not be able to conveniently pay him when the job is done. Therefore, we are asking the help of your good offices at the proper time."

'What this means is that the general does not want to depend on Rashad to be a person of good will and guarantee payment at a precise moment. He does not want to

deliver whatever goods or services he has promised and risk being stiffed by Rashad and his brother. Very wise of him,' thought Delagarde.

"I assume this *favor* that the general will be doing for you will have an immediate result that can be judged of the moment, and therefore payment in full will be due," suggested Delagarde quietly.

"Quite correct," answered Rashad evenly. "We will be expected to pay in full upon...*accomplishment.*"

"I see," remarked the banker as he searched for the deeper meaning of all of this. *'As long as I don't know the details of this interaction, I...the bank...won't be a party to it and it will simply be an arms-length financial transaction. I am comfortable with that.'*

"Well, I am beginning to see some potential for accommodation here, Sharif. What is the amount of money that will be required for the bank to front? We can easily do gold or U.S. dollars, but payment in gold will require a premium of ten percent over the normal transaction fee. That, plus the interest on the funds we advance to your party."

Sharif was growing uncomfortable in his chair and got up and walked to the large window that looked out over the landscape of Zurich. *'How could a people with so few natural resources become so rich and powerful on the world stage while Iran with her vast oil reserves have to grovel for small financial favors? Soon that will all change,'* he thought confidently.

"The minimum amount he will be compensated for his success will be three million U.S. dollars. For superior performance, the amount will be six million. There is also a provision for a one million dollar bonus payment if other provisions are met. Therefore, the total amount remains unknown at this time, but your maximum exposure is only seven million U.S. dollars," explained Rashad evenly.

"Still, a significant amount," Delagarde countered gently. "And I assume there will be little, if any, documentation of this agreement...rather just the verbal assurance of you and your brother that we will be repaid within ninety days of our...*performance?*"

"We would prefer it that way...as I assume you would as well," answered Rashad.

A moment of silence engulfed the room as both men considered their positions in this delicate matter. Rashad felt he had told the banker all he could without compromising the plot, and Rene quickly calculated the appropriate risk-reward ratio given what little he knew about the background.

Technically the bank was not allowed to participate by the gentlemen's convention that overhung international sanctions on currency transactions with Iran, but these were technicalities for the consumption of the media and various overzealous watchdog groups who knew little of the back channel and behind-the-scenes dealings that were necessary to keep international financial dealings civilized. *'In a way, it is the duty of our bank to make such an arrangement workable to all parties. This is the vital service we provide to the world,'* Rene rationalized.

"We, of course, will be pleased to provide this service," said Delagarde, breaking the silence.

"And the fee?" questioned a relieved Rashad.

"A fifteen per-cent transaction fee and ten percent interest per month on the balance advanced. Plus, of course, the additional premium for any payments in gold."

Rashad gazed out the window, looking at nothing in particular for a moment, stung by the usurious terms demanded by the banker. But he had expected nothing less and quickly agreed.

"The fees will be automatically debited from the funds you have on deposit with the bank and we will have to place a hold on those funds in the amount advanced to your contractor as collateral for the loan," explained Delagarde. "Purely routine. I'm sure you understand," he continued.

"Of course," came Rashad's terse reply.

"Then we have an agreement?"

"Oui, Monsieur," answered Rashad in a gesture to Delagarde's heritage.

"Now to some details, Sharif: I assume the contractor will present himself at our bank to receive the funds due him. That will be fine, and I will receive him personally, of course. How will I be able to verify the identity of this person and how will we know exactly what amount he is to be advanced?"

Rashad pulled a crisp, new one hundred U.S. dollar bill from his pocket and cut it in two halves in a jagged pattern. From his briefcase he pulled out a hand operated paper punch with a distinctive cutting die on the head and punched three holes in the half notes as they were held together so that the die cut holes only lined up when the two halves were matched on an alignment scheme that was known to Rene Delagarde.

While it was true that the shape of the die cuttings could be matched by a master counterfeiter, only Rene Delagarde knew how the halves needed to be aligned in relation to each other for there to be a match. When you held the properly aligned notes up to the light the patterns had to precisely line up or there was not a match. The verification process was quite simple. The bearer of the half note would be entitled to the funds if his bank note exactly matched the half that would be held by Rene Delagarde. In order to be authenticated, Zarcash or his agent would have to possess the other half of the note held by Rene Delagarde prepared by Sharif Rashad. As an added precaution, the person presenting himself as the authorized recipient of the funds would have to provide a code to the receptionist at the offices of the bank to meet with Delagarde. That code was the serial number of the hundred dollar U.S. Federal Reserve Note that was on both halves of the note.

"Very clever, Mr. Rashad. This will make the payment foolproof and easy. I assume you will get your half of the note to the contractor. Now, there is the matter of the amount to be paid."

"In order to leave no trace of your involvement, I will make a reservation for dinner on a specific date at the restaurant where you frequently dine in the name of Monsieur Falcone. It will be for a specific number of diners. I will ask the Maître Dei to call your secretary with that information. From that information you will know the date on which the contractor will present himself at your bank and how much to pay him. The number of reservations will represent the number of millions to be paid."

"And your receipt?" asked Delagarde. "I assume you want a receipt for payment made."

"Why, the two halves of the bank note, of course," replied Rashad with a grim smile.

After the briefest moment of small talk, Rashad shook hands with *the infidel,* Delagarde, and took his leave from the offices of the evil but necessary bank. During the taxi ride to the Zurich airport Rashad surveyed the road ahead and tried to imagine the many difficulties that lie ahead in the acquisition of the weapons. But for the advancement of Islam and his personal enrichment, many sacrifices would be necessary. Next on his agenda was to spend a few days of pleasure in Dubai and then back to Islamabad to meet with Zarcash. As he thought of punching the holes in the bank note in Delagarde's office thirty minutes ago, he knew, in more ways than one, the die had been cast.

BOOK VI

*

THE GAMBLE

CHAPTER 16

BANKERS AND SPOOKS

"Borrowers are nearly always ill-spenders, and it is with lent money that all evil is mainly done and all unjust war protracted."
John Ruskin – 'The Crown of the Wild Olive.'

In international banking circles, as in contract bridge, nuance and convention are the preferred ways of communicating important and sensitive information between parties that have mutual interests. Hugo Delagarde was a master at both. Although largely retired from the day-to-day operational aspects of managing the bank's business, each Friday he would have lunch with his son, Rene, in his private dining room at the bank. Here they would discuss the important business events of the past week and exchange ideas about the most effective ways to strategize each opportunity for the maximum benefit of the bank and its stockholders.

This Friday the topic of the Iranian Trade Minister's visit was deemed important enough by Rene to bring to the attention of his father. After going over the preliminaries and presenting Hugo with a summary of what the deal would entail and the potential profits it would bring to the bank, Rene waited for his father to comment or ask questions before going to the next topic.

"I know these men, Rene. They don't have the class or the manners of our friends in the House of Saud. They are clumsy and coarse. They are not my favorite clients. I do think the series of sanctions that have come and gone over the past few years have been disruptive to their economy, which in turn has depleted their currency reserves. But they pay their bills and I am satisfied to have them as clients. And all this secrecy and paying money to unknown people after certain milestones have been met...what do you think is going on here?"

"Of course, Rashad was not forthright with me about the reasons behind this transaction – as is the case with many of our clients – but I got the feeling that he would have bought the deal even if we would have demanded higher fees and greater interest. He desperately wanted to make this deal and knew we could be trusted to be discreet. In my opinion, this is part of a grand or strategic plan that not only involves Rashad himself, but others at a higher level; but the subject is a mystery."

"Rene, in the banking business it is always good policy to try to understand the fundamental needs of a client as part of the assessment of a current need. In the case of Iran, they have one great asset and that is their huge reserves of oil. On the minus side, they have one great intangible need, and they have been frustrated for many years by this need not being met. They lack the respect from the Western and Islamic world that their Sunni brothers, the Saudis, have. They want to be a Shiite version of Saudi Arabia but they have not been able to affect this up to now. If I had to guess, I think that Rashad's visit to you this week may be connected in some way to easing this long standing frustration."

"Father I have always valued your good judgment and sound advice. We shall keep that in mind in case this deal begins to fall apart or becomes otherwise troublesome. A bad outcome for us would be if the money we have lent for this is used for illegal or unethical means and our participation becomes public knowledge. That could damage our relationships with some of our more well-respected clients. On the other hand, the best case scenario for us will be if it comes off without a hitch and we make the profit we anticipate. At this point the die is cast."

Hugo Delagarde did not build his bank or the personal fortune derived from it by waiting for the results of a complex transaction to simply play itself out. That left too much to chance...too much to the random fates that were beyond his control. Fortunes were lost by careless men who relied on the whims of chance or lack of attention to detail to navigate their business or personal dealings. Hugo Delagarde was not such a careless man.

After their luncheon Hugo Delagarde sent what would appear to be the most innocent of emails to a business contact in Washington, D.C.

> Dear Mr. Singleton:
> As you know, our bank is seeking to generate more business in the United States. We have decided to engage the services of your marketing organization to bring prospective clients from both the public and private sectors. I plan on being in Washington, D.C., next week and would appreciate the opportunity to meet with you to discuss this business arrangement. Would Wednesday at 11:00 AM be convenient at your offices? Perhaps we could have lunch at Julio's.
> Sincerely,
> Hugo Delagarde

Of course, there was no "Mr. Singleton" at the firm to which this message was sent, but the message was automatically forwarded to an email address that resided in a server to which the Administrative Assistant to the Director of National Intelligence, Doctor Rachel Hunter, had access. This message was printed and handed to Director Hunter for her attention and action. The three portions of the message that were significant code were the name "Singleton," the date and time of the requested meeting, and the name of the restaurant. Hugo Delagarde's name, of course was real, assuring that the message could survive a modest level of electronic snooping. "Singleton" was related to the reason for the meeting. In this case Hugo wanted to discuss a business transaction between his bank and a country with strong Islamic ties. "Wednesday at 11:00 AM" indicated that this was money that was to be paid to a third party at the initialization of the transfer of funds, and "Julio's" indicated that he would like to meet with the director personally and in private.

Within an hour a reply was sent to Hugo Delagarde indicating that the meeting was indeed set at a previously agreed to time and place.

Of course the marketing firm for which "Mr. Singleton" worked was a front for the CIA and the offices of the fictitious firm were a convenient place away from CIA headquarters in Langley where clandestine meetings between CIA operatives and others could conveniently meet discreetly. There was secure underground parking and controlled access so that the comings and goings of visitors in vehicles with tinted windows would be difficult to trace. The CIA employed its own car service indistinguishable from the many private services in the area.

Hugo Delagarde made the trip from Zurich to Washington by private jet and was staying at the Mayflower Hotel. At the appointed hour on Wednesday he presented himself at the offices and was escorted to a private meeting room with simple furnishings, a small conference table and accompanying chairs, an overhead projector aimed at a wall containing a pull down screen, and a credenza containing liquid refreshment. There were no windows in the room but two doors at opposite ends of the office. Within moments after he was seated, the door opposite the one through which he had entered opened and he was joined by Rachel Hunter. She closed the door behind her with an audible click and they were alone.

"Good morning, Mr. Delagarde, it's good to see you again. Thank you for making the trip. Why anyone would want to leave Zurich to come to Washington is beyond me," she said pleasantly.

"Speaking of which, what brings you here today? Something about money, I'll bet." This elicited a chuckle from the Swiss banker.

"Oh that, and more!" Hugo replied modestly.

The director and the banker continued to exchange pleasantries and innocent gossip about mutual friends for a few moments then got down to the business at hand.

"Doctor Hunter, I have always enjoyed our relationship and your graciousness at being my bridge partner in those rare cases where we have been able to be social. I look forward to such an occasion sometime soon." Rachel Hunter smiled and nodded in agreement with the banker.

"As you know, our bank has dealings with many multi-national companies and international political jurisdictions. Many of these are either based in the United States or are countries with which the U.S. has a healthy political relationship."

"On occasion we even have financial dealings with those entities with who America may not be on the best of terms. I'm sure you are well aware that in order for the international banking community to work efficiently we sometimes have to work, shall we say, outside the public policy pronouncements of certain countries, the USA included. We strive to be financial partners with all of our clients unless it is patently clear that a transaction would be criminal or war-like in nature." Once again, Director Hunter smiled pleasantly and nodded slightly in agreement.

"I came here today because I was recently made aware of a future transaction that is to take place at our bank involving several millions of dollars and gold about which I am somewhat troubled. The truth is that we don't have any evidence that the funds we have agreed to transfer are for an illegal or warlike act, so we agreed to make the transaction for a substantial fee. However, you should know that our guaranteeing client in this case is the Government of Iran."

The only indication of a change in countenance on the part of Rachel Hunter was that she blinked twice in quick succession rather than once. But the mention of Iran and the future transfer of millions of dollars to a mysterious third party made her intellectual and professional antennae pop to attention.

Hugo spent the next 15 minutes reconstructing the details of the meeting that had been related to him by his son. Rachel Hunter asked an occasional question as a point of clarification but took no notes, nor was Hugo speaking from any. But to the Director, this information was pure gold. At times analysis seemed like looking through a glass darkly, but when dumped into the pot of other random information constantly and painstakingly being culled from this most volatile part of the world, a more coherent picture would eventually develop that could lead to an accurate picture of events that impacted American interests, and could be used for actionable decisions made by executive authority.

The hour had passed quickly and Director Hunter asked to be excused, but not before sincerely thanking the wise old Swiss banker for his proactive courtesy in making her aware of information that could be of vital importance.

"It's always a great personal and professional pleasure to see you, Hugo. I look forward to a relaxing game of bridge the next time I am in Geneva or Zurich."

Hugo Delagarde smiled and shook her hand warmly as they prepared to depart. "Please pass my best personal regards on to President Braxton and also the Secretary of the Treasury. The Secretary and I go back a long way."

Both Hugo and Rachel Hunter knew that Hugo Delagarde and, by extension, his bank, had scored some major points here today and the Swiss banker beamed broadly in anticipation of the future benefit this would bring to his international financial enterprise.

CHAPTER 17

ABRUPT CHANGE OF PLANS

"The best laid plans of mice and men often go astray."
Robert Burns – Scottish poet

Pakistan was in chaos politically. There had been three presidents there in the past five years and even though Ali Tariq El Hakim had put together a loose coalition of diverse political leaders to earn the titular position of 'President,' his was a leadership by committee. He himself was frequently at odds with the other members of the coalition in matters of national policy and international relations. Only rare consensus on the part of the ruling coalition produced decisions that were respected by a majority of Pakistan's citizens and trusted by most members of the international community.

Then there was the military. The Pakistani military was the only institution in Pakistan that had a firm structure and a purpose universally respected by the people. Problematically, the head of the Pakistani military was General Jamil Muhammad, an ambitious and colorful second-generation career military officer who was a bitter but clandestine foe of President El Hakim. The cautious competition between the two men was made more pronounced by the fact that El Hakim was a Sunni and General Muhammad was a minority Shiite.

This combination of shaky civilian leadership frequently at odds with a powerful military made it difficult for Pakistan to gain credibility on the international stage and to be trusted as a reliable trading and political ally.

Having few natural resources they could barter for goods and national respect, the one asset that Pakistan possessed that gave other nations pause and created a basis for grudging respect was an unknown number of nuclear weapons that had been developed and manufactured from the 1970's forward. More troubling was the fact that many of these were likely plutonium bombs, much smaller and more powerful than the original uranium bombs developed by Gamal Kahn, the German scientist who was largely regarded as the 'father' of Pakistan's nuclear weapons program.

Rashad and Zarcash had another clandestine meeting two weeks after Rashad returned from Zurich to discuss the plans going forward. Now that Rashad had made arrangements for the transfer of funds when the job was complete, he felt free to discuss the financial details with his co-conspirator. The two men finally settled on a fee that would total two million in gold for each warhead delivered safely to the sovereign territory of Iran. He would also receive one million in small denomination gold coins for 'operational expenses' incidental to the project.

Presumably these funds would be used by Zarcash to gain the cooperation of his fellow military officers and men whose assistance or acquiescence might be required in the diversion of these weapons. How Zarcash split up the money among the Pakistanis who would help him in this brazen plan was up to him. Rashad did manage to bring two hundred thousand dollars with him in used American currency that Zarcash could use as good faith money to capture the interest and gain the silence of those who would help him.

As the two men sat in the upper room of the same smoke shop drinking coffee and going over financial details, Rashad went out of his way to make it clear that only after the warheads were delivered to Iran would he transmit the correct codes to the bank so Zarcash could collect the funds. But this was hardly necessary.

In the nearly three weeks since the two had last met, Zarcash had the opportunity to think over the plan that would possibly bring him great riches at the price of betraying his country. Having invested many years of military service to a second rate power, surviving many political-military intrigues that could have gone badly for him if his cunning had abandoned him, or had he backed the wrong man, he acknowledged privately that he had carelessly squandered what pittance he had been able to put away as savings. Zarcash surveyed his options and, compulsive gambler that he was, reasoned he had no realistic option but to take one last shot at the brass ring. He would risk it all on the Rashad brother's audacious plan to smuggle nuclear war heads out of Pakistan into neighboring Iran. True, it was risky, but over the time he had to contemplate the risk-reward ratio he had decided that the odds were in his favor – if Allah was with him in their great crusade.

THE PLAN

TYPICAL NUCLEAR BOMB, UNASSEMBLED.

Most modern nuclear weapons, wherever produced, have at the heart of the weapon a nuclear warhead, as well as an Arming, Fusing and Firing Mechanism (AFF) specific to the form of delivery that will be applied. The warhead itself, consisting of the plutonium or uranium core and uranium triggering mechanism, along with the AFF, was what the Iranians wanted. All other electro-mechanical portions of the bomb were easily manufactured by Iranian scientists. The challenge for any country or group wanting to be a member of the Nuclear Club was to produce the quality and quantities of highly enriched uranium (HEU) and/or plutonium to produce a nuclear warhead.

This most important stage is what Iran, largely due to significant efforts by the Western world, had been deterred from doing. Now Rashad and Zarcash, driven by entirely different motivations, were taking the initiative and seeking redress of their grievances, as well as seeking personal respect, by redirecting nuclear warheads from the passive arsenal of a country whose best days had faded in memory to the use of a progressive Islamic state with a global vision. In the eyes of both men this was a noble cause.

Rashad and Zarcash talked, planned, war-gamed, and drank chai long into the night attempting to finalize a plan to get a nuclear device into Iran.

The reality - and the problem for the conspirators - was that Pakistan had a very stringent nuclear security protocol in place that protected its nuclear stockpile from incursion by unauthorized personnel intent on theft or sabotage, tampering, or other clandestine intrusions.

Although Pakistan was not a signatory to the Nuclear Nonproliferation Treaty (India and North Korea were the other non-signatories), she saw herself as a 'responsible' member of the Nuclear club, and complied with the provisions of nuclear security as mandated by United Nations International Atomic Energy Agency (IAEA) policies.

Pakistan was well aware that her atomic weapons were prime targets of terrorists groups such as al-Qaeda. Security was extremely tight and her weapons were strategically dispersed so that no one, except those at the highest levels of the civilian and military administration or at the umbrella agency, the Nuclear Defense Complex, could have access to them. As an added precaution, the Arming, Fusing and Firing Mechanisms were kept secretly at sites away from the actual weapons themselves so that even if a warhead itself was compromised, the AFF appropriate to that warhead required to detonate it would have to be diverted as well – an extremely unlikely scenario.

The specifics of Pakistani nuclear warhead capability were unknown. There was significant controversy over the number of warheads she possessed (somewhere between 80 and 120 was the consensus) and the yields of the devices she possessed were estimated to be evenly divided between low yield (20 – 150 kt.) and high yield (300 – 500 kt.) weapons. But it was suspected by American intelligence sources, who had a keen interest in the location and security of these weapons, that the weapons were strategically dispersed in various hardened and protected sites throughout the country so Pakistan could conceivably have a 'second strike' capability if there were either an initial strike by an aggressor, or it was forced to initiate a first strike in response to a serious provocation, such as an armed incursion from her arch-enemy, India.

Although it would be ideal if Zarcash could manage to steal three bombs in their entirety, it was highly unlikely that he, even with his high level of authority by virtue of his military position, could pull off something as audacious as this without causing a major internal security furor and perhaps even causing an international incident. No, as the two men continued to talk it became clear that a multi-point plan was more appropriate – and a step-by-step approach should be the way to make this plan come to fruition without being compromised by Pakistani nuclear security.

Rashad and Zarcash concluded their meeting in the early hours of the morning with many questions left unanswered. It was a critical moment in the planning phase of the operation and both men realized they had some thinking to do to refine their plan.

Two days later Rashad took a commercial flight out of Islamabad to Tehran. He didn't dare make any prior contact with his brother out of concern that direct communications between a Trade Minister and the President of Iran might be eavesdropped on by Pakistani intelligence and suspicions alerted. When Rashad arrived in the evening he took a car directly to his brother's home on the outskirts of Tehran. After friendly greetings were exchanged, Mahmoud Rashad asked quietly, "Are you making progress, Sharif? We are anxiously awaiting details of a plan that will get us the weapons we are seeking."

"Things go well, my brother. I have the financial details worked out and have a reliable accomplice in place in Pakistan to assist us internally – a high ranking military general who has access to places we need to be."

"Who is this man, Sharif; what are his connections? Is he reliable?"

"He is General Pervez al Zarcash, Deputy Commander of all Pakistani Military forces," replied Sharif confidently.

There was no reply from Mahmoud Rashad, but he made a mental note to look into the bona fides of this vital link of his dangerous plan.

"What have you been able to learn about the disposition of the Pakistani nuclear weapons? I am quite sure they are heavily secured. That is the one aspect of the situation that worries me."

"Mahmoud, here are the facts as I have learned about them from my Pakistani connection. First, the Pakistanis have somewhere near one hundred of these weapons in their stockpile. They are dispersed throughout Pakistan for security purposes. Second, the warheads themselves, which are the most critical component of an entire weapons assembly, are stored in various forms of readiness. Some are actually assembled to ready-to-use nuclear bombs that could be carried by their Mirage III fighter aircraft. Some are mounted on their most modern Shaheen II mobile guided missiles. Some warheads are stored so that their deployment and delivery could be flexible, depending on a specific military situation. It seems the most practical goal would be to acquire the actual warheads rather than entire bomb assemblies. Surely we are far enough along in our own development that once we have an actual working warhead, we can retrofit it to our delivery system."

Mahmoud Rashad paced the room in his house as he considered everything that his brother had told him. To Mahmoud every important decision he made as President boiled down to expediency and the risk-reward ratio. Time was running out, and the mullahs would be expecting results soon. He felt that he must at least brief them with a solid plan within a few weeks in order for them to maintain confidence in him about this most pressing strategic project.

"Sharif, I need to consider some things here. Please return tomorrow evening so we can finalize our plan. I have to speak to our chief scientist about this so I may have confidence in whatever plan we make. Now we will have chai and talk about the future of our great country and our position in Islam after we become a nuclear power."

The next day President Rashad called Khalil Aziz Mohammad, his chief nuclear scientist into his heavily secured conference room in the Presidential Palace.

"Khalil, I am going to bring you into my confidence about the state of our nuclear weapons program."

The scientist became momentarily ill at ease because of the failure and delays that had the Iranians without the prospects for even a prototype weapon after all the years of trial and error. He was furiously thinking of rational excuses for their lack of success as he felt this meeting might be an inquisition of sorts about why he had failed to produce a weapon. *'Of course, the military strikes and the damage that resulted set the program back significantly and had not been anything he could control...'*

"Khalil I have brought you here today to tell you that Iran will soon have our very own nuclear weapon...and not just one, but several!"

Khalil Mohammed was at once relieved and shocked at such a stupendous revelation. Khalil, bewildered by this sensational news, replied, "But, Mr. President, how can this be?" he asked looking at Rashad with an expression of incredulity.

"I, too, have been frustrated, but the military raids, the evil Western sanctions...*many things*...have all contributed to these delays. We are making progress, but we are still a far ways off."

"Not as far off as you may think," replied Rashad, conspiratorially.

"Khalil, today I am making you one of the very few of us in the Iranian government who know of this plan. This plan is even more secret than actually building a bomb ourselves, as the Americans, Israelis, and the Western media have been speculating for many years. Although we have denied it publicly, it has taken on a life of its own and is now seen as an unproven fact with them. This new plan is a state secret of such importance that in telling you, your very life is in danger if news of this ever leaks out. Do you understand?"

All Khalil Mohammad could do was to manage a huge gulp of harsh reality and mutter, "Yes, Mr. President, of course."

"Khalil, what is it we lack to build a nuclear bomb? What are the main components that we lack?"

That was an easy question for the scientist, as these were matters he struggled with on a daily basis. "We need much more of the 90 percent highly enriched uranium, and more plutonium 239, Mr. President. Many of our centrifuges were damaged by the Israeli raid and the American computer virus hurt the effectiveness our processing systems substantially. As far as the physics package is concerned, I would also say that we have a great deal to learn about the machining of the metal spheres that will direct the explosive compression the plutonium in the actual warhead. The spheres are critical to the yield of the weapon."

President Rashad paced the room and thought about a response that would startle the skeptical scientist. Finally, he stopped and looked directly at Khalil and asked simply, "What if I could deliver to you a working nuclear warhead? How long would it take for you and your scientific team to disassemble the weapon and reverse engineer the warhead so we could copy it and produce others of the same type?"

"A *working warhead?*...Allah be praised if such a thing could be done," replied Mohammad.

"Well, Khalil? I am waiting for your response as a person knowledgeable in these things. We need to know."

Now it was Khalil's turn to rise and pace throughout the room. He would like to be able to ask some of his colleagues who were closer to this aspect of the program, but he knew this was absolutely out of the question given the dire warning received from Rashad about the secrecy of the program.

No, he would have to come up with an acceptable answer and then be personally accountable for the timing if it came to fruition. Small beads of sweat began to break out on his face and under his frail arms as he formulated an answer that would have professional and personal implications for him. Success would make him a hero of the Islamic revolution and assure his continued status as a respected scientist in Iran. Failure would have many negative repercussions, possibly including death. The silence in the room increased the stress level even further, and he knew he had to give President Rashad an answer now. Khalil Aziz Muhammad lifted his head, straightened his jacket and look President Rashad clearly in the eye.

"Two weeks, Mr. President. Three at the most. Within that time we can reverse engineer the warhead and make the spheres and machine the beryllium surfaces to match whatever we have as a sample. I personally guarantee it."

"Yes, you do indeed. More than you know," replied Rashad grimly.

"But Mr. President," Khalil continued, "that still does not solve the problem of the requirement for greater amounts of nuclear material."

After a period of reflective silence, while one man contemplated his fate based on a promise he had just made, and another contemplated the monumental change that would take place in Iran if they became a nuclear power, Rashad answered, "If I can get you the fissile material, how long would it take you to build three warheads?"

Another deadline to contemplate increased Khalil's stress level even further. Such a decision would have ordinarily consumed weeks of meetings and consultations with specialists from many engineering disciplines, but the need for a dramatic decision descended upon the room like a pall that entombed them. Once again Khalil found himself placed at a once-in-a-lifetime decision point. Khalil was grateful that the silence was broken by Rashad himself.

"I assume we have thought far enough ahead over the years that we have all the machine tools and materials so if the fissile material suddenly and miraculously appeared, we could construct a weapon in a timely manner. Is this assumption correct?"

Khalil Muhammad was relieved at the simplicity of this question and he was able to answer in the affirmative with confidence.

"Yes, of course, Mr. President. Everything is in place in that respect."

"Well, Khalil, all I need is your answer and this meeting will be over. I understand that this is stressful for you, but I, as the person ultimately responsible, feel a significant amount of that as well."

Khalil's mind raced in anticipation of unknown factors that could delay any rational estimate he would make, and he thought of the contingencies that would have to fall into place for the plan to work. Time was running out and he stepped to the edge of the abyss of a fateful decision.

"Two months to construct three bombs, Mr. President. A large part of this will be the computer simulations we will have to run in lieu of actual testing of a prototype bomb. Such testing takes substantial time and many hours of valuable computer time. That is my best estimate."

Right or wrong, Khalil Aziz Mohammad was relieved that he had been able to make decisions about a time frame that evidently agreed with President Rashad as he had expressed no objections. Khalil desperately wanted a cigarette and release from this confining room.

"Thank you, Khalil. You have given me the information that I wanted. For the moment, the matter is now in my hands. Pray to Allah that he bestows his favor on our plan."

That evening President met once again with his brother in his spacious house in the suburbs of Tehran.

"Sharif I have consulted with a trusted source about what is possible for us going forward based on the information I have received from you relative to the Pakistani connection. I have formulated a plan that I will share with you and, if you agree in principle, we will implement it immediately."

As the two men drank strong chai and smoked, the President laid out his carefully thought out plan to his brother.

"Based on your recommendation, I have concluded that it is not feasible to steal a weapon in its entirety. The sheer bulk would make it practically impossible to hide from prying eyes. Besides, I am sure the Pakistanis inventory these weapons on a regular basis and would miss one immediately, even if you and your Pakistani partners were able to divert one to our use. No, we must go *small and basic* to maximize our chances of success. Besides, all we need to make a weapon that is useful to us is the warhead itself. I have been assured by our scientists that once they have a workable warhead in their possession, they can fill in the missing pieces that we currently lack and produce a credible weapon."

"I can see that you have put considerable thought into this my brother. Tell me the rest."

"There is the matter of *testing*, which is an extremely important imperative to our scientists. They tell me that every legitimate nuclear program in the world has had testing at its core. Apparently no one wants to produce a weapon of this magnitude that is potentially a 'dud' as they say in the West. Well I intend to test, but not like the scientists are suggesting."

"But, Mahmoud, we will need to test in order to produce credible evidence that we have nuclear assets," retorted Sharif.

"Exactly my point, brother. After the scientists have done their reverse engineering on the *prototype,* as I have decided to call it, I intend to explode the warhead in the Iranian desert far away from any of our nuclear facilities in an above-ground test. This will be the signal to the world that we have produced a nuclear bomb. The news of this test will reverberate throughout the world for many weeks – perhaps months – before the U.N. and the Western world will arrive at a consensus about what – if anything - they can do.

Meanwhile we will be going into the second phase of our plan and will have produced two or three additional warheads that we will place in strategically isolated locations throughout Iran so no military attack will make any sense to either the U.S. or Israel. Even if we are not successful in stealing the additional warheads, the rest of the world will not know this and they must assume we have additional weapons. Therefore, the success of our plan hinges on a successful first phase. We must get a warhead out of Pakistan so we may copy it and then test it."

Sharif Rashad considered his brother's plan for a few moments before continuing to speak. "I understand phase one and believe your reasoning is sound. However, I have two questions that are extremely important to me – as the executor of the plan."

"Yes...go on."

"Do you have any insights about getting a warhead out of Pakistan, and what will we do for the additional bombs you propose to build after we have detonated the prototype?"

"I do have a suggestion about phase one...the prototype...which I think may work. Please let me present it as a possibility and you and your Pakistani contact may explore it for its viability from a practical standpoint."

"Of course, my brother. We are partners on this project and open to all ideas," replied Sharif Rashad amicably.

"Early next month is the annual Pakistani Armed Forces Military parade in Karachi to which all interested parties in the Middle East are invited, friend and foe alike. For example, even the military leaders of India, Pakistan's nemesis in the sub-continent, will be invited. Like many such parades – the Russian Federation's for example - this event was intended to send a message to everyone, once again friend and foe alike, that in this case Pakistan possesses formidable military power and is not to be disrespected or taken advantage of. For the past two years Pakistan has shown its Shaheen II long range missiles on their mobile launchers and given subtle hints that these missiles have a nuclear strike capability. If they are on mobile platforms I think we can safely assume that the missiles have a nuclear warhead assembled with them. It would not be efficient for these mobile platforms to be wandering the countryside in a stealth mode and not have the warheads attached, or at least contained in the mobile platform itself," continued Mahmoud.

Sharif Rashad began to warm to what he was hearing from his calculating brother whose musings only made his job easier. Sharif saw himself as a simple man and always felt more comfortable with his brother as the planner and him as the executor of any plot they concocted together.

The President continued as he paced the meeting room drinking his strong tea, while lecturing his brother as if he were a student.

"All the top military people in Pakistan will be present at the parade as well as those from other countries. I will make it a point to send our Military Chief of Staff to the event and he will personally host a reception at our embassy after the parade, inviting all the military from Pakistan as well as their visiting peers. This will be a do-not-miss event for any high ranking military officer or diplomat."

"After the parade, the vehicles and weapons that have been on display will have to be re-organized and dispersed back to their secure locations. This activity will undoubtedly be supervised by non-commissioned officers or junior ranking officers. Given the size of previous parades, there will be confusion, movement of many men and their equipment, and large-scale vehicular redeployment in the post parade process."

"I will leave it up to your Pakistani friend to make sure that he is personally supervising the marshaling area and, as such, his orders should be carried out unquestionably. This is where we will arrange for the clandestine removal of one of the nuclear warheads from the Shaheen II missiles and its replacement with a dummy warhead. This should be able to be done rather quickly by a small group of technicians who will have previously rehearsed the procedure, and in the confusion of a busy marshaling area, work on one of the missiles by military personnel should not be critically noticed."

Sharif was impressed by the simplicity of the plan and knew instinctively that it had a chance to work. But the most critical aspect of the first phase was actually moving the warhead from Karachi to Iran, and he questioned Mahmoud about their options.

Once again, Mahmoud Rashad's abilities as a cunning plotter made Sharif proud and confident that this bold plan would succeed. It was evident that Mahmoud had thought through the movement of the warhead from Pakistan to Iran with a minimum of potential difficulties.

"Two days before the military parade, one of our crude oil tankers will enter the Baba channel south of Karachi and dock at Oil Pier One to pump out its cargo of crude. Of course, this will be noticed by the American satellite images, but it is a routine thing that is done many times a month. They will pay no undue attention to it."

Sharif Rashad knew this arrangement would be entirely possible as his brother had virtual control over the Iranian National Oil Company and could direct the timing and placement of the tanker fleet at his discretion.

Mahmoud continued with his explanation of his plan. "After your Pakistani General has taken possession of the warhead and the Arming, Fusing and

Firing Mechanism after the parade, it will be transported by military convoy to the Karachi oil pier where it will be off-loaded as cargo onto the tanker under the cover of darkness. Once secured, the tanker will depart and return to our tanker terminal at Bander-e-Abbas where we will take possession of it. This is a very simple plan which gives us a high probability of success."

The two brothers discussed the technicalities of the logistics associated with the plan well into the night, and the next day, as Sharif flew from Tehran to Islamabad, his concerns deepened as he began to know that the ball was entirely in his court. His brother had conceived of this bold plan and had planned the grand strategy to make it come to fruition. True, he had established the Pakistani connection and worked out the financial strategy, but now it was time for him and Zarcash to execute. Three weeks was a short time to put all the pieces into play.

As soon as the Airbus 380 landed in Islamabad, Sharif was on his secure cell phone to Zarcash requesting a meeting the next day.

Like Sharif, Zarcash was impressed with the sheer audacity and simplicity of the plan outlined by Mahmoud Rashad. Sharif was greatly relieved that Zarcash raised no strenuous technical objections when he finished explaining the details. This meant that the president's plan was probably doable with the right amount of planning and skillful persuasion on the part of General Zarcash.

"We have three weeks until the parade, General," spoke Sharif Rashad. "I will be counting on you to make whatever arrangements are necessary to affect the seizure of the warhead and the AFF device, and get them to Oil Pier One where it will be transferred to the Iranian tanker. Once this job has been done, you will be finished with phase one of the plan and you will be free to go about your normal military duties while you plan for phase two of the project."

"And what about phase two?" questioned Zarcash. "The military parade presents an ideal venue for the diversion of one warhead, but there is only one parade per year and getting the other three may present some formidable challenges."

Sharif Rashad was saving the best for last to impress his co-conspirator.

"We will not be stealing any additional warheads, Zarcash," explained the Iranian carefully. "With the *prototype*, as soon as our scientists have reverse engineered it and we have detonated the warhead in the desert, two-thirds of our plan will be in place. Iran will have concrete plans for manufacturing nuclear warheads that have been extensively tested by your scientists, and we will have shown the world that we have a nuclear capability. In doing so, the technical and international relations aspects of the plan will have been accomplished."

"Not to belabor the point, Sharif, but what about the other three bombs? I thought the plan was to have three that would be your arsenal."

"But we will have three, Zarcash. We will build them in Iran."

General Zarcash was momentarily perplexed as he had fully expected to be responsible for the ultimate diversion of four warheads to Pakistan. Now a much less ambitious plan had seemed to have been revealed – one that offered much less risk, but also far less of a financial reward. His spirit was at once deflated and, for the first time, anger threatened to sneak into the equation.

"Then it seems like my role in the plan has been seriously diminished," General Zarcash said testily to a bemused Sharif.

"I will surely not benefit anywhere nearly as much as I originally thought," he continued. "Here I am taking a very great risk for a small amount of compensation."

Sharif let the tense moment percolate for a theatrical moment before he stepped in to calm the increasingly agitated General.

"Au contraire, mon ami," smiled Sharif. "In fact I have just made your job infinitely easier for the same amount as originally agreed." With

ABRUPT CHANGE OF PLANS

this, Zarcash furrowed his brow as if suspecting a trick and looked as his tempter curiously.

"Easier...how so?"

Sharif continued, "Initially I was expecting you to divert very large pieces of hardware over a long distance, which would have exposed you to grave risks of detection and prosecution. Now that is all changed. Now all I require of you is to deliver large suitcases to a border crossing between Pakistan and Iran, where I will meet you with military transport. You do not even have to leave your country in the process, so your movements will not be suspect."

"A suitcase? What could fit into a suitcase that would complete the plan? Are you sure you are not oversimplifying the plan?"

Sharif got up and began pacing the room for maximum effect. "Inside the suitcases, my friend will be enough highly enriched uranium and weapons grade plutonium for us to make the three additional bombs we need for our arsenal. Less than fifty pounds of raw material!"

Zarcash slumped into his chair and beamed at the idea of so simple a plan and how relatively easy it would be for him, a high-ranking Pakistani general, to make such arrangements.

"You seem relieved, Zarcash," confided Sharif. "Evidently you do not object to this change in strategy."

"But, of course," exclaimed Zarcash. "This is far easier than stealing warheads and transporting them. This fissile material that you seek is manufactured under tight security at the Khan Research Laboratories in Kahuta, Punjab, not far from Islamabad. This facility is under the control and scrutiny of the Pakistani Military and I, as Deputy Commander, have full access there."

"What will you do? Simply scoop up this material, place it in a suitcase and leave with it?" asked a clearly skeptical Sharif. "I doubt it is *that* easy."

Now it was Zarcash's turn to toy with Sharif's mind about this part of the plan.

"As we have previously discussed, Sharif, Pakistan disperses its warheads in secure locations throughout Pakistan. There are many reasons for this, but the primary one is safety and security of these from attack by an enemy or diversion by a radical group such as al-Qaeda. One of our primary hiding places is in a vast natural cave complex in the extreme northwest region of the country."

"Due to the fact that these weapons have to be refueled regularly, it is my responsibility to see that highly enriched uranium and plutonium are taken from the Khan Research Laboratories to the various storage sites on a routine basis. I am the supervisor of this activity, but the technical aspects of this are done by our partners, the North Koreans. For safety and security reasons this is done in a military convoy with a senior military officer in direct command. Only I and a few personnel within the Khan Research complex know when such a convoy will leave, so it will be relatively easy for me to arrange such transport without suspicion."

Zarcash continued, "many of our warheads are kept in a vast cave complex in the northwest region, ironically enough, not far from the Pakistani-Afghan border. This cave complex is also frequently used by Afghan Taliban warriors to reassemble and regroup after fighting in Afghanistan, but our storage facilities are kept separate and apart from their activities and there is never any co-mingling of personnel."

"We're sure the Americans suspect Taliban in this region, but it is doubtful that they are aware of our nuclear weapons storage activities there. When we refuel a weapon, we bring the partially depleted fuel back to the Khan complex for enrichment."

"'Depleted' does not mean the weapon will not function, it simply means that it has a reduced yield, say from 100 Kilotons to 60 Kt. Make no mistake, a weapon with a 60 kiloton yield is still exceptionally powerful – enough to wipe out most of a large city like ...*Tel Aviv, shall we say*," he said with a grim smile.

My plan is simple. Instead of sending the depleted fuel pits back to the Kahn laboratories, I plan to divert the shipment directly to your country. When it arrives you will be able to use these fuel pits in the weapons spheres you are building. Once the depleted pits are supplemented with a few grams of tritium their yield will increase dramatically and these will be formidable weapons that will be more than adequate until Iran can reach full highly enriched uranium and plutonium production of your own in no more than three years. In five years Iran will be a substantial nuclear power with international prestige and perhaps even a seat on the U.N. Security Council."

"And you will be rich," added Sharif.

"And living in Cordoba," Zarcash added with a broad smile.

As if on cue, the door to the room burst open and three men walked confidently into the room, two of them wielding compact automatic weapons. In the dim light Sharif could see that they were of Oriental extraction and wearing civilian clothing. The oldest of the three, and the one of greater physical presence, looked at Sharif carefully and said evenly, "Good evening, Mr. Rashad. Please allow me to introduce myself. I am Colonel Young Ho Kim of the Democratic People's Republic of Korea. I am your new business partner." With that, he turned toward General Zarcash, pulled an automatic pistol from its holster and shot him once through the right temple, killing him instantly.

CHAPTER 18

NORTH KOREAN CONNECTION

"A riddle wrapped in a mystery inside an enigma…"
Winston Churchill (Speaking about Russia)

Sharif Rashad recoiled in shock as the North Korean Colonel stood over Zarcash's body with a look of disdain in his eyes. Rashad's dark eyes darted back and forth between the prostrate body of his former co-conspirator, whose blood continued pouring out of the massive head wound and pooled onto the wooden floor, and the Korean killer still holding his smoking pistol. Colonel Kim's companions looked passively on the scene as if they had witnessed this many times before, their faces showing no emotion.

"What…who are you?" Rashad managed to say as the Korean holstered his pistol, finally looking away from the dead Pakistani general, as if satisfied that he had accomplished his mission.

"Why did you do this terrible thing? The man was my friend!"

"The man was nothing but a degenerate gambler who was about to betray his country. Actually, you will thank me later as I have saved your plan from utter failure and you from the gallows," the Korean smiled grimly.

"The plan…what plan? I don't have any idea what you are speaking about."

Rashad was desperately trying to raise some doubt in the mind of the killer – perhaps to the point of giving the Korean second thoughts about what he had just done and running from the scene. Such an action would allow him time to escape...and to think. He needed to think about his daring plan that now lay in shambles with the death of Zarcash. At first Rashad was fearful that he, too, might be killed, but the Korean had said *"you will thank me later,"* which would indicate that he was to be saved – but for what? Such confusion and sudden terror had chilled any ability to think rationally and Rashad found himself like a drowning man, desperately clawing his way to the surface for life-giving breath and, with it, the hope to live another day.

The Korean dismissed his companions after talking to them at some length. Before leaving they wrapped Zarcash's bloody head in his shirt and then picked up his limp body, taking it through the door feet first. In a moment Rashad could hear what sounded like doors slamming shut and an engine coming to life, followed by the unmistakable sound of a heavy vehicle driving away. Rashad and the Korean assailant were now alone.

"Now, Sharif Rashad, Special Trade Representative of the Government of Iran, please allow me to introduce myself further. I regret that my initial introduction had to be so dramatic, but the secret between you and Zarcash would not have lasted many more days and it was imperative that I take decisive action before you two were found out by those who would have been only too pleased to foil this otherwise beautiful plan and ruin any chance for future success. You are too far along to waste this opportunity, my friend."

"I still think you are bluffing, Colonel," Rashad said confidently.

"It would be impossible for you to have any knowledge of any so-called plan between us. We were simply friends who enjoyed each other's company and got together to drink chai and speak of our mutual interest in Islamic affairs. There is no *plan*, as you say."

The Korean general pursed his lips in silent amusement and finally said. "Well Sharif, apparently you are not on the same page with your brother."

After a moment of dumb silence Rashad found himself at the precipice of sensory overload. Within the past few moments he had gone from feeling more confident than ever that the plan for obtaining nuclear weapons from Pakistan was sound and doable, to witnessing the violent murder of the lynchpin and his trusted partner in the crime, to the devastating realization that his brother – the President of Iran – had apparently doubted his ability to manage the operational aspect of the project and had betrayed him to the Korean Colonel standing before him now. Sharif Rashad felt utterly defeated and unworthy of his manhood as this realization flooded over him like a massive haboob from the Arabian Desert.

Sharif Rashad looked up at the Korean standing triumphantly over the wreckage of his former plan with a forlorn expression and simply said, "It appears as if I am at your mercy, Colonel. It is you in whom my brother has placed his trust and not I. However, if he thinks that I was about to betray him, that is unfortunately incorrect. I have always acted in good faith with him on this vital project. Can you tell me why he suddenly came to mistrust me?"

"Mistrust?" replied Colonel Kim. "Certainly that. But not you, Sharif...may I call you Sharif?...No, your brother has the greatest trust in *you*, for the reasons you just expressed. However, most recently he received knowledge through certain intelligence assets about the man you chose to be your confederate at this end. The man who could affect the diversion of the warhead and subsequent transfer of the fissile material was under investigation by the internal security forces of the Pakistani military. They had learned of his substantial gambling debts and other...shall we say...inappropriate behavior and his effort to cover them up. Therefore your brother made the judgment that, because of the risk this investigation posed to the success of the plan, the man had become a potentially vulnerable partner."

"Forgive me, Colonel. But I am very confused about how you fit into this picture. I was aware that several Korean scientists were working with Iranian nuclear scientists on fissile material enrichment and many of them were killed in that unfortunate raid by the Israelis several years ago. I was under the impression that relationship had ended."

"Yes, well, North Korea certainly scaled back our direct involvement after that, but both countries continued to have a number of common interests. We both view the United States as an enemy and we both have a significant interest in the development of nuclear weapons, albeit for separate reasons. The Democratic People's Republic of North Korea wants to protect ourselves against aggression by the United States and South Korea. We may also use our nuclear weapons as a bargaining chip to get more realistic trade concessions from other countries. In the case of Iran, you wish to threaten and intimidate Israel while leveling the playing field in the Middle East. Then there is the whole Sunni–Shiite Muslim thing, which is a mystery to me, my country, and most of the rest of the world."

"But still, why you?" asked Rashad. "Why are you here in this land that is even more alien to you than Iran? At least with Iran, you and your scientists had a common interest."

"Oh but my friend, we do have interests with Pakistan, and we do not feel like aliens here. North Korea has had to dramatically reduce our nuclear weapons development program to placate the U.N. IAEA inspectors who are mere puppets of the Americans. In exchange for this we have been able to get food and other non-strategic materials for our weakened economy. The men who staged the coup against the youthful successor to the 'Dear Leader' Kim Jong Il, saw this as the perfect opportunity to build trust – and buy precious time - between them and the United States."

"But why would Pakistan be interested in working with North Korea on a joint nuclear development project? Pakistan already has many nuclear warheads and is miles ahead of North Korea in this respect," responded Rashad.

"Nuclear programs do not stand still my friend. The weapons must be refined, made smaller to accommodate tactical weapons development and possibly used as bartering material. In today's world, a non-nuclear country lusting after a nuclear weapon is like a nascent automobile buff lusting after a new Mercedes Benz – there is a wide gap to be bridged before fulfillment of the dream."

"Still, why would Pakistan partner with North Korea?"

"Ah, now you ask the key question to which only a few know the answer.

"The answer is quite simple, really. We can scratch each other's backs. North Korea has significant short and long-range missile technology. We are far ahead of the Pakistanis in this respect. The Pakistanis can benefit by us sharing this with them so they defend themselves against the Indians to the south. On the other hand, due to the drawdown of our development program, we have taken a large number of centrifuges out of service. Pakistan has excess capacity of centrifuges.

"Even a beginning student of economics can see that the two countries have compatible needs that are the basis for a partnership. Several years ago this partnership would not have been possible due to the good relations between the United States and Pakistan. Now relations are so strained that Pakistan is beginning to see American as its enemy, particularly after the recent raid into Pakistan by U.S. forces in the northern frontier rescuing American POWs. This couldn't have worked out better for North Korea's interests."

Rashad thought for a moment as he continued to try to understand the situation better. The North Korean connection to Pakistan and how the Korean colonel was to be of assistance in the project was still murky in his mind.

"Since you seem to have the ear of my brother, Colonel Kim, am I to understand that we are going to proceed with our plan, or have the two of you decided on another course of action? I'm sure you understand that I am in a state of considerable misunderstanding at the moment, given the events of the past hour."

The colonel had finally taken a seat in the chair where Zarcash had been assassinated just moments before. He now seemed more relaxed and somewhat more conciliatory in his conversational tone with Rashad.

"Please rest assured that the plan will go ahead as originally conceived, with a few minor changes," the colonel replied. "Over the past several years the

Pakistani-North Korean partnership has grown into one of trust. Although the Pakistanis do have intermediate range guided missiles, such as the Shaheen III's, they have looked more and more to North Korea for expertise in the missile guidance area. North Korean technicians actually do most of the work on these missiles and their mobile launchers and will be the ones responsible for seeing that these are placed correctly in the military parade and re-deployed back to their readiness configurations after the parade has concluded. Since these men work for me, it will be a relatively simple matter for me to see that a warhead gets removed from one of the missiles and taken to the oil pier for loading on your crude carrier for its trip back to Iran."

Once again, Sharif Rashad began to marvel at the level of cunning oversight that his brother had placed in this grand plan to obtain nuclear weapons and material from the Pakistanis.

Sharif had naively thought that his brother had simply turned him loose in Pakistan to develop a contact and allow him to move forward on their behalf, hoping that things would work out well. But, once again, Sharif was reminded of the executive and administrative ability of his brother who always seemed one step ahead of Sharif, but never rubbed his nose in it.

On reflection, the North Korean connection and the involvement of this Colonel, who was obviously ruthless in his approach to success, was starting to make sense. Despite his revulsion at the brutal murder of Zarcash, Sharif decided that he felt no great sense of loss about his former co-conspirator and he thought he would be able to work amicably with Colonel Kim, even though he really had no choice.

"One more thing, Colonel. I assume you are aware that the primary motivation for Zarcash's involvement in this conspiracy was that he was to be paid a significant sum for the delivery of the warhead and the subsequent fissile materials. Does this mean that we are no longer obligated to pay for these items? I'm sure my brother will be pleased if that is true."

The Colonel paused for dramatic effect and gave Sharif a brief smile before answering.

"Why, no, my new friend. It does not mean that at all. On the contrary, as the price for rescuing your important plan and saving it from becoming an embarrassing international incident to your government, you will now be required to pay me."

"Actually, that is what I expected," replied Sharif Rashad somewhat ruefully.

"What I know you did *not* expect," continued Colonel Kim, "is that such payment will have to be paid to me in gold coins and in double the amount that you planned to pay the unfortunate Mr. Zarcash."

In three weeks, the Pakistani military parade went off as scheduled. Diplomatic and military dignitaries from many foreign countries, particularly their neighbors in the Middle East, were there to witness the latest improvements in the Pakistani military arsenal as well as to observe who – friend and foe alike – were also in attendance and, just as important, who was not there. These events were frequently a clue as to budding military alliances and the disintegration of others. This was as much about people watching as observing the weapons on parade.

Missing in person, but present in a more subtle sense, were representatives of the United States of America.

The United States Naval aircraft carrier, U.S. Abraham Lincoln, the flagship of the carrier battle group cruising in the northern Arabian Sea, had launched stealthy drones to cover the parade and augment images being taken by KH-12 (Victor) reconnaissance satellites. These images would be instantly transmitted to the National Reconnaissance Office and, in turn, to CIA Headquarters in Langley Virginia for computer-enhanced analysis.

Two days prior to the Pakistani military parade in Karachi, Colonel Kim and his technicians readied the Shaheen III missiles on their launchers and moved them by rail from their deployment areas. Over the past three years the Koreans had proven themselves so adept at improving the reliability of the new iteration of the Shaheen and increasing the yield of the warhead without increasing the size of the package that the Pakistani military had ceded virtual control of the management of the Shaheens to Colonel Kim and his technicians.

Of course, a Pakistani officer was in command of each mobile missile and its launcher, but only tacitly so, and many things could be done to the package under the guise of 'maintenance,' in which the officer had little or no interest. In essence, Colonel Kim was in command and control of the missiles themselves and only an actual launch toward a hostile target was out of his direct reach.

The actual parade route was along School Road on the north side of the Karachi Military Cantonment Railway Station near the Port of Karachi. This provided a wide boulevard for viewing of military troops and vehicles while the acreage of the abandoned race course to the south of the cantonment provided an ideal staging place for the many elements of men and machinery that constituted the makeup of the parade.

The mobile missile launchers would be brought in via rail to the cantonment and re-deployed on special trains after the parade. In the post parade confusion of the marshaling area it would be a relatively simple matter for the Korean technicians to remove the warhead from one of the launchers and place it on a truck for the ten-mile trip to the Iranian oil tanker waiting in the Baba channel. Three days later it would be in the port of Bandar-e-Abbas, Iran.

On a bright Friday morning in August the first vehicles disembarked from the rail cars and were driven to the marshaling area of the abandoned racetrack south of the military rail yard. There they were cleaned and made especially presentable for the parade. There were tanks, armored personnel carriers, mobile artillery pieces, reconnaissance vehicles, mobile command centers and, of course several varieties of mobile missiles. There was even a Pakistani mini-submarine carried on a multiple axle lowboy flatbed trailer.

The mobile missiles and submarine were primarily there to make Pakistan's traditional enemy, India, aware that any incursion through the Pakistani frontier along their common border would be met with swift, sure retaliation. Both countries had become nuclear powers through a post-World War II blunder of U.S. foreign policy and this had created a potential flash point in the Asian sub-continent that was to plague the rest of the world for years to come. It was one thing for the established nuclear powers to discourage, or even actively work against the proliferation of nuclear weapons, but once the genie was out of the bottle, it was impossible to put it back.

Colonel Kim and his technicians went through their paces flawlessly, preparing the mobile missiles and staging them for the parade. His technicians were the highly educated and skilled elite of the North Korean scientific and military community and felt privileged to be living and working in the relatively free society of Pakistan vis-à-vis the harshly controlled environment of their homeland. Thus the strict obedience to Colonel Kim's every order, no matter how bizarre, was done immediately and without question. Any deviation could be met with swift discipline from Kim and his security staff including punishment of the disciplined one's family still living in North Korea.

The parade began at noon under a blistering sun with thousands of infantry troops marching down School Road past the reviewing stand in their colorful uniforms accented by white leggings and forest green berets, their right arms moving in unison in an exaggerated manner while the other arm cradled their individual weapons. The Pakistani army was nothing if not well-uniformed and dramatic in its marching cadence, a heritage from its British colonial past.

Next came the mounted infantry on ceremonial horses with their manes festooned in colorful regimental banners and battle stripes, ridden by seasoned horsemen – The Grand Pakistani Lancers – who, with imposing and well-manicured facial hair, sat proudly in saddle, riding as the ancient conquerors their ancestors undoubtedly were, once again a throwback to more genteel colonial times.

Then came the more powerful and sinister weapons, either drawn by motorized vehicles or self-propelled, reminding the observers how the modern battlefield had morphed with technology and science. Politicians still plotted, generals led vast armies, and soldiers continued to fight. But with mightier and more fearsome weapons, leading mankind to the precipice of potential annihilation with each new confrontation and giving rise to a new force on the battlefield, the *soldier-philosopher*.

For once — even if for a day — the political leadership of Pakistan saw itself at military parity with its neighbors and other nations. As its armed might marched or rolled by the reviewing stand, the martial music drown out any doubt or criticism being expressed by those who would oppose such a force in the future.

The parade continued for over an hour, finally disbanding and leaving the civilian observers along the parade route momentarily proud of their heritage and confident of their present place in the world. Meanwhile the visiting dignitaries, diplomats, generals, and knights of commerce mingled in the reviewing stand, each with an agenda of the moment, the memory of the parade as a backdrop to the real business at hand.

Later, Sharif Rashad, in his position as Trade Minister from Iran, and his counterpart, the Ambassador from Iran to Pakistan, lavishly entertained over a hundred important guests in a prestigious hotel in downtown Karachi, plying their guests with food and liquid refreshment as diplomatic camouflage to the nefarious deeds being perpetrated only a short distance from this opulent setting.

Concurrently Colonel Kim and his technicians had an agenda of their own as motorized vehicles from the parade jockeyed for position in the marshaling yard adjacent to the Karachi Railway Cantonment. As Pakistani soldiers barked orders and trucks, tanks and other motorized weapons swirled in the dust of the afternoon to be loaded on railroad cars for re-deployment to strategic sites. The Korean technicians, under the guise of needing to perform maintenance on one of the mobile missile launchers, moved it into a garage on the abandoned race course site, removed the nuclear warhead from the launcher and replaced it with one containing no fissile material.

The actual live warhead was then placed in a special lead-shielded container and placed on a truck that immediately began its apparently unremarkable journey to the oil pier in the Baba Channel.

Apparently unremarkable...except to the ever-probing eyes of one of the stealthy Sentinel Drones that glided noiselessly over the parade and the marshaling area, transmitting high resolution images to a NSA communications satellite in geosynchronous orbit 22,000 miles above the surface of the Earth.

BOOK VII

*

DENIAL BY FORCE

CHAPTER 19

FATEFUL TEST

"Now I have become death, destroyer of worlds."
Bagavad Gita – Hindu Scripture

Three days after the military parade in Karachi, the nuclear warhead arrived in Iran at the Bandar-e-Abbas tanker terminal under cover of night. It was quickly unloaded and, under tight security, began its journey to one of the nuclear processing facilities in a remote area of Iran, where it would be reverse engineered by the Iranian scientists prior to detonation.

Every morning the President of the United States receives a document known as the 'President's Daily Brief' prepared by the staff of the Director of National Intelligence. The DNI is a cabinet level position that coordinates input from various American intelligence agencies and distills disparate information into something succinct, consistent and useful to the President and his national security staff in their decision-making process.

Since 2005, when the position of Director of National Intelligence was originally established to coordinate all intelligence under one roof after the September Eleventh attacks, the Director of National Intelligence and the Director of Central Intelligence had jockeyed for the President's ear in matters of influence when it came to these matters. The reality was that the DCI was rarely out of the loop when it came to the hierarchy of intelligence gathering and interpretation and, indeed, the lead source of information for the DNI was, in fact, the CIA.

In the case of Jonathan Braxton's presidency, the fact that he had a longer and more trusted relationship with DNI Rachel Hunter, as opposed to DCI Raymond Rollins, gave Doctor Hunter — as the President frequently referred to her in the presence of other staff - the edge when it came to the President's go-to person for such matters.

This morning both Rachel Hunter and Ray Rollins were present for the briefing of Jonathan Braxton. Rollins wisely deferred to Rachel Hunter in her technically superior position as DNI. Rollins, a wise man himself, edging close to the end of a distinguished career in national service with the position of DCI as the crown jewel in his impressive resume, was no longer interested in turf battles in Washington and knew of the President's comfort level with Rachel Hunter.

Rachel Hunter began by assuring the President that the important information they had for him this morning was largely developed by the CIA, with assistance from Naval Intelligence and the NSA. "Ray," Rachel Hunter began, "since this information comes largely from your shop, why don't you do this part of the brief?" As the DCI busied himself with the digital images he was about to throw up against the screen in the Situation Room, President Braxton smiled inwardly at the wisdom and intellectual honesty of Rachel Hunter and hoped that in his maturing Presidency he would become as gracious and charitable as this talented woman was, sacrificing her ego for the good of the National Security team.

"Mr. President," the DCI began, "last week was the annual Pakistani National Military Parade. Normally this event is held in Islamabad, but due to elevated security concerns it has been in Karachi for the past two years. There may be commercial reasons for this as well as Pakistan is desperately trying to improve its economy and Karachi, with her maritime facilities and commercial infrastructure, is of equal, or perhaps greater, importance as a commercial showpiece to visitors as is its military hardware."

"Otherwise, they have an ulterior motive," remarked Braxton. "But that's hardly material for the Daily Brief."

"But wait sir, there's more," continued Rollins.

"We have reconnaissance satellite images of the parade and also Sentinel drone images of before and after. Mr. President, there are about 20 people in the defense and intelligence establishment that know what I'm about to tell you, and you are about to be lucky number 21. Our Sentinel drone technology is such that we can now detect gamma radiation emissions from very long distances. The drone we were using over Karachi last week detected gamma emissions from all the missiles in the parade, but similar images of the launchers that left the cantonment after the parade showed one launcher without any of these gamma emissions. It also happened to be the launcher that was taken into a garage in the marshaling area after the parade."

"And?" interjected Braxton, his interest piqued.

"This is educated conjecture, sir. But we believe the Pakistani Shaheen III launchers carry, at the minimum, tactical nukes on board because they are the final line of defense against any mischief that might be perpetrated by the Indians. The gamma emissions are shielded, but there is still leakage due to the packaging configuration. The short summary, Mr. President, is that we strongly suspect that a warhead from one of the Shaheen III missiles may have been removed after the parade and has been diverted."

"But where? The place must have been crawling with Pakistani military. What about their security?" asked Braxton.

"This is the kicker, Mr. President," continued Rachel Hunter, "the people servicing the missiles are Koreans...North Koreans."

Jonathan Braxton looked at his intelligence gurus and said blandly, "So, we have a potential nuke gone missing and a bunch of peace-loving North Koreans in serious need of cash with keys to the nuke locker wandering around looking for a customer. What could possibly go wrong?"

"Mr. President, in the immortal words of the late Steve Jobs, 'One more thing...,'" said Rachel Hunter grimly, "we think Iran may be the customer."

As soon as the Iranian oil tanker arrived in Bandar-e-Abbas Sharif Rashad received a coded signal from his office at the Iranian Trade Ministry indicating that the shipment had arrived. He immediately flew to Tehran, where he was reunited with his brother the next evening.

"Once again, my brother, I am overwhelmed by how thoroughly involved you are with our project and the lengths to which you have gone to achieve success," remarked a genuinely impressed Sharif.

Mahmoud Rashad merely gave his brother a weak smile and nodded in agreement.

"I must admit I was shocked about Zarcash but it seems you knew certain things I did not about our partner. Nevertheless, I am thrilled that phase one of our plan has succeeded and want to know what is next."

"What is next, Sharif, as you may suspect, is that our Korean partners wish to be paid – and soon. I need you to go to Zurich to arrange for payment – in gold coins – by our bankers to the Korean representative. I am, of course, disappointed about the increase in the fee we must pay for these services, but under the circumstances it is unavoidable. Upon receipt of the payment, the Koreans will release the AFF mechanism of the warhead to us and we may proceed with the detonation of the bomb in our desert. My estimate – and what I have committed to the mullahs – is that within two weeks Iran will finally be a nascent nuclear power. This will elevate my status as President of Iran for the foreseeable future and make you a hero of the revolution."

A gratified Sharif responded by saying, "If it pleases you, I will leave tomorrow and take care of the matter immediately. The bankers have assured me that they can make payment in gold with two-day's notice. For security purposes I will not make payment myself, but will give a security code to the banker that will match what is given to the Korean. That way there will be no direct involvement...nothing to tie us to the North Koreans.

Two days later Sharif Rashad was meeting with Rene Delagarde in Zurich.

"My supplier has completed phase one of the contracted work and wishes to be paid in gold," explained Rashad.

"Unfortunately there were some...cost overruns...and the price we have to pay for these overruns has increased the value of the contract very substantially. We now owe him five million U.S. dollars for this phase, and he wishes payment of three million in Krugers and the rest in smaller denomination gold coins of various kinds."

Rene Delagarde had no overt reaction other than to raise his eyebrows when he heard about the increase. The gold would not be a problem, but it might take an extra day to make the transfer from another bank. Rene had gone over the terms with Sharif during their initial meeting and he saw no reason to risk any unpleasantness by reminding him that between the increased surcharges for the payment in gold as well as the increased interest for the new fee, this transaction was going to cost Iran much more. Banks performed a valuable service in international commerce and their fees were simply a means to a greater end for all parties. At this stage Iran had no other options.

"And a new twist, which I hope with not complicate matters," added Rashad.

"My supplier wishes to establish an account with your bank where these funds may be kept safely and discreetly. I'm sure you will appreciate the new business," said Rashad in a matter of fact way, attempting to minimize any further questions.

"Well, of course, like all banks we are looking for new business. May I ask who your supplier is?" asked Rene Delegarde.

Rashad cleared his throat and edged forward in his chair before answering.

"Our supplier is the Democratic People's Republic of North Korea. A Colonel Kim and his commander, General Park, will be the two signers on the account."

There was a moment of silence as the two men considered the gravity of what had just been said and Rene Delagarde finally answered softly.

"I will have to discuss this matter with others before I give you a final answer on this. Although I am the Managing Director of the bank, there are certain elements of our business about which I do not have complete latitude. I hope you understand."

Both Rashad and Delagarde knew what Rene had just said was code for having to think long and hard about doing business with the North Koreans. They had a notoriously bad reputation for not paying their sovereign obligations on time, if at all. This did not endear them to those engaged in international commerce. Even tolerant Swiss bankers had their limits when it came to business relationships, and being a business associate of this unpredictable rogue nation had a potential down side. This was a decision for Hugo Delagarde and, perhaps, others.

Accompanying the nuclear device on its trip to Iran from Karachi were three technicians from Colonel Kim's staff. These men had intimate knowledge of the inner-workings of the stolen warhead and were also veterans of nuclear testing that had taken place in North Korea. In actuality, relatively few tests of nuclear devices had taken place since the implementation of the Nuclear Non-proliferation Treaty of 1968, and the Comprehensive Nuclear Test Ban Treaty of 1996, and most of those had been conducted by the Pakistanis, Indians and, most recently, the North Koreans. These scientists and technicians were the foremost experts in this arcane activity. These were the men who would train the Iranians and supervise the detonation of the stolen warhead.

President Mahmoud Rashad and the ruling Shiite mullahs were intent on showing the world that Iran had acquired nuclear weapons technology. There was no strategy to hide the fact. Therefore, the most fundamental decision was whether this detonation was to be an above ground or an underground test of the device. Although an above ground test would be the most dramatic, it would be viewed by the rest of the world as grossly irresponsible from an environmental standpoint and most provocative. By contrast, the last underground tests by the North Koreans in 2006, 2009, and 2013, even with their relatively low yields, were easily detected by Western seismographic monitoring equipment and there was little doubt that an underground detonation in Iran would be immediately detected. Therefore, the decision was made to detonate underground in a remote spot in the Iranian desert, with no history of any significant seismic activity, approximately one thousand miles southeast of Tehran, well away from Iran's oil and natural gas infrastructure.

As usual, Mahmoud Rashad had put a great deal of thought into the location of such a test detonation. It had to be far away from any significant natural resource infrastructure and population area, yet the site would have to have power and water available to support the preparations and actual test. An existing copper-gold-silver mine in Iran's Kerman Province (approximately 29.56 N, 55.51 E) proved the ideal place to conduct the test, and satellite reconnaissance imagery indicating increased human activity in the area could easily be construed as normal mining activity.

In anticipation of the actual receipt of the warhead, the Iranians tunneled into a mountain in the vicinity of the mine and began to make ready the necessary infrastructure to support the test. Within a week after the warhead had arrived at Bandar-e-Abbas everything to support the test was in readiness.

As Rene Delagarde described his strange meeting with their Iranian customer to his father, Hugo, the elder Delagarde flashed back to his previous dealings with unpopular regimes having poor human rights records. There was Iran under the Shah (now only marginally better), the Soviet Union immediately post Stalin with the abuses by the KGB (now noticeably better after Putin) and, of course, Syria under the father and son Assads (now in continued turmoil after Dr. Bashar al-Assad took asylum in Switzerland in 2013), and several others.

In banking as in politics, change and understanding frequently comes slowly, and exercising patience is often wise before coming to a hasty conclusion about an individual or an institution. One might not necessarily like all one's clients, but the color of money over the years does not change. In the end, Hugo Delagarde advised his son to establish an account for the Koreans, but place severe limits on transfers and watch them closely. Hugo had his own plans to watch his new clients.

Two weeks after Mahmoud Rashad had been notified that the test site was ready, the nuclear warhead was transported from the secret Iranian nuclear facility at Mohammadabad, where it had been painstakingly dismantled and reversed engineered by the Iranian nuclear scientists under close supervision of the Koreans, to Kerman Province in a military convoy. The Iranian scientists and technicians accompanying the warhead along with the Koreans and the Iranian security detail were acutely attentive as this most critical final phase of the scheme was about to become a reality.

There were two final touches that had to take place before the weapon could be detonated. The payment had to be made to Colonel Kim. and that payment would trigger the delivery of the AFF device and associated control software that would be the final piece of the package that would make it possible for the warhead to be detonated.

Hugo Delagarde placed a high value on his relationship with Rachel Hunter. He thought it would be mutually beneficial if he informed her, as a follow-up to their recent personal meeting, of the subsequent revealing conversation he had with his son regarding the financial transaction their bank had entered into with the Iranians, which now included a North

Korean connection. Hugo had long since given up being driven purely by financial gain, and in his old age saw personal relationships and integrity as more important aspects of his life. Dealing with the government of Iran was one thing, but when that equation began to include the North Koreans this brought former President George W. Bush's iteration of the phrase "Axis of Evil" to mind. Although as an international banker he was cautious of being too judgmental of his sovereign clients, he thought he could smell nefarious intrigue in this case, and decided that others whom he respected might have at least some passing interest in the matter as well.

Mahmoud Rashad had a trusted intermediary meet with Colonel Kim in Pakistan to give him the two key items that for receiving the payment in gold that had been agreed upon. One was the United States half-bank note that had been prepared by Sharif Rashad when he made the initial arrangements with Rene Delagarde. The other was a single piece of stationary from the desk of the President of Iran with a complex series of upper and lower case numbers and symbols written on it.

There was no message or signature, just the code. Rene Delagarde had an identical document and the person who presented him with both the bank note half and the coded document would be granted access to the funds. Rene would obtain a signature and a fingerprint from the party presenting the documents and these items would constitute proof of delivery to the Koreans. The day after Colonel Kim received the documents he flew to Zurich to meet with Rene Delagarde.

Hugo Delagarde spent one hour at his personal computer – one not connected to the Internet for security reasons – typing a memo to Rachel Hunter in which he detailed the banking arrangement his bank had made with the Iranians and how the North Koreans had come to be involved. He printed it out on a laser printer connected only by a USB cable to his laptop and placed it in a special envelope that had been given to him for such matters by Rachel Hunter herself in one of their previous meetings. This envelope was couriered directly to the American Embassy in Geneva and, once there, was immediately placed in the diplomatic night bag that arrived at the State Department the next day. Rachel Hunter had it on her desk within an hour. Her assistant scanned it, determined that it was safe and un-tampered with, and opened it for the DNI's viewing. Two hours later she and Ray Rollins, along with President Braxton's National Security Advisor and his Chief of Staff, were sitting in the White House Situation Room.

"Mr. President, I have reviewed some recently acquired intelligence with Ray Rollins, and we both agree that this may be confirmation that Iran is actively working with the North Koreans toward getting a nuclear weapon. In fact, this plot may be in its late stages because there has been payment made to a North Korean military officer by a bank about which we have knowledge."

"I take it this was not made by the Bank of America," cracked Jonathan Braxton sardonically.

"No sir. It was an international bank...I'll give you the details if you wish," replied Rachel Hunter.

"That won't be necessary, Rachel. But I think I hear *yodeling.*"

This brought a smile to everyone's face, as Braxton was frequently able to find humor in many situations, even if they were off beat.

"So, assuming this is true – and it's not exactly news that Iran is intent on acquiring a nuclear capability, what are our options here?" continued Braxton.

Jack Duggan, the President's National Security Advisor, took the floor. "The reality is that we don't have many options here, sir. We don't have diplomatic relations with either country, so a discreet inquiry is not possible. We could go through intermediaries, but that could compromise a sensitive intelligence source. Then, even if we approached Pakistan about our suspicions they would simply deny it. That government is so unstable that even a rumor of a missing nuke could cause a major cave-in there. I would say that increased surveillance is all we can do here at the moment."

Colonel Kim arrived at the bank early in the morning and asked to see Rene Delagarde. He was shuffled to a secretary who, in turn, showed him into the office of Rene's administrative assistant.

"Good morning, Colonel Kim. We have been expecting you. I hope you will not mind if we ask you just one or two questions to verify your identity."

"No, of course," was the Colonel's reply.

"I'm sure you are aware that we have certain security procedures since we don't know you personally. My understanding is that you were to have been given a certain item that we are to compare with another such item. Do you have that with you today?"

Colonel Kim produced an envelope, opened it in the presence of Delegarde's assistant and took out the half of the U.S. currency bank note that had been given to him by Sharif Rashad.

"Please excuse me while I verify the authenticity of this item," said the assistant formally.

Rene's assistant went into his office in a roundabout way and silently gave him the bank note which he quickly compared with his half.

'Well this part checks out,' he thought. "Please have Monique escort the Colonel into my office," he said. "And notify the people in new accounts to expect a new client about which I have briefed them. I think the Colonel is authentic."

After the Colonel had been seated and offered coffee in Rene Delagarde's comfortable office, Rene got down to the business of international banking with the Korean Colonel. Most military people, regardless of their confidence, have had very little experience in sophisticated business matters, particularly international finance, and Rene Delagarde was in total control of this aspect of their meeting.

"I want to welcome you to our bank, Colonel. I am pleased that you wish to establish an account with us. But first, there is one more level of authentication that I must request. I assume that the President gave you a document with some data on it. If I may have this, I will compare it to the information I have and we can complete the transaction."

"I must say, I am impressed with the security you have in place here, Mr. Delagarde," replied the Colonel. "I was beginning to wonder whether I would actually meet you."

Rene merely pursed his lips and gave Kim a knowing smile. "One can never be too careful in matters of this nature, Colonel Kim."

The Colonel took the letter from his jacket pocket and handed it to the banker with both hands as he would a gift. Rene looked at the document for a long moment and announced that it was authentic and that the transaction could proceed.

"Now Colonel, I assume you would like to see the gold that we have on deposit for you. Since we are not dealing in sovereign currency here, but rather gold – as you have requested – any withdrawals must be made in person by you. Also, you, as the signer on the account, will be responsible for transporting any such withdrawals from the bank. For future identification purposes, you will have to use our fingerprint verifier when you register for a withdrawal. It is also our policy that any other signers on the account be notified electronically by the bank of your intention to make a withdrawal. We must have their acquiescence in writing to give you access to your gold. This is normal procedure. I hope you will find this not overly burdensome."

The reality was that these were special, cautious provisions placed on this account by Hugo Delagarde himself as a condition of doing business with the North Koreans.

"Candidly, I did not expect there to be so many conditions," Colonel Kim said guardedly, "but if this is your policy, then I have little choice but to conform."

Kim knew that transporting this amount of gold would require considerable resources he did not have, and he must be content, for the moment, to leave the gold in the underground vaults of the bank, severely limiting his options if something went wrong in the future. The inexperienced Colonel signed the agreement with Rene. He was taken to the vault by Rene and some of the bank's security people, not suspecting that he had left samples of his DNA when he used the men's room.

As soon as one of the North Korean technicians received a coded text from Colonel Kim, he turned over the AFF device for the warhead to the Iranians and the arming of the device proceeded. Mahmoud Rashad was notified that the test was in a state of readiness and the detonation would proceed on his order. Iran was finally on the verge of becoming a nuclear power and, in doing so, changing the political dynamic in the Middle East and all of Islam.

At precisely oh-six-hundred hours GMT the seismographs at NORAD in Cheyenne Mountain, Colorado, registered a disturbance of 6.9 on the Richter scale approximately 1,000 miles southeast of Tehran, Iran. Since this geographic region had no history of seismographic activity and there were no aftershocks, the scientific community came to the collective conclusion that Iran had just detonated a nuclear weapon. The news spread like wildfire through every capital in the world and landed like a thud on the desk of the President of the United States.

Rachel Hunter called President Braxton and simply said, "Mr. President, the genie is out of the bottle now, and I don't think we're going to be able to put it back in."

CHAPTER 20

NUCLEAR FORENSICS

"The only use for an atomic bomb is to keep someone else from using one."
George Wald – American Nobel Laureate

The question in the White House situation room was not 'What?' but, rather, 'How?' and 'What is next?' after the blast, undoubtedly nuclear in nature, was detected in the desert of Iran. After years of efforts on the part of the Western countries and Israel, some diplomatic and some military, some cajoling and some little more than wishful thinking, to prevent such a development, the Islamic Republic of Iran had finally tested a nuclear device and was now forcefully knocking on the front door of the exclusive nuclear club demanding entrance and a seat at the table.

Like many so-called *clubs* and loose associations consisting of members with unique characteristics or mutual interests, the Nuclear Club was originally made up of powerful, if not genteel, members who realized the special responsibilities attached to such membership and, as such, made sincere efforts to restrict future entry only to those nations who demonstrated a clear sense of responsibility toward their newly enhanced status as a possessor of the most powerful weapon known to man. Iran had now presented its application in a most forceful manner.

Jack Duggan, the President's national security advisor, had gathered the National Security Team in the Situation Room of the White House immediately after it was determined by NORAD and the CIA that the seismic event in Iran was most likely a nuclear event. The President opened the meeting.

"By now you've all heard that Iran has detonated a nuclear device earlier today. I can't say this was a huge surprise as we all know they have been striving for this for many years. Now, despite our best efforts to thwart this, it has become a reality. This is common knowledge in the world media, and they will be clamoring for a reaction from me and our administration."

"Already Israel is on heightened alert, although I think this is a precipitous reaction. I feel there is a long way to go between testing a weapon and being able to deliver one as an aggressive act."

The President paused for affect and then continued.

"I would like to hear comments and recommendations from the team at this time."

Jack Duggan spoke up first.

"Mr. President, it is imperative that we determine the origin of this device and get whatever details we can about it. This will go a long way in determining how far along they are with this technology."

"Go on, Jack, we're listening."

Duggan nodded at Rachel Hunter as if giving her the floor, and she was ready with her astute analysis.

"Mr. President, the state of nuclear forensics has been advancing quite rapidly in anticipation of such an unfortunate event. A joint working group of physicists and nuclear scientists has been working on techniques, procedures and timelines for nuclear attribution. Based on these recommendations and some exercises they have conducted toward that end, here are some recommendations.

NUCLEAR FORENSICS

"First, we must determine whether this is a HEU or plutonium bomb. If this was a plutonium-based device once we know this for sure, we can determine what type of reactor the plutonium came from. This will help us determine the source of the fissile material used in the bomb."

"I'll take your word for this, Rachel," remarked President Braxton, "I'm just an old mechanical engineer that knows about erector sets and Legos."

"Sir, I have already taken the liberty of giving the NRO the go-ahead to prepare to adjust the ground track of a KH-12 Victor reconnaissance bird over the site. All I need is a signed okay from National Command Authority...."

"You've got it...please continue," urged President Braxton.

"We've got stealth Sentinel drones being configured at Al Udeid Air Base in Doha, Qatar to fly into Iran and get air samples near the detonation. It's important that we do this immediately before the winds disperse the fallout too far."

"Fallout?!... What fallout?" interjected a suddenly alarmed Chairman of the Joint Chiefs of Staff. "I thought this was an underground test."

"Well, it was...sort of," replied Rachel Hunter. "We think it took place at the end of a tunnel that the Iranians bored into a mountain near an old mine. I think they just took an abandoned tunnel and made it larger. That's what previous photo images show, anyway. There was probably gaseous debris that escaped from the end of the tunnel after the detonation that continues to disperse into the atmosphere. If we can get a low flying drone into the area and get some air samples, we should get some forensics data that will help us."

President Braxton looked directly at the Chairman and said, "Max, make this happen right away. Coordinate with Ray Rollins' DDI for the exact coordinates. Better have another drone on standby in case the first one gets knocked down."

Rachel Hunter continued.

"Sir, this next step is radical and everyone can weigh in on this, but we've got to get some ground debris from the outer edge of the tunnel to juxtapose against whatever the drone can get from the air. Even if we get airborne in the next couple of hours, and assuming we get some good air samples, we can't be sure of getting attribution this way. We've got to get some boots on the ground near the edge of the tunnel, and then get out before the radiation is too intense to cause damage to the men. If we don't do this initial forensic work, we're likely to learn nothing about this test or what capabilities the Iranians have going forward."

"I'd like to hear from the Secretary of State on this," asked Braxton.

"Sir, if we don't do this, I'm afraid the Israelis will," answered SECSTATE, Alexander Randolph. "I'm sure every state in the gulf region is concerned about this, even those friendly to Iran. I think a prudent thing to do would be for us to consult with the Saudis as a show of restraint and good faith, and then take some action ourselves to get this information."

"Here we go again, being the global police," interjected Braxton, knowing he was speaking to deaf ears. *'They don't have to be accountable for our actions, like I do,'* he grumbled to himself. *'The buck stops at my desk, not theirs.'*

The meeting was interrupted by Braxton's Chief of Staff, Phillip Johnson, who was reading from a piece of paper that had been handed to him by a Marine Guard who had knocked on the Situation Room door. "It says here in a piece just off the wire from Reuters that President Mahmoud Rashad has just spoken to a group of reporters in Tehran as follows:

> The Government of the Islamic Republic of Iran announces today that it has successfully detonated a nuclear device in the desert region southeast of Tehran, Iran. This test was conducted consistent with accepted environmental considerations concerning such tests, and has successfully demonstrated our ability to defend our nation against any

armed aggression by those who may seek to do us harm. Like other members of the nuclear powers, as they are sometimes known, Iran intends to be a responsible steward of this weapons technology; but we reserve the right to use it as a last resort in the defense of our nation if we are attacked. In a parallel activity, Iran will continue the development of nuclear technology for energy purposes as we have been doing for many years.

After a moment of silence as President Braxton allowed the words of the news to sink in with his staff, he continued. "There you have it, ladies and gentlemen. President Rashad has abandoned all pretense of using its nuclear research program strictly for energy and is admitting that they are aggressively pursuing weapons development. At least we won't have to dance around the head of that pin any longer."

Knowing what he was likely to hear, Jonathan Braxton asked the Joint Chiefs to weigh-in on this development.

"I'm sure I don't have to remind you, Mr. President that you campaigned hard on the promise that you would not tolerate the Iranians achieving nuclear weapons status. The media, as well as your political opponents, are going to remind you of this and expect some response. I'm no politician, sir – God knows – but a number of influential people here and abroad are going to see this test as a provocation and will be clamoring for an armed response. I doubt you will be able to keep the Israelis on the reservation very long after this."

Jonathan Braxton knew the Chairman was right. This President was one of a long line of U.S. chief executives who had consistently lectured anyone who would listen about the dangers of a nuclear armed Iran, and in this case, the proverbial 'buck' had just landed on his desk. He now had to make difficult and fateful decisions that could have wide-ranging ramifications.

Jack Duggan looked for an entry point and jumped in behind the General.

"It seems to me, sir, that we have only one choice. There is no easy access to this area. We would have to go in at night, grab a soil sample, and get out of Dodge right away. This is a six-hour window, tops."

"And who gets this juicy assignment?" asked a skeptical President Braxton.

"One and only, sir; Navy SEALs. They have the training using radiological suits and have the transport systems...and most important, the cajones to pull this off. "

"Well I'll give you the last part, Jack," smiled Braxton, "but how are you going to get them in there undetected and then get them out with the samples?"

"Mr. President, I have Lieutenant Commander Stinson, the leader of SEAL Team Four, out in the lobby. May I have him come in and explain a potential scenario to the group?"

"Wait, Jack. I thought that only the people in this room were briefed in on this. Who is Stinson?"

"He doesn't know what we are discussing here, sir. He's here to brief on a theoretical access and egress situation that could be applied to any covert operation like we have been discussing. They train for this out in Arizona frequently. Lots of open desert terrain, good flying weather, and nobody looking over their shoulders."

"Okay, Jack, bring him in but keep it light and breezy on the nuke aspect for right now."

Jack Duggan brought Commander Stinson in and made the introductions. Stinson was a graduate of the Naval Academy and a Rhodes Scholar, tall and handsome, but with dark eyes that gazed at the group with a curious intensity. Those who knew about these things instinctively saw him as an earnest and determined man, not to be taken lightly. Duggan had a relief map of Iran that spilled over to adjacent countries shown on the screen.

"Commander, we need to grab an important package around the area shown on the map as Kerman province in Iran. The Iranians would prefer that we not come for this package but will be *out-of-town* for a few days. Can you describe to the group here how you and your people could do this with a minimum of detection within a six-to-eight hour window?"

The SEAL commander looked at the map and assessed that the closest friendly entry points would be the two boundary salients along the Iran-Afghanistan border just east of Kerman Province in Iran. These were approximately 250 miles from the objective.

"I doubt that the Iranian air defenses in this part of their country would be significant as this is many hundreds of miles away from their natural resources infrastructure or population centers. We could probably sneak in there with one stealthy Black Hawk and a back-up. How many bad guys will be there?"

"I think they will have cleared out for a couple of days, so I expect very little resistance, if you were detected, Commander."

"How long on the ground should we anticipate?"

"Maybe ten, fifteen minutes, tops."

"May I ask what it is we're picking up, sir?"

Duggan shot President Braxton a knowing glance and replied, "Dirt, commander...a box of dirt and a few small rocks."

"*Right,*" thought Stinson. '*They don't need a SEAL team to go pick up some ordinary rocks.*'

SEAL Team Four was on the way from Little Creek in an Air Force C-17 the next morning headed for Kandahar, Afghanistan. Commander Stinson had a large whiteboard set up forward as well as a map of Iran and southwest Afghanistan.

"Gentlemen," Commander Stinson began after they had been airborne for about one hour, "we are going to infiltrate from one of the salients along the Iran-Afghanistan border, fly in a ground-hugging configuration to a mine near Kerman, land near the entrance to a mine tunnel, scoop up some dirt, and exfiltrate to the other salient. Time in Iranian airspace, less than five hours. Time on the ground, ten-to-fifteen minutes. This may be the most exciting five hours of your life, as we probably won't be able to do much to defend ourselves if there are bad guys there."

"Must be some pretty important dirt, Commander," imagined the Master Chief.

"That's why we're going to be wearing radiological suits, Chief. When we get back to Afghanistan we're going to be deconned by a Chemical-Biological-and-Nuclear (CBRNE) team and the Black Hawks are going to be incinerated. Just another day at the office...I hope all you prospective fathers out there have banked your sperm," he joked darkly. Nobody laughed.

The stealth Sentinel drones took off from the American air base in Doha, Qatar within hours after the test and flew directly east where they crossed into Iran at the intersection of Iran, Pakistan, and the Arabian Sea. From there they flew north-north-west to Kerman Province at approximately 200 miles per hour. When they reached the objective, the drone started transmitting images and taking air samples from the special evacuated cylinders fastened underneath the fuselage.

Since the prevailing winds aloft in this region were from west to east in a clockwise rotation the drones took many samples in the area directly over the detonation point and then made their way eastward to Afghanistan where they landed at Kandahar. There they were met by a CBRNE team that removed the cylinders from the drones, placed them in special lead-lined shipping containers, and placed them on a C-17 bound for Washington, D.C. by way of Ramstein, Germany.

SEAL Team Four disembarked at Kandahar and spent a half day on a refresher exercise using the new Chemical-Biological-Radiation-Nuclear 'Haz-Mat' personal protection suits to be worn at the site near the radioactive debris field. While doing so they went over the high resolution aerial images of the detonation site that had been provided by the KH-12 'key hole' reconnaissance satellites and the Sentinel drones.

The engineers at Lockheed Martin, the manufacturer of the stealth aircraft, had learned many lessons since losing one of the earlier versions of the Sentinel to Iran in 2012. The newer planes were more robust and the navigation software was now virtually impregnable to hacking, the probable reason for the original aircraft's loss.

Although the Iranians had made substantial efforts to reverse engineer the captured drone, there were many secrets that had been built into it that their engineers would have to be very lucky to see. These secrets were now working to the advantage of U.S. military tracking systems as they gleefully watched the Iranian knock-offs being tested over the skies of Iran. Drones they were, stealthy they were not.

An advance team had gone to the take-off point in extreme western Afghanistan to set up a place where the stealth Black Hawks would begin their journey to the detonation site. There would be fuel, food, medical supplies, water, and the other essentials for the ingress of the team to the site. As soon as the SEAL Team took off in the night, this advance team would pack up and go to the egress point and set up to wait for the return of the SEALs and the debris from the detonation site.

At 22:00 the SEALs lifted off in their Black Hawks on this bizarre mission--one of many they would never speak outside of the SEAL culture for many years, some never to do so.

The plan was for the SEAL Team to fly the stealthy Black Hawks at a ground hugging flight path from the Afghanistan-Iranian border salient to the edge of the debris field formed by the nuclear detonation at the opening to the horizontal mine shaft used for the underground test. There they would set up a security perimeter around the LZ while the three SEALs in the 'sampling group' scooped up samples of dirt and small rocks from the debris field into special containers and take them back to the two Black Hawks that had made the trip. Redundancy was a key, in case one of the choppers was detected and possibly shot down by Iranian forces.

The undetected infiltration to the test site by the stealthy SEAL Black Hawks was aided by an AWACS from the U.S.S. Abraham Lincoln carrier strike group flying over the Strait of Hormuz, jamming the Iranian air defense radar scans facing eastward toward Afghanistan and Pakistan with its advanced software. As far as the Iranians were concerned this night, the airspace eastward into the remote and unoccupied deserts was devoid of any activity and they could rest easy. They had not counted on American technology and motivation to seek out the truth about Iran's new-found nuclear assets.

The evacuated air cylinders from the drones, now filled with molecules and small particles absorbed from the air downwind from the detonation of the nuclear device, had arrived at a testing facility at Aberdeen Proving Ground in Maryland and the results of the preliminary tests were in. The U.S. military and the CIA, in international cooperation with other responsible members of the nuclear club, had meticulously compiled a database of air, water, ground, and actual radiological samples from various nuclear tests and nuclear processing facilities throughout the world since nuclear testing had begun in earnest shortly after the end of World War II.

In spite of the competitive nature of nuclear weapons development, nuclear scientists and physicists, a notoriously cautious lot who were often apologetic about their work on weapons of mass destruction, had been concerned since the earliest days that nuclear proliferation be minimized. Common sense demanded that radioactive 'signatures' from various types of reactors be catalogued into a standardized database that could be used for nuclear attribution in case fissile material was unintentionally or illegally diverted from its ethical use. It was this database against which the samples gathered after the Iranian nuclear test was compared.

"Mr. President, gentlemen."

Rachel Hunter spoke from a podium in the White House Situation Room and used a laser pointer to identify various areas on the Power Point slide that was projected on the screen.

"Based on preliminary evidence from the air samples we were able to obtain right after the detonation three days ago, our scientists think there is a 60 to 75 percent chance that this device was based on plutonium processed in Pakistan. In order to be one-hundred percent certain, we have to get soil samples from the debris field outside of the blast tunnel."

Rachel paused for a moment and asked an Admiral from SPECWAR out of Southern Command in Tampa, Florida, to brief the National Security Team on the progress of the SEALs who had been dispatched on that mission.

"Director Hunter, gentlemen, the latest information I have is that the SEALs are airborne into the objective and should be on site within one hour. We are following their progress with the Sentinels and should have visual confirmation as soon as they reach the LZ. The AWACS is jamming with the new radar suppression software and so far we are seeing no Iranian air defense activity that would indicate they have been detected. With any luck, I think we have a clean operation here."

The mission status light inside the Black Hawk carrying the lead SEAL team went from green to amber as the GPS system tracked it within five miles of the objective. At two miles it began flashing amber, and when the red light came on the SEALs knew they were at their objective, approximately 500 meters from the mouth of the tunnel. As the Black Hawks settled-into the site the SEALs scrambled to unload from their helicopters, looking like something out of a science fiction film. Burdened with their weapons and sampling materials, the SEALs in their ungainly CBRN suits and night vision gear made their way across the site, deploying clumsily to assigned positions and looking all the while like astronauts walking across the moonscape. The pilots, themselves clothed in the Haz-Mat suits in consideration of the overall 'hotness' of the site, reluctantly let their rotors spin down to the idle position in order to reduce the velocity of the soil particles around the aircraft. The SEALs knew this was the point at which they were most vulnerable.

The SEALs forming the security element cursed the HAZ-Mat suits that were not only hot, but reduced their field of vision and mobility – key factors in establishing a secure LZ for the other members of the team. Every man was concerned that a kinetic exchange with Iranian forces could quickly go bad for the Americans if they could not fight as they had trained. Each SEAL counted the minutes, hoping that the recovery element would make it quickly to the debris field in front of the cave, grab their samples and expedite back to the LZ.

As for the SEALs in the recovery team, each of the three men consulted their advanced individual GPS indicators and when they showed consensus as to exact location within 25 feet, they formed a skirmish line running east-to-west, parallel to the direction of the tunnel and spread out at one-hundred meter intervals from the mouth of the tunnel. When each man reached his planned position he quickly scooped up the required sample and placed it in the special shielded and numbered container he carried.

Once the sample was secured, each man sounded off on the command channel.

"One done...two done...three done."

Lieutenant Maxwell, the OIC of the recovery element then commanded, "CLEAR...CLEAR...GO...GO."

At his command the two other members of the team ambled clumsily toward the waiting Black Hawks with their soil samples, but Lieutenant Maxwell stumbled as he made his way across the rugged rock fall. Maxwell managed to hold on to his sample container, but as he rolled forward in an effort to right himself, the fabric of his Haz-Mat suit near his right knee ripped as it caught against a jagged piece of rock. Maxwell's body recoiled in pain as dark red blood spurted from a laceration across his kneecap. He managed to key his microphone and said in a normal tone, despite his pain, "Six this is Max...I'm down. Need help. Shit, I'm down bad."

As the pilots reengaged their rotor transmissions and the SEALs counted off as they gratefully reloaded the quivering reaccelerating Black Hawks, Lieutenant Stinson, the SEAL Commander of the mission used all his substantial physical strength to carry Lieutenant Maxwell across the debris field toward the second Black Hawk. "Chief, this is six; I need a head-count. Do we have everybody?"

"That's affirm, six. I personally counted. Do you need help?"

"Negative, Chief. I'm within 25 feet of number two. I've got Max. Tell the pilots to spin 'em up...we're leaving Dodge."

After thirty long seconds, Stinson dumped a bleeding Maxwell into the cargo bay of the first Black Hawk and threw himself in immediately behind him carrying the two sample canisters with his other hand.

"Black actual, GO...GO! He spoke urgently into his radio microphone to the lead Black Hawk pilot."

In ten seconds they were airborne in a swirl of radioactive dust and the shrill whine of powerful turbine engines, turning east toward Afghanistan. Unknown to anyone on board the two Black Hawks, Lieutenant Maxwell was already getting sick.

Less than two hours later the two Black Hawks arrived at the Iran-Afghanistan salient chosen for the entry point back into friendly territory. The SEALs were immediately taken to the CBNRE decontamination point where they began the arduous process of nuclear decontamination. After going through a series of pressurized water and detergent cleansings, each followed by a Geiger counter scan, they eventually were deemed free enough of any 'hot' material to finally take off the Haz-Mat suits, which were placed in the Black Hawks to be destroyed by fire in large earthen pits dug by bulldozers prior to the mission.

Lieutenant Maxwell had to be helped through the decontamination process as his knee was so swollen that he could barely walk. At this point only the decontamination technicians and the doctor heading up the medical team knew how much danger Maxwell was in due to the large tear in his Haz-Mat suit that had exposed him to radiation at the debris site. The army doctor ordered the med evac helicopter staged at the egress salient to be dispatched immediately to rush Maxwell to the military hospital at Kandahar, but knew that due to the large dose of RADS to which he had been undoubtedly exposed, especially through an open wound, his chances of recovering from the inevitable radiation sickness were fifty-fifty, at best.

The contaminated Black Hawks were soon bulldozed into the deep pits from upwind and all contaminated material from the site was thrown in on top of the multi-million dollar pile of radiologically hot junk and set afire from 55 gallon drums of Jet-A fuel poured onto the wreckage. The intense flames eventually ignited the contaminated material into a conflagration witnessed from afar by the SEALs and the support team of the mission. As the flames subsided, the D-9s moved in again to bury the twisted, unidentifiable conglomeration of remnants of the tools of war under tons of previously excavated dirt. In a thousand years this would be an archeological site for scholars.

Rachel Hunter met with the President and Jack Duggan personally in the Oval Office as there was no need for the NSC as a whole to weigh in on these results.

"Mr. President, based on the examination of the contents of the canisters that the SEALs retrieved from the detonation site, there is now no doubt that the source of the detonation was fissile material from Pakistani reactors. The bomb exploded was definitely a warhead that was produced from Pakistan. We could prove that in court."

"Okay, now Rachel, what do we do with all this intelligence that we have produced at so great a cost?"

"As you know, sir, this is *the news* of the World right now. The Israelis have beefed up their DEFCON to the highest level in years and even the Russians and the Chinese are showing signs of disapproval. If the Euros didn't need Iran's oil so badly they'd be screaming 'foul' even louder."

"Jack, what do you think?"

"*I think*, Mr. President, that our options are equally unappealing. People will be remembering your promise not to tolerate Iran having a nuclear weapon. But, as usual, there are no easy solutions. The U.N. is impotent and if we try to blockade Iranian oil out of the Strait of Hormuz, the Euros are just going to get pissed at us because they're Iran's best customer."

"Okay, okay, Jack. Why don't we start with what we know and what we don't know? We need to make good decisions based on facts, not conjecture."

"Rachel, you're the keeper of the facts about this situation. What you are your thoughts?"

"Sir, what *we know* is that Iran has detonated one nuclear device that they obtained *some way* from Pakistan in a remote spot in their southeastern desert where we have never detected any sort of nuclear activity. Unfortunately, this known fact pales in significance to what we *do not* know. More specifically, did they get more than one warhead and, if so, how many more? Was the government of Pakistan complicit in this diversion and, if not, who, if anyone, assisted Iran in obtaining this capability? Does this mean that they already have or are close to having a home-grown capability and they are trying to confuse us by setting off the Pakistani warhead? Last, what are their intentions, short and long term, regarding the exploitation of this capability? The answers to these questions are keys to us developing a prudent response to this provocation."

"Sir," Jack Duggan interjected. "The Israelis are frothing at the mouth about this. I talked to their Defense Minister earlier and they are seriously considering an air strike against the Iranian nuclear facilities. If they decide to do this, I doubt we can influence them to stand down."

"I understand their concern, Jack. They are the ones most directly threatened and with the most to lose in the near term. *However*...strike *where?* The Iranians have wisely spread out their R & D and processing facilities to many different sites as well as hardening them. Our military planners have told us repeatedly that striking a decapitating blow to this activity is next to impossible. And there are two other things for both the Israelis and us to consider. First, they will not accept a large attack without retaliation. A worst case scenario could be that they have one or more devices ready to use in response to an attack. Second, I believe the Saudis may passively accept *some degree* of prudent response from the West to this provocation – after all they may feel some threat here as well – but too great a response may trigger their Islamic loyalties, even though they are Sunnis."

"That might motivate them to come to the defense of Iran, although purely for economic reasons. So, in the immediate short term, I am sending Secretary Randolph out tomorrow to Riyadh, Tel Aviv, Moscow and Beijing to try to develop a coalition willing to confront the Iranians diplomatically, while at the same time getting answers to Rachel's questions. Any objections or comments on this?"

Lieutenant Maxwell had been taken to the U.S. Military Hospital in Kandahar, where he had been immediately diagnosed with radiation poisoning. Kandahar couldn't deal with this effectively long term, and he was scheduled to be transferred to Ramstein for further treatment.

The night before he was to be flown out, his condition deteriorated dramatically and he died. Perversely, he was the first casualty of the Iranian nuclear era and was yet another Navy SEAL to die in a remote place, on a classified mission, the details of which his family and friends would never know.

Rachel Hunter and her dedicated and diverse intelligence staff had been digging feverishly for answers to the questions she had raised to President Braxton three days ago. As she carefully thought back over the large amount of data amassed about the Iranian nuclear program an important clue seemed to arise from the meeting and the follow-up personal correspondence she had with Hugo Delagarde. It seemed clear to the elder Delagarde, who had communicated this to Rachel Hunter that the North

Korean Colonel had recently been paid for the initial milestone of a larger contract, the subsequent aspects of which had not yet been delivered. This fact begged the question, *'Is the Korean Colonel now engaged in subsequent activities relating to the Iranian nuclear program for which he expects to be paid additional sums?'*

Rachel and her staff decided that this was a good bet. They also thought that the answer to this question held the key to the others.

Max Jenkins' official title was Special Assistant to the Director of Internal Security of the Central Intelligence Agency. This was a politically correct way of saying that he was a trouble-shooter and a problem solver for the executive staff of the CIA. He was a highly educated man who held a degree in Nuclear Engineering from MIT and an MBA from Harvard.

Jenkins travelled the world on CIA business armed with a diplomatic passport and a unique black carry-on bag that virtually screamed 'don't even think about opening this bag.' In it he carried a 9mm Sig Sauer P-226 handgun, an encrypted Iridium telephone, and a laptop that would probably befuddle the most skillful hacker. For emergency funds he carried several multi-domination gold coins, approximately $10,000 in U.S. currency and Swiss Francs, as well as a Black American Express Centurion credit card with which he could make virtually unlimited purchases in nearly any legal environment, Worldwide.

When Max would show up at an American Embassy and present his diplomatic passport he would have automatic access to the Ambassador or his deputy. On the Ambassador's 'Eyes Only' computer files, there would be a simple notation introducing Jenkins as a 'Special Representative' of the CIA with instructions to "Give Mr. Jenkins 'complete cooperation' and get him anything he needs for his work in your jurisdiction." Even the CIA Chiefs of Station at the embassies knew Jenkins either personally or by reputation, and knew enough to stay out of his way unless he was pressed into service by Max, which was infrequently.

Max Jenkins held this unique position because he was highly intelligent, displayed profoundly good judgment, had unwavering loyalty to the USA in general and the CIA in particular, and he could keep his mouth shut and emotions under control. If he wasn't doing the bidding of his masters at Langley, he raised orchids at his bachelor home in Georgetown. A CIA colleague once asked him if he had ever seen a James Bond movie and he had replied, "I wouldn't be interested in seeing a movie about me."

The day after Hunter's meeting with the President, Max Jenkins was dispatched on his way to Zurich by Rachel Hunter, carrying a hand written note to Hugo Delagarde.

> Hugo –
> Mr. Jenkins is my personal representative in this matter. Please provide him every courtesy and your candor, just as you would to me in person.
> Highest urgency!
> Best personal regards,
> R.H.

The bank took its security precautions very seriously, particularly when there were very large sums and new clients involved. Colonel Kim, unknown to him, had been photographed several times while in the building, his voice recorded on high quality audio and video equipment, and his DNA sampled. All this information was turned over to Max Jenkins along with Rene's recollections of Kim's recent visit. Max personally delivered this intel to Rachel Hunter after a red-eye flight from Zurich.

"Mr. President, we have learned several things about the North Korean Colonel who visited the Swiss bank between the times our aerial reconnaissance detected the missing gamma radiation from a missile in the military parade and just before the Iranian nuclear detonation. First, he originally told the bankers that he and a North Korean general would be signers on the account, but then he reneged on that when our banker friend told him the general would have to present himself to become a signer. Therefore,

I believe there is enough evidence to connect the dots here and create a strong suspicion that the Korean colonel was the conduit for the Pakistani warhead and that he may be preparing to complete other tasks associated with the first."

"Rachel, I've known you a long time and I trust your judgment in the extreme. However, I have to have a little bit more than this to connect the dots, as you say, enough to move forward."

"Well, Mr. President, we may just have a clincher here. About two weeks before the military parade, the wife of General al Zarcash contacted the American Embassy in Islamabad through an intermediary who told one of the intelligence staffers that the wife of a Pakistani Army General who had just committed suicide wanted to talk to us about his death. So a meeting was set up promptly at a neutral site but the wife of the officer never showed up.

In situations like this, we seldom follow-up unless we suspect something fishy, and this never made it into the morning report we received at Langley. Well, after the gamma radiation report, I asked the DDI to check back with the Islamabad Station Chief for *anything even remotely noteworthy* that might not have gotten back here.

He did some checking and told me about the woman who never showed for her appointment. I asked him to try to reconnect with the intermediary, and they arranged another meeting. This is where it gets weird, sir. It turns out that the general's wife is now missing and has been so since the day before the scheduled first meeting. However the intermediary friend did agree to meet with my station chief and said that the general's wife had been very agitated about her husband's death and didn't believe it was suicide. Furthermore, she had told her friend that her husband was doing something very important for a *friend from Iran* that might make them a great deal of money so they could retire to Dubai. In his job as Deputy Commander of the Pakistani Army, he had total and regular access to the nukes. I know this is thin, sir...especially the third-hand stuff, but when you put it together with the rest of the intel, the dots get closer together."

"Let's review here, Rachel, and try to connect those dots of yours," replied a suddenly intrigued President Braxton.

"Okay, here's what I think we have," continued the DNI.

"First, we have a detonated nuke in the Iranian desert that evidence clearly shows was from fissile material processed in Pakistan. Then we have pretty decent evidence that the warhead was taken off a Pakistani missile that was being serviced by North Korean technicians in Karachi. This warhead could easily have been moved by sea from Karachi to Iran…no direct evidence of that, however. Next we have a North Korean Colonel showing up at a bank in Switzerland with which we have an excellent, but clandestine, relationship, claiming payment in gold from funds previously arranged for by the brother of the President of Iran. He then insinuates that he will be back soon to collect the remainder of the bounty. I know it's not air tight, sir, but my guess is that the Korean colonel found out about the Pakistani General's plans due to his tight connections with their nuclear program and decided to cut himself in on the action by killing the general and making it look like suicide. In summary, sir, I would say that we need to keep our eye on the North Korean Colonel to see what he's planning next."

"And what do you plan on doing with our North Korean friend, Rachel, other than to foil him in his dastardly plans?" asked a slyly smiling President Braxton.

"What all good spymasters do, Mr. President, when they don't have a good source of HUMINT where they desperately need one – North Korea being an excellent case in point. I plan to confront him and threaten to out him in his disloyalty to his North Korean boss, then recruit him as a double agent, and turn him. He's going to be our Julius Rosenberg with the North Koreans," referring to the American who gave atomic secrets to the Russians immediately after World War Two.

CHAPTER 21

OUT – RECRUIT – DOUBLE

"Espionage, for the most part, involves finding a person who knows something or has something that you can induce them secretly to give to you. That almost always involves a betrayal of trust."
Aldrich Ames – Convicted American Spy

The Democratic People's Republic of Korea was one of the few areas of the World where the CIA had significant difficulty getting solid intelligence. Primarily due to the isolationist attitude and paranoia of the dictatorial regimes that had ruled North Korea since the tenuous truce that ended the Korean War in 1953, the West had found it extremely difficult to get strategic reliable human intelligence out of the secretive nation. Under normal circumstances obtaining information about a backward, third world country with few natural resources would not have been a great priority, except for the fact that the DPRK had developed nuclear weapons, and was close to developing delivery systems that could threaten America's allies, South Korea and Japan, with very little prior warning.

North Korea was chronically short of food for her half-starved population and was in many ways like a cornered animal that might at any time use all of her remaining strength in an attempt to survive. The CIA was most anxious to have a knowledgeable agent in deep cover who could deliver reliable information about the intentions of this secretive government and its cult-like military regime.

Colonel Young Ho Kim of the Democratic People's Republic of Korea was not a spy, not in the strictest sense. But he did possess many attributes that, at least in Rachel Hunter's view, made him as good as one. Colonel Kim was a trusted North Korean Army officer who was also knowledgeable about nuclear weapons and delivery systems. This made him among the elite in their military hierarchy. He was also trusted to be allowed to travel almost at will on a DPRK diplomatic passport outside the closed society that defined the DPRK, since he had been judged as ideologically pure by the past three dictators – of a common genetic heritage - who had ruled that country ruthlessly since 1949.

In a ploy aimed at obtaining much needed foodstuffs and raw materials from the United States and Japan, the current North Korean military leaders had convinced the U.N. IAEA that the nuclear development program that had been so troubling to the international community in the early part of the twenty-first Century had been put on hold. Instead, this work had secretly been moved to Pakistan under the direction of Colonel Kim in exchange for North Korean missile and satellite technology as well as bribes of gold to certain Pakistani political leaders. All these factors allowed Colonel Kim to travel freely without suspicion between Pakistan and North Korea primarily via Air China, which did not have a history of cooperating with other nations regarding sharing information on passenger manifests. In the mind of Rachel Hunter, Colonel Kim would be an ideal agent to have working for the USA, and what better motivation would he have than his already proven love of the world's most coveted currency, *gold*.

The challenge ahead for Rachel Hunter was to track down the elusive Colonel Kim and arrange a pre-planned encounter between the colonel and a CIA operative who could make him aware that they were on to him and give him some options, only one of which would be realistically palatable.

Chang-Sun Yee was a third generation American who had received his Ph.D. in physics from the University of California at Berkeley and was now working at Sandia National Laboratories in Albuquerque, New Mexico. He was also a frequent visitor to the Large Hadron Collider (CERN) near

Geneva, where the long elusive Higgs Boson sub-atomic particle was finally validated in 2012.

To theoretical physicists, CERN was like the Vatican was for Roman Catholic priests, and many scientists made pilgrimages there frequently to meet with peers and exchange notes about their current research. Dr. Yee was also a patriotic American who occasionally did contract work for the CIA. His cover, of course, was his bona fides as a respected nuclear physicist and the fact that he was frequently a participant in international scientific conferences. Rachel Hunter decided it was time to send Max Jenkins to Albuquerque to meet with Dr. Yee.

The CIA and the U.S. Department of Energy, which had oversight of the Sandia facility, had established a safe meeting place for sensitive conversations in the basement of a bank building in downtown Albuquerque. Meetings were set up between CIA handlers and certain scientists such as Dr. Yee through a coded message on an Internet chat room that would only make sense to its intended recipient. At the appointed time he would go to the bank building and make his way to an office which provided access to an elevator that took him to a private room in the basement where he would meet with his CIA handler. No third party would ever witness a personal meeting or see a conversation between Dr. Yee and a CIA operative.

Since Dr. Yee was not a full-fledged CIA operative, the information given him was compartmentalized at any particular time so he would know just enough to accomplish a specific low level task. Therefore, if he was compromised there would be very little to endanger him or reveal anything beyond what he had been told. He was well paid to perform such services and felt it added a sense of intrigue to an otherwise mundane professional life.

Max Jenkins met with Dr. Yee in the secure room at the bank on a Tuesday evening.

"Doctor Yee, there is a conference in Geneva later this month that I think you are slated to attend. We have information that there will be a Pakistani physicist in attendance there, a Doctor Kamal al-Jubar. We know his primary work is at the Khan Nuclear Research Complex near Islamabad. There is a North Korean Army colonel by the name of Kim who also works there from time to time. The simple but vital task we have for you is to give a note to Doctor al-Jubar and ask him to pass it along to Colonel Kim in confidence."

"Your cover will be that you have family connections with Colonel Kim and it is nearly impossible for you to communicate with him through normal channels. This will make the role of Doctor al-Jubar one of innocence – doing a favor for a professional acquaintance – and making Colonel Kim curious that the request might be benign. Do this on the last day of the conference, just before you are to leave, so there will be no opportunity for Doctor al-Jubar to question you further after you have made the request."

Doctor Yee responded that it seemed like an easy enough task and he would be pleased to do it. Max then reached into his jacket pocket and slid an envelope across the desk to Doctor Yee.

"Here is $1,500 in used U.S. currency that has no traces of drugs on it. You may be surprised to learn that such unadulterated currency is hard to come by these days, doctor," said Jenkins lightly.

"We don't want you to ever get held up by Homeland Security or TSA types with the cash we pay to you that could prove embarrassing."

"What about the envelope I am to give to Doctor al-Jubar?"

"The woman sitting next to you in business class on the Delta flight out of JFK to Geneva will pass that along to you covered with a <u>Scientific American</u> magazine after they serve the meal. We don't want to burden you with this until it is necessary."

"Are you at liberty to tell me if there will be any follow-up activity relating to this initial contact, Mr. Jenkins? These occasional small jobs are rather exciting for me," Yee asked hopefully.

"Doctor Yee, we have been very satisfied with what you have done for us so far. Let's leave it at that. But my advice is, *be careful*; remember what Robert E. Lee said after a bloody battle in the civil war: 'It is well that war is so terrible, or we should grow too fond of it.' The same could be said for intelligence work."

The note composed by Rachel Hunter to be given to Colonel Kim was simple and direct, written in Hangul, the written language of both North and South Korea:

Colonel Kim:

I represent the American government at the highest level and arranged for this note to be delivered to you by an unwitting accomplice. Despite their elaborate security procedures, I have detailed knowledge and substantial evidence of your recent business transactions with a certain Swiss banking institution.

I give you the following options to be acted upon within 24 hours after receiving this message:

1. You may choose to ignore this letter and the evidence we have will be turned over to your masters in the DPRK through back channel diplomatic channels. I am sure you are aware of the consequences of this most unfortunate choice.

2. You may choose to meet with my representative at a safe and neutral site in Islamabad to discuss the conditions under which you may safely continue in your present professional duties while providing us with information that is valuable to us.

If you choose option two, you will be well compensated and your cover will be protected. In addition, if you perform well, there may be a possibility for you and your family to come to America and live under our protection with a generous stipend.

There is, of course a third option, and that is for you to attempt to run with the funds you have on deposit at the bank or to kill yourself, hoping that it will look like an accident, thus sparing your family.

This third option will only bring extremely negative consequences for you and your family.

If you wisely choose option two, please post the enclosed pre-packaged note at a Federal Express office in Islamabad within 24 hours.

My representative will be on a park bench near a fountain by the Indus River tributary at University Road Park a week from Thursday at 5:00 PM wearing a red hat.

You will be in civilian clothes carrying a newspaper in your left hand.

(Signed) 'Marker'

The note was passed innocently to Colonel Kim by the Pakistani physicist the day after he returned from the conference. Like a cornered animal, Kim knew that his only options were those that were outlined in the note from 'Marker' and that he had little choice but to pursue the second option. There was no thought of fighting or trying to outsmart the American intelligence apparatus. His instincts told him they had planned this carefully and waited for just the right moment to spring their trap. In fact, it was likely that he was probably being followed at this moment.

If discovered by his North Korean masters, the consequences of his financial greed would mean certain death, torture, or internment in a North Korean labor camp for his wife, children and any relatives that could be found. No, the odds of beating this entrapment were slim and all the fight went out of Colonel Kim within a very few moments after reading the letter from 'Marker.' That evening he posted the Fed-Ex letter at the Islamabad office and went home to a sleepless night.

✱

Rachel Hunter met with President Braxton and Jack Duggan in the Oval Office immediately after her station chief in Islamabad connected with Colonel Kim in the designated place.

"Well, Rachel, tell us how it went down," asked Duggan. "We seldom hear the exciting details of the cloak and dagger stuff."

"The Colonel met with our station chief and was surprisingly cordial, considering the circumstances," confided Rachel.

"This meeting was very short, but he agreed to meet the next day in a more private setting. We reiterated the terms and conditions and emphasized how important it was to trust us. My guys got to spend two hours with him the next day at a safe house in a bazaar in Islamabad very close to his residence. He was not followed. Koreans stand out in a place like Pakistan and that makes security for Colonel Kim very obvious, friend or foe. He speaks good English and I think we have an excellent understanding with him. He is aware that we know a great deal about him and his family, as well as his masters in Pyongyang. This has been one of the easiest turns we've made in a long time."

"Well, what's next, Rachel," inquired Jack Duggan.

"First we're going to help him learn some basic tradecraft so he can get information to us safely and reliably. Then we're going to test him with some easy stuff — some things we already know about the Pakistani nukes that he doesn't know we know. We'll progress from there to see how honest he is...I know, I know...an *honest spy* is a contradiction in terms, but we have a plan here. Once we establish some mutual confidence we're going to get to the hard stuff — the Iranian connection. That will be the real test. The more confidence he has in our relationship, the more willing he's going to be to abandon the Iranians, especially since we're his new paymasters. He asked about the gold in Hugo's bank and we told him that if he plays ball, maybe he'll wind up with *some* of it. We'll see!"

Braxton had been listening patiently to the dialogue and broke in.

"Not to get too far ahead of ourselves here, but I would like to do some war-gaming of the path forward based on a few raw assumptions. Bear with me here, people, while we try to move the needle toward an end-point."

President Braxton was warming to the task here and paced the room as he thought and spoke.

"Let's assume, as a baseline fact, that the Colonel was working with the Iranians as the conduit for getting the nuke out of Pakistan and into Iran. He was obviously doing that for someone at the highest levels of the Iranian government. It's vital that we find out the identity of that person or persons and then to know what the end game is, since Rachel thinks there is a phase two and maybe even a phase three to the plan. Once we know that, we can plan to deal with that and thwart these phases without compromising Colonel Kim. He'll be of no value to us if he's found out."

Braxton cast a conspiratorial glance at both Rachel Hunter and Jack Duggan before continuing.

"Therefore I think we've got to determine who his Iranian contacts were, if there was a phase two, and if so, what that is going to be. Once we know this, we can start planning. We've got to work fast as the follow-up to the first warhead may already be in play."

Max Jenkins was on his way to Pakistan that evening with a personal note from Rachel Hunter to the Islamabad CIA Station Chief. She trusted her station chief, but she knew that Max Jenkins had earned his bona fides in Iraq and Afghanistan in the early days of the conflicts there and knew how to press all the right buttons to get solid intel in a hurry from a wavering source.

It had taken Max Jenkins a little over an hour of face-to-face conversation with Colonel Kim to learn the total story of how his relationship with Sharif Rashad began and then evolved into the successful hijacking of the Pakistani warhead into Iran. That part had been suspected by Rachel but it was always good to get some validation that your antennae were still working. The shocking revelation was that Colonel Kim had been recruited by President Rashad himself when he began to suspect that the Pakistani General Zarcash was deemed 'unreliable' as a partner. This showed Rachel that people at the highest level of the Iranian government were involved in this plot.

Immediately after the interrogation, Jenkins was on his special encrypted Iridium telephone with the DNI.

"Doctor Hunter, I've just spent an amazingly informative time with Colonel Kim. I've got bad news, really bad news, and some 'we-can-deal-with-this' type news. Are you ready…? First, in the bad news category, there *is* a phase two of their plan. So this is not over, not by a long shot. Second – and this is the really bad news – there was a *second warhead* in the original shipment. Presumably, the Iranians still have this and it's hidden somewhere. The way this happened was simple; each launcher carries two warheads, each with different yields, so the missile crew can tailor the war shot to a specific tactical situation."

"With these mobile launchers the crew needs to be able to respond without going through the logistical exercise of obtaining a different warhead if needed. So the Koreans loaded both warheads from the Shaheen III and placed it on board the oil tanker headed for Iran. I'm not sure which one they detonated, but they still have one in reserve."

"In the final category, the plan for phase two is for Colonel Kim to divert *fissile material* and not another warhead from the Khan Nuclear Research facility to Iran. I'll have more for you when I get back. I'm catching a flight in the next couple of hours."

"Thanks, Max, That's enough for right now. I've got to brief the President."

Kim also revealed to Jenkins that prior to the warhead being detonated it had been taken to a super-secret nuclear processing site "somewhere in Iran"

where it had been reverse engineered for two weeks prior to transport to the Kerman desert site where it had been detonated.

"What did he say about the site?" asked Rachel of Jenkins.

"As we know, Iran has several nuclear processing sites with some probably redundant and perhaps even inactive. These are geographically diverse, which makes an attack difficult to plan and execute. It now seems probable that there may be a site we know nothing of. According to Colonel Kim, the Korean technicians that went along with the warhead were taken in aircraft with no windows so they had no idea where they were. Kim said the site had all the state-of-the-art machine tools and equipment needed to construct a warhead. All they needed at this site was the fissile material that Kim was to provide and they could produce warheads within a matter of weeks."

"Mr. President, I think we have been able to fill in the blanks from the information we have received from our new intel source, Colonel Kim," said Rachel Hunter as she met the next day with President Braxton and Jack Duggan. She spent some 30 minutes going over the details of what Jenkins had been able to learn and then waited for the President to respond. Jack Duggan cleared his throat to speak.

"Mr. President, may I suggest a course of action based on what we have heard here today?"

"Please proceed, Jack. That's what we're paying you for."

"We should tell Colonel Kim to maintain his contact with the Rashad brothers and proceed as if phase two of the operation is going forward. Our strategy should be to make the Iranians think it is business as usual and trust Colonel Kim to continue with the plan to bring the fissile material to Iran."

Braxton responded forcefully, "That's all good, Jack, but how are we going to thwart them from making more bombs and acquiring substantial nuclear capability by allowing Kim, or one of his guys, to get fissile material out of Pakistan and into Iran. Once the plutonium gets into Iran they are home free. We will be lucky to find it, let alone do anything about it. We can't allow the fissile material to leave Pakistan, and when the Iranians see that they are not getting it, Kim will be compromised and we will be right back where we started with them. And don't forget they have the trump card in the fact that they have an operational nuke of unknown yield that they could elect to use."

"I agree, Mr. President. We have to have a three-pronged strategy of dealing with these issues. We have to make the Iranians think that the second phase of the plan is going forward, with Colonel Kim as the point man. We need to pin-point the location and yield of the second nuke in their possession. We need to keep them from using this nuke if they begin to think at any time that we're on to the plan and are moving forward to thwart it. We need to execute on all three of these in a carefully choreographed sequence so the Iranians don't know we're on to them."

"Agreed," said Rachel with conviction.

"Rachel, I'm leaving the first part up to you. After all, Colonel Kim is your guy. As far as the second and third are concerned, this is a classic special ops job. Jack we need the Joint Chiefs and the SECDEF ASAP in the Situation Room. Better get that SPECWAR guy up here from Tampa...I'm sure we're going to need his boys at some point."

CHAPTER 22

END GAME

"Failure is not an option."
Attributed to Gene Kranz, Flight Director, Apollo 13 Mission*

In the days following his initial interview with Max Jenkins, Colonel Kim spent several hours each night in a safe house located within a busy bazaar in the middle of Islamabad with his local CIA handlers, getting to know these professionals, learning simple tradecraft, and answering the same questions asked in slightly different ways. The latter was an attempt by the CIA to validate the reliability of the information they received from him and ensure that no detail had been left unstudied. Micro-recording devices transmitted these conversations wirelessly to another room in the house, where technicians transcribed every word and analysts went over every answer, juxtaposing it against what the Colonel had offered before.

In a few days a nascent level of trust began to emerge between these strange bedfellows. CIA felt they had an agent/informant who was intelligent and reliably forthcoming, while the Colonel felt less and less threatened by the American intelligence operators. He was fed well and occasionally offered excellent single malt scotch or premium Russian vodka during breaks from long interrogations.

An added touch was the presence of two ethnic Korean female agents who were useful when a language barrier made technical communications difficult. Both were physically attractive but aloof in their contact with Kim.

They were obviously very well educated and in synch with the protocol of the American agents. Their presence made the frequent meetings less of a chore and gave Kim a sense of being closer to his familiar Korean roots. The CIA station chief, Doug Chambers, was sensitive about the follow-on contacts that would have to be initiated between Kim and Sharif Rashad. He frequently cautioned Colonel Kim to welcome such contacts so as to reassure the Rashad brothers that he was willing and able to carry out his end of phase two of the contract.

Sharif and Mahmoud Rashad met privately in Tehran shortly after the detonation of the first nuclear device had taken place.

"So, my brother, the world now knows that you have succeeded in your quest for a nuclear weapon," offered Sharif Rashad. "I assume the mullahs are pleased that you have elevated their status within Islam and have given you a vote of confidence."

"That is true, Sharif. You, too, have done well. However, there is much left to do as only a very few of our trusted scientists are aware of how much lies ahead to give us a legitimate internal and sustainable nuclear capability. It is vital for you and Colonel Kim to transfer the fissile material as stealthily and as quickly as possible. If we can get enough plutonium to build two more medium yield bombs, that will give us a total of three or four warheads that should sustain us until our enrichment facilities can begin to deliver enough material to build a stockpile of warheads. Once we have twenty or so weapons we will be at parity with the Israelis and have real negotiating power with the infidels."

"I will be connecting with Colonel Kim once I return to Islamabad in the next few days. We will be making a plan to get the additional fissile material into Iran as quickly as possible," replied Sharif.

Shharif, as you have heard, there is a great outcry from the international community about this test we have conducted. So far, from everything we have heard, the consensus seems to be that what we have tested is a home-grown warhead. Even the Americans and the Israelis are saying that we must have been further along with our development that they anticipated. This must be embarrassing to them, but also places pressure on us to accelerate our development and to maintain security of our processing sites. Finally, there must be no active suspicion that we actually diverted this weapon from another country."

"We were exceptionally careful to ensure the Korean technicians had no idea where they were when we took them to the site where we performed our reverse engineering, as this will also be the site where the raw fissile material will be taken to build the new bombs. Their entire trip was done in a sealed transport plane so, even if they were inclined to betray us, they would have no idea about the location of this secret site," confided Sharif. "We have taken every precaution."

"Well done, Sharif. I think our grand plan is coming towards a successful conclusion. Soon our place of honor in the history of Islam will be assured. Allah Akbar!"

Rachel Hunter was not normally a pacer of floors. Thoughtful and undemonstrative, she was by nature a brooder, a plotter, and above all, an analytical thinker who often gazed out over the Virginia countryside from her office considering every possible option and its contingencies before coming to a recommendation for a course of action she knew could have consequences well beyond her tenure as DNI. She was also aware that she served a president in whom she believed deeply as a good and honorable man and to whom she wanted to give the benefit of the best she and her talented staff could offer. The question of how to deal with the Iranian nuclear situation had been on her mind for weeks and she was determined to do what she and her colleagues in the American intelligence community could do to deny Iran membership in the Nuclear Club.

From the standpoint of the CIA, one of the keys to the success of this strategy would be to ensure Colonel Kim's legitimacy in the eyes of the Iranians. Any failure of the plot to divert the fissile material to Iran could not be traced back to Colonel Kim. This would mean devising a strategic plan to make it seem as if Colonel Kim had no knowledge of the removal of fissile material from the Khan Nuclear Research Facility and its ultimate diversion to Iran. The American's interception of the plutonium meant to build warheads in Iranian facilities would have to be done on Iranian soil after the successful diversion of the material from Pakistan. If discovered after the fact, the lack of security on the part of the Pakistani government and its military concerning nuclear weapons would have to be dealt with as a secondary subject and would be more a matter of private diplomacy between the U.S. and Pakistan rather than military action.

President Braxton and his National Security Team met in the White House Situation Room to discuss and approve the operations plan to intercept the diverted fissile material. The President began.

"By way of review since last time, please let me give you the current situation about the Iranian nuclear problem. As we are all aware, the Iranians have detonated a nuclear warhead and have announced that they now have a nuclear weapons capability. At the moment, our public strategy will be to take that at face value, but there are many unanswered questions. Doctor Hunter and Director Rollins have developed substantial information that answers some of these questions – enough for us to be forced to make an operation plan to counter the continuation of Iran's plans to exploit this initial success."

"As for the big picture, here's what we know; this was not a home- grown nuclear device. It was diverted from the weapons inventory of Pakistan. It is highly likely that Iran has at least one additional operationally capable warhead. We're not exactly sure where it is, but we are working on this. We also know there is a plan to produce additional warheads based on the possible diversion of fissile material from Pakistan. Finally, this plan was hatched and managed at the highest levels of the Iranian government. At this time, I would like to have Doctor Hunter and Director Rollins continue the briefing. Then I will ask for input from those of you who will have direct responsibility for the details of the operational plan."

END GAME

The Director of National Intelligence, Rachel Hunter opened the briefing.

"I'm here to make a statement regarding security of this operations plan. I would prefer to be the bad guy, if there is to be one, in place of the President or Director Rollins on this issue. Some of the details concerning certain aspects of this plan are classified at a level higher than some participants in this meeting are authorized for. This may come as a surprise to you since you are all authorized at an exceptionally high security level. Suffice to say that we will be employing certain assets, human and material, known to only a handful of people in our government. Our guiding principles about dissemination of ultra-sensitive information always have been *'the need to know'* and the *'compartmentalization of information,'* and that is what is in play here. I hope none of you are offended that certain details of the plan are not divulged. The success or failure of this operations plan rests in the judgment and planning of a few select individuals, some of whom are not in this room. We will now get a briefing on the overall plan by Director Rollins and the President will finish up."

The briefing continued with Raymond Rollins at the podium.

"Mr. President, gentlemen, I believe we have a good plan that will allow us to accomplish the goals previously identified in the Iranian Nuclear Prevention Strategy."

With that a series of Power Point slides flashed up and cycled through on the 80-inch screen at the end of the room.

Slide 1:
Prevent the fissile material from reaching the Iranian warhead building site.

Slide 2:
Locate and compromise any additional nuclear materials or weapons at the secret site.

Slide 3:
Contain operational security of human intelligence elements connected with this strategy.

Slide 4:
Confront and influence Pakistan about the lack of security of its nuclear capability.

Slide 5:
Discourage and influence Iran from going forward with new nuclear weapons initiatives.

"Some of you might ask, why not go the safe route and prevent the fissile material from leaving Pakistan in the first place? That would be conventional wisdom. However this carries with it the danger of compromising certain human assets we have in place that are of long term strategic value to the U.S., as well as avoiding alerting the Pakistani government at this stage of our strategic plan that its nuclear security has been compromised."

"We want to do that in a more private way, after the fact, as we believe that strategy will have longer-term security implications for the region and increase our influence in the fragile management of Pakistan's nuclear arsenal. Therefore, we have weighed the risks and decided to counter the diversion of this material on Iranian soil where we will have more freedom to employ covert military activity."

With this, the Chairman of the Joint Chiefs of Staff interjected. "Director Rollins, excuse me, but with due respect I believe you are alluding to the U.S. taking military action in a hostile area. I assume you have a rationale for this proposed action."

"Yes, General, I will be getting to that shortly. We will need your considerable expertise for this."

Raymond Rollins continued.

"In general, implementation of strategic objectives of slides one and two will require military intervention."

The CIA Director looked at the Chairman directly and said, "We're thinking a military Special Operations mission, General."

"Objective three will be a common responsibility, but as far as human assets are concerned, this is definitely a CIA imperative."

Rollins looked directly at President Braxton and continued.

"With respect, sir, assuming that we can accomplish items one, two, and three without starting World War Three, objectives four and five seem to be diplomatic initiatives that may bring an end to this misadventure by the Iranians. If we can do this without making a ton of waves this can turn into a huge win for you and your administration and cement you as a peacemaker in a highly volatile region."

"What you aren't saying, Ray," the President said with a wry grin, "is that if this thing blows up in our face, I'll be lucky if they don't impeach me."

No one else seemed even mildly amused.

Chance Lyon had been reassigned back to SEAL Team Two based in Little Creek after a thirty-day convalescent leave following the successful Operation Trinity interdiction mission in the Arabian Sea several months ago and an interim administrative assignment at the Naval Intelligence headquarters at Fort Story. The Navy doctors finally cleared him one-hundred percent fit for duty, and by virtue of his experience and courageous actions in Afghanistan and Operation Trinity, he had regained the prestigious slot as a platoon commander with SEAL Team Two that he had before his medical leave.

His convalescent leave from the surgery repairing his ruptured femoral artery was coincidental with the timing of the annual Army-Navy football game in Philadelphia, and it was there that he reconnected with Judy Zavier, who had made the trip from Sandia for a long weekend to have a mini reunion with some of her classmates from the Naval Academy.

Unencumbered by the highly restrictive security measures that were in place during Chance's SEAL team's training at Sandia months earlier, the two were able to build on their tenuous email correspondence they had initiated after that the training completion. Given the highly classified nature of their respective jobs in the Navy, their notes had been full of banal generalities meant to placate anyone snooping into their mail looking for security breaches, but it was enough to show their mutual interest until they could meet again in a more conventional environment.

The weekend had been mutually enjoyable for Chance and Judy and had cemented the seriousness of their nascent relationship, although it was separated by thousands of miles at the moment.

Seal Team Two received a warning order by their commander three days after the National Security Team was briefed by the President, Rachel Hunter and, Raymond Rollins.

The top secret briefing was begun by their commander, "Buck" Buckholder. "All right men, we are now on 48-hour deployment notice. This will be a desert trip, get that gear squared away – we're going back to the Middle East. That's all I can tell you for now. I'll see my platoon commanders at thirteen-hundred."

It was late at night in the Oval Office. Present were the President, Raymond Rollins, National Security Advisor Jack Duggan, and Rachel Hunter, who began, "Gentlemen, I think we may have a break in the location of the secret site where the two warheads were taken and where the Iranians intend to take the fissile material for making additional warheads."

Colonel Kim has learned from one of the nuclear technicians who accompanied the nuclear warheads to the engineering site that he carried a miniature GPS device with him on the flight. This device had a tracking feature that recorded his movements over the two-day period and, believe it or not, it shows the exact location where they landed on the interim basis prior to detonating the first warhead at Kerman. He hid it away and brought it back with him when the tech team returned to Islamabad, perhaps intending to sell the information at a later time. Colonel Kim told him he didn't believe him and the guy actually showed it to the Colonel. Kim wrote down the grid coordinates and gave them to my station chief. If this is accurate, we now have the location for the engineering site. And we can use this information to intercept the fissile material before it finally arrives there."

"This is exceptional news," replied President Braxton. "But how do we verify it?"

"Agreed, Mr. President, two things." offered Jack Duggan.

"We can redirect the ground track of a KH-12 Victor satellite and also try to get some drone images. For the latter I would suggest trying for IR images at night to minimize the risk of detection. I need an authorization for the NRO guys to change the KH-12 track. This will take about 24 hours."

"Hang around, and I'll draft and send one with an e-signature to the NRO right now. Thank you all. Keep me posted. We're adjourned."

Colonel Kim met with Doug Chambers, the Islamabad CIA station chief, three days after the revelation about his technician's GPS tracking device.

"Colonel, we have confirmed that there is some activity at the site of these grid coordinates you gave me. It could just be any number of activities. All we know is that there is something there in a complex of buildings. My question to you is, how reliable is your guy? Any chance he is now working for the Iranians? If we base an operation on this location and it's not the correct site, we risk the whole mission and a lot more. We've got to be sure."

"The man has been with me for almost ten years. I brought him here with me when we transferred most of our work to Pakistan. He is unquestionably loyal to me and North Korea, in that order. I will ask him one more time, privately, but if he told me this was true, I would believe him."

Colonel Kim and Chambers planned well into the night in the Islamabad safe-house about how to get the fissile material out of Pakistan into Iran. Chambers felt it was to their advantage to be pro-active with a plan that Sharif Rashad and his brother could react to rather than having one imposed on him by the Iranians.

"How do you propose to divert the fissile material, Colonel?" inquired Chambers.

"The easiest way will be for me to accompany the replenishment convoy that takes fresh fissile material from the Khan Nuclear Research facility to the nuclear weapons the Pakistanis have stored in the large cave complex in the Northern Region.

"This is not unusual, as my technicians are always in charge of the technical aspects of this activity. As their immediate supervisor, it would not be seen as unusual for me to accompany them. When we leave the Khan facility, the material we take out is closely scrutinized and logged, because the security is very tight there. However, once we get to the cave complex, the soldiers there are as much guards as anything else and they always defer to me and my men when it comes to changing out the degraded fissile material."

"Of course, there is a Pakistani military watcher with my men, but it is always the same man, a Colonel Hasbani, and he is usually very lax in his supervision. We will, of course, change out the material – we call them 'pits' - in the number of warheads for which we have new material. However, we will simply disregard changing out the depleted fissile material from three of the warheads and divert the material intended for replenishment to the shipment that goes to Iran."

"What about inventory control back at Khan," asked Chambers, "don't they expect you to return with the same number of pits you took with you?"

Colonel Kim pursed his lips and smiled thinly before answering.
"Mr. Chambers, do you remember the angst officials in the West had about accounting for warheads and missiles after the breakup of the Soviet Union? Well, imagine that in spades with the nuclear weapons control in Pakistan. To tell you the truth, I doubt that every warhead ever produced in Pakistan can be accurately accounted for, let alone the replenishing pits for the warheads," he chuckled.

"And what will you do to ensure the secrecy and security of the diversion plan, Colonel?" inquired Chambers.

"The Koreans are completely loyal to me personally, Mr. Chambers. They owe their relative freedom and, indeed, their lives, to staying in my favor. As for the Pakistanis, everyone one of them is expendable as far as I am concerned. I will kill any of them who I feel imperils the mission, and make it look like an accident or treachery on their part."

For a moment, Doug Chambers blanched at the callous disregard for human life expressed by Colonel Kim, but was suddenly jolted back to reality when he recalled the brutality of the Colonel in the murder of al-Zarcash in front of Sharif Rashad. *'No, we are not dealing with a person with any scruples here,'* thought Chambers.

Colonel Kim continued. "Meanwhile your Pakistani operatives will pick up the container of fissile material in a military vehicle and drive it to a border crossing on the Pakistani-Iranian border near the town of Zahedan, Iran. This is a distance of about 1,700 kilometers which will take them a little over 21 hours. They will be posing as military couriers with a frequent border crossing permit, and the Iranian border guards will not give them any problem. That completes my end of the transaction and no one will suspect that there will have been any security breach involving the nuclear material. The rest is up to the Iranians."

"Yes, indeed," Rachel Hunter confirmed to the SPECWAR Commander who had been dispatched to Washington by CENTCOM to plan the military interception of the material, "we think there is only one way they will do this."

She was referring to how the Iranians would transport the material once it got into Iran.

"General, we are ninety percent sure that the secret processing facility is in a small town in southeast Iran named, appropriately enough, Mohammadabad. This town has no airport and that may be one of the reasons it was selected for this facility. However, it is only about 100 kilometers from the city of Bam, which does have an airport. Our guess is that the fissile material will be flown from the town of Zahedan near the border, to Bam, where it will be loaded into a truck and driven to Mohammadabad."

Accompanying the SPECWAR Commander were a U.S. Navy SEAL Captain and Army Ranger Colonel who were his liaisons with those components and the principal mission planners for the SPECWAR arm of CENTCOM. The SPECWAR Commander gave the Captain and the Colonel an outline of the plan that had been approved by CENTCOM and the Joint Chiefs.

"Gentlemen, the mission is two-fold but simple. We will simultaneously stage a combined forces operation – meaning SEALS and Rangers working in concert – near the suspected nuclear complex at Mohammadabad, Iran, shown here on the map. The Rangers will ambush the convoy of vehicles bringing the nuclear fissile material from Bam to the Mohammadabad complex, and seize the fissile material while reducing all the Iranian escort personnel. There will be no wounded or prisoners that could provide intelligence to subsequent Iranian investigators of the ambush.

Simultaneously, the SEALS will enter the nuclear complex and take it down to a *level of zero capability*. Having done so, they will locate the nuclear weapon that is believed to be in building six of the complex and render it unusable by removing the AFF device and attaching timed explosive devices to the warhead. This resulting explosion will be like a 'dirty' nuclear bomb exploding, destroying the device itself and rendering the entire complex essentially unsuitable for human use for several years by scattering radioactivity throughout the site. Having completed their missions, both forces will extract by the 160th SOAR Black Hawks that delivered them, back to a geographic salient along the Afghanistan – Iranian border. Total mission time: approximately twelve to eighteen hours."

After several minutes of silence while the two Special Operations officers poured over the detailed map and aerial photos of the site, the SEAL Captain finally spoke up.

"Sir, the range from the Afghan salient to the nuke site makes it doable, logistics-wise for the rotary wing package, but we need some intel about the layout of the site and some detail about how we're going to take it down. I assume they have security there."

"That's right, Captain. We have that intel from knowledgeable people who have actually been working at this site recently..."

'...*Really?!*'

This revelation caused both of the SPECOP officers to exchange a startled glance as they did not expect the benefit this kind of first hand intelligence.

"This site is brand new and they have yet to do the type of deep excavating that some of their other sites have, so most of the operations are on the ground level. The Assembly and Testing building – building six - is on ground level. We believe that is where the nuclear warhead is."

"How are we going to take this site down to *zero capability status*, as you say, with only 16 SEALs? That's a pretty tall order unless you're expecting a protracted kinetic engagement," observed the SEAL Captain.

The SPECWAR commander smiled and replied, "Captain, I'm not expecting much of a fight. You're going to walk right in there just like you owned the place, do your work and leave quietly, just like the gentlemen you are."

"With respect, sir, how's that? Sounds like fantasy to me."

"We're going to do it the old-fashioned way, Captain. We're going to *gas* them...just like World War One in the trenches, except more high tech – and less lethal."

"*Gassing?!*" exclaimed the SEAL Captain. "Isn't that a little barbaric...not to mention against the Geneva Convention and a few other laws of war protocols? Is this going to make us war criminals?"

"I understand your concerns, Captain, but we're not quite that barbaric with this new technology. Actually it's quite humane and most harmless. It is a new odorless, invisible strain of nerve agent that is released upwind of a target, and when it comes in contact with humans and animals immediately puts them to sleep for several hours – just like a strong sedative – and when they awake they can't remember anything about the time they were asleep. We've been experimenting with this for a few years and now we have now found the ideal situation to use it against a hostile force in this circumstance."

"What about my guys?" asked the clearly skeptical SEAL Commander. "We're bound to get a whiff or two of this stuff ourselves. I don't see how I can pull this off with a bunch of my guys knocked out by some new kind of gas."

"You'll be issued a new kind of gas mask that is a lot less bulky and is very effective against the gas," replied the SPECWAR General.

"Don't worry Captain, this has been thoroughly tested and this stuff is extremely effective. Also, it leaves no detectable traces in the blood, so it can't be found and used as evidence that we are using gas on their personnel."

The SPECWAR officers studied the maps and aerial photos for the next thirty minutes, frequently conversing with each other and twice on a conference call to some unknown colleagues at CENTCOM in Tampa.

Finally, the SEAL Captain addressed the SPECWAR General. "I think we have a plan for insert and extract, sir. Both the SEALs and the Rangers will have pre-mission work to do. Some of the SEALs have to do the gassing of the nuclear compound before the assault element of SEALs arrives to search for the nuke, and the Rangers need to set explosive charges on the road that will detonate just ahead of the convoy to initiate the ambush. These elements will HALO in from a C-17A to their respective drop zones to be followed by the assault elements inserting from Black Hawks after the pre-mission work has begun. The timing of the mission will be dependent on the actual progress of the convoy from Bam to Mohammadabad. My SEALs will begin their take down of the compound when the Rangers initiate the ambush just in case there are some personnel in the compound who haven't been overcome by the gas. If things work out, both the SEALs and the Rangers should finish up within 60 minutes, and we should extract about the same time and exfiltrate to the egress salient."

He continued, "Having said that, sir, what we do not know is by what conveyance the material will be transferred once it reaches Iran. The two obvious choices are by road or by air. This choice will dramatically impact the timing of when we launch the mission from the Afghan salient. I recommend that we have a plan for each contingency and be prepared to execute it based on the intel we get from aerial reconnaissance after the fissile material crosses the border. We can be flexible if we have a plan, the prep time, and the logistical support to carry it out."

The SPECWAR Commander answered, "Okay, Captain, Colonel – I'll need to run this by the CENTCOM Chief of Staff on a video conference and then we'll be heading back to Tampa. SEAL Team Two out of Little Creek is being assigned to this and a platoon from the 75th Ranger Regiment at Fort Benning will be the Ranger component. Get those commanders and key NCOs down to Tampa tomorrow for a briefing at ten-hundred hours. You've got a week to work out the details and get your people prepped. This is a balls-out op, gentlemen, and it will be going on live in the White House Situation Room."

Rachel Hunter, Jack Duggan, and the SPECWAR Commander were briefing the President in the Oval Office shortly after the operations plan for the Iranian interdiction operation had been approved by CENTCOM.

The SPECWAR Commander began.

"Sir the SEALS and the Rangers are very comfortable with this plan and we're going to have a ton of support staged at the Afghan salient for every contingency. This Iranian site is only 250 miles from the salient, in an extremely remote area of Iran with no significant military support within hundreds of miles. I'm confident that the AWACS radar jamming that we used in the SEAL op at the Kerman detonation site will keep the Iranians from detecting our C-17 and Black Hawks upon insertion. The round trip for the helos is at the edge of their range, so we're bringing along extra fuel in another Hawk and will refuel at the site just to be sure. We will have air assets from the carrier Abraham Lincoln staged in case we need combat air support at the site. We'll have drones with surveillance cameras operating at the ambush site and over the compound, sir. Just like the Bin Laden raid in 2011, the Situation Room will be able to hear this in real-time audio."

Colonel Kim and Sharif Rashad greeted each other as comrades in the traditional Arab way of touching both cheeks in a light embrace and voicing the traditional "Assalamu alaikum" peace greeting as they met and walked along a pathway in a park along a tributary of the Indus River near Islamabad.

"All is in readiness, Sharif. The replenishing convoy of fissile material is set to leave the Khan Nuclear facility next week for the nuclear storage complex in the northern region. As usual, my technicians and I have a key role in this activity, and I have a well-considered plan to divert enough fissile material for two or three medium yield weapons."

Colonel Kim went on to describe the plan in great detail including the identities of the men who would be transporting the hijacked fissile material, the exact description of their vehicle, and the exact date and time they would be making the border crossing from Pakistan into Iran.

"It is none of my business, of course, but what will you be doing with the material once it is in your hands?" Kim asked innocently.

"As soon as you have verified the contents, it is my expectation that the execution codes will be immediately given to the bank so that I may collect my funds," he continued. "It is important to me that there is as little delay in this process as possible."

"I appreciate your position, Colonel. You have been of immeasurable assistance to us in the acquisition of this capability and we intend to honor our commitment to you. In answer to your question, we will have a team of technicians at the airport in Zahedan to inspect the cargo. Once verified, they will signal me and I, in turn, will notify the bank that they may release the balance of the funds to you. I hope that meets with your satisfaction."

"Of course, Sharif. I believe you are a man of honor. But don't forget that I hold the trump card in this transaction. I'm sure the Israelis and the Americans would be very interested in the details of our business arrangement. As you know, I have no love for either group and with the funds I receive as payment for this partnership, I will be wealthy enough to be immune from any enticements from other sources. In fact, I am looking forward to doing business with you and your brother again."

Colonel Kim passed the information that Rashad had agreed to his plan to the Islamabad CIA station chief and this intel, in turn, this was transmitted to CIA headquarters in Langley. The stealth drones with the gamma ray detection equipment would then follow the progress of the fissile material along the way within Iran.

C-17A GLOBEMASTER AIRCRAFT

The SEALs and the Rangers were soon on their way to Afghanistan in their C-17A Galaxy aircraft and their commanders were in regular contact with their SPECWAR commander in Tampa about any OpPlan updates. Each commander had an encrypted Iridium telephone handset and could conference up with SPECWAR as well as with the commander of the logistical staging activity at the Afghan salient.

Rachel Hunter, Raymond Rollins, Jack Duggan, and President Braxton were video conferencing with the SPECWAR Commander about the progress of the Iranian Interdiction operation as the SEALS and Rangers were headed to their Afghanistan salient insert point via Kandahar Airbase.

"General, can you give us a status review of the operation as it now stands?" asked President Braxton.

"Yes, Mr. President. Based on the intel we've received from CIA, we believe that the fissile material will arrive at the Afghan-Iran border crossing at Kuh-i-Taftan sometime in the next few days. There the material is to be off-loaded and trucked approximately one hundred kilometers north to Zahedan where they have a major airport; this will take maybe two hours. They could elect to move it by helicopter, but we're betting they use a motor vehicle because the road is good and they don't want to risk flying it in a helicopter a short distance at night. If we're right about Mohammadabad being the final destination, they will likely fly the material in a fixed wing aircraft to Bam, which has a good airport. Loading, flying, and unloading time should consume another few hours. Finally, they will probably take the material by vehicle from Bam to Mohammadabad for the same reasons stated before. They could always opt for a chopper, sir, for this final phase and then we would have to abort the mission, at least the Ranger phase – unless we want to change the plan for an option to deal with a helicopter transfer from Bam to the site. We have the flexibility to deal with that."

"Rachel, I would like to get an assessment from you on this," replied the President. "This is so crucial to the mission timing, I think we have to make a bet one way or the other. What would you do if you were in their shoes?"

At this moment Rachel felt the walls of the Oval Office slowly closing in on her as she knew that her instincts were going to be put to a profound test. The success of the mission and perhaps the lives of many brave American men could hinge on how she answered this question from the man she was so proud to serve.

Moments passed before she answered.

"Sir we have arranged for the material to cross early in the evening, just after dark. Colonel Kim has made the point that this will reduce the chances of the crossing being observed by satellite or other means. I'm betting on the original scenario, that is by ground to Zahedan, air to Bam, and ground again to Mohammadabad. Here's my reasoning:

The plan has been long in the planning stage and the execution is the final phase. The Iranians have already achieved the publicity value they sought, so there is no urgency in making the new warheads that the fissile material will provide. There is, however, a prudent need to get the fissile material to a safe place. Therefore, it will be to their benefit to be cautious about transporting this material to the final assembly site.

Helicopters are inherently more dangerous than single engine planes, particularly at night, so I would be using ground transport wherever possible, especially on short hops like the first and third legs. The proof of this will be how the material is received at the border crossing at Kuh-i-Taftan. If there is no helicopter there at the time the material crosses from Pakistan into Iran, I think we can be ninety percent sure the transport scheme I have outlined will be their plan. If we can get a drone over the site at night with IR imaging and gamma ray detection, and can confirm that the fissile material gets loaded on a vehicle, I think we can use that as the trigger to start the operation."

As the Pakistani nuclear fissile material replenishment convoy arrived at the Northern Region garrison complex, it was met by the Commander of the guard battalion, who was in charge of security for the nuclear weapons that were to be serviced by Colonel Kim and his technicians.

"I'm, glad to see you again, Colonel. I hope that we will be able to socialize for a couple of days while your men service the weapons."

"Just so, Colonel," replied Kim. "I have not forgotten your appetite for good Scotch whisky and have brought along three bottles of the best I could find in Islamabad. This whiskey is difficult to find, even on the black market, but your hospitality has always been excellent, and I want to gift these to you."

The Pakistani Colonel's eyes lit up at the idea of sharing such a rare treat and he shook Kim's hand vigorously.

"Something else that might ease the monotony is the company of the two guests that I have brought along on this trip. I have two new technicians that have recently come from North Korea and they are both anxious to learn while working on real live weapons. They also happen to be young ladies who have recently graduated from one of the prestigious engineering universities in China and have been placed in my care for six months. I think you will enjoy their company."

"Colonel Kim, your thoughtfulness is overwhelming," enthused the Pakistani commander. "I am looking forward to meeting them."

"If you like, they can join us for dinner tonight at your quarters," replied Kim. "I think you will find them to be pleasant company and very eager to socialize. They both have learned that many advantages accrue to ladies who are agreeable company for men like us. They have gotten used to some of the finer material things during their stay in Beijing. I can personally vouch for the intelligence and advanced social skills of both these young women."

The Pakistani commander was now nearly beside himself with anticipation and immediately called his house boy to prepare a sumptuous meal for four and to spare no amenities for him and his guests.

"Colonel, I will tell the captain of the guards that you and your men are to have full freedom of movement throughout the facility when you begin your work tomorrow. If there is anything you need, please let me know and it shall be done. Meanwhile, we must think ahead to an evening of enjoyment. May I expect you and your two guests at six at my quarters? If this is agreeable, I will send my car for you."

Colonel Kim smiled and nodded in response. But the expression of pleasure was because his plan was working, rather than anticipation of spending the evening with the pretentious and ill-bred Pakistani commander.

Early the following morning after Colonel Kim's technicians had completed the servicing of the Pakistani nuclear warheads hidden in the cave storage complex, the North Korean Colonel organized the motorized convoy for the return trip to the Khan Nuclear Research Facility near Islamabad. The long journey, some of it over less than optimal roads, would take the entire day, possibly into the evening, depending on weather and road conditions.

Although the nuclear weapons were under the command and control authority of the Pakistani military, and the titular commander of the warhead servicing activity and the convoy was a Pakistani Army Colonel, Omar Hasbani, the reality was that Colonel Kim was, for all intents and purposes, the actual convoy commander. Hasbani was a degenerate gambler and womanizer in the same class as the recently departed General al-Zarcash and was only too happy to have the technical expertise and competence of Colonel Kim to rely on when it came to servicing these sensitive weapons. As long as he had let Colonel Kim have logistical matters his way during these regular servicing missions there had never been a slip up, and the missions had always been unblemished successes. If Hasbani was ever to advance to the rank of General, and make his eventual retirement pension more comfortable, he intended to maintain his laissez faire attitude toward the reliable Colonel Kim.

Kim approached his counterpart, Colonel Hasbani, just as the convoy was scheduled to depart at 08:30. "Colonel, we have had a problem with the vehicle loaded with the depleted plutonium pits and my mechanics are working on fixing it now. We may be delayed for a couple of hours. That will put us back in the nuclear facility well after dark, but we have made this trip many times and I am not worried. I would wait until tomorrow to leave but the weather report is predicting rain by midday which will make the roads more difficult." Colonel Kim was careful not to overstep his de-facto authority and carefully continued. "With your permission, Colonel Hasbani, I recommend that we forge ahead even though we will not return to Khan until after dark so we may avoid the deteriorating weather expected tomorrow."

"As you suggest, Colonel Kim. We can never be too careful with the fissile material. I'll make the security people at Khan aware of our plans for a late arrival," Hasbani said, relieved that he did not have to exercise the responsibility to make such a decision.

As their conversation continued in sight of the numerous Pakistani soldiers and Korean technicians making up the convoy, Colonel Kim made a point of overtly bragging to Colonel Hasbani about winning a large amount of money playing cards with the Pakistani garrison commander the night before. He laughed boisterously about his good luck and flashed a large amount of cash to the impressed Colonel Hasbani, making no attempt of hiding his good fortune. As the Pakistani Colonel congratulated the North Korean on his winnings, Colonel Kim thought to himself, *'I will use this scene to my advantage as the circumstances of our journey back to Khan come to be known later.'*

At a little after 11:00 Colonel Kim announced to Colonel Hasbani that the repairs to the vehicle had been made and they were ready to depart the Pakistani garrison for Khan. "May I suggest, Colonel Hasbani, that you take the second position in the convoy after the point security vehicle? I will take up the rear with the repaired vehicle carrying the fissile material immediately ahead of me just to make sure there are no further problems. You and I can maintain radio communications for security purposes."

Once again, Colonel Hasbani viewed the North Korean's organizational rationale with relief and as sound as anything he might be forced to conjure up as the convoy commander. "That is an excellent plan, Colonel. We will meet at the halfway point when we stop for refueling to compare notes and double check security."

The first half of the journey from the Pakistani garrison to Khan went uneventfully. As the truck convoy bounced along over the combination of paved and unpaved roads toward the Khan facility, Colonel Kim rehearsed his plan over and over point by point, making sure that no detail was left to chance. Colonel Kim was confident in the absolute loyalty of his Korean driver. He was equally comfortable in the knowledge that the two Pakistanis driving the fissile material transport vehicle directly ahead would be easy pawns in his plan to divert the fissile material to Iran.

At the halfway point in the journey just before dark, Colonel Kim signaled the lead vehicle to stop for a refueling break. The Pakistani soldiers filled five-gallon gas cans from the refueling truck that was part of the convoy and topped off each vehicle for the balance of the trip. Colonels Kim and Hasbani conferred in the road as the refueling took place coordinating their actions for the remainder of the journey. Satisfied that all was normal, the two Colonels shook hands and agreed that they would share chai and smoke American cigarettes at Khan when they returned hours later.

Sharif Rashad had recruited two former Pakistani military non-commissioned officers with the payment of a modest amount of gold - with the promise of a substantial bonus upon completion - to meet the convoy returning from the Pakistani garrison to the Khan facility as part of the fissile material diversion plan. If things went as planned, the diversion would take only a few moments, leaving no evidence of a conspiracy and the guarantee of success. These two men, along with their carefully reconditioned transport vehicle, looking identical to a Pakistani military vehicle of the same type, were waiting on a side road perpendicular to the convoy route.

As the convoy prepared to restart, Colonel Kim had his Korean driver replace the driver of the fissile material transport truck ahead of him on the pretense of giving the latter some relief. Colonel Kim's driver was replaced with another Korean so Kim could concentrate on orchestrating the tasks ahead. That being done, the convoy lumbered off into the enveloping darkness toward Khan.

Colonel Kim carefully watched his satellite GPS receiver and as they came to within one-half mile of the side road where the Pakistani diversion conspirators lay in wait, he had his driver signal the vehicle ahead with a pre-arranged coded on-off headlight flash to slow down. This increased the gap between the last two trucks in the convoy and the others substantially, but in the darkness and winding road conditions, this was not noticed by Colonel Hasbani.

According to plan, at precisely the right moment, the conspirators moved their vehicle out from the side road creating a blocking force that caused the truck carrying the fissile material to come to an abrupt stop. Both Korean drivers were aware of the plan and reacted exactly as they had been trained to do by Colonel Kim.

The two Korean drivers and the Pakistanis immediately dismounted the stopped vehicles to investigate the blockage ahead of them. Now, in the middle of the darkened road, with the rest of the convoy lumbering well ahead, Colonel Kim took advantage of the confusion of the scene and the limited visibility to carry out his nefarious plan that would provide Iran with enough fissile material to build at least two more warheads and, in the process, enrich him personally beyond his wildest dreams.

As the two Pakistani drivers argued with the conspirators who had blocked the road with their truck, Colonel Kim emerged from the darkness and shot the Pakistanis dead. He then retrieved a pistol from one of the dead Pakistanis, aimed it at his Korean driver and killed him as well. The only witnesses to these brutal events were the Pakistani conspirators and Colonel Kim's loyal driver. In the aftermath of the shocking events, Colonel Kim turned to his driver and said to him in Korean, "I had to kill Mr. Song to give credibility to our cover story about the attempted robbery by the Pakistanis. If it was only them who had been shot, the cover story would have been too suspicious. Two Pakistanis killed with no Koreans even injured would not have washed with the Pakistani investigators. Besides Mr. Song had no family and was of little use to me as a technician."

Within moments, under the direction of Colonel Kim, the four conspirators had removed the fissile material from the blocked convoy vehicle and transferred it to the other truck. After confirming instructions to the Pakistani operators, Colonel Kim dismissed them and they moved down the road in the opposite direction of the convoy, beginning their journey to the Pakistani-Iranian border some 1,700 kilometers and 21 hours away.

Colonel Kim waited for several more minutes before radioing his counterpart, Colonel Hasbani, now several miles ahead. "Colonel, we have had some trouble back here in the convoy. We experienced some further mechanical troubles with the transport vehicle which was resolved in just a few minutes. However, while we were delayed, the two Pakistanis took this opportunity to try to assault and rob me of my cash at gunpoint. Of course, I resisted and I was forced to shoot them in self-defense. However, they did return fire and killed one of my Korean technicians. I have loaded the bodies in the transport vehicle and we will rejoin you shortly."

Within 30 minutes Colonel Kim and his driver had rejoined the main convoy and the two colonels had stopped to conference about the recent difficulties reported by Colonel Kim.

"These events are most unusual and quite tragic, Colonel Kim," said Colonel Hasbani. "There will have to be a complete report and an investigation, of course."

"Perhaps it was unwise of me to display my gambling winnings so overtly back at the garrison. I think my enthusiasm about my good fortune got in the way of my better judgment," replied Colonel Kim.

Colonel Kim continued. "In some way I am grateful that there is a surviving witness in the form of my driver. But, being an ethnic Korean, I don't want him to have to report this to the authorities back in North Korea - perhaps jeopardizing our mission here in Pakistan. Perhaps if you, Colonel Hasbani, allow me to write the report in my own way and you agree to endorse it, we can avoid any complicated investigations by the Pakistani military. This way you will be in the clear and there will be nothing in your file showing any personal involvement in the unpleasant events whatsoever."

Colonel Hasbani didn't have to think much beyond the moment to know what Colonel Kim was suggesting was the easy way out for him, and he quickly agreed. "I agree completely, Colonel Kim. These men committed a crime and they paid the price. Let us hear no more of this. We will proceed to the Khan facility and the two of us will make our report together. You have my complete backing in this matter."

As was imagined by the two experienced Colonels, upon their return to the Khan Nuclear Research facility there was a cursory investigation about the deaths of the two Pakistani soldiers. Without any conflicting statements from any other source, the supporting statements of the two respected colonels went into the record as delivered and the matter was concluded.

Chance Lyon's SEAL element had drawn the assignment of taking down the compound after the other SEAL unit had HALO'ed in before them and set off the gas canisters upwind from the compound. Past reconnaissance had shown that the prevailing winds were from west to east and blew consistently in the harsh desert terrain around Mohammadabad.

Chance and the Ranger Platoon Leader, Lieutenant John Olyphant, sat in the shade in a camouflaged HUMMVEE at the Afghan salient site to escape the blistering heat of the late afternoon sun and the intense activity of support operations all around them. They poured over maps of the Mohammadabad vicinity and the latest aerial images, both IR and visual, to ensure that no detail of the site and the surrounding area had changed or had been overlooked. It seemed clear from comparing these with historical images that the Iranians did not suspect that any potential foes knew of this secret site in the remote desert of southeast Iran.

As they compared notes about the logistical aspects of their joint mission, Lieutenants Olyphant and Lyon carefully rehearsed the timing and tactics of their respective missions and how these individual actions impacted the common goal of seizing the incoming fissile material and demobilizing the second existing warhead.

STRATEGIC MAP – OPERATION DRAGON CLAW

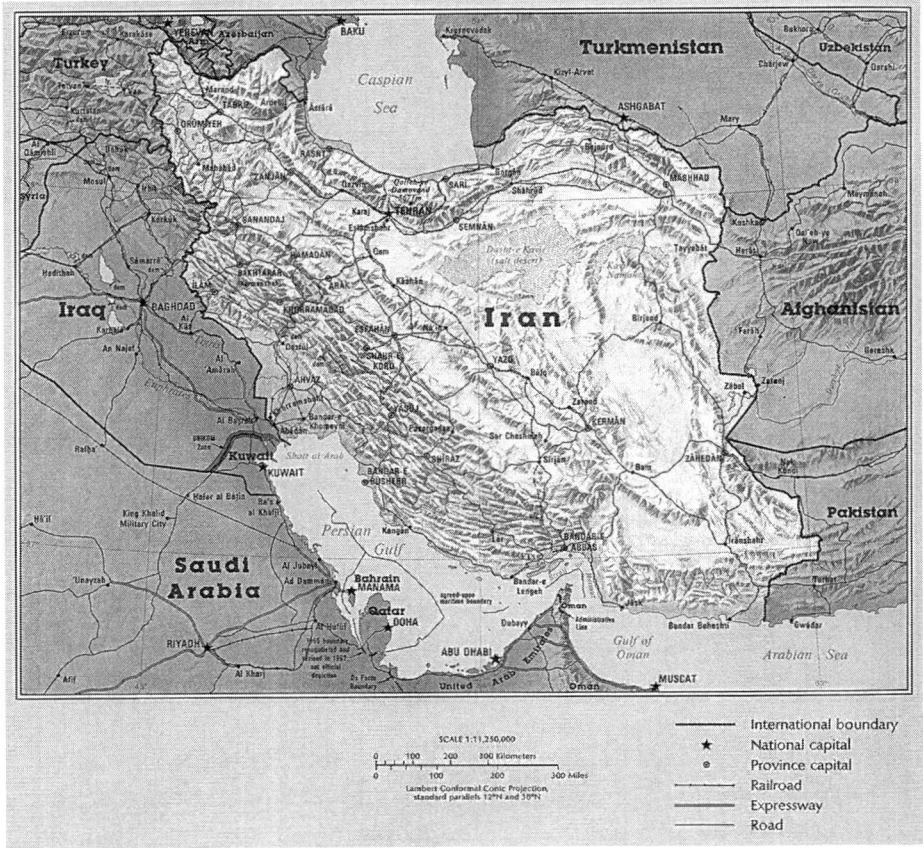

Map Credit: U.S. Central Intelligence Agency

At 18:00 hours Lieutenants Chance Lyon and John Olyphant received their final briefing from Colonel Howard Williamson, Commander of the 1st Battalion, 75th Ranger Regiment, who was the overall mission commander. He would be the tactical command and control element for the operation based at the salient. The briefing confirmed that the Pakistanis carrying the fissile material were about to arrive at the border crossing and also – perhaps most critically – that there was no helicopter seen near the border crossing. This clearly meant that the Iranians intended to transport the fissile material, held in lead shielded suitcases, on the first leg of the journey to Zahedan by motor vehicle.

Once the Pakistanis crossed the border, this would be the signal for the operation to begin. The first element of SEALs, who would be responsible for the gassing of the nuclear engineering compound at Mohammadabad and the Rangers who would be setting the charges at the ambush site were waiting in their C-17 at Kandahar airfield in Afghanistan some 400 miles northeast of Mohammadabad for the signal to take off on their two-hour flight to the drop zone, thus initiating one of the most important American military Special Operations missions of all time. The stakes were high; the risks of failure held many unforeseen consequences, and the rewards of success would mean the end of Iran's quest for nuclear weapons -- showing the mullahs and Mahmoud Abdul Rashad the lengths to which the United States was prepared to go to prevent this acquisition of deadly power.

The Pakistani couriers of the fissile material grew nervous as they approached the border crossing in the early evening hours. So far the trip from the diversionary hijack site in the northern region had been uneventful. In this heavily militarized country the movement of military vehicles went virtually unnoticed in the sea of human and vehicular traffic that transited the country in pursuit of commerce and national security. Colonel Kim had provided his couriers a letter of transit from the commander of the secret nuclear garrison site, who had been grateful for several gratuities provided by Colonel Kim during his visit. Such a document would not be questioned by any but the highest military authority if his men were stopped. By showing the Pakistani border guards their impressive military credentials and the letter of transit signed by an important military officer, the couriers would be routinely waved through the dusty and little used crossing with little or no inspection whatsoever.

The opposite was true of their reception by the Iranians. Upon arrival just as it turned dark, the couriers and their vehicle were directed to a garage set aside from the border crossing. As they drove inside the doors were closed and many men, some in military dress and some in civilian clothes were waiting to meet them. The couriers were greeted in an official, business-like manner and offered food and drink while several men removed the contents from the vehicle and set out examining the suitcases. They took some preliminary tests with what was essentially a high resolution Geiger counter to ascertain whether there was any radiation coming from the suitcase.
After a few brief nods among the group, men dressed in radiation suits appeared and gingerly hefted the suitcase onto a rolling table and wheeled it into another room within the garage. After twenty minutes, the men reappeared, removed their suits and nodded enthusiastically to the military leader of the group. He in turn picked up what appeared to be an Iridium telephone and spoke earnestly into it for less than a complete minute. He then listened to whomever it was he was speaking to for several minutes, occasionally answering and frequently nodding in agreement. When the conversation ended, he approached the couriers.

"You job is complete and you have performed well. The content of the package is what was promised and you are free to return to Pakistan. Please tell your commander that his portion of the contract has been completed satisfactorily and we will proceed as agreed. Thank you."

The National Security Team consisting of President Braxton, the SECDEF, SECSTATE, DNI Rachel Hunter, DCI Raymond Rollins, and Jack Duggan, plus an assortment of support staff, gathered in the White House Situation Room to listen and watch as events began to unfold half a world away that would have profound implications for the future of peace and stability in the Middle East and beyond. The Situation Room was wired for audio and visual feeds from dedicated satellites owned by the National Reconnaissance Office and all the policy makers and strategists could do now was to wait for events to unfold.

After two hours of flying time from Kandahar, the orange light came on in the cargo area of the C-17A flying at 25,000 feet above the Iranian desert as the signal for the SEALs and Rangers to get up from their fold-down web seats on either side of the cargo area and do one final equipment check before the giant deck in the rear of the aircraft yawned open for their High-Altitude-Low-Opening (HALO) insertion into the night sky above their respective drop zones. The plan was for the SEAL element to go first and make its five-minute descent to the drop zone while the Rangers circled above before making their run to their DZ.

Both groups had rehearsed this moment many times in the last few days and were confident as they waited in silence for the green light that would initiate this adventure into deadly combat that each of these highly trained and motivated young men both loved and, in the deepest part of their psyches, feared in a perversely enjoyable way. If they had to explain it, most outside their unique community wouldn't understand.

Within one hour after the fissile material had been delivered by the Pakistani couriers to the border crossing, the lead shielded suitcases had been reloaded into two separate Iranian military trucks and were headed north toward Zahedan for the next phase of the journey to the secret Iranian nuclear site at Mohammedabad. This movement was detected by the American stealthy drone flying at 10,000 feet silently over the border crossing and relayed simultaneously via satellite to the mission commander at the Afghan salient, CENTCOM in Tampa, and the White House Situation Room.

Colonel Williamson signaled his SEAL and Ranger platoon leaders and the pilot of the C-17A that the mission was in a 'go' status indicated by the yellow light in the cargo bay that had changed to flashing. The cargo bay ramp in the rear of the aircraft began to descend, causing the inside of the plane to buffet moderately with frigid air that pulled a vacuum throughout the cavernous interior. The pilot banked slowly to begin his insert run to the SEAL LZ. Two minutes later the cargo bay light abruptly turned from flashing yellow to green. The 14 SEALs bunched up as they shuffled toward the ramp and tumbled out in unison into the rush of cold night air, protected only by their oxygen masks and tactical parachutes that would not open until they had streaked silently in what appeared as a choreographed stack of individual silhouettes against the night sky, some 23,000 feet toward the desert floor below.

The SEALs and Rangers were well-prepared for their HALO insertion. At 25,000 feet altitude the outside air temperature would be at least 25 degrees below zero and the partial pressure of oxygen would be very low. Therefore, the SEALs and Rangers prepared by inhaling pure oxygen for the last thirty minutes of the flight. They would also be inhaling oxygen from portable flasks strapped to their bodies during their descent, which would purge any nitrogen in their blood that could potentially cause decompression sickness, more commonly known as the 'bends.' In addition, each operator would be protected from the sub-zero temperatures by highly efficient thermal underwear, gloves, and a face mask that would serve the dual roles of distributing the oxygen and protecting their faces and lungs from the sub-zero temperatures during free-fall.

At that altitude, approximately 2,000 feet above the ground, they would deploy their chutes and, with the help of their night vision goggles, guide themselves to a drop zone marked by IR strobe sticks dropped by the lead SEAL jumper. They would land within a few hundred feet of each other after traveling downward for nearly five minutes.

As soon as each SEAL did his 'walk-up' landing on the ground, the first order of business was to bury their parachutes as thoroughly as possible and then gather together to begin the mission sequence that had been rehearsed at least a dozen times in the days leading up to the mission. With all SEALs and equipment accounted for, they checked the GPS tactical maps strapped to their wrists and rapidly made their way off in the dark desert night toward their objective a little over one mile away.

With the first group of SEALs safely on the ground and proceeding to their objective, it was time for the Rangers to begin their HALO insertion in much the same manner. The pilot banked to the designated glide path run toward the Ranger drop zone some 10 miles away and the cargo bay light began to flash yellow, while the rear deck started its descent in a whine of hydraulic pumps and a rush of cold night air. The two DZs were planned to be located upwind of the nuclear complex and the insertion to them by HALO parachute drop was to avoid detection by any security patrolling the grounds. At an altitude of 25,000 feet the aircraft noise would be negligible to those on the ground. It would be unlikely that the parachuting Rangers would be detected as the tracked noiselessly against a dark sky and deployed their chutes at a low altitude far away from the nuclear site. Just as the SEAL element had done moments earlier, when the status light turned green, the Rangers shuffled down the ramp and off into the dark night air descending toward their DZ six miles away. Their deadly cargo of explosives and high tech weapons strapped to their bodies made this group of confident and determined warriors a formidable death-dispensing machine, aiming for an unsuspecting hostile target on the desert floor below.

Once Chance Lyon and his Ranger counterpart, Lieutenant John Olyphant, received the signal from the C-17A that the insertion of the SEALs and Rangers at the objective had been accomplished, they loaded up their assault teams into the idling Black Hawks and took off like determined beasts of prey, hugging the terrain to avoid detection, toward their respective objectives.

In the early stages of the two-pronged attack, all the observers in the Situation Room could hear were infrequent radio communications encrypted on a secure radio channel and relayed from a NRO satellite. Most of this was 'mission chatter' that made little sense to the civilians in the room. Occasionally one of the Generals would clarify one of the remarks, but most of the communication was just evidence that the mission was in its early precarious stages. A nervous Jonathan Braxton broke the silence.

"General, what do you give our chances for success here?" he spoke idly to the JCS Chairman, "there are a lot of pieces to this puzzle."

"Sir, I give us a 95 percent chance of taking care of business and getting this done according to plan. These are some of the best people we have out there and I like our chances...today and going forward. I wish I was out there with them."

"Well, General, you might be a little old to play with this bunch, but I'm glad you're doing the job you have. Keep us up to speed with the communications chatter."

"Will do, and thank you, sir."

The SEAL element charged with gassing the compound split into the groups and moved toward their assigned positions guided by their GPS units and acetate copies of the compound map that had been provided to Colonel Kim by the Korean technicians who had been there with the original warhead delivery. These would prove invaluable as the mission progressed.

The small anemometer carried by the SEAL gassing element validated that the prevailing wind data was cooperating this night at a brisk rate of five-to-seven miles per hour, which would help disperse the immobilizing gas over the compound evenly, based on experiments that had been conducted previously in Utah desert, terrain that was remarkably similar to where the SEALs found themselves this evening. The mission meteorologists had run computer analysis regarding the best places to release the gas based on wind conditions, temperature, and terrain conditions. This data had been made into a matrix that the SEAL team leader would use to position his men for the initiation of the gas attack. Once again, the precision GPS positioning devices the SEALs carried attached to the arms of their multiCams assisted them in finding the optimum positioning of each man and his SEAL buddy prior to the attack.

After a final whispered briefing shortly after the SEALs collapsed on the LZ, the team leader dispatched his men and ordered them to dig in at their respective spots while the balance of the team established a security position protecting their flanks and the western side of their gassing positions. Lieutenant Schields found a position on a knoll overlooking the nuclear compound from approximately 100 meters to the west and carefully scanned the compound for a full ten minutes aided by his night vision goggles looking for signs of human habitation or security personnel. Within a few minutes he could see that there was a security force of six men patrolling the interior perimeter in a coordinated fashion. For Lieutenant Brian Schields this was a nearly perfect scenario as he could judge the effectiveness of the gas dispersion by watching the security force and its reaction after the gas had been released. Lieutenant Schields waited until the elapsed mission time indicated Chance Lyon's SEAL team assigned to the compound take down was less than one hour out before giving his men the signal to release the gas.

Meanwhile, First Sergeant Lyle Roger's demolition squad, assigned the task of setting charges to blow the bridge to stop the convoy carrying the fissile material shortly after it turned off Highway 93, had collapsed on its LZ with no injuries and with all equipment intact. As with the SEALs, the Rangers had a quick final briefing from Sergeant Rogers before they made their way to the bridge. "Okay guys, we get to start this surprise party. This may be the most fun you have all day," he said.

Aerial reconnaissance from the FLIR feeds of the stealth drones revealed that the fissile material shipment had arrived in Zahedan airport. It was a waiting game now to see how the material would be shipped on the second leg of the trip. Critical to the mission as planned was the calculated assessment that the next stage would be by air in an ultra-reliable fixed wing aircraft between Zahedan and Bam. If this turned out to be correct, the timing of the mission would be ninety percent guaranteed and the prediction for success would be elevated in probability. The planners in CENTCOM–Tampa and the White House Situation Room were waiting for this next step with crossed fingers.

The Ranger platoon of 40 men led by Lieutenant Olyphant and one senior NCO was split into two units. The demolition team would set the explosive charges in the bridge and the ambush team who would assault the convoy ahead of the bridge when it came to a stop.

All of the events at the Mohammadabad site were carefully choreographed in the operation plan to occur in sequence. Once it was determined that the fissile material had left Zahedan by air in a fixed wing aircraft, it was a near sure thing that the journey between the Bam airport and Mohammadabad would be by motor vehicle. Therefore the mission timing on the ground at Mohammadabad was dependent on when the flight left Zahedan.

Flight time for the Zahedan to Bam leg would be approximately two hours, and the ground travel time between the Bam airport and the ambush site would be another two hours. The Ranger demolition team would move from the LZ to set the charges on the bridge one hour after the flight took off from Zehedan, and the SEALs would release the gas immediately after the last security radio check from Mohammadabad to their support site some 200 miles away – which occurred every two hours - was intercepted by the supporting drone.

Both the SEAL and Ranger assault forces had arrived at their LZs from the Afghan salient in their Black Hawks and were ready to begin their respective assaults when the motorized convoy turned off of the Highway 93 Road toward Mohammadabad. This would give the SEALs taking down the site no more than one hour to do their work and leave before higher authority would expect to hear a security radio check from the nuclear site. With good luck and precision execution, the fissile material would be hijacked, the second bomb destroyed, the complex rendered radioactive, and the American Special Operations teams should be on their way back to the egress salient before the Iranian security people many miles away suspected there was any trouble at the nuclear site.

A voice came over the loudspeakers simultaneously in the operations centers at the Afghan salient, SPECWAR in Tampa, the White House

Situation Room, and most important, the earphones of the Ranger and SEAL commanders on the ground in Iran: "Attention, attention. We have confirmation that a fixed wing aircraft with a radioactive signature has left Zahedan airport flying westward in the past ten minutes."

The die was now cast. All the planning, reconnaissance, analysis, rehearsing, and execution came down to what would happen at the Mohammadabad site between now and first light the next morning. Every individual's ounce of effort, pain, sleep deprivation, and personal sacrifice that had been made by the Navy SEALs and Army Rangers in their formal training and subsequent preparation for a mission of this intensity and importance would come into play in the next few hours.

The SEALs and the Rangers were not alone in their mission. In addition, an AWACS aircraft circled over the Arabian Sea near the coast of Iran jamming Iran's eastward looking air defense radar; two F-35C fighter aircraft waited on the steam catapults on the U.S.S. Abraham Lincoln in case they were needed for close air support of the mission; the crew chiefs of the Black Hawks furiously refueled their helicopters at the LZs for the extract and return from the mission; and finally, the computer 'jockeys' of the unmanned stealthy drones operated their high tech eyes-in-the-sky observation platforms from their darkened bunker at Al Udeid Air Force Base in Doha, Qatar. All were vital support pieces of this most complex mission. Every man was motivated, focused, and pumped-up for the challenge of a mission they would long remember but never speak of outside their warrior community for the rest of their lives. This was American Special Ops – brave men supported by sophisticated technology and equipment - in its finest hour.

With the signal from the reconnaissance drones that the flight from Zahedan was aloft, the Ranger demolition team made its way to the bridge to set the charges, and the SEAL gassing element leader waited for a coded confirmation of a radio check call from the Security Building team in the nuclear compound, as relayed from the support drone. Tension mounted for the SEALs, who knew that for maximum security, they should not commence the gas attack until the radio check was made. The closest Iranian military base that could support the nuclear site was over 200 miles away to the northwest and it would take helicopters with troops an hour and a half to two hours to muster and get to Mohammadabad in support of any security breach. Time was both the SEALs ally and their enemy.

The Rangers reached the bridge within 45 minutes of the signal for "go" and began placing the charges on the old wooden bridge. At first there had been a spirited controversy about whether to blow the bridge well before convoy arrived or wait until it was nearly upon it. The latter scenario prevailed because it would create confusion within the convoy, giving the Iranian Army security team less of a chance to organize and summon help, and there was less chance of an early detection of an explosion, the noise of which would carry easily in the cool desert air around Mohammadabad. After the explosives were planted, inspected, checked, and double-checked by a Ranger explosives expert, the bulk of the demolition detachment withdrew to the ambush site to provide security for the ambush team, leaving a small Ranger force behind to detonate the charges upon command.

The moment of truth for the SEALs responsible for the gassing of the compound was now at hand. The SEALs were nervous about deploying a weapon that was seen in their eyes as passive in nature as well as one with which they had little experience. But SEALs were known as combat innovators and they had been assured of its effectiveness by many civilians and a few military colleagues who had been testing the immobilizing nerve agent, so they proceeded with confidence and a splash of hope that this modern variation on a ghastly old theme would do the job as advertised.

After receiving the coded signal from the drone that a radio check had been transmitted from the compound, the SEAL team leader gave the site one final look through his night vision binoculars and gave the signal to his four strategically placed 'gas men' to open the pressurized stainless steel cylinders and begin allowing the gas to escape and float on the prevailing winds toward the compound. Even those SEALs upwind of the gas men wore the new protective gas masks as a precaution against becoming accidentally immobilized by the nerve agent. There was now little to do but wait and watch to see how those in the compound would be affected as the gas drifted their way on the desert wind.

The flight carrying the fissile material from Zahedan touched down at the Bam airport nearly two hours after departure and was immediately met by a small convoy of light trucks and a platoon of Iranian soldiers. Also in the welcoming group were a contingent of scientists and a few civilians representing the close inner circle of President Mahmoud Rashad. The decision had obviously been made to have the cargo proceed under cover of darkness directly to the Mohammadabad Nuclear Facility. All this was observed and reported by the stealthy drone that was recording and transmitting both IR and gamma ray signals in real time to war rooms on two continents as commanders and civilians anxiously watched the mission unfold in real time. Rachel Hunter's intuitive wisdom and good judgment had been vindicated, and her valuable service to the President of the United States was about to be cemented into posterity.

All the SEALs assigned to the gassing of the compound looked through their night vision binoculars with curious fascination to see what, if anything, would give them a clue as to the effectiveness of the immobilizing gas. The closest they could get to the western edge of the compound while maintaining the camouflage was approximately fifty yards and it was difficult to know how fast and in what concentrations the invisible gas would travel. The SEALs had been assured by the training technicians that a very low dose of the potent gas was all it would take to render the personnel in the compound unconscious. All they could do was watch and wait.

Anxious moments passed with no change in the walking routine of the security personnel as the gas continued to spew from the cylinders. *'Perhaps we're not close enough; maybe the winds are too high...or too low...preventing the gas from working correctly,'* thought Lieutenant Schields. *'What do we do if this doesn't work? They said not to worry, it WILL work. Shit, I hate working with something that doesn't make noise and blow things all to hell!'*

Then, just as his anxiety was reaching a point of serious discouragement, one, then two...and then a *third* security guard abruptly fell to the ground without even a gesture of astonishment or resistance. Each man just collapsed in mid stride as if cut down by a bullet, though in this case the weapon was a noiseless, odorless collection of organic molecules ginned up by a bunch of chemical engineers at Dugway Proving Ground in Utah and delivered on the desert winds.

The SEALs looked upon the scene with a measure of astonishment as all human motion within the compound ceased in front of their eyes. The next question was whether the gas would permeate the interiors of the various buildings on the site, especially the large dormitory and mess hall on the southwest corner of the compound where most of the personnel would probably be this time of night. The hope was that the HVAC make-up air intakes would pick up the gas and put the building occupants into an even deeper sleep than they were currently experiencing.

After another 10 minutes, the SEAL team leader ordered the gas men to close the dispensing valves of the gas cylinders and advance to the western and northern edge of the compound where they could get a closer view to determine any human activity. As the SEALs advanced closer to the perimeter fence they crouched in what little cover they could find and listened anxiously for voices from within both the dormitory and the security building that would tell them the gas had not been totally effective. Instead the only sound they could hear was the low humming of air conditioning units and diesel generators that supplied the air conditioning and electricity for the sprawling compound.

"Clear!" came the radio signal from the SEALs on the northern edge just twenty meters from the Security building. "Clear!" came the whispered expression of status from the SEALs observing the west and south edges of the dormitory and mess hall.

"Phase two," came the order from the gas element leader and all the SEALs in the gassing element moved to their assigned positions on all sides of the compound near the gates. Within three minutes the ghostly looking SEALs in their combat gear and Star Wars looking gas masks had defeated the locks on the gates and had opened them to allow access to the assault team flying to the SEAL LZ at this very moment.

Lieutenant Schields switched radio frequency and radioed to Chance Lyon, "Compound Secure." After that order he watched as his men advanced to the several entrances of each building breaking down the doors to each and tossing smaller hissing gas cylinders into the interior as insurance that no occupants remain conscious enough to foil the activities of the incoming assault team. Within ten minutes only an eerie silence hung over the compound as the Iranians had been induced into a deep sleep from which they would not fully recover for ten or twelve hours. The gassing element had done its job. Now it was up to Lieutenant Chance Lyon and his assault team to find and neutralize the second warhead, and in the process render the secret site uninhabitable for the foreseeable future.

First Sergeant Lyle Roger's demolition team was waiting for the command to detonate its charges as the rest of the Ranger platoon organized the ambush point to maximize the kill zone so the ambush would be swift and sure. The "kill all with no prisoners" edict had been harsh, but there was a strong desire within President Braxton's National Security Team to make the attack as *sanitary* as possible so that the Iranians would have a difficult time planning and executing any retaliatory effort. Yes, the Iranians would certainly strongly suspect the Americans or the Israelis – or both – but lacking any smoking gun evidence, they would probably remain a supremely confused victim of some identified enemy who had been determined to make a show of force designed to counter Iran's nuclear ambitions.

The Rangers were stoic about their mission imperatives and now, with their ambush set as it had been rehearsed thoroughly, they awaited the signal from Colonel Williamson at the Afghan salient that the convoy had turned off Highway 93 and was headed for its imminent rendezvous with death.

THE ASSAULT

Chance Lyon's SEAL element swooped into the LZ in their Black Hawks upwind from the nuclear site and donned gas masks in preparation for the assault on the compound. The assault plan was for the team to split up into four-man teams and proceed to the gates on each side of the compound marked by the IR chemical lights. Chance and three of his specially trained enlisted men would enter the Weapons Assembly and Testing building and search for the second warhead. They had little to go on except the verbal description and two small photo images of the device that the Korean technicians had given Colonel Kim. Other potential complications were that the warhead might have been moved from this building somewhere else and that location might be on a different unknown level in this or another building.

Once located, the placing of the explosives would have to be done as they had been carefully trained, so as to render the warhead useless but not detonate the fissile material in the process. This would be a delicate balance of damaging the internal workings of the warhead while spreading fissile material contamination throughout the building-- making further human use of the site impossible. For yet another time in Chance Lyon's relatively short military career he was being put to the test in the most severe of circumstances. In his mind, he wouldn't have it any other way.

The convoy from the Bam airport consisted of six light vehicles. As they turned off Highway 93 their progress was continually monitored by the stealthy drone 'piloted' by a 25-year-old Air Force officer at a glowing computer terminal in Doha, Qatar, United Arab Emirates. Although his Air Force training had prepared him well for this task, the pilot's actual training had begun when he was merely an adolescent playing computer games online against faceless opponents with aliases like 'Foo Fighter,' 'Angry Master,' and 'Avenger.'

Tonight his thoughts became, *'I can't believe they are paying me to do this shit,'* as he viewed his computer monitor with the glee of a seasoned gamer.

However, in his maturity, he knew tonight's activity was far removed, and had more profound implications, than the online games of his youth.

The Iranian truck convoy lumbered along the dirt road connecting Highway 93 with the Mohammadabad Nuclear Site at the reduced rate of speed demanded by the worsening road conditions and the need for security of the cargo. The convoy commander had been briefed prior to departure that he commanded the end of a vital mission that was *very near* to completion after years of frustration, and they were *too close to success to fail now*. Success would mean that in mere months they would be on equal military footing with the Israelis and at the top of the heap of a fractured Islamic world. Every officer riding in the convoy had been told his personal reputation as a hero of the Iranian Revolution rested on getting their secret cargo to the nuclear site securely.

The advance scouting element of the Ranger ambush party half a mile southwest of the ambush site caught the first glimpse of the convoy and triple-clicked its radio microphone, alerting the Ranger assault element leader that the convoy was moving in its direction. In just a few moments this was confirmed by the headlights of the lead vehicle glimmering into view and moving deliberately toward the Rangers, who were dug into their ambush positions waiting patiently for the signal to initiate the assault.

The assault plan was to concentrate fire on the two lead and two trailing vehicles that would be carrying the bulk of the security forces. Once these four vehicles were taken down the residual personnel would likely either surrender or be ineffective fighters in opposition to the Rangers, who had numerical and firepower superiority. The Rangers had been thoroughly briefed on what the suitcase containing the fissile material looked like, so there would be no trouble finding it in the carnage of the convoy. Once located, all Iranian soldiers would be reduced, and the Rangers with their package of fissile material would exfiltrate to their LZ and their waiting Black Hawks.

Those officials sequestered in the White House Situation Room watched and listened in fascination as the faint video feeds from the two drones supporting the SEALs and the Rangers cast eerily green ghost-like images from onboard cameras on the large flat screen monitors. In separate corners of the screens FLIR images from the Ranger drone indicated receipt of faint gamma ray detection and IR blotches from heat generated by the vehicles and the men riding in them. Similarly, the SEAL drone showed IR images of the SEALS moving into position around the periphery of the compound and the stationary images of the six motionless security guards immobilized by the nerve gas. The Chairman of the Joint Chiefs muttered aloud, "Keep your fingers crossed sir, the moment of truth is upon us."

As soon as the convoy reached a designated point along the road Lieutenant Olyphant signaled his demolition crew to blow the bridge. Within five seconds a series of muffled explosions spread over the stillness of the desert night with accompanying dull white lights that broke up the darkness above the surface of the bridge. Debris and smoke filled the air ahead, causing the lead vehicle in the convoy to brake to a sudden stop. Simultaneously, a pattern of pre-planned fire from the automatic weapons of the hidden Rangers raked over the individual trucks blowing out tires, shattering glass, and ripping through the canvas covering the back of the trucks, tearing it to ribbons while delivering a hail of sudden death to all the human occupants.

For a full thirty seconds the withering fusillade continued, as one after another of the trucks began to smoke and burn from ignited diesel fuel. A few dazed, and perhaps brave, Iranian soldiers staggered out of the middle vehicles making feeble efforts to return the fire coming from unseen sources, but their actions were in vain as they were cut down in place by Ranger snipers. At the shrill sound of a whistle from Lieutenant Olyphant, all firing ceased and stillness hung over the length of the convoy as suddenly as the cacophony of death had begun. Light flames flickering in the darkness surrounding the convoy and the moans of the wounded and dying were the only sounds to be heard.

The sounds of the explosive charges and the automatic weapons' fire of the deadly Ranger ambush borne on the desert air were the signals for Chance's SEAL element to begin their assault phase. As the two SEAL elements consolidated on the nuclear site, each four man team concentrated on one of the six main buildings at the site, entering each and making sure that no occupants remained unaffected by the gas. The results showed that the gas had been stunningly effective, stopping the occupants in their tracks, most of them in their beds at this time of night. But there were exceptions. The SEALS found men in various positions, some even all too humanly so, such as sitting on the commode, urinating into a urinal, or even showering. Perhaps most important, the Security Building seemed to be occupied by two duty personnel, an officer and an enlisted person, both of whom were sleeping blissfully with their heads planted on their desks. It would seem that the gas attack had been so stealthy and swift that there was no opportunity for anyone in the compound to set off an alarm or communicate with higher authority that they were under attack.

Meanwhile Chance and three of his specially trained SEALS had penetrated the Weapons Assembly and Testing building where, according to the Korean technicians, the second nuclear warhead hijacked from Pakistan had been taken. Having only an inexact idea about its size and where it might now be, Chance's SEALs began a frantic search as the elapsed mission time clock steadily blinked along. Their initial interest concentrated on the easternmost section of the building where the Koreans last saw the warhead when they had been there.

The building contained a bewildering array of equipment, hand and machine tools, high-tech testing apparatus, and long tables loaded with computerized devices of unknown functionality. In addition, there were wooden shipping crates containing cargo manifests describing the contents and their places of origin as well as details about business entities that were providing, either surreptitiously or boldly in defiance of international convention, the items necessary for Iran to fuel its nuclear ambitions. These manifests would be taken from the site by the SEALs and perhaps used at a future time by the United States as leverage against uncooperative nations or companies who were willfully cooperating with Iran's pursuit of its nuclear agenda.

Each SEAL in the Weapons Assembly building was wearing a 'helmet cam' device that continuously recorded in high definition video every action the man took as he ran from room-to-room searching for the warhead. As the search team methodically searched westward into the building, revealing weapon sub-assemblies in some state of final assembly but no complete warhead, they came upon a semi-conscious man reeling drunkenly from room to room, seriously disoriented and showing effects of having become physically ill, presumably from the effects of the nerve gas. By his dress, he was not military and his lab coat had his name embroidered with the prefix of 'Doctor.' His presence was perhaps one of a threat or an opportunity, and he was immediately half dragged to Chance Lyon.

Chance looked earnestly at the man, both amazed that there was a human being in the compound who had not been immobilized by the gas and shocked by his physical appearance. Chance asked him a logical question; "English...English? Do you speak English? I will not hurt you...I want to talk to you! Please...English?"

The man looked drunkenly at Chance Lyon and spoke deliriously, "You... American? Do not shoot. I am sick. Please help me," as he dropped to his knees in front of Chance and vomited once again.

"Great," muttered Chance. *"Now I've got a drunken scientist on my hands and he's puking his guts up in front of me."*

The ill scientist looked up pathetically at Chance Lyon and slurred, "Yes, English...speak English. Please don't kill me. I am only work on science projects. Who...you kill me? I am very sick...don't know why."

"Hurley, Hurley...get this guy something to drink," Chance yelled at his closest SEAL partner. "Make him drink some water. We gotta get this guy alert so he can help us...hurry."

The other SEALs in the building collapsed on the situation, feeding off Chance's urgent instructions and began to deliver assistance to the Iranian scientist. The one SEAL who was trained as a medic dropped to his knees, inserted an IV line into the arm of the reeling Iranian and started squeezing saline solution into his system in an effort to rehydrate him. Chance was hoping that this semi-conscious Iranian might be a key to their success at the nuclear site.

As the SEAL medic forced the saline into the dehydrated Iranian scientist his anxiety began to decrease and he slowly began to understand his life was not in danger from these mystery men who had confronted him in his heretofore cloistered laboratory. Gradually he started to come around. The SEALs, however, cautiously resisted the temptation to remove their cumbersome gas masks, having no idea at what concentrations the gas could render a man helpless.

Chance anxiously watched the medic work with the Iranian and looked at his chronometer that showed local time, EMT, and a stop watch. The stop watch indicated that they had been on the site for 30 minutes but had still not found the remaining warhead. Time was getting away from them and something had to be done immediately to find it.

Lieutenant Olyphant listened and watched carefully as silence enveloped the Ranger ambush site. Satisfied that there were few, if any, survivors who could mount a credible defense, he advanced the Ranger platoon to the vehicles to check the status of the soldiers and to look for the suitcases containing the fissile material. Logic and gut instinct told him that this could be found in one of the two middle vehicles in the convoy, and he made his way up the embankment to the road.

Carefully, the Rangers went from vehicle to vehicle finding no one fully alive, but some in the final stages of dying from their wounds. Lieutenant Olyphant and six of his men rushed toward the middle two vehicles that had been relatively undamaged in the ambush, knowing that there might be soldiers there who had not been killed or wounded. But the first priority was to find the suitcases containing the fissile material and get it away from the ambush site before the fires that were now burning in adjacent vehicles caused explosions of fuel that would spread to the middle two trucks.

In a pre-planned move, Olyphant took truck number three and sprinted toward the cab to check personnel status. As he stepped up on the running board on the passenger-side he came face-to-face with the driver and his passenger in the cab, cowering in fear, with the only light provided by the flickering flames from the truck ahead. He could feel the truck bounce roughly as other Rangers jumped up into the back of the truck bed using their IR flashlights to allow their night vision goggles to aid them as they searched among the contents for the suitcase.

From the darkness within the convoy came an excited shout: "BINGO! BINGO! Lieutenant. Here it is...we've got it!" one of the Rangers shouted out from inside the truck. Momentarily distracted by the shouts from inside the truck's cargo area, Lieutenant Olyphant looked away toward the rear of the vehicle, providing an opportunity for one of the Iranians to draw his sidearm and shoot in the direction of Olyphant's head. The shot was wild but shattered the glass in front of the Lieutenant's face, propelling shards of thick, broken glass into his face and neck. Only his night vision goggles saved his eyes from the sharp debris of the broken truck window. As blood spurted from his face and neck the shot sent Lieutenant Olyphant reeling away from the truck and onto his back in the road below.

"L.T.'s down! Get a medic!...MEDIC!" cried out a Ranger closest to the third truck as he looked with shocked concern at his prostrate and bleeding platoon leader.

"Get that shooter!" he yelled to no one in particular. As the Iranian shooter from the truck attempted to scramble out of the cab to finish off Olyphant, another Ranger grabbed the Iranian by the arm as he opened the door from the passenger side, dragged him out, pulled him to the ground and executed him with his Sig Sauer 9mm pistol in one fluid motion. By this time the driver had recovered and was crawling over the seat to help his partner but was shot by a Ranger assaulting the third vehicle from the driver's side. Additional shots coming from the fourth truck echoed through the night, indicating that final vehicle was being taken down, but all attention now was being given to the removal of the lead-lined suitcases and attending to the wounded Lieutenant Olyphant. Shouts of "Clear, clear...clear" echoed from each truck in the convoy, indicating that the Iranian personnel had been accounted for. Now the Rangers set up their security perimeter and waited for the command to reorganize and exfiltrate to their LZ, leaving nothing behind but spent shell casings, a wrecked, blazing convoy, and dead Iranian soldiers.

The faint streaming video feeds to the Situation Room came in an eerie green format, showing very little of what the SEALS were doing in the compound as all the action was inside the Weapons Assembly and Testing Building but, in contrast, showing a great deal of personnel movement around the ambushed convoy, as well as the vehicles burning more brightly from the igniting fuel. There was not enough detail to see the Ranger lieutenant going down but the flurry of activity around the third truck made it clear that something important was happening there. In a few moments all the command and control elements in the communications loop heard the welcome news from Colonel Williamson, the overall mission commander.

"Package secure. Extract phase imminent," meaning the Rangers had succeeded in finding the suitcases with the fissile material and were breaking off from the convoy headed toward their LZ. The SECDEF took a call on his secure Iridium from SPECWAR in Tampa.

"Understood, thanks, Tom." He turned to the President and said, "Sir, the Rangers have secured the suitcases. Casualties: one WIA...could be serious. We're thirty percent home."

Chance Lyon was making little headway with the Iranian scientist who was still woozy, but slowly coming around. Time was running out and

Chance had no time to play games with the scientist whom he hoped was their best shot at finding the nuke. He decided to get straight to the point with the quivering and drooling man who might either faint dead away – or even *really* die – at any moment, thus becoming useless to them. Chance pulled his service pistol and pointed it right at the man, whose bloodshot eyes widened even further as he must have thought that his life was now over.

"Take me to where the nuclear bomb is," shouted Chance, his eyes a blazing fury of frustration with the knowledge that time was running out for the SEALs to carry out their mission.

"No bomb here...no bombs!" shouted back the scientist with a strange conviction.

Nearly beside himself with frustration, Chance pressed the muzzle of the pistol to the man's neck and seethed in anger saying, "Look you fucker, the Koreans said there is a bomb here. You remember the Koreans? WHERE'S THE BOMB?! If you don't tell me I'm going to shoot your nuts off and then I'm going to kill you."

The Iranian scientist frantically looked left and right, hoping got elicit some sympathy from this raving American mad man, but he saw nothing but resolve from the hard eyes of the other SEALs.

"Yes...yes. The Koreans brought two warheads, but no bombs! We have to make the bombs using the warheads."

Chance looked at the other SEALs in astonishment, realizing that he had gotten tripped up by simple semantics. He had asked where the *bomb* was instead of the *warhead*. 'What a dumb shit you are, Lyon!' thought Chance.

Now in a theatrically controlled tone, he continued to the Iranian, "Okay, asshole, where is the *warhead*?" waving his pistol around the room for emphasis. The Iranian scientist gulped, looked earnestly at Chance and had the presence of mind to say, "If I show you, you will not kill me?"

Chance, exhaling a sigh of great relief, responded, "if you show me and help me blow it up, I won't kill you. In fact, I'll take you to America and get you a blond girlfriend with great big tits!"

The now bewildered scientist stared at Chance with a quizzical look and asked, "What are tits?"

With this innocent remark all the tension in the room momentarily collapsed and even the highly stressed Chance Lyon was smiling.

In five minutes the scientist ushered the SEALs into a locked area in the far west end of the building containing a single stainless steel table on which had been placed the larger of the two previously stolen Pakistani warheads. The SEALs quickly took photos, measurements, and serial numbers from every part of the device that was visible to document what they had found.

'Now, how are we gonna kill this thing?' thought Chance.

Realizing that he had gained a partial element of trust with the scientist and that he might benefit from his technical assistance for this part of the mission, he asked the Iranian for help.

"We have come here to destroy this weapon. I have explosives and the means to escape unharmed. What's the best way to destroy this weapon? If you help me, I will let you escape with us and take you to America."

"I have a wife and child in Tehran. I cannot leave them," replied the scientist with resolve.

Chance took a leap of faith and quickly replied, "If you help us, I will assure you we will rescue your wife and child and bring them to America so you can be together."

"And if I do not? I do not trust you Americans," replied the scientist confidently.

"Then I will tie you to this table and you will be in this room when the explosives go off. You have a simple choice today. Help us destroy this warhead or die."

The scientist remained quiet for a moment and then replied, "It would seem I have no choice in this matter. What about my colleagues? What will be their fate? Some of these men are my friends," he said sincerely.

"I have no time for moral judgments," replied Chance. "They will probably become victims of the consequences of hubris and lust for power of your political leaders. I am a soldier with a military mission that I intend to carry out, with or without your help. Tell me how I should place my charges to destroy this warhead. If you don't, I will do as I think best."

Here Chance was faced with the kind of moral dilemma that Special Operations leaders are faced with that demands the application of sound judgment, courageous decision-making, and dedication to the mission at hand, making them the loneliest of leaders. Given the many thousands of planning hours, the exposure to great danger for hundreds of dedicated operations and support personnel, the expenditure of many millions of dollars in hardware and mission support, and finally, the enormous political stakes surrounding success or failure of the overall strategic mission, compassion for a single individual – in this case the fate of the Iranian scientist and the potential danger to his family – had to be weighed in proportion to the bigger picture. To Chance, the choice was clear if not entirely a comfortable one. If the scientist cooperated he would be spared. If not, he would die. There were no other options.

"If you set off explosives around the device without it being armed by the arming-fusing-firing device, the fissile material will not detonate with the effectiveness of a nuclear device. Instead, the explosion will merely scatter the fissile material about the site like a 'dirty' bomb rendering the site useless for human occupancy for several years and the fissile material will not be recoverable," replied the Iranian scientist.

"That was our original intention. I'm pleased you could confirm that," responded Chance.

"This building is shielded to prevent the spread of radioactivity in case of an accident. Depending on the intensity of the explosives, many of my colleagues will likely be spared but they will have to be evacuated from this site and the government will not be able to use it for some time," offered the Iranian.

"Pity," replied Chance. He motioned for the SEALs with the explosives to get them set so the mission could proceed and they could get extracted. Sunrise would be in three hours.

After the successful ambush, the plan was for the Rangers to exfiltrate in their Hawks from the ambush site and to consolidate at the SEAL LZ to provide back-up for the SEALs and refuel their Hawks for the flight back to the Afghan salient. The Rangers had been instructed to remain at the LZ and not extract until the SEAL mission was secure in case there was a need for back-up. However, Lieutenant Olyphant was bleeding badly from the glass shrapnel wounds and he would need surgery if he was to survive many more hours. In the command absence of Lieutenant Olyphant, Sergeant Lyle Rogers used Olyphant's Iridium to call Colonel Williamson at the salient. Given Olyphant's condition and the fact that the fissile material was safely in hand, Williamson gave the go ahead for a squad of Rangers, including the wounded Lieutenant Olyphant, to extract in one of the Hawks, leaving Sergeant Rogers and the balance of the Rangers at the LZ as the local Command and Control component and back-up for the SEALs.

As the demolitions specialists set the charges, Chance carefully reviewed all the items on his mission checklist to ensure nothing was left undone for the successful completion of the SEALs portion of the mission. All his men were accounted for and an advance party had been sent to the LZ to ensure everything there was ready for extract. The fuel drums had been pre-'sanitized,' leaving no identification markings, so there could be nothing to trace them back to American forces. The gas canisters had been accounted for and were to be taken back with the SEALs. Whether he wanted to or not, the Iranian scientist would be going with the SEALs because he knew too much to be left behind and he didn't deserve to be killed anyway. As for the Rangers, all that would be found at the ambush site were many hundreds of 5.56 mm NATO shell casings from their M4 rifles. This military round was so ubiquitous in global weapons systems that trying to use this evidence to pin this complex operation on the United States or the Israelis would have no credibility except in some of the more gullible and lazy-minded news media. Lacking any response to Iranian accusations from the American political administration or the Israelis would leave the world, including the Iranians, with nothing but a huge mystery. Even the Iranians would be at a loss as to who, in reality, placed their latest and most ambitious attempts to develop a nuclear weapons capability on the trash heap of history.

Under the direction of their commander, Chance Lyon, and assisted by the Iranian scientist, who had now identified himself as Ahmed, the SEALs began working feverishly to carefully set the charges that would compromise the warhead without detonating the fissile material into a nuclear explosion. The latter event would have disastrous consequences for the strategy of the mission while imperiling the lives of all the American military commandos taking part in the raid. In addition, within the debris of such an unintended outcome, could possibly be clear evidence of American involvement. The Iranians would surely spin the event as a direct nuclear attack on Iran by the United States, painting them as nuclear aggressors in the Middle East, with all the negative consequences associated with such a trumped up scenario landing on the doorstep of the White House.

Such an unintended consequence would change the entire dynamic of the West vis-à-vis Middle East strategic relationship, roil World oil markets for months to come, and lead to cries for the impeachment of Jonathan Braxton. Truly, the most important aspect of Operation Dragon Claw was unfolding and there was no margin for error. The actual moment of detonation of the charges and the immediate critical aftermath would have ramifications throughout the world for many years to come, and, once again, Chance Lyon was at the point of the trident.

One of the SEALs who was part of the security team keeping watch outside the Assembly and Maintenance B building charged breathlessly into the building shouting out to Chance Lyon and his search team. "Sir, a helicopter is circling the compound and playing a searchlight on the grounds. They may have spotted the guards who collapsed from the gas. What should we do?"

Chance looked anxiously at Ahmed and asked urgently, "Do you know anything about this? Where did it come from?"

Ahmed spoke rapidly in return. "Sometimes a helicopter comes at night to test security. It circles the compound and then lands on the helipad and the co-pilot goes to the Security building. It is a test of security. Its presence and timing is not predicable."

Chance was now in a momentary quandary. He had to supervise the setting of the charges – that was his primary mission and one not to be left to anyone else. Dealing with the helicopter would have to be assigned to another leader. Chance keyed his mike and spoke to Lieutenant Brian Shields, the leader of the SEAL gassing element.

"Brian, organize the men and take care of the chopper if and when it lands. We have to assume we have been compromised to some degree as they probably have radio contact with their headquarters. If they land, we can't let them leave. Do what you have to do to take down the chopper and the pilots, but don't' let them leave...and Brian, this is a no witness situation – you know what I mean."

Lieutenant Shields understood this to mean that, once on the ground, not only would the Iranian helicopter not be allowed to leave, but the pilots could not be left in a position to give future testimony to what they might have seen in the compound.

Chance completed his transmission with, "We have about fifteen more minutes here before we finish and exfil."

"Roger dodger," was the terse and confident reply of Brian Schields.

Schields was a Naval Academy graduate and a newly minted SEAL, but he had proved his bona fides in a recent deployment to Afghanistan with another SEAL team. He had been chosen as Chance's back-up and gassing element leader as Colonel Williamson felt it prudent to have two SEAL officers at the compound in case of serious trouble with the mission. His concerns were now vindicated by the imminent arrival of the unexpected helicopter carrying Iranian security personnel.

Chance had been correct in his assessment that the pilots in the security helicopter had detected something amiss in the compound. There had been no reply to their radio transmissions to the Security building and they had, indeed, seen the disabled guards with their searchlight. They had reported this back to their headquarters from where they had left more than an hour ago. "We have no reply from the compound, Colonel," radioed the co-pilot. "We have seen at least two guards who appear to be disabled on the ground. Our intentions are to land to further evaluate," was their situation report to the airfield nearly 200 miles away.

"We suggest you continue your reconnaissance for five more minutes, Lieutenant," was the telephonic reply. "Try to get a better understanding of the situation on the ground before you risk landing. We are sending troops to support you. They should be airborne within twenty minutes."

These unencrypted telephone transmissions were being intercepted by the U.S. Air Force drone supporting the SEAL mission and were being bounced back to Chance's SEAL team by an American communications satellite that was simultaneously relaying them in real time to Colonel Williamson at the Afghan salient, SPECWAR in Tampa, and the White House Situation Room.

Colonel Williamson called Chance Lyon on the encrypted Iridium telephone to inform him of the Iranian's security team situation.

"Yes, sir, we're aware of the helicopter. We're dealing with that as we speak. Thanks for the head's up about the reinforcements."

"Lieutenant Lyon," replied Colonel Williamson, "get it wrapped up there and exfil ASAP. When the Iranian cavalry arrives we want them to find nobody home and nothing but a radioactive LZ."

"Roger that, sir, we're doing everything we can," was Chance's reply.

Ahmed's technical assistance was extremely helpful and increased the SEAL's confidence that the explosives they were rigging would make this a dirty bomb event and not a nuclear detonation that everyone feared. Nevertheless tensions were running high in the bomb assembly building and Chance was wondering if there could be any further complications that would delay the team's exfiltration and egress from the mission site. *'The pucker-factor is definitely increasing,'* thought Chance.

Meanwhile, Colonel Williamson decided to delay the release of the balance of the Rangers in case they would be needed as security for the SEALs in the event of an untimely arrival of Iranian troops. With Lieutenant Olyphant having been med-evaced, he directed Sergeant Rogers to leave a security team at the Ranger-SEAL extract LZ and move the balance of the Rangers to a blocking position between the Assembly building and the helipads. When the SEALs were finished setting their charges, the SEALs and Rangers would exfil in double-time together.

He then called Commander Glenn Forsey, the Air Boss on the Abraham Lincoln and asked him to launch two F-35C's and hold them just off Iranian air space in the event he needed fighter cover at the nuclear site.

Forsey replied that the fighters were staged and would be airborne in one-minute and he continued, "Colonel, AWACs shows no air activity coming your way, but we're focused on your situation. I'll keep you in the loop." The Lincoln had turned into the wind and the fighters screamed off the carrier's deck itching for a dog fight with any Iranian fighters.

Williamson called Chance and said, "In case you need them Lieutenant, I have Rangers covering your back and fast movers headed your way with AWAC's guidance. You are not alone."

Meanwhile Lieutenant Schields and three SEALs broke away from the security of the Assembly Building and headed cautiously toward one of the buildings closest to the helipad, taking care to stay in the shadows out of direct sight by the circling Iranian helicopter.

Once in position, Shields had a simple and direct plan that was based on the assumption that the Iranians had sensed there was something amiss in the compound. Shields positioned two of the SEALs so they could bring fire on the pilot's side of the observation helicopter after it landed, while he and another SEAL made their way to the Security Building. One SEAL would bring fire on the pilot after he landed while his buddy provided security for the shooter. In turn, Shields and his SEAL buddy would enter the Security Building and ambush the other Iranian who would undoubtedly attempt to enter the building immediately upon landing. The shooting sequence would be Schields first, and then followed immediately by the SEAL focused on the pilot when he heard the Lieutenant's gunfire.

In five minutes the Iranian helicopter landed, but there was an unexpected hitch. Just prior to touchdown, the helicopter dropped two canisters of white smoke that, with the aid of the rotor downdraft, completely obliterated the area around the helipad from conventional observation. The SEAL's NODs revealed only a fog of green smoke obscuring anything over ten feet away. As the rotor's thrust died sown, the smoke still lingered and it was impossible for the SEALs to see how many people exited the helicopter or where they headed. This changed the SEAL's ambush plan dramatically.

The reality was that two men had exited the passenger side of the helicopter, while the pilot stayed inside the Plexiglas cocoon with the engine idling, obviously anticipating the potential for a quick get-away. As anticipated by Schields, one man did begin to make his way toward the Security Building, but none of the SEALs had any view of the second. In the green fog and confusion of the compound the second Iranian made his way past the SEAL security perimeter and into the Assembly Building.

The Iranian was familiar with the layout of this most important building in the compound and immediately began wending his way to where he knew the precious warhead was stored. As he drew closer to the room, he could hear voices that were clearly American excitedly discussing something with urgency. The Iranian drew his pistol and silently moved toward the doorway, hoping to surprise whoever was in the room.

One of the SEALs setting the charges at the direction of Ahmed saw a flash of movement in his peripheral vision and shouted out to Chance, "Threat in the door!"

Chance instinctively dropped into a crouch, drew his Sig Sauer P226 9mm service pistol and instinctively fired twice at the movement in the door. The high velocity rounds struck the Iranian in mid-chest, killing him instantly, but not before the Iranian had fired off a round from his pistol that struck Ahmed in the back of his skull and exiting his forehead, scattering remnants of brains, blood, and bone all over the nuclear warhead on the table in front of him.

Simultaneously, the other Iranian burst through the door of the Security Building with his pistol drawn, expecting trouble. He might have been expecting trouble, but he didn't exactly anticipate it in the form of Lieutenant Brian Schields, who stepped out of the shadows and double tapped the surprised Iranian with his Sig-9, killing him instantly in the standing position. Meanwhile, the SEAL by the building nearest the helipad emerged like an apparition from Hell from the swirling green fog of smoke being gently blown by the decelerating helicopter rotors and blew the pilot away as he sat in his pilot's seat.

Shouts of, "Clear"...,"Clear"...,and "Clear," echoed over the compound and through the SEAL's radio network.

Chance announced over the net and to the SEALs in the room with him, "Exfil...exfil. Collapse on the LZ." He looked without emotion at the bodies of Ahmed and the Iranian who had shot him, before saying to the others, "We won't have to keep a promise to Ahmed about his family now. Our work is done here; let's head to the LZ."

The SEALs had attached multiple timing fuses to the explosives they rigged around the warhead and moved out for their LZ. As their fully loaded Black Hawks lifted off from the desert LZ in a swirling storm of dirt and debris a huge non-nuclear explosion filled the night air over the Mohammedabad nuclear site. Chance Lyon looked over at his demolitions Chief Petty Officer and gave him a thumb's up, accompanied by a grim smile and an affirmative nod.

The Black Hawks reached altitude, and turned in formation, heading east toward the safety of the Afghan salient as the eastern horizon greeted them with the first faint light of a new dawn. Lieutenant Chance Lyon, US Navy SEAL operator, could not help but think that what he was witnessing was a metaphor for what lay ahead in his professional life.

To be continued…

*There is considerable speculation that Gene Cranz did not use these exact words in his admonition to the NASA Apollo engineering team when he charged them with finding a solution to getting the astronauts home safely, but it was implied.

EPILOGUE

PRESIDENT JONATHAN BRAXTON

President Braxton became the first American President in many years to actually back up his rhetoric with action, in the form of stopping the Iranian nuclear weapons development in its tracks, while doing so without creating an international incident. Of course, there would be no public utterances about this as the military operation that did so was totally black. It really didn't matter from a domestic public relations standpoint because Braxton was not up for election again after his second term. However, the international rumor mill - far more sophisticated and subtle than that which existed in the United States - soon began to speculate that something had happened in Iran to create a major stir resulting in a change of secular leadership. Cocktail gossip at embassy receptions throughout the world soon became rife with speculation that there had been an 'accident' shortly after the initial testing of Iran's weapon that had delayed any further weapons development indefinitely. Iranian diplomats were uniformly silent on the matter. The Braxton administration consistently denied any knowledge of any such accident.

MAHMOUD AND SHARIF RASHAD

The ruling Shiite Muslim mullahs in Iran were not without secular political sophistication. They simply preferred to leave such trivialities to secular men such as Mahmoud Rashad over whom they had ultimate control. To the mullahs, Mahmoud was like a domesticated dog on a long leash - at some point he would come to the end of his tether and be brought to heel. First the magnet incident, and now the destruction of the Mohammadabad nuclear site and the loss of Iran's only other nuclear warhead was the end of Iran's nuclear development program for many years. The Mohammadabad incident resulting in the loss of the second nuclear warhead was the last straw in the gradual loss of confidence the mullahs had been feeling for Mahmoud Rashad, President of the People's Republic of Iran. Shortly after Mohammadabad, both Mahmoud and his brother, Sharif, were arrested in the dark of night by agents of VEVAK and brought before the Ruling Council of Clerics. There they were denounced as 'traitors to the Revolution,' and sentenced to hang. As the brothers stood together on the gallows inside a prison in Tehran, Mahmoud Rashad looked at his brother tearfully and cried out, "Allah Akbar!" as the trap door opened, sending them on their way to meet their god.

COLONEL YOUNG HO KIM

In retrospect, Colonel Kim had the most to lose and the most to gain personally from the outcome of the deception surrounding the subsequent denial of nuclear material to the Iranians. He also became the sole active survivor of this elaborate plot orchestrated by Rachel Hunter and Raymond Rollins. If VEVAK would have been more patient and thorough in their investigation beyond the Rashad brothers they might have made the connection with Colonel Kim and outed him to the North Korean Government, but the mullahs wanted their pound of flesh and it ended far short of Colonel Kim. The Colonel, having become used to the finer things that being a conduit of information to American intelligence brought him, continues as an enthusiastic and valuable human asset to the CIA under the codename of 'Gamma.'

CAPTAIN HANS FRIDRICH ('HERR KALEUNT')

In truth, Hans Friedrich, Captain of the Pacific Dawn freighter, was without culpability in the disabling and hijacking of his ship. After two weeks in an Iranian prison, during which he and his crew were systematically interrogated by agents of VEVAK, the Iranians could not discover any conspiracy among the crew, nor could they determine the nationality of the group that boarded the freighter and placed the radiological dispersal devices irradiating the cargo. With little or no evidence as to 'how' or 'who' it was difficult for the Iranian government to make much of a public outcry relative to the incident. Friedrich, a seasoned and cunning international traveler, who frequently purchased prohibited items in many ports of call, hid the Euros he received from CPO Schultz on the ship in a cleverly hidden lining in his custom-made boots and escaped Iran with his bribe intact after he and the crew were released. Prior to returning to Shanghai for another assignment, Friedrich made a detour to a certain bank in Hamburg to claim a promised withdrawal. Included in the balance of the funds promised by Chief Petty Officer Schultz during the SEAL interdiction of the Pacific Dawn was a note. The note suggested Captain Friedrich contact a certain phone number in Hamburg and ask for Herr Schnider, and identify himself as Herr Henkel, a freighter captain. Friedrich cautiously did so, and a meeting between the two was scheduled for the next day. After several more clandestine meetings in Germany and in Shanghai, where Friedrich kept an apartment, he was recruited to spy for the American Central Intelligence Agency. The Captain continues to provide valuable information to his American handlers about shipments of strategic material between China and her customers, such as the Democratic People's Republic of Korea, Iran, and other nations of interest to the United States' intelligence community. His former ship, The Pacific Dawn, continues tied up at the isolated quay in Bandar-e-Abbas, Iran, subject to an uncertain fate.

LIEUTENANT JOHN OLYPHANT

If not for the protection provided by his night vision devices, Lieutenant Olyphant would probably be blind or, possibly, dead, from the thick glass shards exploded into his face and neck by the gun wielding Iranian soldier in the truck at the Ranger ambush site near Mohammadabad. His life was saved by Army surgeons at the U.S. Army Hospital in Kandahar, Afghanistan, and he was evacuated to Ramstein for rehabilitation. Lieutenant Olyphant received a Silver Star for his actions at the ambush site and retired with a disability discharge from the Army. He is now semi-retired on his cattle ranch in Arizona, but stays in touch with Chance Lyon and other members of the Special Operations community. He works on his marksmanship daily, becoming accustomed to shooting with one eye, the other covered by a rakish black eye patch.

MAX JENKINS

If one had access to the activity on Max Jenkins' Black Centurion American Express Card, or his U.S. Diplomatic Passport scannings, much more could be known about the activities or whereabouts of the CIA's most reliable trouble-shooter. Lacking such, Max Jenkins remains a mystery man to everyone but Raymond Rollins, Director of Central Intelligence. From time to time Max can be spotted at Washington, D.C., area flower shows displaying his champion orchids.

RACHEL HUNTER, PH.D.

Rachel Hunter continued her extraordinary service to President Jonathan Braxton and his administration. The Mohammadabad Operation was presumably the final national security crisis faced by Braxton and, as his second term began to wind down, Doctor Hunter began to explore her options for the future. A clandestine effort was beginning at the Board of Trustee level at Harvard University to replace its aging President and Rachel, as a distinguished alumnus with a storied career, was on the short-list as a candidate. However, when uber-liberal Board member Solomon Lewis heard of Rachel's place on the list he objected strenuously and threatened to take the secretive search out into the open, exposing his objection. Lewis's mean-spirited threats intimidated the staid Harvard Board and Rachel's name was quietly withdrawn. Unbeknownst to Lewis, Quinton and Loretta Darlington - prominent New York and Geneva philanthropists - were on the verge of quietly donating one-hundred-fifty-million dollars to the Harvard endowment fund. When Loretta Darlington got wind of the snub of Rachel Hunter by Lewis from a frequent bridge partner, the bequest was abruptly cancelled in a private telephone conversation between her husband and the Chairman of the Harvard Board of Trustees. The Chairman pleaded with Quinton Darlington to hold off until the matter could be *reconsidered* by the Board. But his request was met with an audible 'click' on the line, indicating that the potential donor had hung up on him. Two days later Loretta Darlington telephoned her bridge partner to tell him of the news. "Thank you for making Quinton and me aware of the Rachel Hunter matter. She's a wonderful person and was an excellent candidate.

EPILOGUE

Lewis is a fool and a crank...I loathe him. But tell me, darling, how *do* you find out about these things? Quinton tells me these boards of trustee proceedings are *most* secret!"

"Well, Loretta, we bankers have our connections...must have been quite a blow to Harvard to miss out on this most generous contribution," answered Hugo Delegarde. "I'm looking forward to seeing you and Quinton again very soon."

Two months later, Rachel Hunter was offered the Presidency of Stanford University. A year after Doctor Hunter took her position at Stanford, the Board of Trustees announced that the Darlington Foundation for Advancement of Higher Education had made a gift of one-hundred-fifty-million dollars to the Stanford University endowment fund.

LIEUTENANT CHANCE MACKLIN LYON, U.S.N.

Two months after Mohammadabad, Lieutenants John Olyphant and Chance Lyon met privately in the Oval Office with President Jonathan Braxton, the Chief of Naval Operations, and the Army Chief of Staff, where they were awarded the Silver Star and the Navy Cross, respectively, for their leadership at Mohammadabad, Iran. The citations for these awards remain classified Top-Secret.

Early in his next assignment as Operations Officer of SEAL Team Two in Norfolk, Chance began to have headaches severe enough for him to miss duty. This information reached Doctor Mack Lyon through Chance's father, Bernie Lyon, and Doctor Mack immediately contacted Doctor Robert Spenser, Director of the world renowned Barrow Neurological Institute in Phoenix, Arizona, describing Chance's medical history in detail. Doctor Spenser agreed to take the case and one week later Chance and the Lyon family were in his office being shown images of a CT scan done on Chance a day before. Doctor Spenser revealed that there was evidence of considerable scarring from the previous neurological procedure that was placing pressure on Chance's brain. The scarring needed to be completely reduced and required Chance to spend at least two months of complete rest after this surgery to heal properly, once and for all. Doctor Spenser himself performed the four-hour procedure and predicted complete recovery for Chance - if he re-habilitated as directed.

In the eyes of BUPERS of the U.S. Navy, the second neurological procedure disqualified Chance from serving in anything but an administrative position for the balance of his career. For a warhorse like Chance, this was akin to a death sentence. In the frequent email correspondence between Anne Lyon and Marilyn Wheeler, wife of Admiral Steve Wheeler, Chief of Naval Operations, and this information was revealed and gradually passed up the food chain from Admiral Wheeler to President Braxton.

Admiral Wheeler and President Braxton discussed the matter privately and came to the collective conclusion that, given Chance Lyon's distinguished service to the United States in his relatively short naval career, he would be offered a medical discharge and a discharge promotion to Lieutenant Commander.

This concludes Chance Lyon's career as an active duty Naval Officer serving his country...,

...But it does not conclude Chance Lyon's service to the United States of America in his new capacity of private citizen!

Made in the USA
San Bernardino, CA
01 November 2013